The Silversmith

The Silversmith

Book One of The Selvaren Series

LJ CLAREN

SECOND SKY

SECOND SKY
First published in 2025 by LJ Claren
This paperback edition published in 2026 by Second Sky

8

A CIP catalogue record for this book
is available from the British Library.

PB ISBN 978-1-83618-950-3
EB ISBN 978-1-80550-663-8

Printed and bound in Great Britain by
Clays Ltd, Elcograf S.p.A.

Papers used by Second Sky are from well-managed forests
and other responsible sources.

Second Sky
An imprint of Storyfire Ltd.
Carmelite House
50 Victoria Embankment
London EC4Y 0DZ

An Hachette UK Company

The authorised representative in the EEA is Hachette Ireland
8 Castlecourt Centre
Dublin 15 D15 XTP3
Ireland
(email: info@hbgi.ie)

www.hachette.co.uk
www.secondskybooks.com

For anyone who's ever felt like they aren't enough:

You are. Keep going.

Author Note

This novel contains explicit language and sexual scenes as well as some graphic descriptions of violence, gore, loss, grief, torture, death (including the off-page death of a child), food insecurity, disordered eating, traumatic bleeding, panic attacks, hallucinations, animal death, attempted rape, and sexual assault, and may be triggering for some readers.

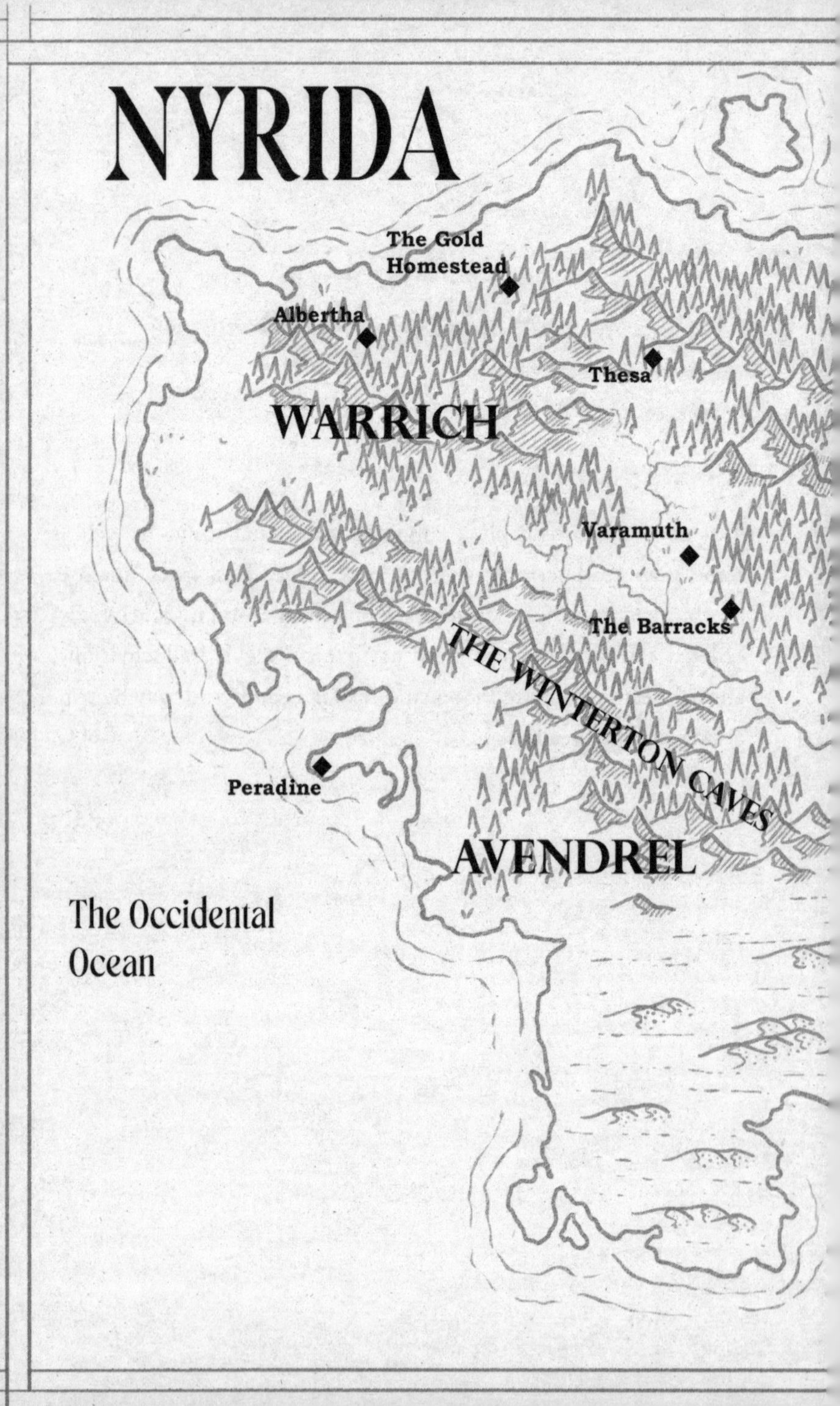
NYRIDA
The Gold Homestead
Albertha
Thesa
WARRICH
Varamuth
The Barracks
THE WINTERTON CAVES
Peradine
AVENDREL
The Occidental Ocean

Freyburn
WYMARA
Tovick
Brinnea
The Brinnean Sea
TUGAF
Anacos

Chapter One

Two more steps. Two more villagers in front of me. Once they were done, it was my turn to barter with what I had, which wasn't much.

At this point, it was that or starve.

I focused on breathing despite the ache of hunger blurring my vision. Clouds of mist escaped my lips and every breath trembled, along with the rest of my body.

Through flurries of snow, people hustled down the gravel road beneath ominous gray skies. The tips of my fingers—even in my wool gloves—threatened to lose feeling. I gulped. It was already early afternoon and wouldn't get any warmer than it was right now.

Warrich in early winter was cold enough to kill if one wasn't careful. Only the boldest travelers ventured to the northernmost region of Nyrida. And the bitter wilderness, given the chance, spared not a single one of them. Towns were small and sparse. It had taken me four hours to walk here from my home in the forest.

"Next."

The person in line behind me shoved me in the back. I gasped and almost fell to the ground. My knees ached from overuse and exhaustion. And I still had to survive the walk home after this.

Removing my stiff fingers from my pockets, I presented the stall owner with two small coins and cleared my throat.

"Bread, please. Whatever kind you have."

The man was middle-aged with a crooked nose and chestnut hair speckled with gray. He stared down at my offering and scoffed. "Bread is three coins."

My stomach plummeted. "Please." Panic gripped my heart and sent my pulse faster than my body could handle. "This is all I have. There has to be something. I'll—I'll come back. I'll work for it."

The stall owner looked up at me and narrowed his eyes, a licentious gaze lingering on my face, lips, and a small bit of exposed neck. An eerie smile tilted his mouth. "On second thought, I might consider other forms of payment."

"What...other forms?" My throat went dry, but while fear burned in my chest, my stomach protested hunger in equal strength. If another form of payment could be requested in the middle of the village market, it couldn't be so terrible.

He smirked and scanned me from head to toe. I wasn't dressed in anything fancy—a gray linen shirt, my thickest undergarments and pants, bundled up in all the layers I could find. My well-worn boots were laced tight and my green shawl was thick but tattered in places.

My gut soured when he leaned forward, so no one else could hear, and hissed, "You'll have to use those pretty pink lips of yours."

I took a step back and tightened my shawl around my shivering body.

"I—n-no," I stuttered, horrified that, in my desperation, I had hesitated for a moment.

But I no longer had any solid food left. In a week, maybe less, I'd have no choice but to butcher our last two hens, Daisy and Penny, and I'd never . . . *killed* before. In the last few weeks, they'd stopped producing eggs, leaving me with only vegetable broth. And after they were gone . . .

I gulped and surveyed the small marketplace for another booth selling something I might possibly afford.

My mother would have known what to do.

But it had been eight weeks since she left me alone here, without an explanation. I wondered once again where she had gone, with less concern than I should have. The thought that she might be freezing to death, lost in the wilderness, should have horrified me. I should have longed to see her again, but I didn't. No, the ache of hunger was stronger. I only craved the food and drink she'd know how to provide.

Shreds of hope that my mother would return had carried me through the last eight weeks. It felt unlikely—she had *chosen* to leave me—but I still hoped she would return to the home she'd known and loved for so long. Even if her daughter's welfare wasn't enough to motivate her.

A vibrant red cloth snapped in the wind a few stalls away. My breath vanished. Icy sweat beaded at the nape of my neck. Disoriented, I centered my feet in the gravel and tried not to sway. The color reminded me of them . . . of the discovery that still haunted my dreams.

For months now, I had woken every morning in a cold sweat. And it was always the same bloody, inescapable nightmare that brought me there.

Only now, I wasn't asleep. I was brutally awake and freezing. So it seemed I wasn't free of the nightmares while conscious, either. I blinked once, twice, swallowing down the urge to scream the way I had that day. But I refrained and forced tears to clear my vision and dispose of the memory. So much red.

But it was hard to rid myself of those all-consuming memories when I had little else to fill the space. These days, blood was just about all I could remember.

"Move!"

A body much bigger than my own slammed into my back again, knocking me to my knees. Sharp rocks bit through the cloth of my pants and the thin wool of my gloves. I'd been too stuck in my own head to see the assailant. Not that it mattered. I didn't have an ounce of strength or skill to defend myself, and they were already gone down the rocky path.

I got up and looked around the market. Ramshackle buildings shuddered in the brutal wind, proof of the village's lack of resources. Signs on the stalls showed the price of goods, and nothing cost less than three or four coins. None of the stall owners looked any kinder than the one who'd requested *other* forms of payment.

I resigned myself to returning home.

If I made it back before dark, at least I wouldn't die today.

But you'll starve.

I winced at my mind's voice. Dying today or a few weeks from now. What a choice the gods had given me.

Many times over the past six months, I'd wondered where the gods were. If they were anywhere at all. If only they would humble themselves and use their divine magic to aid the hungry and insignificant. What would my life, and the lives of anyone else starving in this frigid north, look like if they did? I focused on the sharp cold in my lungs and gathered all of my energy for the journey home.

The trip back through the forest took me more than five hours. I counted every step, and when I lost count, I started over, and over again. It was all I could do to distract myself from the gnawing aches in my feet, calves, hips. From the blisters that split the skin of my ankles. Everything hurt, and it took all my willpower to pretend I hadn't suffered all this exhaustion and agony in vain.

Finally, the weathered stone chimney of my home poked out above leafless trees. I pressed forward, every inhale a challenge. The cabin had been built by my parents before I was born. Though I couldn't remember how it looked in its early years, it was clear that the cabin's exterior had worn throughout time.

Six months ago, I woke up without memory of my first nineteen years of life. I'd suffered a fall and struck my head in the cellar, my mother said, and since then I'd felt like a blank piece of parchment waiting for someone else's story.

Unfortunately for me, *blood* was the brightest stain on that parchment. That recurring nightmare was not just a nightmare, but one of the few memories I kept against my will. A horror I would never forget, no matter how hard I tried.

Before going inside the cabin, I trudged to the barn and checked on the hens. Opening the door required the full weight of my hungry, trembling frame.

Penny greeted me with a string of hungry clucks.

"I know, girl." I sniffled, grabbing the dwindling bucket of half-frozen grain and scattering a half-handful across the floor. Rationing was crucial to keep the chickens alive, just as it was for me. "Come here." I lifted the hens from their nests and set them on the cold floor of the barn to eat their food. "I'm sorry. I'm hungry, too."

With a heavy sigh, I stepped outside and marched toward the house, pausing only to tighten the shawl around my neck. Dried leaves crunched beneath my feet as I moved. In early winter, the branches of trees formed a cross-hatched landscape that faded into endless distance. On the forest floor, the leaves provided a haven for small creatures seeking shelter from the cold. Despite my loneliness—how I sometimes craved anything but painful quiet—I felt there was strange, silent beauty in such a desolate place.

Twigs crunched to my left. My heart pounded in my ears and my body tensed with anticipation. But when I turned and saw a white-tailed deer dashing into the woods, my shoulders relaxed. I wondered what it was to have the bravery to truly run free. Wondered if I would ever find that. I wouldn't even know where to begin.

A nasty wind swelled out of the trees into the clearing. It bit at my skin like shards of glass, and I picked up my pace to get out of the cold.

Once indoors, I slid my stockinged feet from my boots and lit our wood-burning stove to heat some broth. The cabin had one living area, crowded with a sofa and a chair, the stove, and a tiny kitchen with space for two people to sit and eat, and an insulated chest for preserving food. Just off the main room were two small bedrooms and a room for bathing, the latter of which I entered to start a fire below the bathtub. Beneath the large stoneware basin, my father had dug a small, contained fire pit, which could be easily lit and extinguished as needed. Our home wasn't much, but it had been enough for the four of us once.

My gaze lingered on the larger of the two bedrooms, where I'd found the dead bodies of my father and five-year-old brother, Phillip and Oliver Gold.

Each time I remembered, I felt the scrape of the wail that tore through my throat when I found them. I'd only seen the aftermath. Three months after waking without memories, I found them in my parents' bed: eyes closed, asleep, with no signs of fear in their peaceful expressions. No worried creases had distorted their features. No bruises on their bodies. No signs of struggle. Either it had been so quick, they were both dead before they knew what was happening, or they'd been staged that way for me to find.

The cuts across their necks had been deep and precise. A merciful execution. But on each of their torsos, an X had been carved through their shirts. A mark, or a target, maybe. For what, I didn't know.

I stood near the hearth and stared at the worn leather sofa. Some nights, in the weeks after finding the bodies, I had woken to find my mother asleep there, hair cascading behind her head. Her own chestnut pillow.

Groaning, I rubbed my eyes with the heels of my hands. Perhaps out of some guilt-driven desire to punish myself—and ruin one of the only fond memories I had of her—I recalled the last thing my mother said to me before leaving eight weeks ago.

"I would give you up to have my boy back. I am done being your safe haven."

That made two of us. I would have switched places with him in a heartbeat.

It should have been you.

I shuddered at the vicious internal voice insistent on reminding me, entered the bathroom, and drew the curtains closed. As far as I knew, no one lived within miles of this cabin, but I couldn't shake the fear of being watched. Like someone had been waiting for me to return.

I shuddered the thought away and stopped to undress in front of the broken mirror that hung askew on the wall. From what I *could* remember, my pallid skin had once held color but it had gradually faded here in the wilderness. Now, all that was left was the bright pink of my near-frostbitten cheeks after nine—no, ten—hours in the freezing air. I had never hated my reflection, but it pierced me with sadness to see the skeletal lines of my body. Where strong, healthy curves had once arched and bowed through my chest, hips, and thighs, now I was frail and flat. But my mother had assured me, for reasons I didn't understand, that I would be wise to keep a thin stature.

"Delicate and light, Ary. Anything more is unbecoming."

My long, silver-blond hair was tangled at the ends and in desperate need of a trim. Loose strands escaped my braid and trailed down the sides of my face. A string of light freckles painted my cheeks and cascaded over the bridge of my nose. My green eyes were rimmed red with exhaustion.

I watched my reflection as I let my fingers linger over the small scar directly over my heart. Lower down, there was a faded horizontal smile on my abdomen from some surgery I'd had when I was young—a growth that had to be removed, according to my mother. But the scar on my chest was more prominent. I always called it my mystery scar, because my mother didn't know where it came from. Or perhaps she did know and chose not to tell me.

It wasn't the scars themselves that bothered me, but the fact that

I didn't have the memories to explain either of them. I might have found power in my scars had I recalled living through the pain.

I stared at the burning flames beneath the basin, aching to feel the heat. Most days, I let the fire burn longer than it should, but I looked forward to the steaming water. Hot enough to hurt, but not hot enough to peel the skin off my body.

It anchored me to the present, and made breathing just a little easier.

I climbed into the wide basin and let the water engulf me. Sweat prickled my forehead and my limbs burned. I suffered through the heat until I felt my body relaxing. Every muscle in my body was tired, so I laid my head back and let exhaustion take me.

When I woke, the candles I'd placed in the window were out and bathwater licked my naked body with a sinister chill.

I dried off, dressed in my nightgown, and lay down in the bed of blankets I had made for myself on the floor beside the hearth. Oliver and I had shared the smaller bedroom, but since his death, I found it difficult to sleep in a half-empty bed. Every time I tried, my fingers grazed the spot where his little body had once lain tucked up against me. I tried to imagine him there, but my imagination would drift too far, and instead of finding comfort, I found ghosts.

Hours later, a sound above the wailing wind stirred me from sleep. I sat up, wondering if my mother had returned. Unlikely but . . . just in case.

As soon as I rose, a loud, abrasive knock on the front door startled my stiff, frozen limbs to life.

"Ary!"

My eyes shot wide, and panic gripped my throat. That wasn't my mother's voice.

"Ary, you know who this is!"

I threw the covers off my legs, pinched my thigh, and waited to see if I was hallucinating. I hadn't heard that sharp, raspy, indignant voice in months.

I'd had an inkling someone was watching me earlier. I shouldn't have ignored it.

"I know you're in there! Don't pretend you can't hear me!"

"Impossible," I whispered. I pressed my ear to the front door and waited for her to speak again, if only to prove I hadn't fallen into a fever dream.

"Open the damn door, Ary!"

A tight ball of fury began to coil in the pit of my belly. Did she think she could come back like she never left? After . . . everything? I rested my hand on the knob and froze, cold air snaking up my bare legs from beneath the door, pricking at my skin.

"Damn it, Ary! I understand if you hate me, but it is cold as shit. I'm out of food and rum, and I am not afraid to break down this gods-damned door with a pickax—"

I yanked open the door and found myself staring into the angry, determined, bright-eyed, and beautiful face of my only true friend—Gemma Tremaine.

Chapter Two

Gemma had matured over the past few months. Her mahogany skin seemed a little darker and more worn from the sun. That made me think she had been in the south. The sun was scared to show its face this far north, especially with winter looming.

I remembered her ebony curls, disheveled from the wind. They were longer now, and pulled into a loose, messy bun. Stray strands framed her high cheekbones and striking amber eyes.

Gemma was a filthy-mouthed, relentless force of a woman. My parents had welcomed her into our home from one of the nearby villages, and while I only remembered a month with her, it had been enough time to form an attachment even stronger than any I'd formed with either of my parents.

Gemma was twenty-four—four years older than me. She'd shown me the kind of fire a woman could brandish with her tongue. During that month she'd told me stories of our world. Every one felt like a wonder to me, because history and travel—the world beyond this forest—were things my parents never spoke about.

A few weeks before Phillip and Ollie's deaths, however, Gemma had left us to seek new "living arrangements."

"There you are!" She reached out a foot to block the door before I could close it on her. I wasn't going to leave her out there. But I didn't plan on allowing her in right away, either. She would have to earn it.

I was still trying to recover from the shock of finding Gemma on my doorstep when she tried to step over the threshold. To her annoyance, I didn't budge. "You've got to be shitting me, Ary. Let me in."

"No."

"No?" she repeated, eyes wide and disbelieving.

"No," I said, but Gemma shifted forward to lean more of her weight against the door. "I said no. You can't come in."

"Ary—"

"What do you want?" I demanded.

She grumbled something unintelligible and, with just enough force to unbalance me, shoved past into the house.

"You've become such a gracious host, Ary." She wiped her boots on the bare floor, unslinging a crossbow from her back and placing it on a chair. Irritation burned my throat. I had just scrubbed that floor the day before in my desperate need to control…*something*. "Thanks for the warm welcome. 'What do you want?'" she repeated, scoffing, as she moved toward my father's dusty old liquor cabinet, inspecting the contents. "You don't seem to be overwhelmed with options here, do you?"

"I could say the same for you."

Gemma's body was curved, defined, and strong, but I could tell she was tired. She smirked, but that didn't hide the bags under her eyes. It was clear she hadn't bathed in days, either. She smelled a little, honestly.

"I won't deny it." She opened and closed the insulated chest. "I haven't had a drink since I stopped in Albertha, and that was two days ago. So you can imagine I'm parched." I picked up a half-empty glass of water and held it out for her, though I knew water wasn't what she desired. She took it anyway, eyeing me carefully.

"You haven't told me why you're here," I said.

"Well—"

"Or why you left when I needed you."

She paused abruptly, with my glass halfway to her lips. Her eyes narrowed.

"If you think it was my choice to leave, you never knew me at all."

My damn mother.

"She forced you out?" I asked, indignance pressing at my throat.

Gemma nodded, then scoffed. "Said I was getting a little too *mouthy*. Is she here?"

"No."

"I'm not surprised. When exactly did she leave?"

"Eight weeks ago."

"Eight weeks!" Gemma gasped. "Gods." She leaned against the counter, waiting for me to elaborate.

"I found . . . something," I began, uncertain whether to reveal the contents of the note that had sparked our final argument, "and I confronted her about it."

"Good." She pursed her lips and assessed me. "I hope you gave her hell."

When she'd lived with us, Gemma had worked to cultivate in me a little of her own biting wit, but defiance and aggression didn't come as naturally to me. She said I was too timid, dangerously so. Gemma had spoken of teaching me to fight as well, but we hadn't had much time or opportunity before she'd disappeared from my life.

"I doubt she's coming back," said Gemma.

My heart sank. I knew it was true, but hearing her say it cut deep. "I figured as much, but... how do you know?"

She pursed her lips but didn't answer. "You don't seem too devastated."

"I'm angry, not devastated." I folded my arms over my chest. "And don't avoid my questions. Why are you here?" I mindlessly scratched my elbow just to keep my hands busy. "Why now?"

"Well, you weren't supposed to be alone for eight damn *weeks*!" she hissed. "I was originally given the order to come back two weeks from now, right after your twentieth birthday, but the timeline changed."

"Given the order by who?"

"Elowen wasn't supposed to leave," she said without answering my question. "She was supposed to stay with you, but that woman does as she wants."

"She's alive?"

Gemma nodded. "Last I heard."

Sighing, knees trembling with relief, I sat down across from Gemma. My mother and I hadn't parted on the best terms. The bond between us had always been weak, and I might not have wept for long over her death. That didn't mean I'd *wished* for it.

"I need to show you something," I said.

I unfolded the letter to S and placed it in front of her. It was crumpled and torn in the corners, having lived in my pockets since the day I found it. As punishment for being the only Gold child still living, I had been forcing myself to read it every day.

Gemma glanced for less than a second then covered it with her palm and crinkled it into her fist.

I wasn't sure why I'd kept it with me, that damned note. Perhaps so I didn't forget the day I'd found it as I'd forgotten so many other things. I remembered the grim luster of the overcast sky, the dread I'd felt when descending the rickety stairway into the small cellar beneath the house. Knees protesting against the gravel as I knelt behind three boxes of my little brother's things.

A few weeks after Phillip and Ollie were murdered, I'd gone down into the cellar to grab a jar of jam. When I turned to leave, I noticed the corner of a small note with tattered edges peeking out between two of Ollie's old children's books. I saw his name scribbled in my mother's script and couldn't *not* read it.

Swallowing down my nerves, I'd unfolded it.

S,

Oliver has pneumonia. Ary has the same cold that caused it. Please send for help or come with provisions yourself. I need you.

Elowen

Supplies *had* mysteriously arrived on our doorstep the week we'd both been sick. At the time, I hadn't thought much of it, but now I wondered if someone else—this S, perhaps—had sent those supplies.

I'd confronted my mother about the note. Her response had been short and cold.

"You know what you need to know, and nothing more."

I scowled at the memory. Those hazel eyes had never been a maternal refuge, not for me. A protective, loving fire had burned in them for Oliver, but a chilly indifference fell across them when they were trained in my direction.

I blinked as if to shed tears that never fell for Elowen Gold.

"Do you know who he is?" I pressed Gemma. She took a swig of water and avoided my pleading eyes. I snatched the glass from her hands so she had little choice but to match my stare. "Gemma, who is this letter written to?"

"Damn Elowen for leaving me to do her dirty work." With a reluctant sigh, she met my gaze. Her eyes held curiosity and pity that irked me. She gestured for me to return the water. "Did you ever wonder why Phillip was a drunkard?"

My mother had never confessed to blaming me for Phillip's drinking. But she didn't have to. The melancholy expression he'd often worn in my presence made it clear there was something about me that haunted him, and she resented that. Resented *me*.

"Of course I wondered," I answered softly, sliding her glass across the table.

"Did you ever wonder why you don't look like him?"

I looked down at my hands. My father and little brother had tawny complexions with dirty blond hair, a stark contrast to my pale skin and strange silvery locks.

"I never looked like Elowen, either." I'd envied her stunning chestnut waves, high cheekbones, and hazel eyes.

"That's because you look like your father." Her fingers danced on the small oak table. "Your real father."

I gulped and rubbed my hands together to soothe the

quickening chill in my fingers that had nothing to do with the temperature of the air.

"*S?*" I asked, barely whispering.

"Simeon. Simeon Whitlock."

I thought I'd heard the name before. Maybe once or twice, my father—*Phillip*—or my mother had spoken of him when they thought I wasn't listening. Something about his wishes, his orders, and it not being "time."

"My mother had an affair?"

Gemma nodded, apologetic.

I expected to feel more anger than I did, but a part of me might already have suspected the news. Phillip had always seemed detached and we'd never formed a strong bond. Still, I'd always thought of myself as his child and Oliver's sister.

But now I realized his detachment…I must have reminded him of my mother's lover.

"What about Ollie?"

"Theirs," she replied. "He was Phillip's."

Numbness coated my throat. At least Ollie and I shared a mother. He *was* my brother. I could hold on to that.

My mother was right, though. It should have been me that died that day.

The belief that I was *theirs* had been a thread tying me to both of my parents. Until now.

Now, that weak thread snapped. I recognized myself for the burden I had always been—and a constant reminder of marital betrayal to Phillip.

"I know that look." Gemma's sharp, stunning features twisted with pity. "It's not your fault Phillip drank."

"That's not—" I sighed, attempting to steady my voice. "I'm not so worried about that."

Though I'd had no control over the circumstances of my birth, I couldn't help but feel guilty for the trail of consequences left in its path. When I'd asked my mother why we lived in solitude here in the forest, she'd often told me, "Conflict breeds more conflict." I'd taken it to mean that staying quiet and reclusive would keep us out of trouble. But if I was the product of betrayal, then perhaps conflict had followed me—followed me here, to Phillip and Ollie.

The deepest, darkest parts of me—parts that wanted to blame myself just to have answers—wondered if it had.

"Am I the reason they're dead?"

Gemma's lips parted, but she gave no answer.

Horror clawed at my stomach. I turned my back to her, nauseated and struggling to breathe.

"I don't know," she admitted softly. "Word of their deaths got to me, but I . . . I don't know who killed them."

Elowen blamed me for their deaths, though—I was certain of that. She had never said it outright, but she didn't have to. Whoever had killed them must have been there to kill me, but I had been out in the forest collecting berries.

She blamed me. That was why she had left me. Because after they were murdered, she could barely stand to look at me.

My shoulders remained sore and heavy, laden with guilt.

"Ary," Gemma gently implored. "I'm so sorry. I shouldn't have let her force me out." The wooden floor creaked as she drew closer. "But you're the one trying to force me out now. Don't," she pleaded from behind me. I felt her touch my hand, and I recoiled. "Please, listen—"

"I don't think I can listen to any more right now." I stepped away with every intention of locking myself in the bedroom I never slept in. But halfway there, I paused, fists clenched. "I'm not forcing you out. You can stay, if you want."

Please don't go, I silently begged. Saying the words aloud was too exposing, like showing an open wound.

And mercifully, Gemma stayed. For the rest of the day, she and I coexisted in silence. More than once, I tried to speak, desperate to fill the void that her news had carved inside me, but I couldn't find the right words. That night, though I'd tried and failed to sleep in the bed—it was too cold—I returned to the floor beside the fire. I wanted to be alone, but I wanted to sleep even more. To quiet the hateful voices snarling at my soul.

It took me a while to settle that evening, and I could feel her nervous gaze flickering over me as I lay on the floor by the fire. When she wasn't peering at me by the light of the flames, I began to watch her, too, and I noticed things I hadn't before.

A pale, jagged line of a scarring—a stark contrast to her dark complexion—began behind her ear and disappeared deep into her collarbone. That wasn't the only scar. There was another one, less noticeable, to the left of her forehead, receding into her hairline. Both were new. Marks of the rough and ragged life she'd lived. They were half hidden, and I wondered what else she hid, realizing that I had never thought to ask much about where Gemma came from. She had been orphaned, but where? And how long ago?

I frowned, as my stomach twisted with unease.

Was it possible she'd also been lied to? She was always tough and honest, often cold to anyone but me. Had she been abandoned? Then accepted by two strangers, Phillip and Elowen Gold, only to truly be forced back out by the closest thing she knew to a family?

Having her back set relief and unease warring in my mind. She was a cure for my loneliness but brought with her a whole host of mysteries.

My stressed mind was finally dulled by exhaustion, and I drifted to sleep—a dreamless one, thankfully. When dawn broke, I rose wearily from my floor bed and caught Gemma half asleep, leaning against the front door.

"Gemma?"

"Shit!" She startled awake and took inventory of her surroundings—bright eyes frantic—before rising to her feet. "Sorry. I was going to try for a hunt but didn't want to leave you before you woke. Fell asleep here. All you have is vegetable broth and the eggs are gone. The cellar is out of reserves. You have no food, Ary."

I worked my throat through a swallow and nodded. "I went to the nearest village to try and trade or buy something, but..."

I hadn't had enough to give. And for a while after my mother left, I hadn't even cared if I starved. But I had no desire to discuss why I hadn't done more for myself.

I decided to change the subject instead.

"Where did you come from, Gemma?"

"You mean where did I go?" She pushed against the front door handle to stand. Her brow was furrowed, and she was massaging her neck, undoubtedly sore from the position she'd slept in. "Before I came back here, I was bouncing back and forth between Avendrel and Wymara to—"

"No, I mean... I know your parents are gone, but are there others? How did Phillip and Elowen come to know you? Where are your people?"

"My people?" She snickered. I crossed my arms, then uncrossed them again, nervous. Her expression softened as she noticed my anxiety.

"My people are your people, Ary, and I'll tell you about them, but first, we... *you*," she emphasized, gesturing to my frail form, "need to eat. If you start some tea and the stove, I'll fetch some more eggs from the barn, and then I'll take you on a hunt."

"I'll go to the barn," I offered. "The hens haven't laid in a while, but they need their food and I could use the fresh air."

Gemma opened her mouth to protest but refrained as she watched me slide my tattered leather boots on. "Hurry. It's cold. Do you want me to come with you?"

"I'll be fine." I paused with my hand on the doorknob and turned around to see her watching me, beautiful light brown eyes rich with sympathy. "You'll be here?"

"Yes." She nodded, smiling brightly. "I promise."

The woolen interior of my boots did little to keep me warm as I stepped outside. I tightened my shawl around my neck and increased my pace, but last night's thick layer of snow and my lingering hunger made it impossible to escape the cold.

I inhaled the crisp air to clear my throat. The wind swirled around me, and my eyes watered, but no tears fell. A powerful sense of relief washed over me. I pinched the skin of my forearm to remind myself this was real. Someone else—Gemma—was *here*. I let out a sigh and trudged through the predawn darkness to the barn, eager to be back within four walls, if only to block the wind.

A gust in the night had blown the door to the barn wide open. It knocked against the wall in an unsettling rhythm. With heavy feet, I moved inside and grabbed the rusty handle to wrestle the door closed. I didn't fasten the lock, to avoid fumbling with it in the dark on my way out, hopefully one or two fresh eggs in my hands. To allow in more light, I opened the creaky shutters on the window nearest to the hens.

When I turned to face Daisy, I gasped. She wasn't perched in her nest, fluffed up against the cold. Brown and white feathers were strewn about the floor with drops of red intermingled.

Red. So much red.

My pulse pounded in my ears.

"Daisy?" I whispered, spinning around in my search. But the trail of feathers and blood led nowhere. "Penny?" I turned to my right. Penny wasn't in her nest, either. No, her nest had been demolished, and there was a large smear of blood on the side of it. "Penny, where…"

A pair of deep golden eyes peered at me from the corner of the barn. They belonged to a dark shape partially hidden in shadow. I could just make out a bird's limp and mangled body—Penny's body—hanging from the mouth of the creature. The slow drip of her blood from its mouth. My throat tightened. I felt a draft and thought for a moment of Penny's spirit escaping through the partially open window.

Drip… drip… drip…

Penny's lifeless form fell to the floor. The wolf lunged at me. I retreated quickly enough to avoid its jaws, kicking it once in the snout. The wolf reeled back, disoriented, and I lunged for a garden hoe a few feet away.

I held up my improvised weapon as it closed in once again.

"No!" I screeched, but the wolf had me cornered. I jabbed at its gnashing teeth.

I had only ever seen a wolf from afar. Up close, the creature's jaws were far larger and more terrifying than I could ever have imagined. Bloody saliva dripped from its teeth.

I had never been trained to fight a human. Certainly not a vicious animal like this.

"Get back!" I shouted, threatening it with the hoe. It would not be long before the wolf realized my garden tool was no match for its brute strength and insatiable appetite. "Get away from me!"

When I shifted to the left in a meek attempt to escape, it snarled and advanced a few steps. I jabbed at it again, which only seemed to anger it more.

Before I could react, it leaped at me and locked its jaw around my right arm. The sting and pressure of the bite dragged a wail from my throat.

The wolf tossed my body across the floor of the barn, and my head crashed against an empty feed barrel. My vision blurred. Tears formed in my eyes, on my cheeks, but I had forgotten how to breathe. And if I could not breathe, I could not weep.

"Please!" I tried to gasp an appeal to my attacker. My unwounded left arm was my only defense. Blindly, I held it up, waiting for the final strike.

Chapter Three

But the attack never came. The wolf had stopped snarling, and in a confused moment, blurred by tears and terror, I could have sworn I heard a yelp.

The room whirled around me like I was at the center of a spinning top. I focused on my palm, which grasped the hay-covered floor of the barn, trying to maintain my balance. Though my vision was still blurred, I could see a large figure hovering above me. Not Gemma. A man. The early morning light that snuck through the windows revealed him: massive, clad humbly but sturdily in dark, worn leather.

A clang pierced the taut silence: his blade, dropping to the floor. He stumbled in shock then fell to his knees before me. His hands went straight for my face. I froze, defenseless and afraid. But his hands, though rough and calloused, were gentle on my skin. Focusing on his face helped me stabilize and kept the room from spiraling around me. He had brown eyes, like hickory, plagued by something like… sorrow.

On the right side of his face was a jagged scar beginning over his eyebrow and fading down his cheek, disappearing into his dark beard. His shoulder-length hair was the same dark color, tied back partially in a knot.

"Who—who are you?" I stuttered, trying to calm my shaking body. I shifted to pull away from him, startled by the way he'd touched me. Like he *knew* me. But my balance was still faulty and I had no idea which way to go.

At the sound of my voice, he exhaled sharply, like the wind had just been knocked out of him. He moved his hands from my face to my shoulders, where they carefully rubbed, warming me. This man, whoever he was, could snap me in half with one squeeze of those powerful hands. But he was gentle, the careful movement of his fingers wildly at odds with his size and rough appearance. Not to mention the way that he just killed a wolf like it was nothing.

And then . . . three simple words.

"I found you."

My chest tightened and my body trembled. But I found myself fighting the strangest urge—to relax at the sound of his voice. Its deep soothing timbre filled me with a sense of safety that was impossible to explain. I didn't know this man. I reminded myself of this again and again, sucking in a breath as he shifted closer. As one rough hand returned to my cheek with a soft caress. When he moved, the early morning light streamed in through the cracks of the rickety barn and over his face, revealing brimming emotion in his gaze. "You're safe."

I found the courage to look past him. The wolf lay dead on the floor of the henhouse, neck contorted and bleeding, bones crushed.

"It's dead," I breathed.

He cleared his throat. "Yes. Are you hurt?" His eyes shifted to the right of my face, where I could feel a slow, trickling warmth. "You hit your head?"

I nodded and lifted a wavering hand to the rapidly rounding bulge by my right temple. My hair was warm and damp with blood. He tilted my head to both sides to assess the damage.

"Is your vision blurred?"

"I . . . I don't know." Because I was still shaking.

He held up three fingers.

"How many?"

"Th-three."

He nodded and fastened his grip around my elbow. I flinched. Not because it hurt, but because it clearly could if he wanted it to. "Can you walk?"

I swayed when I tried to stand, even while using him for stability. His forearm was so hard and thick, my small hand couldn't fit even halfway around it.

"I . . . I . . ."

My feet were off the ground before a coherent thought could form.

In one swift movement he lifted me into his arms. Now he cradled me, one arm beneath my knees, the other strong and firm against my back. Instinctively—and I didn't have the slightest clue where that instinct came from—I wrapped my arms around his neck and let my cheek rest against his chest. My impulse was reckless, but . . . he smelled like whiskey, leather, cedar, and fire, and his swift, solid movements made me wonder if I could close my eyes and rest. Just for a second. Under the light of dawn I could see the veins pressing against the skin of his muscular neck, the tightness of his jaw. He was holding something in.

As soon as we crossed the threshold of the cabin, he lowered me gently to the floor but kept a hand on the small of my back to ensure my steadiness. I was about to turn to get a better look at him in the light when Gemma rushed into the room.

"Ary, there you are! These idiots just arrived while you were out, and—shit!" She gasped when she saw my battered form and rushed over to me. "Are you all right? What the hell happened?"

The man's hand still rested against my back, and as Gemma grew closer, it flexed. "There was a wolf in the barn." I cleared my throat. "The chickens are gone."

Gemma pulled me in for a tight hug. She moved away to reveal three young men standing around the kitchen table. Two had black hair, one sandy blond, and all three had kindness in their eyes. While none were as intimidating as my wolf slayer, these men—all here at once—made my family's humble cabin look comically small and crowded.

When I shifted to remove my shawl, pain flashed through my arm. Beneath it, I saw the wolf's bite for the first time.

"Ugh," I whispered, studying my own ragged flesh and trying not to grow nauseous. It looked even worse than it felt.

"May I?"

A startled noise—part squeak, part gasp—escaped my throat when a deep voice rumbled beside me.

Before I could answer, his long, rugged fingers locked around my other arm, pulling me to the chair next to the fireplace. I gulped down nerves when he knelt on my right. He made a motion for me to reach out my wounded arm. I paused, eyeing him warily. I knew I absolutely *should* be wary of a massive, menacingly handsome older man touching me with hands that had effortlessly killed a wolf mere moments ago.

"That bite needs to be treated," he commanded, his deep voice beguilingly soft but stern. "Let me help you." His appeal cut deeper than the wound on my arm, but it also warmed my chest. I sucked in a breath, startled by my body's hasty reaction.

I cautiously obliged, peeling back the sleeve of my shirt. Gemma gasped in horror at the sight of the wound.

The wolf slayer wasted no time. Unfazed by the gore, he fastened an iron grip around my wrist and reached for a bottle of foul-smelling liquor from his bag. He pulled the cork out with his teeth and held my arm still. I flinched and sucked in a breath at the stinging pain when he poured it over my wounded skin. His eyes flashed to mine.

It was clear this wasn't his first time tending to a wound, and I was glad to be in the hands of a man who knew exactly what he was doing.

"The bandage will need to be changed no later than this time tomorrow. Sooner, if it bleeds through." When he had finished, he gently fastened and closed the bandage. I flinched at the pressure and friction of the cloth. Our eyes met briefly, my pulse climbed sharply, and sweat dampened my palms. "Then you should change it daily, or more often if it gets wet, until you heal."

"Thank—" I cleared my throat, but my voice was still a mere whisper. "Thank you."

He gave me a single, stern nod and stood, towering over me. His deep brown stare lingered on my face. So intense I could hardly stand it.

"You're lucky it didn't get your whole arm, aren't you?" One of the men spoke up from the kitchen table, mercifully cutting the tension in the room. When I glanced back at my wolf slayer, he'd already retreated to stand against the wall beside the hearth.

"Don't scare her!" Gemma had started to prepare drinks for each of my visitors. She used her foot to shove a pair of casually outstretched boots off the table. "She's not exactly used to four *dirty* men showing up in her cabin."

I had little knowledge of men, but all the newcomers appeared to be in their mid- to upper twenties—older than me but younger than my wolf slayer.

Gemma brought me a glass of water and, upon seeing the goose egg on my forehead, wrapped some ice and snow in a cloth to reduce the swelling. And the rest of them stared at me. It was an effort not to recoil from the attention. Their gazes were friendly, but the way they all watched... I felt on display. They were all very attractive, and I didn't know how long to look or if I *should* look or if it was rude to stare, but *they* were all looking at *me.*

So I couldn't help but stare back with wide eyes, politeness be damned.

"Gemma?" I hissed nervously, afraid to take my eyes off them all. "Who's in my house?"

She moved to stand behind my chair. With a hand on each shoulder, she guided my attention back toward the sofa, where the three younger men had settled.

"They are here to help."

I pulled back from Gemma and shot her a nervous glare.

"Caz Sinclair," said the first of the men, his voice cheerful and smooth. He was the tallest of the three, lean with shiny black hair and hazel eyes. I guessed he was the oldest, too, though younger than the man who'd saved me. He presented himself with a dramatic, playful bow. "And my brother, Finn," Caz added, gesturing to the man sitting beside him. He looked a year or two younger, with almost all the same features, including those hazel eyes. He was slightly shorter than Caz, but what he lacked in height he made up for with greater brawn.

"An honor." Finn bowed more reservedly than his brother. "We have waited a long time to meet you."

The third of them—the young man with sandy blond hair and freckles—gave me a shy smile and nodded. "Yes, an honor," he echoed Finn's sentiment. "I'm Ezra Hart."

I shot a wary glance in Gemma's direction.

"You—" My throat scraped, drawing heat to my cheeks in embarrassment. "It's good to meet you, too," I finished shyly.

"Why so quiet?" Caz's eyes twinkled. "We are here for your protection and companionship. Nothing more."

"Why do I need protection?" I glared at Gemma.

She didn't answer, only winced and turned to the others. Vexed, I crossed my arms over my chest, careful to avoid brushing against my wound. What else had she *forgotten* to tell me?

I turned to my mysterious savior, who still hadn't introduced himself. He was standing by the fireplace, without a jacket, illuminated by the cabin's dim light. He stood with his arms crossed, too, though he was at least a full head and shoulders taller than me. Huge. His expression was cold, grumpy, and the muscles of his jaw were flexed. He looked... brutal.

I noticed, though, that his dark brown hair and matching beard were well kept. Wild, yet reserved. He wore all black, shirtsleeves rolled up to his elbows, top button undone. Both forearms were covered in tattoos, uniform tally marks that spiraled up, around, and into his sleeves. His muscles were clenched so tight that the veins in his thick, corded forearms were visible.

Yet despite the tension in his body, those warm, hickory eyes glowed like honey.

He was so savagely beautiful and exhilaratingly terrifying that I had to remind myself to breathe.

When the air caught in my throat, he noticed. His stern expression turned tortured, and his dark eyebrows drew together.

He silently observed while the other three exchanged small talk about their journey, drinks, supper, and the weather. The tension that radiated off him should have irked me. Instead, the power of his stare was so magnetic that I couldn't help but feel it centered me, for better or for worse.

"I was told there would be three, not four." Gemma's voice was unnaturally high pitched in the way it often was when she was stressed. She brought a tray of hot tea, coffee, and mugs to the sofa. "I expected the Sinclair brothers and Ezra. That is what Simeon, Elowen, and the Wintertons agreed to. Three. No more, no less." She scowled at my wolf slayer in the corner of the room. "So who are *you*?" Something I, too, was quite interested to know.

"That's Smyth. Simeon's orders, last minute," retorted Caz, then nodded at me. "I bet our girl here is glad he tagged along."

My cheeks flooded with heat. Words—all of them—were trapped in my throat. My pleading eyes sought out Gemma, desperate for aid. I should have been more than nervous in this situation. I should have been *angry*...

But there were six people in total in my home, including

Gemma and this . . . Smyth. More presence, more *life,* than I could ever remember inside these walls. Against my better judgment, despite my nerves and inability to speak, I found I was enjoying the sudden and welcome warmth of company.

Loneliness had made me irrational.

"Not *your* girl, you creep." Ezra flashed his bright blue eyes at Caz, his voice a teasing groan.

"Oh, don't act like you didn't spend the entire last week talking about anything but meeting her, Ez." Caz took a casual sip of his coffee and lifted an eyebrow at Ezra.

"Yeah, but she's my—" Ezra stopped himself, glaring at Caz before turning to me. He had an uncanny resemblance to Oliver, both with his sandy blond hair and dimples. And those deep blue eyes . . . those were Phillip's and Oliver's eyes. "You're my cousin." His awkwardness was endearing—though it did little to help my nerves. At least I wasn't the only anxious one. "By marriage anyway. My mom was Phillip's older sister," he rushed out.

"What?" I sucked in a ragged breath. I didn't know Phillip had a sister, or *any* extended family now that I thought about it. "Gemma?"

"He's telling the truth." Gemma spoke slowly, like she feared I was having a hard time understanding. She rested her long fingers on Ezra's forearm. "He's your cousin, Ary. He's family."

"My family is gone."

The words flew from my lips like blades. And I hated myself for saying them. Finn and Caz both crossed their hands in their laps and pursed their lips, waiting patiently for someone else to fill the silence. Ezra sighed. I expected anger, but his blue eyes were rich with empathy, and I hoped he wouldn't hold my outburst against me.

I stole a glance at the man they called Smyth and saw he had trained his unreadable eyes on the floor, muscles still flexing in his jaw.

"I'm sorry." I sighed, forcing my attention back to Ezra. "I'm sorry, that was uncalled for."

Ezra waved it away and shrugged. "You've been through a lot." He looked at me, then at the others, then chuckled. "If it was dropped on me that I was destined to save the world, I'd be a bit miffed, too."

Gemma rubbed her eyes and sighed.

"What?" I choked. I was still very angry with Gemma, but that anger didn't rival the fear rising from deep inside me.

"You haven't told her?" Finn nearly shouted, his expression a mix of stress and amusement. "Well, *shit*."

"This should be fun." Caz leaned back in his seat and folded a pair of toned arms behind his head. His eyes twinkled beneath a few strands of black hair—far messier than his brother's.

"I was getting around to it," Gemma grumbled, scowling at them both. "Elowen didn't exactly fill Ary in on the situation. I just told her Simeon's her real father, and she needed time to process." She wrung her hands together before throwing them in the air. "Such a gods-damned mess!"

I swallowed hard and looked around at them all, attempting to garner a look of encouragement or confidence, *something* that didn't make me feel completely and utterly lost. My gaze landed on the towering mass of man in the corner. Smyth's gaze locked with mine immediately. Almost as if he'd been waiting for me to turn his way.

The sense of safety I'd felt when he carried me back from the barn still soothed me. But it was...wrong. I knew that I was so desperate for connection that I yearned to trust whoever walked through my front door. For some reason, my instinct had chosen him, but I had a feeling it probably shouldn't have.

"What do you need to tell me?" I retrained my eyes on Gemma, feeling slightly steadier. "Tell me."

Gemma sat down in the empty armchair across from me, folded her long fingers in her lap, and cleared her throat. "Do you remember me telling you about the Dark Ages? Over four hundred years ago, when the Rexus dynasty ruled over Nyrida."

I nodded. The Rexus family had been eradicated long ago, but before that, they had held power for centuries. They were ruthless. They used fear and lies to demand subordination from the people.

"Nyrida was starving to death under their rule. Those who weren't starving were fighting each other, while the ruling tyrants kept all the wealth and power to themselves. Until the people found a way to overthrow them. People—or specifically, two men." Her eyes darted to the others while she divulged details she'd never given me before. "Some say those men made a deal with the twelve gods. Others say they just got lucky."

I shifted in my seat. Phillip and Elowen never let me read any books about our pantheon of twelve gods—the Selvaren. I knew there were twelve, and I knew they offered no help and no mercy to the poor and desperate. Beyond that, they were a mystery to me.

"What do *you* say?"

Gemma sighed. "Wherever they got their abilities, I say we

should have known that humankind cannot handle unlimited power without misusing it."

Apprehension snaked like a prickly vine around my neck.

"Those two young men, childhood friends..." Gemma straightened her shoulders and continued. "They went looking for the magic of the Selvaren—a magic only spoken about in legends. They knew it might be a lost cause, a silly story for children with overactive imaginations, but they were desperate to find some way to overthrow the tyrants. It took them over a decade, but that magic? They found it hidden somewhere beneath Nyrida's surface. They never disclosed exactly where or how. But they kept this power for themselves and used it to destroy the Rexus family. The battle was quick and bloodless. The future was meant to be peaceful and sustainable—a better world for our people. And it worked. For a while, this world had a new start. The land was cultivated through good magic. The people were treated fairly, resources shared, power distributed equitably. For the first time in centuries, Nyrida held hope for a future."

"Okay." I shifted in my seat. "Go on."

Gemma's eyes darted around the room again before confessing, "One of those two men was Simeon, your father."

Disbelief sent me staring around the room, gauging the others' reactions. But they were all unsurprised. My brow rose. "I thought these men were alive over four hundred years ago."

I jumped at the sharp flick of Caz's tongue on the roof of his mouth. He wiggled his fingers in the air. "Magic of the Selvaren, Your Highness."

Finn rolled his eyes at his brother and muttered, "Read the room." Caz chuckled. I took note that the older of the handsome, black-haired brothers seemed to think there was no time or place too serious for a lighthearted joke. Maybe I'd appreciate that later, but not right now.

"Magic," I repeated skeptically. Yes, sure, *magic*. The magic of the gods was a myth.

Even if they were telling the truth, this Simeon fellow had made no effort to be a part of my life. If Elowen was writing to him, he knew about me and knew what I was to him. Yet he remained absent. Not a single effort to connect with his daughter. He had no right involving me in whatever mess he'd gotten himself in. I would let Gemma say her piece but decided I didn't have to accept it.

"After the Rexus family was overthrown, Simeon became one of the rulers of these lands. As his only daughter, that makes you a queen, Ary." Gemma bit her lip, her eyes filled with apology for what she was about to admit. "*The* queen, actually. Of Nyrida."

Chapter Four

"The queen," I repeated slowly.

Gemma nodded.

With a low groan, I closed my eyes in an attempt to reject all other stimuli beyond her words.

"I mentioned there were two men." Gemma's voice lowered. "The other is named Molochai."

Is. She had said *is*, not *was*. My apprehension spiraled. This had to mean Molochai was still alive after four hundred years, just like Simeon. And if that wasn't enough to churn my stomach, his eerie name did the trick.

"Simeon prefers to work through herbs, potions, and spells. He was—*is*—by the book, while Molochai has been more... experimental with the magic. Back then, they ruled Nyrida together, and the new world flourished. But eventually, Molochai found he wanted the one thing he couldn't have."

The dread in Gemma's stare mirrored my own.

"Simeon had a sister," she continued, "ten years younger than him and Molochai. Her name was Christabel. She was angelically beautiful, and while Simeon and Molochai were worshipped like gods, they let Christabel be the queen of the people, loved and unconditionally revered. Simeon—even Molochai, at the time—knew they needed to rule differently than those before them in order to gain the people's trust. The males in the Rexus family had been ruthless, and they felt Nyrida would be far more amenable to a woman in charge."

"Or at least, the appearance of a woman in charge," Finn added, tipping his mug at me. "They made most of the decisions themselves but made Christabel the figurehead. And they said that as long as there was a female alive in the bloodline, a female would rule."

"A ruler with a softer heart," added Caz, resting his hand over his chest. "Less chance of a revolt."

"So they used her?" I asked.

"She agreed to it." Gemma shot both Sinclair brothers an annoyed look. "And Molochai loved her—was obsessed with her—but the moment *she* was old enough to know love, she gave her heart to someone else. While Molochai treated her with gifts, with magic, with anything she could possibly want, she didn't love him back. Her heart belonged to someone else. A young, well-respected soldier. When Christabel married him and became pregnant with his child, whatever goodness kept Molochai at bay was destroyed. His rage was unleashed. After she had the child, Molochai killed Christabel's husband, and then he killed the babe. Stabbed it through the heart at only a few days old."

Bile rose in my throat. The kind of evil it would take to kill a child, an *infant*…

Gemma paused to let the information settle, searching me warily. I looked at Caz and Finn across from me, Ezra beside me, all three sitting quietly with their hands folded in their laps. Though their expressions were solemn, they seemed otherwise unperturbed, as if this was a story they were hearing for the hundredth time. A morbid yet inescapable part of history.

"Why am I just hearing this now?" Resentment gripped my heart in its angry vise. My nostrils flared. Instinct drew my attention to Smyth, whose mouth was pressed into a line, jaw firmly clenched, rage imprisoned. Perhaps on my behalf. I soaked in the welcome sense of solidarity.

"Because your parents have been trying to protect you." Gemma stood from the table and paced back and forth across the kitchen. Only three steps each way, it was so small. "You see, killing Christabel's child was not enough revenge for Molochai. He went back to the place he and Simeon found their magic, and he took more. He took something dark and evil—all-consuming shadows. Then he cursed Christabel with a horrific illness that forced her to die a slow, agonizing death. She died eighteen years later, childless, at thirty-nine. For years, Simeon and Molochai fought for control of Nyrida. Simeon is strong, but his spells could not hold back Molochai's shadows. Eventually, the land was divided between them, with Simeon ruling in the north and Molochai controlling the south."

"And now, after four hundred years, Simeon got my mother pregnant and Molochai wants to kill me?" I guessed.

Gemma sighed, as if she had the right to be just as overwhelmed as I was, then continued. "It's believed that when Simeon and Molochai unlocked their magic, it latched on to their families. Christabel began to have visions of the future. Within the last few years of her life, many of those visions proved to be legitimate.

Three days before she passed, she woke in the middle of the night and summoned Simeon into her room with one final premonition."

I stared out the window and tried to remember hints of this story in the hopes Phillip and my mother had told me *something*. That they hadn't kept me in the dark. And maybe they hadn't, not before the accident, but since then my memory was gone, any attempt I made was futile.

Whenever I got close to anything whole, it was torn back by some mysterious force, as if whatever injury I sustained—whatever constraint kept my memories from me—was alive and actively fighting me.

"What was the premonition?" I asked.

Gemma cleared her throat. "'A young queen born of ancient blood will abandon a life of solitude, wield her gods-blessed power, marry the prince of the people, and resurrect this world from Molochai's darkness.'"

Young. Ancient blood. Abandon a life of solitude. *Power.*

Oh, no. No, no, no.

These people thought it was me.

My eyes widened while Gemma's words—Christabel's words—played on a loop in my mind. Was that why Phillip and my mother had kept me here, to shelter me from all of this until I was old enough? Would I ever be old enough? Ready enough? Had they wanted to give me a normal childhood? That might have worked had I remembered any of it.

Had *Gemma* been sent to our home just to socialize me? After waking with no memory at nineteen, I *had* begun to withdraw. But to give me a friend just to take her away... something felt off.

Especially when I looked down at my frail hands.

"No." The filthy old mirror on the wall mocked me with the

reflection of my growing unease. "That's not right. I don't have any power."

"Ary." She stopped pacing. Her tone slowed and softened. "You're far from alone in this. When Simeon retreated into the north, he allied with a powerful family called the Wintertons. From the horrors Molochai wrought upon our people in the war came solidarity. Together, they built a fortress under the walls of a mountain, to keep Molochai's forces contained out of our lands. And their stronghold has grown over the last four hundred years."

Gemma bent down and took my hands. "Molochai still controls most of our regions to the south, but we still hold the north. And the fortress—the Winterton Caves—that's where your mother is now!" Gemma added this with a smile, as if news of my neglectful mother would make it all better. "Our leader, Alistair Winterton, and his wife, Ophelia, are currently in charge there. And that's why we're here. To escort you to Simeon. He will train you in your power, and then you'll go to the caves."

I shook my head, but she squeezed my hands, nodding, attempting to comfort me. "Thousands of people waiting for you, ready to fight at your side, ready to serve you."

Ezra cleared his throat and gave Gemma a pointed look. She shot a glare of warning right back.

"There's more?" I choked out.

She sighed in resignation and cringed. "The 'prince of the people' in the prophecy? We know that must be Alistair Winterton's grandson, Elias. He's the commander of your army, and he's going to be your husband."

Husband. The word caught in my mind like a prickly burr.

"Why?" I trembled, looking frantically between each of them

until landing on Smyth—the man that gave me an unexpected sense of safety—in a final, desperate plea for help. "I don't... I don't want a husband."

How could I? I was only nineteen. I had never lived, had never even been kissed. Smyth's broad shoulders sank with a heavy sigh, and out of his tortured eyes poured unexpected compassion.

"Because you need his army," Gemma answered, drawing my attention back to her. "The people will fight best under a united leadership."

"And I have to *marry him* for a united leadership?"

"Simeon made a deal with the Wintertons." Ezra shrugged. "And it's in Christabel's prophecy."

Finding Phillip and Oliver dead with their throats slit had nearly destroyed my sanity. But not completely. Now, I was afraid I was losing my mind once again. I could imagine it giving way, in a single, audible *snap*.

I was prophesied to destroy the darkest, most powerful sorcerer in the world. But first I had to marry some random prince. Gemma mentioned my marriage like... an afterthought. As if giving my heart to some man I didn't know was a reasonable expectation.

My heart raced. My breaths grew shallow. Tears swelled behind my eyes. I could try to run. If Gemma, Ezra, or the Sinclair brothers didn't catch me, Smyth would. Only an imbecile would think they could *run* from a man like that. And something else tugged in my chest, begging me to weigh the options more carefully before letting my flight response take over.

Would it be better to live a dull, lonely life of my own choosing? Or would I enjoy a life full of travel and adventure, even if every important choice was already made for me?

If I refused, would they drag me out of here anyway? And if they let me stay, did I really want to spend the rest of my life in a house full of nothing but hunger and ghosts?

"I need some air." I nearly knocked over my mug of tea as I rose abruptly from my seat.

"Ary!" Gemma stood to follow, but I was halfway out the door. Quick when I wanted to be. "Ary, wait—"

The cabin's door slammed behind me, cutting off her words and granting me immediate reprieve from the suffocating truths within walls that now felt like a prison cell.

Her story wheeled through my mind on a loop until I memorized each and every detail. Details of the world I lived in but was hearing for the first time. At least a thousand people desperate for my arrival and eager for guidance I was incapable of providing. A betrothal to a renowned soldier I had never met and would likely disappoint with my lack of confidence and abilities. Two 400-year-old men, one of them my real father, the other an evil sorcerer who, according to a prophecy from my dead, clairvoyant aunt, only I could kill.

But I weighed 110 pounds and certainly had no magic.

It all felt like a cosmic joke, and I couldn't shake the image of the gods, or god, or whoever was out there, reclining in their golden chairs with a refreshing drink, watching me scramble, laughing at me.

Behind me, the door of the cabin squeaked open.

"Gemma, I need to be—"

I froze. It wasn't Gemma. The sight of Smyth's towering form in the eerie light of the winter moon glued my tongue to the roof of my mouth. I sucked in a breath as he covered the distance between us, my tattered blue knit hat and gloves in his large hand and a thick wool blanket draped over his forearm.

"What are you doing?" I wiped away my tears with the back of my hand. He carefully slid my hat over my head, my gloves on my small hands, and laid the blanket over my shoulders.

"I could ask you the same thing." He stepped back and folded his powerful arms across his broad chest. He gave a subtle nod of approval at my covered body and gave me space. "You just ran outside into the dead of winter without a coat. You're asking for frostbite, hypothermia, or both."

"I wanted to be alone."

"That's not happening," he answered tersely. "But you won't know I'm here."

I wasn't sure that was possible. His rigid stare burrowed into my back, like a fox hell-bent on making me its den.

"What happens if I say no?" I gulped, glancing back, then up at him. *Gods*, he was big. "What happens if I stay here?"

"If you're lucky, eventually you'll die of starvation," he answered brusquely. Quickly—almost imperceptibly—his tense gaze scoured over my thin, quivering body from head to toe. "But something tells me you already know that, so I'll humor you." He watched me wrap my trembling arms around myself, a flash of annoyance—no, *anger*—darkening his brown eyes. "If, by some miracle, you manage not to perish from cold and hunger, it won't be long until Molochai finds out where you are. When that happens, the wolf in your barn will seem like a friendly stray mutt compared to the monsters—both men and beast—that he will send after you. They will abuse your flesh before they feast on it. After a long, horrible while, they *will* kill you—gradually, torturously—and then they will gnaw on your bones."

My stomach roiled, even though it was empty.

"So I *don't* have a choice?" I breathed, tears welling, threatening to flood my cheeks.

"You *do* have a choice, Ary." His mouth thinned into a stern line. "It's just a very shitty one."

A surprised, tearful laugh bubbled up and out of my throat. He was harsh but honest, and I found myself grateful for that.

"Why me?" My breath billowed in front of my face, and my voice cracked. "Gods, why is it me?"

I would have thought it impossible for Smyth's rugged, scarred features to soften. But when he saw my tears, they did. All of him softened. The tension in his muscles released, and a comforting wave of solidarity washed over me like scalding hot water. It burned me, only for a second, then cooled and left rejuvenated skin in its wake.

"I suppose we'll have to figure that out together."

I puffed out a ball of mist, faking irritation, but his comforting words were a soothing balm over my aching heart and confuddled mind.

Smyth kept me company until I had enough of the cold and turned back to the house. He reached over my shoulder, gripped the door, and pulled it open for me. I trembled at the heat of his body so near. At the alarming and irresponsible—but undeniable—urge to ask him to wrap me up and shield me from all this.

"Thank you," I mumbled, hoping he knew I wasn't just grateful for him getting the door.

The others stood when I entered. I let the warmth of the indoors soothe my trembling breaths, and I took note of a steady Smyth standing behind me.

"Okay." I forced the word out.

"Okay?" Gemma repeated hesitantly.

I straightened my shoulders and tried to feign confidence. If I faked it long enough, maybe it would stick.

"I don't know how I'm going to do it. I can't say it's what I want because I don't really know what I want." Frustration welled in my chest at the sympathy in their eyes. I felt no malice for Gemma and these men, but their sympathy seemed hollow after presenting me with an offer I had little choice but to accept. I think I preferred Smyth's brooding to the pity of acquaintances. "Even so, what I want doesn't matter when the life of every person in this world is at stake, does it?"

Silence.

My pulse raced, guilt threading through me for my sour words. But was I wrong? What would appease them, if not my acceptance? I tried to concede without holding back the truth of my feelings. It was a delicate balance I'd need to learn in order to lead.

"We won't disappoint you," Caz finally assured me with a wink and a smile. I blushed, unacclimated to the attention of men. The overwhelming amount of testosterone in the air made me want to retreat into myself.

Ezra cleared his throat. "Can I have a moment with Ary?" He glanced at the others. "Alone?"

Smyth gauged my reaction and, when I didn't object, gave a terse nod to Caz, Finn, and Gemma and ordered, "Outside."

Smyth had been mostly silent since tending to my wound. He'd let Gemma and the others take the reins for a while, but it was clear he was in charge. They grabbed their coats and braved the cold. Smyth followed, not without shooting a warning glare at Ezra before closing the door behind him.

The silence between us was awkward, like prickly little spikes suspended in the air, waiting to strike if the wrong move was made, the wrong word spoken. That wolf must have left behind some of its fighting spirit when it bit me, because I found myself speaking first, even though Ezra was the one who asked to talk.

"Do you..." I cleared my throat, sticky with nerves. Ezra sat down on the tattered crimson sofa in front of the fire and gestured for me to sit across from him. I obliged. "Do you have any other family in the caves?"

My cousin fiddled with a stray thread. "My dad passed away when I was young, but my mom is still alive."

"I'm sorry," I whispered. "About your father."

"We've all lost someone." Ezra shrugged, and I sensed he didn't want to discuss his own losses. "We take care of each other."

Having a community like that did sound comforting, even if it meant thrusting myself into a role I would never be ready to fill.

After a long pause, Ezra released the sofa's thread from between his fingers and sighed.

"I can't imagine what all this feels like." He looked around from where he sat, hands resting on his lap. I took my time assessing his boyish features. He, too, was handsome. His dimples crinkled when he smiled, and his dirty blond hair was thick and disheveled. To me, Ezra's most familiar trait was that blue-eyed curiosity I had seen in Ollie. They weren't brothers, but they could have been. "And I know Gemma said it, but I hope it helps to hear it from me...you're not alone in all this."

I forced a smile and nodded.

"You look like them." I faced the fireplace and watched as the heat of the flames danced languidly. "Phillip and Ollie." I waited for Ezra's reply but was greeted again by silence. "I never did," I explained further, turning to face him. "I never looked like them."

"Do you look like your mom?"

"Not really." My mother's chestnut waves always flawlessly framed the sharp angles of her face and her hazel eyes. Her skin was warm and tan. Quite a contrast to my soft face and pale flesh. "She's beautiful."

They all had been beautiful. Of the few memories I had, my favorites were Ollie's bright blue eyes, his little hand in mine, and his giggles trailing behind me through the yard. I could remember the joy I felt with him on those days. We had played in the fields by the house on the rare occasion it was warm enough to forgo our hats and gloves. He had been a brilliant little boy with a mind fueled by excitement and imagination.

"I always blamed myself for Oliver and my fath—Phillip," I corrected, knowing I could never call him my father in good conscience again. "Gemma doesn't know who killed them. I would venture a guess it had something to do with my parentage."

"It's not your fault."

I flinched, not convinced by his words.

"That chair there in the corner," I pressed on, "Phillip, your *uncle*... used to sit in it, and I would sit on the floor with Oliver in my lap. Not every night, but some." Not every night because some nights Phillip began early with the rum and his speech slurred too roughly for us to understand. I left that out, how I used to take care of him when he got lost in his drink. So my mother didn't have to and Oliver never saw. "He would read to us."

"What was he like? Phillip?"

Phillip had been an intelligent man with a tortured soul. He'd been a sad drunk, never violent or belligerent. Soft-spoken and full of thought. He'd been the type of man to keep his burdens to himself until they crushed him.

When I woke up that day after falling in the cellar, my family had felt like strangers. I'd loved Oliver immediately—was impossible not to—but even with him, there were times I felt…kept at a distance.

Now I knew why.

"Kind," I finally told Ezra. "Phillip was kind. He loved his family as best he could."

"Gemma mentioned that he was drunk a lot."

"He had his vices." I gestured to the bottle of rum half empty on the bookshelf. Neither my mother nor I had found the strength to move it. Even Gemma must have known it was Phillip's, because she hadn't dared touch it. "He was sad. I didn't understand why I never felt…*enough*, but now I do. I wasn't his. He knew it, but he still called me his daughter."

I remembered the last thing he said to me and realized he must have known. Maybe not that he was going to die that night. But about me, about the prophecy, about what I might have to become.

"Sweet girl, I pray you'll be free one day."

I hadn't known what he meant at the time. But freedom, true freedom, seemed less likely by the minute.

"He did love you, then, as his own?"

I shrugged, attempting a smile. "I think he tried."

I'd never shared that feeling aloud, but I shared it with Ezra. It felt necessary to give him all I could of Phillip and Oliver, even if they felt less like mine to give. I shared everything I could remember: Ollie's favorite toys and books, the small mole on his forehead, his little laugh that turned into a squeal when he got excited. Ezra asked how exactly they died, but I decided to spare him from the gory details. No one else needed the weight of that burden.

"I don't think they felt much pain," I answered. "They looked peaceful." That mark—the X—was deep but smooth, and I'd hoped that meant they hadn't struggled. That they'd been carved up only after death.

Ezra accepted the details with a solemn nod, then leaned back in his chair. "Probably wasn't the Butcher that came for them, then."

My interest peaked. "The Butcher?"

"The Butcher of Nyrida," Ezra clarified. "He's been doing Molochai's bidding for centuries." Ezra mimicked a knife across his throat. I flinched at the visual. Too familiar to the scene I'd stumbled across months ago. "He's got more murders under his belt than Molochai does. There's not a person in the caves who hasn't lost someone by his hand. He even killed Elias Winterton's parents and his little sister."

I shuddered. "And don't you think he killed Phillip and Oliver?" I wasn't too concerned about the horror stories Ezra had heard as a child, but I would take any chance to figure out what had happened to them.

"Well, the Butcher... he *butchers,*" Ezra emphasized. "From what I've been told, if he'd done it, they would have felt pain. It would have been... messy."

I nodded slowly. "Is he... human?"

"Yes. Or something like it. Molochai's used blood magic to keep him alive for four centuries." A shiver rippled through him. "It's a dark, rogue type of magic Simeon refuses to use."

I couldn't decide if that was selfish or valiant, choosing to live—maybe suffer—alone for eternity, watching every loved one come into the world and then leave it.

"Does Simeon live in the caves?" I asked. I wondered whether he would even want me for anything other than what the prophecy foretold?

"Sometimes. He comes and goes as he pleases." My cousin resurrected the fading fire with the metal poker, then he turned to me. "I know this is a lot to take in, but I promise, things will get a lot easier once we get you back to the caves," Ezra assured me, his eyes brightening. "Elias will be there, and he can take over your training and protection. He'll help you."

An unnatural cold settled in my bones at the thought of my... *betrothed.*

"Do you know him?" I fidgeted with my thumbs. "Elias."

Ezra's face illuminated with pride. "I know him well. He's a good man. You'll like him."

Doubt lingered in the back of my mind like an itch. Wouldn't a good man come fetch his bride on his own?

"What's the deal with Smyth?" My thoughts lingered on the man who had helped me. The man who was *here.*

Ezra rolled his eyes. "The plan was always for Finn, Caz, and me to follow a few days behind Gemma and take you back to the caves just after your twentieth birthday. Elowen was still supposed to be here." His brow furrowed. "Sounds like she disobeyed

Simeon's orders, but...we were one day into our journey when Smyth showed up with a note from Simeon claiming he was now in charge. I questioned it, but the letter had Simeon's seal on it. His handwriting, too."

"What's his motive?" It was clear he wanted to protect me, but the reason *why* eluded me. Had Elias been too busy to come fetch me and hired some muscle to drag me out of hiding instead?

"I don't know." Ezra sighed. "But he hasn't cared much about anything but getting to you. It's odd if you ask me, but your protection is our objective, and I can't deny he'll be helpful with that..." My cousin shrugged, then chuckled. "He's an absolute beast. Two days ago, we were jumped by a band of thieves, maybe six or seven of them. Finn, Caz, and I had barely grabbed our weapons by the time Smyth was halfway through them." Ezra shuddered. "Can't say I like him much, but he's already saved my life once. With Molochai's forces pressing north, I can't exactly object to him being here."

"Same," I mumbled, taking my bottom lip between my teeth with a heavy sigh.

And with the way Smyth looked at me—tense, assuring, warm, *certain*—I prayed that he would, and thought that he might, teach me exactly how to save myself, too.

Chapter Five

The others came back inside, and we spent the rest of the morning discussing our route. We were to depart in a few days' time. Between now and then, I was to eat, rest, and learn to defend myself. I had to know "how to break a nose and punch a dick," as Gemma so elegantly put it. I thought of Ezra's story about bandits on the road and agreed that was fair.

If we went to the Winterton Caves directly, the journey would take us only two weeks on foot. But before that, we were to trek southeast to the city of Brinnea, where Simeon had requested we meet him. Few details about Simeon's plan were given to them, but they suspected it had to do with my power. About me being ready to wield it.

The more they apprised me of the world south of Warrich, the less convinced I was that I would ever be ready for Simeon *or* those caves.

Finn and Caz told me about monsters that stalked humans like prey. Many different kinds—some with wings, some with claws, all with very sharp teeth. They apologized for overwhelming me with information. I laughed nervously and told them I'd been overwhelmed since the moment I heard the word *queen*.

The monsters were Molochai's creation, crafted with the dark magic he stole from the earth. There weren't many this far north in Warrich owing to the lack of prey—well, people—but the farther south we went, the more we might encounter.

Midday arrived and I was hit with a feeling of sheer panic and embarrassment at not having anything to feed my new visitors.

"I'm running low on food." Shame crawled up to my throat. "I…I'm sor—"

"When was the last time you had any meat?" Smyth asked as he rummaged through the cabinets and the insulated chest. There was nothing there but a few bottles of vegetable broth. "Grains? Vegetables? Milk?"

"I've had eggs. Each of the hens usually produced one a day." My chest twisted at the thought of the hens. The night before, I'd begged the others to bury them, not cook them, if we could stand to spare them. Mercifully, Smyth had given me one long, assessing glare before he went outside and began to dig without argument. "And broth. I've eaten broth," I added, following Smyth's movements through the kitchen, smooth and urgent. "I ran out of meat a week after my mother left."

"Seven weeks." He grew rigid. That strong, menacing jaw pulsed. "You've been eating only two eggs a day—at *best*—and vegetable broth for seven weeks?"

"Yes." I glanced at Gemma, but she was no help. Her attention darted nervously between me and Smyth. "The blight took most of the crops last year," I explained. "We made broth from what we could save. My mother said eggs and broth are all I need to…keep my figure."

Something violent and terrifying blazed in his eyes at my words. My throat tightened while discomforting awareness slithered across my skin. My body had slimmed near to its bones over past months. My mother had never objected to it, though I had once heard Phillip tell her I didn't have much weight left to lose.

"I see." His voice was cold, his expression empty and unreadable—that violence gone, tamped down. An inflexible pause gripped the room, broken only by his swift, sturdy footsteps as he crossed the full length of the house in a few long strides. He dug through his bag, withdrew a package bound with twine and butcher's paper, and set it on the table in front of me. My mouth watered at the delectable sweet and savory scent.

"Isn't this yours?" I was *so* hungry, but I couldn't take the man's food.

"It's yours now." He nodded toward the package. "Go on."

I glanced at the others. Finn and Caz shared amused smirks while Ezra looked away.

"I'll share with—"

"No," snapped Smyth gruffly, pointing firmly to the package. "You will not share. It's yours."

I carefully unwrapped the twine and parchment and gasped when I saw what was inside. My stomach roared. Jerky. I looked up to see Smyth watching my hand, fury and woe spiraling in his hickory stare. I followed his glare and saw that my fingers were trembling. From hunger, from anticipation, maybe from low blood sugar. Embarrassed, I tucked my hand into my lap beneath the table and reached for a piece of the jerky with the other.

It tasted so good, like smoky, sweet sunlight bursting on my tongue. My eyes watered, maybe from the taste, definitely from the gratitude.

"Thank you," I said after swallowing the first piece. He gave a firm nod, and the strong muscle in his jaw throbbed beneath his beard. My pulse stumbled over itself.

"Caz. Ezra." Smyth strode over to his coat hanging in the corner and pulled out a worn leather pouch heavy with coins. He tossed it in Caz's lap, where it landed with a *smack*. "Go to Thesda. Buy all the food and drink you can with that."

Ezra opened his mouth to object. "Thesda is nearly a day's trek southwest—"

"Then you'll be back by sunset tomorrow if you leave now," Smyth concurred coldly. "Quick stop for a rest if you'd like. You'll be fine." I watched Ezra's shoulders slump in annoyed resignation. "Finn." Smyth turned to the younger Sinclair brother. "Think you can manage a hunt today?"

"I'll do my damnedest." Finn nodded without protest and turned to Gemma. "Care to join me?" A warm half-smile lit up his handsome face.

The corners of Gemma's mouth twitched upward as she began to stand, ready to go. But then she glanced at me, apprehension flickering through her expression, then at Smyth, her shoulders tensing. If she left, I'd be alone with him. While that didn't scare me as much as it should have, I knew Gemma wouldn't allow it.

"I'll stay." She rested her hand on my arm and narrowed her eyes at Smyth, who regarded her dispassionately. "With Ary."

"Can I go?" I asked.

"Not with that injury," Smyth replied with a terse nod at the bandage on my arm. "And not when we don't know who else is in these woods. You're not leaving my sight."

I gulped, fear chilling my blood, and conceded.

Finn wasn't gone for long, and when he returned with a large hare, I felt ashamed that I'd never tried to hunt for my own food when it seemed so easy for him to do. And now, I sat at the table, useless, with a blanket wrapped around me while Gemma and Finn argued over whether or not a knife was even needed to skin the hare.

"The skin's thin." Gemma reached for the hare. "Just snap the ankles, grip with your fingers, and pull."

I flinched at the visual and turned my attention away, knowing I was going to have to learn how to do things like this but deciding... not today. Before his death, Phillip had always taken care of hunting and preparing the animals for us. Afterward, any meat my mother traded for—which hadn't been much—had already been skinned and gutted. But I found this was a skill I wasn't eager to learn. I had no desire to disassemble a living thing.

"You've got to give the tendons a clean cut first with a good blade." Finn sighed and jerked the dead animal out of her reach. "Just let me do it, woman!"

Smyth stood next to the sink, thick arms folded across his chest, looking incredibly bored with their dispute. I wondered how well *he* could prepare an animal. Did he flinch like I would? Did the thought make him nauseous?

Who was I kidding? That man could skin a creature in his sleep without remorse and wake up to eat a full meal afterward.

I sat with my hands folded in my lap and stole the occasional glance at him. Each time our eyes met, I averted my gaze before I had a chance to decipher his expression. But I felt him watching, time and time again.

Finn and Gemma eventually compromised: Finn cut the tendon and Gemma did the rest without a knife. I watched him watch her with quiet fascination, the curve of a smile accenting his tan face, those hazel eyes gleaming.

The smell of freshly ground coffee wafted over my nostrils, and Smyth placed stoneware mugs on the table before us. I lifted my eyes, too grateful for the gesture to tell him I only liked the smell of coffee, not the taste. Gemma groaned and lifted her mug to her lips. The taste wasn't all that bad, and I could put up with one mug of it to avoid being rude. I moved to take a sip.

But I paused, staring at the clear, green-tinted liquid in my mug, absorbing its light, leafy scent. Not the rich, earthy scent that drifted from the mugs in Finn's and Gemma's hands.

"You gave me tea."

Smyth leaned up against the wall, his expression blank, waiting patiently for me to elaborate.

"Everyone else has coffee, and this is tea," I clarified.

"You don't like coffee." The intensity in his gaze sent a shockwave of warmth straight to my stomach. He was right. I didn't like coffee. But even if I did, his conviction could convince me otherwise.

"I—I..." They all watched me, including Gemma, who shrugged and mouthed, *I said nothing*, when she saw my inquisitive eyes. "I never told you that."

He didn't react. He didn't even move, save to blink. I took a sip, and my body relaxed when the warm verdant sweetness touched my tongue.

"Is there honey in this?"

"Yes." He crossed his arms over his chest and took a sip out of his own mug.

"I never told you I liked honey in my tea, either."

"But you do." It was a statement, not a question.

"Yes. How'd you know?"

His thick brows rose. "Lucky guess."

My mother mentioned it to Simeon, and he told Smyth. That was the likeliest explanation. But it was hard to believe that my mother cared enough to share information that might help me adjust in this moment. She'd hardly remembered my preference for green tea and honey when she lived here.

Finn and Gemma spent the afternoon telling me more about our lands and people. Elias maintained a loyal network of spies even in southern Nyrida, who passed back information. Molochai's army was strong, but we still managed to hold them out of the north.

For four hundred years, our growing army fought back the Insidions: what Molochai's forces called themselves. In large cities like Tovick and Brinnea, and the Winterton Caves, Simeon's wards were the strongest. Other places throughout each province, like smaller villages and camps, were protected only by occasional army patrols.

I watched Finn add marks to the map he and Gemma had sketched. It took up the entirety of the small dining table. I tried to follow, bound by frustration that I barely knew what I was looking at. Had I known all of this once, before the accident? Why had my parents never bothered to teach me about it since then?

"In the past, this region"—Finn waved his hand over the

north—"was mostly safe from Molochai. But lately, his forces have been pushing north across the border. Insidions could be anywhere, so Simeon doesn't want you to stop for very long in villages where there aren't wards. We'll make haste until we get to Tovick. Smyth has a friend there who can offer us shelter."

Warrich had always been my home. I had never been to—and I knew little about—any other province. My knowledge of our world was limited to what Phillip had told me or I'd read about in books. The names and climates, mostly. Southwest of Warrich was Avendrel. Tugaf—the largest, hottest province—was far south. Phillip had told me a little about the dense foliage and mountains in Avendrel, the seafarers in rocky Wymara, but I could only imagine what it felt like to see it all for myself.

"We'll travel to Tovick," continued Gemma, "rest for a few days where the wards are strong then move on to Brinnea, where Simeon's waiting for you."

"And after Brinnea?" I asked.

"You'll stay in Brinnea with Simeon for as long as he deems necessary. Then we all go west, to the caves." Gemma smiled as if expecting me to share her excitement. "To take you home."

I looked up at Smyth, towering over the table, one hand rubbing his bearded chin, expression stoic and guarded as he fixated on the map. Odd, that he was so quiet. That he let Gemma and Finn take the reins on explaining this to me while he stood back, silently assessing.

"Why doesn't Simeon go straight to the Winterton Caves in Avendrel?" I asked. "Would that not save time? We're adding at least three weeks to the journey when we could be at the caves in just over a week."

Gemma shrugged. "Simeon has his reasons. I imagine there is something important in Brinnea. And perhaps he wants time alone with his daughter as well."

"And we listen to him without question?" I felt Smyth's eyes dart to me when I spoke, that unfamiliar defiance settling in my chest, nagging me.

"No." Smyth's deep timbre sliced through me. "But you need time before you go to those caves, so we'll go to Brinnea."

Ultimately, I agreed. Not because Smyth said so, but because he was right. Though I was beyond nervous about meeting Simeon, extra time to process, to learn and grow, felt like exactly what I needed.

Deciding to retire early, I washed in the tub. I allowed Gemma to help, if only to keep my bandaged arm from getting wet. The goose egg on my temple was gone, bright blue and green hues already yellowing the edge. Thankfully, I wasn't concussed. That wolf had tossed me against that feed barrel with vicious fervor. Perhaps my body was more resilient than I thought.

"Both bedrooms are open for whoever wants them." I shuffled across the floor in my slippers, old wood squeaking and settling beneath even my light weight. Finn looked up from a book I'd read at least ten times and lifted a curious eyebrow.

"Ary," Gemma began as I rearranged my blankets. "Maybe you should—"

"That's where you've been sleeping?" Smyth snapped, eyes blazing. "On the floor?" I swear he *growled*. "Like a *dog*?"

I nodded and rubbed at my elbow, embarrassment snaking up my spine. "I like sleeping here." He cursed under his breath. I couldn't make sense of the rest of his angry grumbles, but I knew they weren't nice. Why did this grumpy, attractive man care where I slept? His concern over my diet was one thing. Eating nothing but eggs and broth for two months was, at best, mildly concerning in any stranger's eyes.

"You're not sleeping on the floor."

"It's okay. I'm used to it."

"No." His mouth pressed into a thin line. "The floor is hard and cold, even by the fire."

"My mother didn't mind—"

"Your mother isn't here."

Trepidation trickled through my veins. His intensity could eclipse anyone else within a fifty-mile radius. And yet I felt... ignited.

"Fine." I stood and folded my hands in my lap. "If you feel the need to make any more obtrusive demands, you know where to find me." I turned, each step toward the bedroom requiring unreasonable effort. The embers in my chest were not born of anger, but excitement. It felt good to be defended. To be cared about enough that a perceived mistreatment made him angry. Gemma cared, but this was different. It was an unfamiliar feeling, and I liked it.

As my hand tightened firmly on the doorknob, I turned to see him studying my form with an impenetrable gaze. I gulped down my nerves and added, "Just make sure you knock first."

I closed the door behind me and pressed my back against it, unsure how to quell the strange, defiant emotion flickering to life inside me.

And wondering if I even wanted to.

Chapter Six

An hour later, Gemma joined me in the bedroom. I'd waited for her on the bed with my bony knees tucked into my chest.

"You could have gone hunting with Finn today." I sighed. "I would have been fine."

Gemma sat behind me and brushed my hair, smoothing any knots into silver-blond silk.

"No." She shook her head and clicked her tongue twice in thought. "I wasn't leaving you with that beast."

"Smyth," I corrected her.

"Whatever," she murmured. "He scared the hell out of me the moment he burst in the door. Didn't bother saying hello. Barged in, looked around, demanded to know where you were and was back outside before I could tell him. I'm grateful that he found you before that wolf could hurt you, but I don't trust him."

"He saved my life." The words spilled out before I could stop them. Despite hardly knowing him, I felt the need to defend him.

"Yes," she conceded. "But something's off with him. He spent the last hour pacing back and forth in front of the fire, ignoring me like I was nothing more than a throw pillow. I finally gave up trying to figure out what he was doing and came in here."

"What?" My stomach burned with nervous excitement.

"Yes, and he's probably still at it."

I lay beside her and listened for those strong, swift footsteps. Was he still pacing? It took all my restraint not to check for myself.

Just before sunrise the next morning, I heard three solid knocks on the bedroom door. Gemma rolled toward me and groaned. The smooth, heavy footsteps informed me of our visitor's identity. I nudged Gemma and whispered, "It's Smyth." That was enough to get my snarky sentry up and standing in front of me.

"Come in," she called warily.

Smyth ducked, almost too tall for the doorframe, and nodded at my right arm. "Your bandage. It's been twenty-four hours."

Gemma offered to help. He ignored her and sauntered to my bedside, waiting for me to offer up my arm.

"Gemma, can we have a moment?" I summoned up the courage to ask. Day by day, I was going to get better at speaking up for myself.

"No!" she snapped. "I'm not leaving you alone with him."

I rolled my eyes. "You'll just be in the other room."

Her eyes darted skeptically between us.

"Scream if he touches you anywhere but that bandage."

Smyth bade her farewell with an annoyed grunt.

He knelt down on one knee beside the bed, careful to give me space. While he unwrapped the bandage, I stared at his scars. The one over his right eye, reaching down across his cheek. Another on his thick neck beneath his ear. A third at the top of his forehead receding into his hairline.

When he caught me staring, a flicker of shame passed through him. Did he think I was afraid? The scars were brave, not ugly. He had something to show for his pain. Ridges, like a map through his past. He had a story, memories, a life, even if it was violent. I couldn't remember receiving my scars, and they served as a reminder of the emptiness I felt.

"I, um..." I cleared my throat. "I never really thanked you for saving me."

"You don't have to thank me."

His deep timbre lifted the hairs off my neck. Goose bumps textured my forearms while confusing heat crawled from my chest to my belly, leaving a strange exhilaration in its wake.

I swallowed hard. "But I do... thank you."

Smyth stood and reached for the cloth bandages on the chair in the corner. I shivered at the sight of the muscles in his neck and shoulders flexing. I hadn't known a man could be so intimidating. How would my mother feel about him here? Like Gemma, she'd probably be wary.

"Did Alistair Winterton and his grandson send you along with the others?" I asked. "To fetch me?"

"I don't answer to the Wintertons." His voice was curt.

"Simeon then?"

Smyth turned to face me. "I don't answer to him, either. But"—he winced—"he and I have an agreement of sorts." He tore a piece of cloth wrapping.

"What kind of agreement?"

He didn't answer, but he knelt back down, and waited patiently for me to extend my wounded arm. I obliged. He cradled my arm like it was porcelain and might shatter.

The exposed wound was hideous. Teeth marks sinking deep into torn flesh.

"Will my arm be okay?" I closed my eyes to stave off the mounting dizziness.

He must have sensed my imbalance, because he shifted closer and barricaded his knee between my hip and the edge of the bed. His leg felt like a boulder pinning me to my seat.

"It will likely scar," he said, "but yes, your arm will be fine."

I opened one eye, peering down at the ragged flesh. The light ointment he applied to the wound burned, then cooled.

I opened my other eye and admired everything else about him. The wild crease of his brows as he focused. His strong, straight nose. The powerful cut of his jaw, covered by a well-groomed beard, which managed to be thick without being too bushy. And my favorite thing about his handsome face: his deep brown eyes that sparkled even though he wasn't smiling. It was difficult to look away.

Curious how he might react, I asked, "Have you met Elias Winterton?"

Flames of anger flickered through his steady gaze, visible for a mere second before disappearing. A failed attempt to hide his disdain.

"Can't say I've had the pleasure." The words leaped off his tongue like a spark off hot coals, stinging me, even as I tried to pull away. He didn't fasten the bandage as tight as the day before, and when I went to tighten it, he ordered gently, "Leave it loose. The wound needs to breathe."

I obeyed, flinching only from the friction as I slid my arm through the sleeve of a light blue cardigan my mother had left behind.

"Do you need anything for the pain?" Smyth asked, his knee still pressed against my hip like he was afraid I'd slither right off the mattress. "It might be worse today than it was yesterday."

"What do you have?"

"Nothing conventional." I didn't really know what that meant, so I waited. "Alcohol," he clarified. "But no more than one drink for you."

"Oh, I don't know if that's a good idea. Phillip drank a lot, and it wasn't…good."

The wound was now clean and freshly bandaged. I thought Smyth was about to leave when his fingers twitched against my elbow. His eyes snapped to mine, concern and rage melding into… *worry*. My heart stuttered.

"Did he hurt you?"

"No," I said breathily, then cleared my throat. "No." Surer this time. "He was just sad." Smyth's eyes narrowed, assessing me…for lies? "Probably because he had to look at me every day, and I was a reminder of my mother's affair."

"None of that bullshit was your fault." I jumped at his startling aggression. "They were lucky to have you."

"I don't think they wanted me here," I muttered bitterly, the words slipping out of me before I could stop them.

"What?" he snapped, his intense stare on me. "What did you just say to me?" The heated edge to his voice demanded a response.

My eyes widened in shock. "I…I said I don't think they wanted me here."

"Why the f—?" His voice was strained, his face contorted in pain. "*Why?*"

Rather than retreat, he stayed where he knelt, his body close.

"Because I was so . . . *numb*. I used to feel like there was nothing alive in me," I confessed, my body ejecting the words like a poison. I cringed at my candor. I hardly knew this man, but I was a moth with thin, fragile wings drawing too close to his incinerating blaze. "After my accident in the cellar, I felt like I was missing so much of myself and—"

"The accident?"

I nodded. "Six months ago I fell in the cellar and hit my head. It injured my brain somehow and I can't remember anything before that moment."

Smyth stared at the bed beside me and slowly nodded. "Do you feel that way now?" He rubbed a gentle thumb over the skin of my elbow, which he still hadn't let go of. "Numb?"

"No." I gulped, looking up at him.

He met my gaze earnestly, and my stomach clenched.

"They must be paying you a lot to take care of me." I laughed nervously, anxious to fill the silence. "You seem overly concerned about someone you just met. Someone you only need to transport from one place to another."

"I'm not here for *money*." The words snapped out of him, deep and seething.

"Okay." I spoke past the lump in my throat. "I'm sorry. Are you always this . . . grim?"

"Grim." He raised his eyebrows, chuckled humorlessly, then carefully lowered and released my arm. "That's a new one."

"You just seem . . . weary. Angry, maybe," I added, cringing. "Who hurt you? Or 'who pissed in your porridge?'—as Gemma would say." I cringed again. So awkward.

"It doesn't matter."

"It matters to me." I surprised myself with my boldness.

"Of course it does." He sighed. "That's just who you are."

His eyes darted to my mouth as I scrambled to retort. "You hardly know me."

He studied his hands, eyebrows creased in thought. My eyes wandered to the tattoos on his forearms. They spiraled around his triceps, past his elbow, likely up and over his biceps, shoulders and chest, maybe beyond. I wondered what they counted. Where they ended.

"You're right." He stood. "And I guess you could say I'm here because I'm good at killing. You will need to be good at killing, too."

The heat in my belly chilled to ice.

"I'm not sure that's something I want to be."

"I can't tell you who to be, Ary." He sighed, discomfort flickering through his gaze, gone as quickly as it came. "I can teach you to think for yourself and survive."

"Think for myself?" I laughed ruefully. "Within the last two days, all I've heard is who I'm required to be, what I'm obligated to do. There's no space for my own thoughts." The words poured out of me startingly easily.

"Then *make* space," he countered. "Don't let them tell you who you are. May I?" He gestured to the basin of water on my dresser. I nodded and watched, mesmerized as he rinsed his massive hands.

"You sound confident that you know me quite well after only

twenty-four hours," I continued, my voice a little too squeaky. "Enough to tell me what to do."

"I do what it takes to ensure you learn how to fight back rather than concede to others." He gestured to the room, the house around us, implying that... I had already given up. "So that you're prepared to stand up for yourself when Alistair Winterton, his grandson, and their people realize you can't be confined to their pretty golden throne."

Was it an insult or a compliment, to not... comply? A challenge, perhaps? To be something different than what they would ask of me. Something... more.

Or had he decided, after only a few hours, that I would fail before I'd even begun?

"Don't you think it's a little presumptuous to assume you know what I need better than I do?" I feigned defiance.

His nostrils flared. "How could you know what you need if you aren't even sure who you are?"

I gritted my teeth, eyes narrowed up at him. This man—so brutally forthright—lit a spark of anger in my chest. He made me want to fight back.

"Why did Simeon send you instead of Elias Winterton?" I asked. "Given his reputation as the army leader and my... betrothed."

Something dark and hot burned through his gaze. His strong jaw flexed in discontent. "Would you rather your *betrothed* had come?"

"I don't know, I... I never said that," I answered. "I just thought you were supposed to train me to lead them, to save them, not hate them."

"There's a difference between what I've been told to do and what I plan on doing."

My eyes shot open wide. "What do you plan on doing?"

Smyth's assessing stare lingered on me while he dried his hands. His silence should have scared me. Instead, it intrigued me, frustrated me, and I locked my stare on him.

"It's still early," he said, turning his back to me. "You should get some more rest today." He paused with one hand on the knob. "And if you ever feel *numb* again or that you're . . . *missing* yourself, come to me."

Go to *him*? Someone I hardly knew? Was he serious?

"That's not a suggestion, Aryella," he added tersely.

My skin prickled with heat. "How do you know my full name?" I rushed out. Phillip, my mother, Gemma, and Oliver had never called me by my full first name. They called me Ary. It had always, always been Ary. I couldn't even recall how *I* knew what it was. A lingering truth from before my fall, perhaps, rattling around in my brain, waiting to fit back into place.

He stopped with his hand on the doorknob. "You're my queen." His other hand flexed at his side. "Of course I know your name."

And with that, he left.

Tension poured out of me in a shaky sigh, and my pulse raced in my ears.

My full name, in his voice, bowed me over, igniting something angry and foreign and relentless in my chest. Like a recurring dream I knew I'd had, but the details were . . . gone.

How did he know something I hadn't thought about in ages? I hadn't told anyone in this house that my full name was Aryella.

But it was.

Chapter Seven

Smyth had told me to rest, and my body begged to obey, so I stayed in bed for two more sleepless hours. Gemma's story and the prophecy preoccupied my thoughts. When I got up, she cooked the hare meat into a hearty stew and served me a heaping bowl. Smyth watched silently to ensure I ate every last drop. When I was finished, I retreated to the bedroom to *rest* some more. I reread a book for the tenth or twelfth time to distract myself. It kind of worked.

But I spent most of the morning staring at my pale, feeble hands. Hands that were meant to draw power from Nyrida's gods and destroy an evil sorcerer.

Frowning at my delicate fingers, I shook my head. Unlikely.

I returned to my book and let myself escape in *that* fairy tale instead.

By the time I had finished reading, the fading winter sun shone through the small boxed window and signaled dinnertime was soon. I slid on my slippers and climbed into the chair under the window, shivering at the frigid air whistling through thin cracks. I absorbed the beautiful winter image. Memorized it, because I knew that soon I would look upon the clearing for the last time.

Birch trees, tall and thin, poked out of a thick blanket of snow. Leafless and towering, they reached for the golden red sky with their spindly branches, like strands of hair hiding the forest beyond. I could see hills from this angle on the south side of the house, and I wondered if I even possessed the strength to trek across them.

For the first time, I desired that strength. The strength to move freely, to explore, to learn. So for the first time in days, maybe months, I smiled—a *real* smile—despite my trepidation of all that would soon uproot my life.

Caz and Ezra would return that night, and after hours of self-imposed seclusion, I actually looked forward to being social, even if it meant braving Smyth's consuming presence.

There would be more options for food once they arrived, but Gemma insisted on heating up the rest of the stored vegetable broth first. Caz and Ezra arrived minutes after the sun set, burdened with canvas sacks full of food and supplies. Gemma handed me a hot bowl of broth and scurried over to help unload the cargo. The bowl was still steaming, so I waited to avoid burning my tongue and watched the others.

Ezra hoisted freshly cut meat from one bag—venison, by the look of it. Caz unearthed multiple canvas bags of bread and eight ears of corn.

Smyth was shameless about watching me eat. Not a single ounce of regret in those burning brown eyes. When the others made jokes, he didn't laugh, and his eyes held no joy. I wondered who or what had stolen the light right out of him.

"Here." I finished my bowl of broth and looked up to see Smyth handing me a plate of whole grain bread and freshly cooked venison. My mouth watered when I saw the steam coming off it. "Eat."

"I'm okay." My stomach still growled, but I told myself I was fine. There were more of us now, and we had to make sure we didn't run out. "We can save it for later. I finished my broth."

"I don't care. You've only had rabbit stew, vegetable broth, and water all day. Not enough. Not even close." He grabbed a clean fork and knife from beside the sink and placed them on the table next to the plate. "You're hungry. Eat."

But I thought of my mother, and her insistence that I stay thin. Now, I guessed, for Elias Winterton, my . . . betrothed.

I sighed, preparing the lie. "Thank you, but I'm not very hungry."

"I'm not asking."

My throat clenched. "Elowen told me I can't gain weight—"

"I don't give a shit what that insufferable cow said to you." Smyth's voice was calm and even, but his hands clenched into fists at his side. Like a monster ready to pounce. His anger rerouted from his fists to his eyes, which burned hot with rage. I sat, lips parted, gaping. That was my mother he spoke of. I should be angry, but just like yesterday . . . it felt good to feel defended.

I made the choice not to mention my mother again. She was far from mother of the year but I wasn't sure she deserved whatever wrath this man had in store.

"*Eat*," he commanded again.

Gemma and Ezra watched from the other side of the table, their expressions caught between horror and amusement.

"You better do it, Ary." Caz's voice was muffled through his own bite. He pointed at my plate of food with his fork. "I've seen him lose it over a lot less."

I sighed and complied. He and the others had gone to great lengths to ensure I was well fed. And he was right—my mother was not here.

The venison's flavor was rich with the herbs and greenery the deer had eaten. Hints of sage filled my nostrils, and I breathed in the luscious aroma like my life depended on it. It was an effort to keep from groaning while my taste buds worshipped the gift of warm, buttered bread. I shoved away the shame of being helpless and found comfort in feeling full.

"I should have tried to hunt, or... *something*." I infused my voice with gratitude. "I can't thank you enough for this. All of you. I should have tried harder. I should have—"

"Rather than denigrating yourself for struggling when you were left alone in a frozen wilderness, you should perhaps wonder why you were left here," Smyth uttered, his rumbling voice firm and cold. "There is no need to thank us for ensuring you are warm, fed, and cared for. Those are bare minimums."

Ezra and Gemma opened their mouths to protest, probably to defend my mother, Simeon, or whoever else made the call to hide me here. But they took one look at my pale, bony form—even with the warmth and life the food and fire brought to my face—and thought better of it.

"Besides, you need your strength. You begin training tomorrow, bright and early." Smyth leaned against the wall beside the hearth, arms crossed. He tilted his head forward, eyes blazing. "With me."

Sleep was again a reluctant companion that night. My thoughts were preoccupied with images of a poised warrior prince destined to be my husband, simmering flames, twisting vines, dancing wind, rushing waters, spiraling tally mark tattoos, and a pair of hickory eyes…

The inside of the coffin was gold and decorated with carved, delicate vines and flowers. Roses. Odd, because one could assume the quality of a coffin's interior wouldn't matter to a dead person.

Above me, a frosted glass top distorted any view of the outside. Something small and warm was nestled beside me, breathing rapidly, but evenly. I couldn't see what it was, and it was too tight a space to try and look. I focused on my own breathing, but the air felt thin.

Something moved outside the coffin, drawing my attention. A looming figure stood over where I lay trapped, watching me. I gasped. They shifted.

"Help," I cried weakly, light-headed. "Please. Let me out." When I tried to lift my hand to push against the glass, I was too confined. The small thing beside me stirred and whimpered. "No, no, no," I sobbed feebly.

My breaths quickened, but I drew in less air, like it was dissipating, like I was losing it. I screamed. And screamed. And wailed. And…gasped…and…the figure on the other side of the glass did nothing.

"Let me go—"

"Ary! Ary, please wake up!"

A feminine voice, sharp and warm. Familiar.

I jerked in the coffin to find myself still trapped.

"Ary, stop! Oh holy gods, stop!" The voice again, from somewhere else, somewhere…far away. Panicked. Crying.

A shrill wail erupted from the tiny thing beside me. But I couldn't help it, soothe it. I couldn't even help myself.

From that distant place, with the panicked voice, I heard a deep rumble—a demand. I screamed, hoping they could hear me from inside this casket.

"I can't get her to wake up," replied the familiar woman on the other side. "Please... please help her..."

Strong, swift footsteps.

Then, a lifeline.

"Come back to me, Aryella."

My eyes shot open. I sat up, spine ramrod straight, salty tears running down my face as I escaped the night terror's grasp. Gasping for air, I anchored myself to the warm, strong presence keeping me steady. "Breathe." I focused on his smooth, even voice. Sucked in a tattered breath and dug my fingernails into the rigid arms holding me steady. "That's it. Again." I took another trembling breath. "And again. Good girl."

I blinked away the tears and saw that Smyth was the one who anchored me. The moonlight from the window glowed on his dark brown hair. His eyes fixed on me as he said, "You are *safe*."

Gemma stood behind him, her ebony curls wild and eyes shining with fear and tears.

A small, broken noise escaped my throat. Equal parts relief and fear—but not fear of him, but of whatever... that was. Wherever I had been.

"I... I was locked in a golden coffin with a cloudy glass top." My voice trembled. "I could breathe, but the air was thin. There was someone watching me, waiting, but they never let me out no matter how much I begged, or h-how loudly I screamed."

Gemma shuddered. Smyth's only response was the muscle in his jaw that always flexed.

When I noticed my finger's white-knuckling, my nails pressing into his skin, I eased my hold and lowered our hands to the bed. The bedside lamp spread a gentle glow across the small bedroom, enough light that I looked down and gasped. At what I'd done to his skin…

"You… you're bleeding." Tiny little half-moon cuts, right where my fingers had been. "I'm sor-sorry."

"I've had worse," he assured me. True, if his scars were any indication. Something warm and precious tugged in my chest at the realization that he hadn't pulled away, even as I'd hurt him. "I'll make you some tea." Panic gripped me by the throat when he moved to get up, and I might have reached for him out of instinct if he hadn't added, "I'll be back," like he'd read my mind.

Gemma approached me carefully after Smyth had left.

"You were screaming and crying and I couldn't wake you up. You were…" She shuddered. "You were scratching at your chest and your neck like you were trying to get out of your own body."

I lifted my cold fingers to my neck and felt the sting of the thin lacerations. The familiar burn of tears returned. I lowered my hands and saw the blood on my fingertips, on my palms—not Smyth's blood, but mine. Bile rose in my throat. It was an effort to force it down.

"He heard you screaming and nearly busted the door down." Gemma glanced to the door, her beautiful brow furrowing. "I couldn't get you to wake up, but he…" She sighed. "You're all right." But her smile didn't reach her eyes. "That's what matters."

Smyth returned with hot green tea—with honey, of course—

and a few warm, damp towels. He watched, leaning against the doorframe, while Gemma cleaned the blood off my neck and collarbone and I sipped from the cup. Though my hands were unsteady, he didn't fill the cup to the brim, to avoid spilling. His usual impenetrable stare was filled with worry.

"Do you think you'll be able to go back to sleep?" Gemma surveyed the cuts on my neck to ensure they had stopped bleeding. They were mild, but they stung.

I nodded, unsure if it was true. But it was still dark outside, so I had to try.

And I did sleep a few more hours. Peacefully, which may have had something to do with the soothing sounds of his steady pacing outside the bedroom door.

Even the nightmares cowered before him.

Chapter Eight

As Smyth promised, when the winter sun peeked out from the clouds to offer a sliver of warmth against the chilly air, I was summoned outside to begin training. I stood next to a snow-dusted spruce tree, arms crossed, elbows gripped by each palm, waiting for Smyth to finish sharpening a knife. He turned to face me and immediately stopped, running his fiery gaze up and down the length of my body.

"Why are you standing like that?"

I rubbed my elbow nervously. "Like what?"

Concern flickered through his expression. His face tightened, eclipsing any escaping thoughts. I sucked in a breath when he marched toward me, his broad, towering form closing in. He unfolded my arms—his touch like lightning through my body—and laid them at my side. It irked me, how I *wanted* him to arrange me like a limp doll. As if he could show me the way, and I could trust it was the right one. But I let him, because he made me feel safe.

"You have nothing to hide and no reason to cower." His blended words and touch were a panacea for my nerves. Smyth's gaze darted to my lips, parted in surprise, and his fingers twitched on my arm. He cleared his throat, dropped his hand, and averted his eyes. "You also have a long road ahead of you if you intend to survive."

"I know." My shoulders sank with a sigh. "I'm too . . . timid."

"You've been shaped into what's been allowed. Can't expect a lion cub held captive for years to survive in the wild." He watched and waited, and I quickly straightened my form. The need to please him ran through me, a beckoning river. "But until you gain your strength back, you have one option if you wish to survive hand-to-hand combat against a person twice your size. You have to be faster, and you have to be smarter."

"I can do that." I said it over and over again in my mind. *I can do that. I can do this. I can.*

"I know." He withdrew a small weapon from his pocket—a knife—and pulled it from its sheath. "This is yours."

The hilt of the knife, small and unthreatening in his palm, consisted of a taper wrapped with black leather and a silver pommel in a crown-like shape with three tips. The cross guard was curved, its ends pointed in the same direction as the blade.

"Mine?" I took the hilt. The feel of a weapon in my hands was foreign. I'd held a knife for only run-of-the-mill homestead tasks. This blade had been forged with violent intentions.

He nodded toward my thigh—where there was a pocket in the gray pants I'd borrowed from Gemma. "Yours. Store it there. It will be a few days until we get to weapons."

He started by teaching me the stance for simple hand-to-hand combat. Feet offset, shoulder-width apart so I could shift my weight to throw a punch but still maintain my balance. I felt ridiculous standing there poised to fight as if I was anything more than frail bones wrapped in thin skin. Smyth could envelop my clenched fist in one of his hands and shatter my wrist and knuckles with a single squeeze.

Then we focused on my breathing. I hadn't realized how erratic it was until he taught me to do it properly. *Inhale. Exhale.* Feel each movement, each muscle in my body as it took in air and released it. His gaze locked on me while I practiced, gauging each rise and fall of my chest like my breathing captivated him.

His gaze sent warmth to my belly and made me feel…alive. I wasn't sure I wanted him to ever stop.

But I also needed to strengthen my core. Just as important as breathing, he said, to master the place in the body where energy and power originate. So, on top of learning to breathe, I was tasked with a daily full-body workout. Push-ups, sit-ups, lunges, squats, and an abhorrent exercise where I was to position myself parallel to the ground and support my weight between my forearms and toes, with nothing to think about, nowhere to look but the frozen ground as my stomach clenched and burned.

It *was* effective, Gemma assured me when I told her about it. I couldn't disagree. With every shift of my body, I could feel my abdominal muscles howling, the tiny fibers breaking down so they could build back stronger. When I looked at Smyth's entire body, corded with muscle, I wondered how many times he had broken and rebuilt himself.

Smyth showed me the first places to aim for when attacking a man's body—temples, eyes, nose, throat, if I could reach them.

Otherwise, the center of the chest, and of course, the groin. But I refused to practice that one with him.

At supper, I ate everything Smyth placed in front of me—green beans, potatoes, another venison steak, even a sweet cheese spread across a warm, grainy bread roll that had me exerting effort not to groan in delight. I was too hungry, too tired to say no to him or the delicious food.

The next day was the same as the day before. I woke at dawn ready to train with Smyth, this time more excited but still nervous. I dreaded the achiness and discomfort but welcomed the sense of accomplishment I felt from doing something other than sitting alone in that house.

To warm up, Smyth instructed me to run ten laps around the edge of the clearing. Soon, Smyth told me, I'd be running for thirty minutes nonstop, then an hour. Eventually longer. That was difficult to imagine, because after the third lap around the clearing, I was ready to heave up my breakfast. As long as I continued training and giving my body the sustenance it needed, he said I would soon be able to go faster and farther.

For the most part, I liked the sharp bite of the cold at my throat, as if what I breathed in was pure. It hurt, but the whipping winter wind on my face also thrilled and motivated me until I clenched my teeth together and grunted through that last lap. I decided I liked running. Or how I felt when I was done with it. At least I had that going for me.

"Again." Smyth stood towering before me with his large palms open as I threw a punch into each of them, the sound of it smack-smacking at his every command. His massive palms wouldn't budge even with my full body weight thrown against them.

"How is this going to help if someone is trying to kill me?"

"You have to rely on being quick and precise. Your enemies are like wolves and boars, and you are like..." A trace of a devilish grin flickered across his face. It frightened me and took my breath away. "A kitten. You may only get one strike, so it has to be an effective one."

"A kitten?" I asked, mouth agape.

"Small, adorable, fearless." Something like hunger flashed through him. "And born to be lethal."

I rolled my eyes to pretend the comment annoyed me, to try and draw attention away from the blush that was rising in my cheeks.

"I highly... doubt... *that*," I grunted, using the momentum of my body thrust forward against his palm, which gave this time, just a little. When he shifted, I noticed a black leather cord holding two silver rings—one large, one small—around his neck. I wanted to ask about them, but now didn't feel like an appropriate time.

"Good one." He nodded in approval. "And doubt all you want, Aryella. Doesn't change what I know, and it doesn't matter how powerful an adversary you face if you're quick enough to slip right through their fingers." A sly smile pulled up the corners of his mouth. Heat pooled in my belly.

"Well, I'm not fearless." I dropped my hands to take a much-needed rest.

"Maybe not now." I sucked in a startled breath when he reached forward and gently brushed my cheek with the knuckle of his index finger. My eyes widened at the warmth of his touch. "But you will be when I'm done with you."

I shuddered at the thought of him being *done with me*, whatever that meant. And yet his confidence made me feel... taller.

"I should be good at this, right?" I gulped water from the metal canteen Ezra had brought out to me, and I thought of my newly discovered heritage. Generations of powerful people. "It's in my blood."

"You'll be better than good if you *choose* to be, and practice, whether it's in your blood or not."

For as long as I could remember, I had shied away from the weight of making a wrong choice. Both the fear of being wrong and the attendant consequences were debilitating. With few memories, I already felt like I had lost so much.

Now that so many decisions were being made for me, I would give a lot for the freedom of choice again. Even if I wasn't sure what I would do with it. Here Smyth was, trying to give that back to me, understanding what I would be asked to give up once I got to those caves.

Then again, had my choices only ever been an illusion, like my fake life and family, crafted to keep me hidden and docile until someone else decided my time had come?

"Choices." I laughed ruefully and shook my head.

"You always have a choice, Aryella." His stare was fierce. As I soaked in his fervor, I felt that warm, tight pull in my chest. "Don't ever let anyone take your choices away from you."

I bit my bottom lip in thought. His eyes darted to my mouth. Something startling flashed across his face, and I saw his throat bob with a heavy swallow. It passed quickly, but self-conscious warmth flooded my cheeks.

"How did you sleep last night?" he asked, distracting me.

"Better." I forced a smile, still unsteady from the spark in my nerves. "Thank you." I cleared my throat. "For the night before last." I touched the thin lacerations on my neck. They were nearly healed—a testament to how little damage I'd done. How little I was capable of doing. For now. "I know it wasn't real, nightmares never are, but..."

"Does it matter, when you're in the throes of them?" He withdrew a sleek black flask from his pocket, unscrewed the top, and took a drink. I fought the urge to ask him what was in it. Probably not water. "Nightmares hunt you in the quiet and devour your peace. When you are silent, sleeping, nightmares cover the blank canvas of your resting mind until you can't discern what is light and what is feeding on the light. They may not be real, Aryella, but that doesn't make them any less powerful."

I tightened my threadbare scarf around my neck, any lingering sweat from exertion now chilled on my skin. As was the case with many things he said, I struggled to formulate a worthy response. So I swallowed my pride and said, "Thank you." Because I could at least show I was grateful.

"Eat some lunch." He nodded toward the house and took another drink from his flask. "Then we'll continue."

And we did continue, until supper, during which Caz, Finn, and Ezra took bets on which one of them I could defeat in a fistfight now that I had learned to throw and dodge a punch.

"My money's on you, Caz," Finn said to his older brother. "If only because you'll be the first one to piss her off with your smart-ass mouth."

Caz didn't deny it. He winked at me and grabbed a turkey leg—another delicacy he and Ezra had brought back from their trip.

"You're all idiots," muttered Gemma through a mouthful of

potatoes. "Just wait until she finds her power. None of you will stand a chance."

They laughed good-naturedly, but I stiffened. And out of the corner of my eye, I saw that Smyth did, too. He had already eaten and now stood in the doorway with a stoneware mug of coffee in one hand. Intense eyes on me, as usual.

"Do we know what my power is?" I folded my hands in my lap and resisted the urge to add *if I actually have any.* But. . . I was tired of sounding like a pessimist. It was a choice, to think that way. And while I was scared and frustrated and highly doubted my ability to take on *any* of them in a fistfight—much less liberate my people from Molochai—I made the choice to be hopeful. Or at least fake it.

"Christabel never specified," Finn answered. "Only that it's meant to be given by the Selvaren."

"You will find it when you're ready." Smyth took a sip of his coffee and gave me a single, firm nod. Ever my teacher, stoic and sure.

As soon as supper finished, we retired early to rest up for our first day of travel. Caz and Finn shared the other bedroom while Ezra slept on the sofa. I wasn't sure where Smyth slept.

Probably not on the floor.

My nerves and nausea woke me before the sun. Gemma slept soundly for another two hours, and I focused on the rise and fall of her breathing to keep me sane. To her, this was nothing more than the next leg of our journey. She was accustomed to traveling. Alone, even. She had few emotional ties to this place. The Winterton Caves were her true home.

And despite a lingering sense of dread, I had to hope that they—those caves and those people—could be my home, too.

I quietly sat on the edge of the bed while Gemma fastened my silver-blond hair into a braid long enough to touch my lower back.

"How do you feel?" Her voice was pointedly soft. Careful.

"I don't remember ever leaving this place." I fidgeted with my thumbs in my lap. "It feels as if I've been here forever. Was I here before the accident?"

"As far as I know, yes." Gemma tightened the band at the bottom of my braid and scooted off the bed to stand beside me. "Had it been my call, you would've been with us in the caves from the beginning, not hidden up here like some prisoner. Elowen is good at her core. Phillip and Oliver, they were good, and I know you loved them, I just...I don't think you belonged here." She sighed and shook her head. "But Simeon does what he believes is best."

I looked up into her warm amber eyes and wondered if she felt that way while she'd been here. If she felt forced to keep her opinions to herself. If those opinions might have helped me.

"It will be all right," she assured me, squeezing my hand before tossing her bag over her shoulder and leaving the room. "Simeon knows what he's doing."

I was irked by their faith in Simeon. But was I in a position to criticize? Was their blind trust in him any different from the reckless faith I felt in my teacher?

I brushed my fingers against the maroon-and-violet patchwork quilt beneath me, remembering how I used to tuck Oliver in and trace the floral designs over his back because it soothed him. My knapsack was packed light—I had grown attached to very little in this house. Caz would carry the larger bag with the food. Finn would carry any extra weapons. That left me with clothing, my canteen of water, and toiletries. Without much thought, I dragged the quilt off the already-made bed and folded it tightly into my knapsack. It was the one item from this house I would allow myself to bring. Practical, to keep me warm.

The thin layer of snow from days before had melted. For once, the dead grass of the clearing was almost dry save for a thin layer of frost, and the sky was clear of harrowing clouds. I wanted to take it as a sign. Perhaps our gods were on our side.

We ate a large and quiet breakfast because all but Smyth seemed too preoccupied with staring and silently assessing my state of mind instead of partaking in their normal banter. They meant well, but I felt like a child whose dog had just died, with every family member waiting for me to burst into tears.

Finally, I found myself standing in the clearing, my back to the others, who walked on. Only Smyth stopped when I stopped.

My limited memories were all in that house: joyful, terrible, everything in between. As long as that house stood, I had the ability to return to it. To hide. But I was so damn tired of hiding, of starving my body and soul. Even if that meant walking right into the unknown world before me, to marry a man I'd never met.

"I want to burn it down," I told him. "All of it."

He said nothing, only nodded in silent understanding before removing the knapsack from his shoulder and digging around inside, eventually withdrawing two full bottles of clear liquor.

It took effort not to ask why he carried all of it with him. Didn't seem necessary, but neither was prying.

He uncorked one of the bottles, strode over to the house, opened the door, and disappeared inside. Moments later, the sound of shattering glass echoed through the clearing. Even the whipping wind was not powerful enough to drown out the noise.

He burst through the back door of the house and to the barn, where he stuffed a rag into another half-empty bottle that he'd found inside. He lit the end with a match, and tossed it inside. The glass shattered, and the flames rose. There was enough hay and dried wood in that barn that it wouldn't take long to burn to ashes.

From behind us, I heard Gemma gasp. Ezra cursed, Caz and Finn remained silent, and that was all we heard out of them. Maybe they recognized I needed this. Anyone trying to move on from being completely trapped would need this. It was a home, but it was also a prison.

I watched as Smyth prepared another bottle and rag on his way over to me. I recognized both from the kitchen and Phillip's old liquor stash, respectively. I expected him to light and throw it himself like he had with the barn. But this time, he placed the tools in my hand, gave me the lit match. "You want it to burn?" he asked in a deep, steady voice. "Then burn it shall."

My eyes widened at the flame dancing dangerously on the tip of the match in my fingers. Heat and flame and light. I lit the rag and, before it could burn me, tossed it inside the threshold of the house, where Smyth had poured the rest of his liquor.

The moment I let go, Smyth took my shoulders in his commanding grip and backed me away from the flames. I felt the heat rise up, drawing out tears from my eyes that burned with relief, not sorrow. The house went up in flames, and the bright heat filled and soothed the aching emptiness I'd felt the last six months lost in.

I didn't want to be the numb, fragile girl that house had belonged to. With it gone, I didn't have to be.

Still, when we reached the edge of the clearing, our backs to the flames, I found myself pausing at the edge, terrified of all that lay before me. The others had gone ahead without realizing I'd stopped. But again, Smyth noticed.

"I don't know if I can do this." I shuddered, gulping. Walking into those woods. Facing my mother, meeting Simeon, marrying Elias Winterton, and being whatever idyllic queen Alistair Winterton and his people expected me to be. Confronting Molochai after learning to fight in the first place. I was not a leader. I was not a fighter. I didn't know what I was.

"You can." He offered me his hand. And a smile, unexpectedly soft and encouraging, tugged at the corners of his mouth. I sucked in a breath. The first warm and true smile he'd shown me. It was beautiful. "I'll help you, Ella."

His promise tore the air from my lungs. This scarred man with his unflappable, coarse exterior was here to guide me, show me. His unexpected comfort filled the cracks of my spirit with molten silver. Shaped by him, I'd be much harder to break.

Ella. My heart leaped once at that name, and again when I matched his gaze. No one had called me Ella before, but... I liked it—a name that was mine and his. Separate from all this. He nodded toward his hand, his next words a promise. "Whatever it takes."

I let him take my hand in his unwavering grasp, and I believed him.

Chapter Nine

The forest surrounded us on all sides, the trees so tall in places, I had to stretch to find where they ended, up, up, up into the sky. A thin blanket of frost crunched beneath every cautious step I took. Mercifully, that caution waned—as the morning sun peaked higher above the horizon—and disappeared entirely when I could turn back and no longer see even the faintest wisp of smoke from the fire we'd started.

My old home. Reduced to ashes.

Phillip and Oliver, their souls flying free on the wind. I could feel their contentment, their peace, like a powerful sigh in the early winter air.

As if Phillip was free from his vices. As if he whispered to me, *Be free.*

Indeed, I focused on the world around me and tried to be free. There was light from the sky, all around us. In some spots, it was almost too much. The sun blinded me as I walked underneath breaks in the forest canopy, as it reflected off the icy sheen coating the ground.

Ezra and the Sinclair brothers found humor in my childlike awe of new things. That first day, I saw a lynx and a grizzly bear. The latter from afar because, upon spotting it, Smyth gripped my arm and led us all in the opposite direction. He didn't seem afraid of the bear, but irritated. As if he could kill it like he did the wolf in the barn, but it was still an inconvenience.

I resisted when he pulled me away, just so I could stare at the creature. The bear was *huge*. Finn guessed it was pregnant. We saw a moose, plenty of rabbits and squirrels. Gemma claimed it wouldn't be long before we saw black bears, too. Oliver and I had been allowed to watch from the window when animals were present, but venturing outside was prohibited. Where there was prey, there would always be a predator.

More often than not, Gemma had to grab my arm and pull me ahead so I could keep up with the rest of the group. It was an effort to focus when there was beauty everywhere I looked. The world outside of my old home was breathtaking, and at times I forgot that darkness could exist out here. But one glance at the scars on Smyth and I remembered how much I didn't know.

He hovered close to me at all times. Despite the low temperatures, the consistent movement and the energy it took to push forward through those woods kept me warm. Comfortable, despite the exhaustion. When the sun rose to its highest peak, we paused for a midday meal. Smyth insisted I eat a considerable amount to regain any energy I'd lost that morning. I didn't mind the insistence, for better or for worse. He made me feel safe out here, too, like I could venture freely but sink back into his protection if needed.

I walked next to Finn now. Gemma and Caz led our pack, Ezra

walked in front of us, and Smyth was behind—watching to identify threats on all sides.

I said to Finn, "Gemma said that Simeon and Molochai *found* the power from Nyrida. How did they find it?"

He shrugged. "No one truly knows except Simeon, and he keeps it to himself to protect us in case Molochai were to ever capture one of us." Finn noticed my confusion and added, "Molochai would know if we know anything about it. If we never do, he would hopefully make it . . . quick."

Nausea roiled in my stomach. No escape, just a quick death. The only mercy one could ask for if dragged into Molochai's dreadful abyss. The image of two other deaths flashed through my mind. Two bodies, one large, one small, limp in pools of cooling blood—

I forced out a sigh to silence my thoughts. They were gone. They were at peace. No pain.

No pain, only peace. I repeated the assurance three times. If I could tattoo it on my heart, I would. Make it a permanent part of myself so it couldn't come and go. So it couldn't haunt me.

I shuddered against the cold of the air and my thoughts. I couldn't help but wonder if Simeon—my *father*—kept the power's origin hidden from his people for other reasons. Was he afraid that, in sharing the information, he would be risking it happening all over again? Did he feel guilty for playing a part in Molochai's descent into darkness, for helping create the monster that killed his sister, his brother-in-law, their *infant* child?

"What's Simeon like?" I asked Finn.

"I've only met him twice." He offered me his hand to help me over a fallen oak. "When he does come to the caves, he mostly meets with the Wintertons and their inner circle." He nodded to me to imply that I would be included in that. "He's quiet. Wise. I'd say old, and he is, but he only looks to be in his forties."

Indeed, the benefits of suspended aging.

"What is your reason?" I asked. "Is there a reason they chose you and Caz to come along with Ezra?"

"Besides the fact that Ezra's like our little brother and we didn't trust anyone else to keep him safe? Well, Caz's wife had something to do with it."

I frowned. Caz had a wife, yet he'd left her in the caves to come fetch me?

Finn, noting my concern, explained with a warm laugh, "Marin practically volunteered us herself. She's pregnant, due the second week of Rainar. She said if the queen doesn't arrive before the baby does, it'll be bad luck, which she certainly would not tolerate. She might as well have kicked us out the door." He glanced ahead at his brother and smirked, his voice lowering. "Between you and me, I think Caz was driving her crazy, waiting on her hand and foot. Wouldn't leave her alone. Marin is a gem of a woman, but she certainly doesn't like being coddled."

I smiled, thinking this might be my favorite part. Hearing about others I would come to know. A family I could make for myself if the burden of being queen didn't draw an unbridgeable void between them and me. I hoped they could see me as…me. Just me. I hoped that would be enough.

"What about you?" I asked Finn. "Do you have someone?"

Finn's olive skin blushed red, and I caught him throwing a glance toward Gemma, who walked a long way ahead of us. "Not at the moment."

I bit my lip, suppressing a grin, wondering how long Finn and

Gemma had known each other, and if there was *more* between them.

By the end of the first day, we had walked a total of ten hours. My body screamed for rest. I had no idea how I'd make it through the coming weeks unless someone picked me up and carried me. And *that* would be humiliating. I bit the inside of my mouth to keep from groaning as I lowered myself down on a rock near the place we'd decided to make camp. I failed to keep quiet, Ezra hearing me and cringing apologetically from where he unrolled his sleeping mat a few paces away.

"It gets easier." Gemma walked by and squeezed my shoulder. I was angry for a moment—not at her or because of her—but because my mother or Simeon or *someone* could have prepared me enough to spare me this shame. This uselessness.

I grunted and heaved my knapsack off my shoulder, collapsing along with it.

Smyth ordered the others to check the perimeter in pairs to ensure there were no signs of travelers, thieves, or Insidions. He stayed with me, even after I insisted I go with them. Even after Gemma objected, less than thrilled about leaving me alone with him.

I sat on my sleeping mat, legs tucked into my chest, arms wrapped around my knees. My body was grateful for the rest, but I was heavy with guilt that the others had to do all the work. A knowing warmth brushed against my skin. I could feel him watching me.

"There's no indignity in rest, Ella," he said finally.

I looked up at him and sighed. Easy for him to say. When did he need to rest? Probably never, he was so used to the cold, the wilderness. I hadn't seen him *rest* once in the past four days.

"They should never have kept me in the dark."

"One of many things that you and I very much agree on." He sighed, squatting down to build a campfire from the dried leaves, pine needles, twigs, thin sticks, and a few larger pieces of wood he'd gathered.

I took note of how he placed the kindling in a center pile with slightly larger sticks crisscrossed over the top, just in case I ever had to do it myself. He lit the fire with a match and discarded it into the flames. When he noticed me watching, he instructed, "Keep the fire small, controlled, and any additional fuel upwind, away from the flames."

I nodded and memorized his instructions.

"I don't remember much at all from before the accident," I rushed out, unsure why I felt the need to explain myself to him. "But at least I should have plenty of room in my memory for all you teach me."

I stared, waiting for his reaction without a clue as to what I was looking for. Praise, perhaps. Confidence that I could become something. He gave me nothing. His features were like stone, but I thought I saw his knuckles whiten from the grip of his folded hands. Frowning, I focused my gaze on the dancing flames and absorbed the warmth that soothed my aching muscles.

"Is Smyth your real name?" I asked, unable to stand the silence. The name seemed to fit him: direct, strong, unembellished. And yet a name so simple didn't sit right with me. He was . . . more.

He glanced up from the other side of the campfire, his dark brows lifted. "Does it not sound like my real name?"

"I just think if you're going to call me whatever variations of my name that you want, like *Ella*, I should have other options, too."

He assessed me, jaw pulsing. "It's Gavin."

It was a softer name than I had expected. A testament, maybe, to a warmer, gentler man hidden behind that cold, gruff exterior.

"*Gavin.*" His lips twitched when I said his name. "You know, I never *really* agreed to keep training with you. You just demanded that you be the one I learn from."

"And?" He rose to his feet without denying my claim.

"And I'll keep training with you if you allow me to call you by your first name—your *real* name—*Gavin.*"

He chuckled. "Happy to see your negotiation skills are developing." I arched an eyebrow, not backing down. The corner of his mouth curled into a smile before he leaned in against the nearest tree, crossed his arms, and resigned with a single nod, "Fair enough."

It was a futile effort to suppress my grin.

"What is it?" he asked.

I bit my lip and shrugged. "I just hadn't seen you smile much until we left Warrich, and you're smiling. It's…nice." I groaned internally. *Nice* was such a stupid, empty word for the way his smile made me feel.

Smyth—*Gavin*—gritted his teeth, cocked his head in thought, and replied, "It's easier to smile when there's finally something to smile about."

I felt a fluttering in my belly, and I had to endure a few minutes of silence just to gain back my good sense. *Endure* watching him withdraw the cover from an ax head and prepare a few logs to be split.

"So your real name is Gavin." I crossed my legs and folded my thinly gloved hands in my lap. "Can I ask more questions?"

He drew in a long, contemplative breath while he studied me with narrowed eyes. Finally, he gave a noncommittal grunt. All the approval I needed to proceed.

"What's your favorite color?"

To my surprise, he laughed, and for the first time I noticed the dimples poking out of the edges of his beard, his warm smile, and the faint laugh lines in the corners of his eyes. A comforting heat flushed through me, chasing away the nagging fears of the present. He was so handsome, and his ruggedness gave him an edge that stole my breath.

"Green," he finally answered, removing his worn black leather jacket. "Yours?"

"Blue," I answered, which was my normal answer, but I did love the way the navy cloth of his shirt gripped his intimidatingly corded biceps and rippling forearms, so I specified, "Navy blue. Though there's nothing quite like the orange and pinks of a sunrise, too."

"Tough decision." He eyed me warmly.

I shrugged. "When's your birthday?"

"The thirteenth of Helios."

"Born in the summer." I smiled. The thirteenth day of the seventh month of the year. I would have to remember.

"Mine is—"

"The third of Nyxar," he finished for me. "A few weeks before the Winter Solstice."

"How did you know that?"

"Because I know everything about you."

I scowled, biting back nervous laughter and an indignant snarl as they battled each other, begging to break free. His arrogance, his presumption... they made me want to fight back.

And he knew it, too. He smirked and proceeded to split a log in two with one effortless swing of the ax. Clearly something he had perfected.

"How could you possibly know everything about me?" I demanded.

"I told you." He rested another thick log on the stump and prepared to swing. "You're my queen."

I leaned forward and admired his powerful legs. They were like long, thick trunks, effortlessly supporting his solid core and vast shoulders. Despite his toying, his provoking, I had the urge to draw close to him and touch him, just to see what a dominating body like his felt like.

I shivered and shoved the urge away.

"Can I help you with that?" I asked, pointing to the ax.

"Rest. I'll teach you later."

"You should teach me now." I unwrapped the sandwich Gemma had packed me for supper and took a bite. "It would be a tragedy if you died and we didn't have anyone to cut firewood for us."

He laughed again, a deep, husky sound I was quickly becoming addicted to. "Later." When he saw my lifted brow, he added, "I promise."

Smiling, I forced my head clear and stuttered the first question that came to mind, desperate not to lose the flow of our conversation. "If your name is Gavin, why does everyone call you Smyth? Is it your surname?"

"My occupation, what I used to be, long ago."

"Like a blacksmith?"

He gave a short nod.

"What is your surname, then, if not Smyth?"

"Don't have a proper one," he answered. "Just Smyth."

"You don't have one?" I narrowed my eyes. "Everyone has one."

"Not me."

"What about your mother and father?"

"Born a bastard." Rage rippled through him, there one moment and gone the next. Surely his mother had a surname. If there was no father, Gavin would have taken hers. "My mother died in childbirth," he explained. "She bled out and didn't have time for much beyond a first name."

My pulse stuttered in my chest. "I'm so sorry."

"It's been . . . a while, and I don't remember her, of course," he muttered, unbothered. "You don't need to worry about me, Ella."

"Who says I'm worried about you?"

"Good girl." He smirked. My stomach tightened and tingled at his praise.

Keep talking, I told myself. *Keep talking, stop thinking, or you might pass out.*

"So." I cleared my strained voice. "How did you go from being a blacksmith to one of the *prophesied queen's* escorts?" I emphasized the latter with as much sarcasm as I could muster.

Gavin stared at me in sudden brooding silence, arms full of firewood.

"Is that what I am to you, Aryella?" He dropped the wood in a pile with irritated force. "One of your escorts?"

Panic choked me. "I—I don't—"

"Did it ever occur to you that you might mean more to someone than some bullshit prophecy?"

My mouth fell open. "I take it you don't believe in my aunt Christabel's prophetic abilities?"

"Your aunt—" He cut himself off with a clenched fist, shook his head, and released a joyless laugh. "When you're with me, let's focus on *you* learning to take care of *you*. Forget the rest. Can we do that?"

Nodding, I gulped down my nerves and compulsively steered the conversation in a direction that was less confusing.

"It sounds like you all have been anticipating me and my power for quite some time," I rushed out, my voice brimming with anxiety. "Has Molochai really cursed our world with four hundred years of death and suffering all because of one woman?"

He released his tension with a heavy sigh, answering, "There is no limit to what a determined man will do for one remarkable woman."

"More like an unhinged, obsessed man," I grumbled.

His mouth twitched upward. I'd never been so relieved to see the faintest traces of a grin. "That, too," he answered.

It was an effort to avoid his gaze—if only to give my pulse a rest—as we sat for a long while, listening only to the early winter wind, the rustling woods around us, and the crackling fire.

Until a gold coin landed in the dirt before me.

"A coin for your thoughts?"

I looked up at him sitting casually with his large, clasped hands resting over his bent knees.

"I can feel your discontent from here," he explained, noting my suspicion, "and you wear your thoughts on your face far, far too much for your own good."

Something I would need to work on, if I was going to be a queen.

I sighed, defeated. "Molochai…that part is terrifying, but

straightforward. He wants to kill me. He'll either succeed or he won't. It's the rest of it that doesn't... sit right."

He waited for me to elaborate. I opened my mouth to speak, then closed it. Like an idiot.

"I will not judge you, Aryella," he finally said, his deep voice steady, soft, like a warm breeze relaxing my muscles. "Everything you say to me belongs to us. No one else."

I fidgeted with my thumbs and stood to my feet, pacing.

"I am trying to be happy and brave about all of this." He watched me, glued to my every movement, as I walked back and forth, back and forth... "I am *trying* not to pity myself, to be grateful for being chosen and wanted and revered when I know there are hundreds—thousands, likely, if not more—far, far worse off than I was or ever will be, but I—" My fists clenched, knuckles cracking. "I'm nineteen years old and I'm supposed to save the world with some kind of mysterious power from the Selvaren."

I picked up and studied a frozen berry, then threw it back into the bushes.

"The man I'm supposed to marry is already picked out for me. I don't know him, don't know if I want him, and hate myself for being selfish enough to think about what I want—at least in *that* way—when lives are at stake." I threw my hands in the air. "And come to think of it, I don't even know my own middle name." Not that it mattered. It just felt like something I should know. "If I'm bound to die sooner than later, I'd at least like to have a say in who I am and how I lived."

"Jay."

"What?" My hands fell to my lap. I released an exasperated breath and sat down on the withered tree stump he used to chop wood. "What are you—"

"Your middle name." He stood up this time. "It's Jay. Your mother loved blue jays."

"Elowen?" I laughed. "She hates birds." It was true. She always left the hens to me.

Smyth's eyebrows furrowed. His closed mouth was a tight barrier holding something back.

"How would you know that?" I asked quietly.

"My queen," he reminded me nonchalantly and pressed on. "Blue jays represent courage and intuition in the face of fear. Confidence. Do you know what Aryella means?"

"No."

"It means 'lion of the gods.'" He covered the distance between us and squatted down in front of me so that our eyes were level. My pulse raced at his closeness, less than a step away, and the way his shoulders rose and fell with each breath, how the wind seemed to move with him, like he commanded the air itself.

"I won't lie to you, Ella, I've seen and felt a lot of things that make me doubt the existence of the gods, but if they're out there, you're proof. So forget Simeon and Elowen, forget Elias Winterton, forget everything and everyone else." I inhaled sharply when he placed one strong, warm hand over my heart, the other cupping my jaw. "You are magnificent. You will forge your own path. And your voice—a lion's roar—will send those who try to control you cowering at your feet."

"That doesn't sound like me." My voice was barely above a whisper.

Indeed, I struggled to breathe with him so close, so . . . warm and strong and sure of himself. And *this*—his gentle assertiveness—was the reason I was drawn to him. He spoke as if my status as queen meant nothing to him. As if he saw through the walls I put up. He saw *me*. The others cared for me, but around him, I didn't feel the weight of expectations. With him, just him, I felt light. I felt seen and known and *real*. I felt capable. I felt free.

"What's your middle name?" I asked softly.

"I don't have one of those, either." He saw my face fall, chuckled softly, and squeezed my hand. "I don't need one. I've known who I am for a very long time." His thumb caressed my cheek. My lungs came close to collapsing at the warmth, the care of his touch, his intoxicating scent, that mix of leather and cedar. "Didn't I tell you not to worry about me?"

I nodded and smiled at the gentleness glowing brightly in his eyes. He smiled back—that half-smile I was beginning to admire so much. My lips parted and my breath quickened. His eyes darted to my mouth, and I thought he might—

"Perimeter's clear!"

At the sound of Ezra's voice, Gavin cursed under his breath and withdrew. He pulled away from me so quickly that I could've been a live flame. He ran his hands through his dark, shoulder-length hair and walked away.

As if he shouldn't be touching me, shouldn't be so close, and he damn well knew it.

Chapter Ten

He disappeared for over an hour. After returning, he hardly looked at me for the rest of the night. I tried not to let it bother me, not to feel as if I'd said or done something wrong that upset him or angered him.

I gave my best effort to forget about it and mostly succeeded. I slept hard and without nightmares, probably thanks to complete exhaustion.

On the morning of the second day, we would pass by the town Caz and Ezra had gone before in search of food, but we weren't to enter it. Another, larger village was a few hours beyond that one—Freyburn, it was called—and we would be able to seek a fresh meal and shelter there for the night, as well as stock up on additional clothing and supplies.

I was nervous and eager as we drew closer to Freyburn that evening. Eager for warmth, a fresh meal, and one less day sleeping in the cold.

We approached the village around dinnertime. Wooden structures—some broad and tall, others small and homey—were covered in a dense layer of snow, heavy and wet. Fresh. Perfect for snowball fights and building figures and animals like I had with Ollie the winter before he passed. The faded colors of wood were dulled by the thin white blanket but provided a perfect backdrop for the wreaths and holly boughs that villagers had placed over windows and thresholds.

"Preparing for the Solstice," Caz explained, walking beside me. "It's also the day that Simeon and Molochai liberated our lands from the hands of the Rexus dynasty."

My eyes widened. "They still celebrate, despite . . . everything?"

"We do." Caz gestured to a group of children laughing and playing in front of a small oak cabin on the corner of a gravel road. "Molochai has taken enough from us. And many of these more remote villages remain mostly untouched, especially this far north." I smiled as a little boy, no older than five or six, formed a snowball in his small hands and tossed it at his older brother, only to squeal and dash away when the playful throw was returned.

"Some of the eastern seaports, like Brinnea," continued Caz, "have lavish celebrations of their own, but you won't find this further southwest."

Southwest of Avendrel, into Tugaf, where Molochai's forces were far denser. Where the monsters lurked. The map Finn showed me had marked the Winterton Caves as a barrier between those hellish, southern lands and the moderate safety of the north.

Moderate safety . . . for now. In recent months, he'd begun to push north, and our forces were beginning to struggle.

Still, I found I was grateful that we were headed east to Brinnea to meet Simeon rather than to the caves. I needed time, and I was grateful my father—my *real* father—knew it.

I watched the children and fought the sorrow that tightened my throat and nipped at my eyes. What could have been, for Ollie.

"Come with me."

Gavin's deep, commanding voice startled me out of my thoughts. He gently nudged my lower back, guiding me toward a line of shops down the village's main street.

"Keep your hair tucked under your hat," he leaned down to tell me. "It's unusual and easy to identify."

We stopped before a shop with wide windows that exposed a warmth inside I craved. Boughs of holly similar to the ones the villagers hung framed the glass, the snowflakes stuck to the leaves, glistening as light danced off them from the flame torches lining the street.

"Will they know who I am?"

Gavin opened the door for me, uncompromising when he said, "I'm not risking it."

I nodded and shoved down my embarrassment. My shame. Did he think my hair was bizarre like I did? I cursed the gods for not giving me simple, sleek brown locks. Or golden blond, perhaps. Black, even better—like Gemma's sensuous curls. Anything normal. Anything other than the unnatural waves of silver that reached down my back.

I stopped inside the shop's threshold, twisted my silver waves into a quick, messy bun, and tucked all of it beneath my hat. Gavin watched me do it. And though his steel-walled expression betrayed nothing, I thought I saw his hand flex at his side before he tore his eyes away.

"The others are finding us a table for dinner and rooms at the inn." He gestured around the shop. "Pick anything you want."

Eyes wide, I took in the abundance of fabric and color exploding around the shop. Coats, fine dresses, scarves, hats, gloves, blouses, and pants—the shop had them all. Never had I seen so much clothing, so much luxury packed into a single space.

"Anything?" I looked back at him.

"Anything." Generous, but he remained a colder version of the man whose warm assurances wrapped so generously around me yesterday.

The owner of the shop—a round, cherry-cheeked woman with white hair—stole my attention when she hustled over to greet me. "Good evening, dear." She smiled brightly. "What can I help you find?"

"Umm," I replied, forcing a nervous smile. Where would I begin with so many options? I saw a dark purple, wool-lined, hooded parka and a pair of silver-buckled leather boots with more insulation than my current pair. Not to mention the wall to my left covered in shawls and hats and scarves and stockings and—

"We know what we're looking for, thank you," Gavin stated coldly, shifting closer to my side.

The woman looked at my massive, gruffly scarred, bearded companion, then back to me—young, small, timid—and suspicion flooded her gaze.

"I am just in the back, dear," she said with a forced smile. "Please shout if you need me." The older woman moved toward a doorway at the rear of the building, tossing a worried look at me from over her shoulder.

Gavin leaned down and sourly muttered, "She thinks I'm your captor."

"Are you not?" I teased, giggling. "You hardly let me out of your sight."

"If I was holding you against your will, Aryella, you'd know it." No hesitation in his dangerous tone. Only simple, brutal truth.

I gulped, cheeks flushed, and began sifting through the shelves and racks of winter wear. He claimed a new pair of boots was nonnegotiable, so I tried on and chose the silver-buckled, sturdy, sleek black pair. He set them on the owner's counter, where I would need to pay.

Pay.

"Oh." I moved to put the boots back. "I don't have any money."

"I said pick anything, did I not?" He returned the boots to the counter. "Did you think I was joking?"

"I can't let you—"

"You aren't *letting* me do anything." He ran his hand through his hair. I stole another glimpse of the inked notches that began on the side of his forearm. "I do what I want, Ella, if you haven't figured that out already."

I'd try not to read into that. Instead, I focused on the circular wooden rack with a colorful array of scarves, each fastened at the top with an impeccable knot and draping down almost touching the floor. One scarf—emerald green with tiny threads of gold dispersed throughout—caught my eye.

"Do you like it?" He nodded toward the green-and-gold fabric draped between my fingers.

I dropped the scarf. "It's very pretty, but I have a scarf al—"

He grabbed the scarf and draped it around my neck in one swift motion. A matching hat sat on a shelf beside it, which he handed to me. My eyes flashed wide at the cost.

"You can afford this?" I flinched when the invasive question left my lips.

He merely chuckled. No smile. "I've had time to accumulate some wealth."

"You really don't have to buy all of this for me."

"Elowen and Simeon clearly neglected to give you what you need." He studied a pair of luxurious but sturdy fur-lined leather gloves that would fit me perfectly. "I'm happy to compensate for their failings."

Gavin rolled up his sleeves, revealing more ink around his forearms, disappearing beneath his shirt. Tiny beads of sweat glistened above his brow. Built into the wall of the shop was a massive stone fireplace, and the heat now had me wishing I could shed a layer or two myself.

"What do your tattoos mean?" I asked timidly. Hoping I wasn't prying too much.

He studied me, carefully weighing his words before he spoke. "They're a reminder of what's passed." And before I could press for more—"Do you want or need anything else?" He took a silent inventory of all we'd gathered and gave a satisfied nod. "I'm sure the others have found a table for dinner by now."

My stomach growled at the mention of food. "I'm ready to go."

We—*he*—paid for the gloves, boots, scarf, hat. Added in a new coat and long, wool stockings before I could object. He knew my size. I supposed he had been with or around enough women to accurately guess.

The shop owner shot me at least five warning looks before we left, and the last thing I heard before Gavin led me outside was a frantic, "You're always welcome here, dear!"

Beside me, there was an annoyed sigh and Gavin muttered something unintelligible, which the cold wind swept away.

I bit my lip and smiled. I was afraid of many things, but not my wolf slayer.

The tavern was loud and smoky. The six of us sat together around a weathered wooden table in the corner, reinvigorated by the shelter and warmth of the indoors.

Our hostess was a tall, busty redhead, whose confidence I immediately envied. Her red lips curled into a seductive smile at all four men in our group. She even went so far as to place a set of long, thin fingers on Finn's shoulder while she gave her suggestions for our meal. Much to Gemma's chagrin.

Finn smartly shifted out from beneath the hostess's touch, not daring to look her in the eyes. She then switched her attention to Gavin. My cheeks heated as she ran her sharp gaze up and down his intimidating form.

Before she could open her mouth, he uttered coldly, without a glance in her direction, "Will I be paying you to serve us a meal or are you just here to ogle me like a bloodthirsty succubus?"

The woman—shocked—cleared her throat and straightened her shoulders. And then proceeded to take our dinner orders, not a coy little grin in sight.

Even Gemma was pleased with Gavin's bitter words for once.

I just hoped the waitress didn't spit in our food.

When she left, Finn and Caz told stories about their time in the Barracks: a large army base about a day's walk north of the caves.

Every spring, my betrothed, the army commander, took a new batch of trainees to the Barracks to complete the final phase of their training and initiate them into the army. The trainees were exceptionally strong men or women who had turned eighteen the previous year. Elias had gone himself three years early, at fifteen, and had taken over leading the tradition for the past nine years.

"It's called Commencement," Caz explained from two seats to my right while we waited for our meals to be served. "Elias and his top commanders come up with a series of challenges—different each year—and each trainee must pass each one in order to matriculate into the army."

"What happens if they don't pass?"

"Besides lifelong humiliation?" Finn shrugged. "They can choose some other role in the community, or they can repeat the following year."

"The last task is usually some form of combat against his second or third commander," Ezra chimed in. "You fight them, and they decide if you did well enough to give them a true contest. Most of us do, eventually. There's the rare occasion that Elias steps in to fight a candidate himself, though that hasn't happened since—"

"Hendrix Sharpe and Otis Stoll." Finn tilted his drink toward Ezra. "Both my year."

Gemma snorted. "That's only because those two and Hendrix's smarmy brother Micah were hanging around Alec Gerard, and Elias was trying to scare them off from becoming his cronies."

I made a mental note of those names to be sure and keep my distance once I arrived.

"What's wrong with Alec Gerard?"

The four of them traded apprehensive glances. Even Gavin, usually the image of disinterest, had a darkly curious gleam in his eyes.

"Elias used to have two sisters. One older, one younger," Ezra explained. "I told you what happened to the younger one, Willa." I nodded, shuddering. Slaughtered, along with her parents, by the Butcher of Nyrida. "The older one, Helena, was being courted by Gerard, one of Elias's top soldiers. It ended abruptly, with some suspecting that he did something . . . unsavory. But there was no proof, and weeks later, Helena died during a run-in with some Insidions on the southern border, between Avendrel and Tugaf. Her death was unrelated to Gerard—he wasn't even there when it happened—but it meant there was no opportunity for Elias and his grandparents to figure out what occurred between them."

"Not that Winterton *would* do anything," Caz offered, brushing his black hair out of his eyes. For the first time that I remembered, disgust tainted his usually cheerful gaze. "Gerard's too valuable a fighter to be thoroughly punished."

But... Elias's *sister*. I frowned at the mug of honeyed tea warming my hands—Gavin had demanded it from our nervous waitress—and I watched the steam curl up and disappear in the wintry nighttime air.

"This... Commencement." I took a sip of my tea, allowing myself to be soothed by the trail of glorious warmth from my throat to my chest. "Does it happen every year?"

Finn nodded. "You're eligible once you turn eighteen. We've all done it."

"Well, I'm nineteen, almost twenty, and I haven't done it."

Caz chuckled. "You don't have to, Ary. You're the queen."

"That's horseshit."

Finn choked on his beer. Gemma and Ezra echoed each other's surprised laughter.

"Language!" Caz gasped.

I pushed on, fueled by flames of defiance. "They're training to put their lives on the line and fight for a cause I'm meant to lead, and I'm not even expected to undergo the basic rite of passage to be in my own army?"

Everyone but Gavin stared at me like I had sprouted an extra limb. He, on the other hand, appeared all too pleased, that addictive half-smile lighting up his ruggedly handsome face. The scar over his right eye crinkled. He looked... proud.

"You'll teach me, won't you?" I said to him from across the table. "Make me good enough to beat Elias Winterton?" Perhaps it was bold to consider I could ever reach that level. But maybe with my power . . .

Gavin arched an eyebrow and said, "I can think of no better way to spend my days than training you to pummel that pompous shit into a pulp."

Ezra scowled and rolled his blue eyes. "You've never even met Elias."

"Don't need to," Gavin replied coolly, sipping his whiskey.

Caz snorted. Ezra shot an angry glare in my wolf slayer's direction, ever loyal to his friendship with my betrothed. And it wasn't that I wouldn't try to keep an open mind—because I *would*—or be kind, or do my damnedest to be a queen for these people. But sitting on my throne while others did everything for me didn't sound appealing. To prove myself to them, I needed to be just as skilled as they were, if not more so.

"You just seem quite a bit more enthusiastic than you did just days ago." Gemma's face was filled with worry. "What changed?"

I shrugged. "If my fate has been decided by the gods, then so be it. I was born into this. Maybe I didn't ask to be, but I was."

"I suppose that's true." Caz sipped his beer and threw a mischievous half-smile my way. "Though one look at you, and Elias Winterton will be praising the day you were."

Heat filled my cheeks. Not because of the lighthearted teasing but because, out of the corner of my eye, I caught Gavin shooting daggers at Caz. And—though I couldn't be entirely sure, owing to the clamorous sounds of the tavern—I thought I heard him snarl.

"What would Marin think of that, hmm?" Gemma shot Caz a look. "Hearing you admire another woman?"

"Admire!" Caz laughed and tipped his glass at me. "How could

I not? Look at her! Face of an angel." I flinched. "Marin would've said it herself and slapped me for denying it. In fact, I think she might leave me for our queen the moment she sees her."

Finn rolled his eyes. Ezra groaned and buried his face in his hands. I heartily echoed the sentiment, wishing I could erect a shell and crawl inside it forever. Or at least until the end of this conversation.

"What I'm trying to say is..." I cleared my throat, beet red and desperate to make my point and move on. "I can either sit here and mope that things look difficult and terrifying, or I can do something about it. And I certainly will not do *nothing* while everyone *else* does something about it."

I saw the corner of Gavin's mouth curl upward into another smirk, rich with pride.

"I'm sure you can participate in Commencement, Ary," Gemma consoled me, smiling. "You might have a difficult time convincing Elias, but you *are* the queen."

Our food arrived minutes later, causing a comfortable silence to descend upon our group as we recovered from the past two days of travel. After we ate, the others continued with their stories for another hour or two until chatter and laughter were replaced with heavy eyelids and languid yawns.

The room—only one—was small, but we all squeezed in. Gemma and I were forced to take the only bed. All four men insisted they could sleep on the floor. Caz and Finn both snored, which kept me awake late into the night. Though admittedly, I felt secure with all of my friends so near. Being alone in that house had worn me down more than I realized.

As I lay in bed beside Gemma, tucked beneath a quilt, I tried not to focus on the implication that Elias Winterton might try to discourage me from proving myself to him and to members of his army. Did he not want his wife doing any dirty work? How could I not, with my potential power? *Because* of that power, did he feel threatened? I didn't consider myself above Commencement. The need to develop my control and abilities drove me through each training session with Gavin. I had gone so long without both, and now that I felt a sliver of each, I wouldn't let them go. I needed to know I could hold my own among my people. How else could I feel validated in my position, both to them and myself?

I decided then that I would become one of them before I could lead them. Somehow, I would earn their trust, their honor. If we were to defeat Molochai—and if he was as evil and powerful as the others let on—I needed my people as much as they needed me.

If not more.

A woman's scream—shrill, desperate, and brokenhearted—woke me from my slumber. I gasped and shot up in bed.

I looked down to see a trembling hand—my hand—resting on my abdomen. Sharp pain was radiating across my lower back. I whimpered out a sob, feeling only the ache in my stomach and the hot tears streaming down my cheeks. What was happening to me?

Small embers fought for life in the fireplace. Other than Finn's and Caz's snores, the room was silent with sleep. Even Gavin's eyes were closed as he sat on the floor beside the door, head resting against the wall.

I slid from beneath the covers, careful not to wake any of them, but the floor creaked as I took my first step.

"Ary? What's the matter?" Finn's concerned tone centered me enough to notice the sudden absence of snores. I became uncomfortably aware that all eyes in the room were on me. Gemma lit the lamp on her nightstand. Caz, Finn, and Ezra sat up from the floor.

Gavin was immediately moving. He fastened one calloused hand around the back of my neck, the other on my shoulder. He assessed me head to toe. But I retreated from his touch, feeling dirty. Feeling…too broken to be held. He searched my face for answers, but I had none.

I shrank away from his touch and his hands remained frozen, empty, airborne, as if he still held me there.

I made a break for the door, desperate for crisp, fresh air.

"Ary!"

"What are you doing?"

Their frantic calls followed me into the dimly lit hallway, and a sense of panic crept up my spine. I wasn't running from my friends. Rather, the hollow horror of some distant memory nipped at my ankles like a devil's hounds.

Gavin's strong, swift footsteps were behind me. I ran faster.

Down the rickety stairs, through the heavy back door, and into a circle of dead, leafless trees behind the tavern.

"Aryella."

That deep, rich timbre tried to anchor my feet to the ground, my mind to my body. Tried. This time, something else was tugging in my chest. Something that needed me even more than I needed him.

My trembling breath became mist before my face. The same rippling ache from before pulsed through me.

"Leave me be. I just…I just need to be alone."

"You're not going into the woods alone." The crunching of snow as he moved closer. "It's the middle of the night."

My head spun. I looked down, focusing on a spot between my feet as I tried to control myself. On the snow beneath me there was a round, dark spot about the size of my thumb. Reddish in color by the looks of it, illuminated just enough by pale moonlight. Another spot appeared, then a third.

It was coming out of *me*.

Frantically, my trembling fingers searched for the source until stopping between my thighs, where there was a sticky wetness seeping through my underwear.

I gasped at my hand, now damp with blood, trembling. The icy wind was quick to dry it, leaving behind an unsettling crimson pattern. As if ink had spilled and seeped beneath my skin, marking me permanently. A horrible symphony of sound would have forced me to my knees had I not stumbled over to an oak tree for support. There was ringing in my ears, a wailing infant, a woman weeping, and the panicked voice of a man.

"No," I breathed, closing my eyes, clutching my stomach. "No, no, no—"

And then I lurched forward without warning, heaving up the contents of my dinner into a puddle at my feet, visible only in the moonlight. It took me a moment to realize he was there. Gavin had moved to my side so fast that he had saved my hair from my vomit. I whimpered and let him support my weight.

But the pain in my belly worsened—right around that old, curved scar on my lower abdomen—and the sadness carved deeper into me, so deep that I thought it would crawl through my spine and out of my back. I wept, utterly empty, like something precious had been taken from me, torn out of me, the blood with it, leaving me hollow.

Gavin draped his coat around my shoulders but kept his palm beneath, consoling me with smooth, circular strokes on my back. Just like my last nightmare, he was all that kept me from crumbling into the snow. From digging through to the core of Nyrida's earth just to retrieve whatever it was I had lost.

"Smyth, what is it?" Gemma's demanding voice came from behind us. When she went unanswered, she mumbled under her breath and trudged toward me through the thick, wet snow. She stopped and surveyed me. When she saw the blood on the snow between my feet and the crimson stain of my hand, she gave a heavy sigh. "Oh, Ary, you're all right." Gemma squeezed my shoulders. "It's just your cycle. You've always had it terribly."

I winced. Cramping, sure. But not like this.

"I don't think—"

My blood curdled as I heard the woman's scream again. This time a mere echo, but it was there.

"Did you hear that?" I gripped Gemma's forearms. "The screaming?"

"Screaming?" Gemma looked around, then at me. "There was no screaming." A sharp tug in my stomach brought me back to the pain. "You're exhausted and cold. Come on." Gemma wrapped her arm around me and turned us toward the tavern. "Let's get you changed into something of mine. We can wash your nightgown in the morning."

Chapter Eleven

My now blood-free hands were my sole focus during breakfast the next morning. Anything that spared me from looking anyone else in the eye.

No one mentioned a word about my bloody midnight meltdown. Gemma promised she'd told the others how bad my nightmares could get. How I sometimes felt lost along with my memories from before the accident. How, when my nightmares weren't about Phillip's and Oliver's deaths, other horrors erupted in my sleep. She'd also told them I would rather not discuss them. I was grateful for that. I just wanted to pretend they never haunted me.

The frosted forests of northern Warrich gave way to rockier terrain as we traveled to the southeast. The climate grew warmer, as well—a small mercy. Still cold, but far more bearable.

Wymara—with its green, rocky highlands—stole my heart. The trees were sparse, but the sky was broad and blue. The prowling, dipping mountains were beautiful and terrifying, and the lakes scattered across the terrain were clear and sparkled beneath the early winter sun. I had never been able to see so much or so far at once.

Especially at dawn and dusk, when the sun and the moon moved through a graceful dance, a selfless give-and-take, one of them no better than the other. The colors…I could hardly find words to describe what they made me feel, only what they were. Cerulean pools in the sky peppered with rosy pink clouds. The ochre waves off the sun. I was mesmerized.

Along with the blue and orange hues of dusk came the camaraderie and laughter I looked forward to every night we stopped. Before the nightmares waged their wars on me.

Whether over a campfire glowing defiant against the winter winds or huddled around a table in a crowded tavern, I loved listening to my new friends share stories about their lives. The stories gave me a glimpse into some of what could be. What was already developing. Friendship. A family.

My will was strong, but my body was still weak from exhaustion. Despite the Wymaran sun and the endless supply of food Gavin insisted I eat. The rocky hills were steep. I was so very tired and ashamed at how weak, frail, and out of shape I had become hiding away in that house.

One morning later in the week, I tripped over a rock and lost my footing, despite my new well-gripped boots. Mercifully, I caught myself, but Caz whistled for my attention and told me to hop on his back. Just for a little while, he said. The least he could do for his queen.

Gavin appeared sorely displeased with the idea, but I did it anyway.

At one point during the third night—spent below the stars and among the chilly air—I was awakened by the sounds of pine needles crunching beneath sturdy footsteps. When morning came, I had one more blanket tucked around me and Gavin was already awake and cooking deer sausage over the fire.

He served me first—honeyed green tea hot and ready—before the others woke to the mouthwatering scent of charring meat.

"Thank you." My mouth widened when I realized how effortless it was to smile. It had been a while since I felt this type of contentment. It was morning, there was a whole day ahead of me, and daytime was good. Gavin nodded, his mouth curling into my favorite half-grin.

The others woke and ate, their clamorous conversation echoing throughout the frigid forest. When they had finished eating, they split off in different directions to relieve themselves and left me alone with Gavin.

My long hair was loose from its braid and in need of taming. I brushed through it with gentle strokes, careful not to yank at my cold, sensitive scalp. Gavin trained his eyes on me, his stare lingering, as usual, while I packed my sleeping mat into my bag along with my quilt and the other necessary items I carried.

"Are you still hungry?" he asked.

"No."

But his question was a mere courtesy. He pulled a bread roll out of his bag and handed it to me.

I laughed softly. "You don't have to keep giving me your food."

He waved a hand. "Took it from Freyburn. Don't want it. Too sweet."

Indeed, the roll he gave me was more of a pastry—round, with a jam-filled center. Strawberry, by the smell of it. When was the last time I tasted strawberries?

"Hurry." He nodded toward the pastry with a smirk on his face. "Before the others get back and fight you for it."

I gave in, playfully gasping. "Do you have a secret stash of goodies?"

His gentle chuckle caused warmth to pool in my belly. "There's a lot your friends don't know about me, Ella."

When I bit into the pastry, my eyes rolled back in my head and an involuntary moan slid out of my throat. It tasted so good.

"Fuck."

I looked up, shocked to see Gavin Smyth, one hand pinching his nose, the other gloriously muscular arm pressed against the tree, glowering at me like I had just kicked his imaginary dog. All traces of that playful smirk, that gentle laugh—gone.

"Don't do that again!" he snapped at me, body tense.

"Wh—" I swallowed down my large bite. His eyes widened. "What? Eat this delicious treat you so generously gifted me?"

"That... *noise.*" He waved his finger at me. "That sound you just made. Don't do that again."

"I... why?" I glanced nervously at the others, who had just returned.

"Because I said so!" he shouted, storming toward me. I tensed, unsure what to expect. He was careful not to touch me. But he stared at the treat in my hand like it had... *wronged* him. Then he stopped, a brief, unexpected hint of sadness passing through his angry glare at the sight of me. With an irritated grunt, he pointed at me and ordered, "Finish your cake!" before stomping away.

"What on earth did you say to him?" Gemma sidled up to me, watching him storm off.

"I didn't *say* anything," I answered, still in shock. "He got mad at me for making a noise because the pastry was so good."

"A noise." Gemma's eyes narrowed in suspicion, scanning me

from head to toe. "Interesting." She scratched her chin with her index finger. "It has to be a woman that has him on edge. I've never seen a pair of balls wound up so tight."

"Right. Must be some woman," I grumbled, stomach souring.

"*Ary,*" she hissed. I glanced up and found her studying me suspiciously. "What was *that*?"

"What was what?"

"You, just now." She pointed up and down the length of my body. "I mean, I suppose he could be attractive under all that... *disapproval.*" She shuddered.

"Gemma!" I hissed, glancing to make sure the boys hadn't heard. My cheeks flushed with embarrassment.

"Well, forget about it," she muttered under her breath. "He's too old for you."

I cringed and blushed. Finn and Ezra looked at us warily, like they didn't want to know what we were discussing.

"I'm almost twenty years old," I whispered back.

"*And* you're Winterton's bride." She winked at me, her beautiful smile bright in the light of the sun.

I forced back a scowl at the reminder and mentally apologized in advance to Elias Winterton for not wanting to give him a chance. "How old is Elias again?"

"Twenty-five." She nodded toward the thicket of trees Gavin had disappeared into. "Older than you, but not as old as him, that's for sure."

"Is Elias Winterton...attractive, at least?" I felt ashamed for wondering. But was it shallow to *hope*?

"*Oh*, yes." Gemma raised her eyebrows suggestively. "That's not something you need to worry about, Ary." She smirked. "Elias has the kind of hair you'd kill to run your fingers through—thick and shiny and bronze. The face of a god. Tall. Lean muscle, tight ass." She shivered with delight. Finn shifted uncomfortably. I immediately felt bad for him, and for every other perfectly handsome man trying to compete with Elias Winterton.

"You know what, though?" Gemma's eyes darted fleetingly behind me, her mouth curling into a mischievous grin. "I think you could benefit from your own bit of fun before being married off. The gods know Winterton's had his share of it."

"What kind of fun?" My words were laced with apprehension.

"Well," Gemma said, and sighed, "there's nothing more refreshing than a nice, proper *fuck*."

Ezra choked on water and suddenly found the view of his feet wildly interesting. Caz—the last to return to the group—snorted. Finn ran a hand through his neat black hair and cringed.

And a terrifying *growl* from behind me lifted every hair on my body to attention.

Stiff with alarm, I spun toward the source of the noise.

There Gavin stood, his knife in his left hand, and his right… wet and red with his own blood. Two halves of a fresh apple lay on the ground before him. It took only a moment to realize what he had done. Cut straight through the fruit with enough force to put a gash in his own palm.

But that bloodied hand just dangled at his side. It seemed to be the least of his concerns. His deep brown eyes burned with inhuman fury, and his face was curled into a nasty snarl. He was predatory. Terrifying.

And that, I knew, was the look of a killer.

Pointed right at Gemma.

"I knew it," she mumbled, a smug grin on her face, arms tucked behind her head as she eased her back against the large oak tree that sheltered us.

I turned back to Gavin, but he had already disappeared.

"Was that necessary?" I snapped.

"Why, Ary?" Gemma scoffed, waving a hand in the direction he'd gone. "Why should *he* care who you fuck?"

That was a good question. One I didn't have the answer to.

But I could try to get one.

So I turned to follow him.

"Ary, where are you going?" Gemma groaned.

"To make sure he's okay."

Caz threw his head back and cackled while the others watched me in skeptical silence. The man had made it very clear that his top priority was to care for me. To teach me. To protect me. To make sure *I* was okay.

How could they expect me to do anything other than try to return the favor?

"Someone has to," I muttered under my breath, and followed him.

It took only a moment to find him. The heavy sounds of his footsteps dominating the rocky ground were easy to follow.

His menacing, rippling shoulders and torso threatened to split through the black, long-sleeved shirt he wore.

All black today, perhaps to match his attitude.

"Are you okay?"

He laughed humorlessly, shaking his head. "That friend of yours really needs to learn to keep her damn mouth shut."

I lifted my eyebrows. "I don't think you have the right to decide that for her, but even so, she was probably just trying to get a rise out of you." His fists clenched and unclenched—the bloody one, too—and it looked like he was itching to... *hit* something. "I'm surprised how well it's working. What's gotten into you?"

He ran an enormous hand—the clean one—through his dark hair. And for the first time—perhaps since he'd found me that day in the barn—he looked flustered. "Tell me you're not going to."

"Not going to what?" I asked carefully.

"You..." His chest heaved with heavy, frantic breaths, clearly irritated with having to explain himself. "You deserve infinitely more than a *quick fuck*, Ella."

My lips parted in shock.

"I... what?"

The glowing fire of his eyes licked me. But finally, he stated, voice low, cold, and uncompromising, "Tell me you're not going to let anyone touch you."

I straightened my shoulders and crossed my arms over my chest. "That's not fair. It's not for you to decide."

"Well, Your Highness," he sneered, stepping toward me, "I'm not fair."

"Yes, you are." I held my ground, chin up. "You are. I can tell that about you."

He grimaced. "Then you don't know me as well as you think you do."

"Maybe I would like to."

"No." The chill in his tone sliced through me. "You would not."

I rolled my eyes and turned from him, very much over this ridiculous conversation, when—

"Do *not* let Elias Winterton touch you."

I halted, turning back. Fury flickered inside me.

"Excuse me?" The gall of the man. This domineering need for control. What gave him the right?

Gavin stepped forward, shaking his head in warning. "Don't let that little shit put his hands on you, Ella."

"You can't—that's not—" I forced a deep breath. "You don't get a say! It's already decided. I'm going to marry him."

He took another step closer, only arm's length away now. And there wasn't just wild anger in his eyes as he looked at me, but... a silent plea. "I'll kill him if he touches you, Ella."

I forced my shoulders to straighten. "*You* can't protect *or* keep me from the man meant to be my husband!"

"Then I'll be his fucking nightmare."

My mouth fell open, shocked into silence by his brutal honesty. Though I couldn't deny that the thought of having Gavin Smyth as an impenetrable barrier between me and all those wanting to control my life was enticing.

A shield. *My* shield.

So even though he was wrong, even though he had no right, I gave in. Just that little bit. For my sake, not his.

"Fine," I surrendered.

"Fine?" he countered, eyes narrowing. "You're giving me *permission*?"

"Yes, *fine*," I bit out. "Be his nightmare."

His mouth curled into a snarling grin, and his jaw clenched. I inhaled sharply at the menacing sight. I hated how he drew out my fury and comfort like twin peaks of a staggering mountain I could not climb. But we had come to a compromise.

Before I could object any further, he brushed past me, adding coldly, "You've had four days off. Too long. We resume training tomorrow. Two hours, every morning, before we get moving."

I started to remind him that walking for ten to twelve hours straight was not what I would consider a day off. "But—"

"This discussion is over."

I groaned. "Wait, what about your hand?"

He just clenched that hand, blood trickling out through his fingers like it was nothing. Like that pain was nothing.

Nothing compared to what he felt at the thought of me with another man.

We walked for twelve straight hours. Gavin led the way and everyone—including Caz and Finn, the fittest of the rest of us—struggled to keep up with him.

I tried to hide my limp and how my sore body trembled with exhaustion. That shooting pain from just nights before, when I'd started my cycle, still nagged at my lower back, through my hip, and straight into my thigh. At least the wolf bite on my arm was healing well enough that when I rolled up my sleeve and left it exposed to fresh air, it didn't hurt.

Regardless, even though I was exhausted, we began training the next morning, just as Gavin said we would.

At least he was a man of his word.

The sun was warm enough for me to forgo my scarf and hat. After a run to stretch my sore legs, I shed my jacket, too. Underneath, I wore a forest green wool turtleneck with black linen pants. The chill bit at my cheeks, but I was comfortable. My silver hair was loosely braided and rested over my right shoulder.

My body ached, but I stood as tall as possible in front of Gavin, arms at my sides, head held high. Waiting.

His cold gaze assessed my defiance and my thin but slightly stronger form. Yesterday's all-black ensemble had been traded for a navy blue long-sleeved shirt and stone-colored pants, which looked just as irritatingly good on him.

"Well?" I gestured for him to begin. "Waiting on you."

His eyebrows rose, and a surprised grin lit up his normally grumpy, bearded face. "Good morning to you, too." I glared back at him, revealing nothing. He sensed my anger and nodded, grin fading. "I was a prick yesterday."

I blanched. Definitely wasn't expecting that.

"I will not bore you with an explanation," he continued. "But I apologize. And you should know that you're doing much better, Aryella. You're stronger than when I found you, and I'm proud."

I lifted one wary eyebrow, silently encouraging him to continue.

"When I found you, I thought you looked..." That pulsing jaw muscle raged beneath his cheek. "Barely alive."

I scoffed. "Apologies for giving such a disappointing first impression."

"That's not what I mean."

"Then what *do* you mean?" I challenged, crossing my arms over my chest.

"You were cold," he hissed, stepping forward. "You were hungry, scared, alone, and I—" His now-bandaged hand flexed at his side. "I did *not* like it."

I focused my gaze on a reddish-brown rock at my feet before kicking it away. It had only been a week, but that week felt like a lifetime. A new life, and a new world. I felt just a little stronger. My stomach was almost always full, and I could feel the color returning to my cheeks. I could feel hope. A reason for living.

So, agreeing with him, with my eyes still on the rocks near my feet, I muttered, "I didn't like it, either."

The ground crunched beneath his steady footsteps. I felt his index finger beneath my chin as he tilted it upward. My lips involuntarily parted at the sight of his scarred, handsome face, the dark beard I wanted to touch, and the scar over his right eye.

"Five more laps to that boulder and back, twenty lunges each leg, thirty push-ups, core and balance exercises, and then I'll teach you something more interesting than throwing punches. We have little more than an hour before the others are ready to leave, so hurry." I opened my mouth to object, but he held his index finger to my lips and tutted. "Can't let you get lazy, can we, Your Highness?"

I scowled and shoved his hand away. "Never call me that again."

And I ran, hearing his deep laughter echo behind me.

"A choke hold?" I gasped, eyes wide.

I'd hurried through my warm-up as quickly as my aching body would allow. It took determination to push through, but I'd done it. I would need even greater will in the coming days, months, likely years, if I was to accomplish all that was expected of me.

"Do you think you can one-two punch your way through a fight?" Gavin replied, smirking. "I haven't taught you to disarm or, better yet, fully eliminate a threat. And you should learn to do so first without a weapon."

Eliminate.

He meant *kill*.

I swallowed down a bit of bile.

"You're small, so to get a good sleeper hold on someone my size—"

"No one is your size," I grumbled. "You're huge."

He let out a low, surprised laugh and cleared his throat. "You'll need to jump your enemy from behind and apply immediate pressure to the trachea with your forearm. If you fail, they'll easily flip you."

"You want me to jump on you?" I nervously rubbed at my elbow.

"Jumping on Caz's back didn't seem to bother you any," he bit out, brown eyes flaring with unexpected scorn.

My eyebrows shot up, and I rushed out, "Fine, okay."

He came around behind me and fastened his arm around my neck.

My heart thumped in my chest at being so close to him, so completely wrapped up in him. And then when I repeated the exercise, I would be wrapped *around* him.

If he wanted to, he could snap my neck in the span of a single breath. His immense biceps covered the entirety of my neck, past my collarbone. I breathed in the rich scent of him and—

"Take your right biceps in your left hand, behind your victim's head, and squeeze." He showed me the pressure without hurting me.

I expected the word *victim* to rattle around my brain for quite some time.

When he was confident I had those few details memorized, he motioned for me to jump onto his back.

In response to my hesitation, he gave an annoyed grumble. "I don't bite, Aryella." Hints of darkness danced in his gaze and he smirked. "Unless you ask me to."

Groaning, I lunged forward, up, and he caught me without stumbling, like my weight was nothing. For a man his size, I supposed that was true.

"Wrap your legs around my waist and hook your heels inside my thighs."

I did as he commanded, fastening a weak but accurate choke hold around his thick neck. He was so broad that I could hardly fit around him, but I did my best.

His dark hair brushed against my cheek. A ripple of lightning, flanked by desire, shock, pleasure, and a little bit of terror, struck my stomach.

What compelled me to lean my mouth closer to his ear, to brush against him, lips on his skin, and say what I said, I'm not sure I will ever know.

"Why do I have the feeling I'm the first person in a very long time to have you in this position?"

His powerful body shuddered. His fingers tightened against my sleeve. And his pulse… it stuttered. A feline smile tugged at my mouth as I bit my lip—wholly uncharacteristic of the person I knew, the person I *was*.

"Are we interrupting?"

I was dropped to the ground as swiftly as possible without being thrown onto my rear.

Gemma and Ezra stood behind us. Ezra, scowling at Gavin. Gemma, arms crossed. Neither of them was pleased.

"He's teaching me to kill someone with just my arms," I explained, a little too rushed. Gavin distanced himself from me by a few steps.

Gemma's eyes darted suspiciously between us. "Uh-huh."

"Time to go!" Finn broke the uncomfortable silence. A gift from the Selvaren if there ever was one.

Gavin made off in the direction of camp without another glance. Gemma followed, and I meant to, but Ezra stopped me with a gentle grip on my wrist.

"Hey." His blue eyes were touched with worry. "You know he's dangerous, right?"

I watched Gavin—the rough, violent man they knew—as he walked away. Naïvely, I replied, "I don't think he's dangerous to me."

Ezra cringed at my words, eyes plagued with a sad pity I hated. As if I were blind, stupid prey, running straight into the den of a predator.

"Just be careful, okay? I don't know enough about him. None of us do, other than it was Simeon who sent him, and I don't—" His eyes darted nervously in the direction Gavin had gone. "I don't want him to hurt you."

I thought of Gavin's touch, his presence, how it made me feel—safe, warm, alive. That solace I felt whenever he was close. I thought of all these things more than I cared to admit, and I simply couldn't imagine him hurting me.

But Ezra was right. He wasn't the type of man I could simply be attracted to. No, he was the type of man I could get lost in.

Truly, Gavin Smyth's effect on me had the potential to be devastating.

"Okay." I placed my hand over Ezra's and squeezed. "I'll be careful."

And I meant it.

Chapter Twelve

One downside of craggy hills and plunging valleys was a brutal, unforgiving wind that dipped through fewer trees, soared, and threatened to literally blow me away. More than once, I stumbled.

But the wind's attempt to steal my joy, albeit ferocious, was no match for the thrill I felt simply existing in the Wymaran highlands. While Gemma and Gavin threw worried glances in my direction every time I shivered, I remained enamored with the magnificent valley to the south, disrupted by veins of rivers going every which way. The same wind that bit into my cheeks flowed over the rich landscape below, creating the illusion that the earth itself was breathing.

Around midday we came across a mountainous range of ashy black rock, quite different from the rolling verdant hills speckled with gray and brown we'd so far seen. It was far away, but I could see from where I stood how dominating the blackened terrain was, claiming no desire to share space with anything living.

"You see those rocks?" Caz rested a hand on my shoulder and pointed east, toward the range. "They're formed from volcanoes."

"Volcanoes?"

"There are cracks deep beneath Nyrida," he explained. "And even farther below that, the core of our world is on fire. Melted earth seeps back up through those cracks and hardens up top, creating ridges like that."

"Won't the fire... burn through?" I cringed, well aware how idiotic I sounded. I would have to "thank" my mother for failing to teach me basic geography.

"Give it another four hundred years, and maybe it will," Gavin muttered grumpily. He brushed past us, tossing a nasty scowl at Caz.

Caz shook his head and snorted, watching our grumpy leader hike forward.

"I don't know that he likes you very much," I muttered so only Caz could hear. At least, Gavin didn't like whatever friendship was developing between Caz and me. If I ever had an older brother, I thought he might be like Caz, and I was simply giddy at the thought of meeting Marin. I already adored her, just based on what they'd told me.

Caz laughed, free and lighthearted. "I think he doesn't like *himself* very much, Ary." With a gentle squeeze of my shoulder, he forged ahead.

We continued southeast, leaving the ashy cliffs in our wake. One day, I thought. One day I would stare right into one of those pools of burning earth just to prove to myself I could.

That night, I was so exhausted that I hardly saw where we stopped and my dinner almost became my pillow. Someone must have taken my near-empty bowl and laid me on my sleeping mat, because I woke the next morning, cozy and comfortable like I'd gone to sleep of my own volition.

I opened my eyes to daylight, taking in our camp. Above me,

gray rock—a wide, but short overhang—sheltered us, leaving open air on all sides save one. A fortunate shelter from the rain. No wonder I slept so long. The sound of rain always soothed me.

"Good morning, lovely." Gemma smiled down at me. Her outstretched hand offered my daily mug of honeyed green tea. "It seems you slept well."

I sat up and accepted the mug. "Thank you."

Caz and Ezra were laughing and talking next to the campfire. Finn saw me sit up and came over.

"Where's Smyth?"

"Hunting." Finn sat down with his map and unfolded it. "He was gracious enough to insist we stay out of the rain."

Gemma rolled her eyes. "Yes, what a delightful fellow."

Finn nudged her leg and shot her a look of warning. I failed to suppress a grin.

They made sense, the two of them. Finn Sinclair was remarkably levelheaded and unflappable. Gemma was... not. It was a balance between, just as Marin sounded like the stalwart calm to Caz's boundary-pushing levity.

Over the past few days—after many sessions of persistent nagging that I was quite proud of—Gemma explained her feelings for Finn. Feelings that had been developing for a decade. Her parents died when she was young, and she'd grown up in the Winterton Caves just as he had. They had been close friends as children, but Finn—three years Gemma's senior—refused to pursue anything until Gemma was at least eighteen.

But then she was picked to participate in Commencement and chosen by Simeon and the Wintertons to be my social guide and secret emissary. Since her time with me in Warrich, she'd floated from village to village in Avendrel and Wymara, occupied with various surveillance and reconnaissance missions for Elias's army. For Gemma and Finn, the pieces had yet to fall into place.

She wanted it to work. She even said she might love him, though nothing physical had happened yet. I knew it was only a matter of time. And their happiness made *me* happy.

"We're two days away from Tovick." Gemma's voice dragged me back to the present. She and Finn focused on the map. "I've never been there, but it's supposedly bigger than Freyburn. With Simeon's wards in place, it'll be safe from Molochai's shadows."

"It's unlikely Molochai knows you exist," Finn added when he noticed my worry. "Simeon knew what he was doing, keeping you hidden all your life." Gemma nodded in agreement, not without an apologetic look for what being hidden away had done to me. "But still, we need to be careful. Most of Nyrida knows about Christabel's prophecy. It's likely Molochai does, too, so any suspicions about you could be dangerous."

"Being inconspicuous is key." Gemma sighed. "Which is why we can't use horses unless necessary. They're harder to hide and cover tracks. A real shame, as we would likely be in Brinnea by now, *and* my ass wouldn't be on fire."

Finn snorted, folded up the map, and tucked it back in the pocket of his brown canvas jacket.

Using horses had never crossed my mind. I'd only seen them in drawings. I added those to the list of things I needed to see, touch, maybe even ride, before going to the Winterton Caves. How embarrassing would it be if their queen couldn't ride a horse?

"Damn."

We heard Caz's voice, followed by swift, strong footsteps

echoing off rock. Gavin, returning from his hunt. Completely soaked through his long-sleeved slate gray shirt, which gripped his hard, mammoth shoulders and arms. The sight of him might have stolen the air right out of me, but my admiration was replaced by shock at the sight of the massive dead animal slung over his shoulders.

A red deer. With antlers. He'd killed and carried a full-grown red stag over his shoulders for the gods knew how long and how far.

I cursed myself for enjoying such a savage sight.

He thrust the animal over his head in one fell swoop. Effortless, like everything else he did. The dead stag hit the ground with a sickening *smack*. Then Gavin looked right at me, no one else, and said, "This should cover your next few meals."

He knelt down on one knee beside the stag and unsheathed a razor-sharp blade from its place on his belt.

"Oh, *shit*!" Gemma hissed. "I swear on all the sons and daughters of Sussurro, if you do that right here, right now, I will *murder* you and—"

Gavin sliced open the gut of the red stag with unnatural precision, earning groans of objection from Gemma and Ezra as he proceeded to physically remove the guts from the animal and toss them aside, away from us.

Caz nudged Gemma toward Gavin. "Sounds like Sussurro's going to have a bone to pick with you."

She rolled her eyes and gagged. I doubted one of our twelve ancient gods would bother with Gemma, even if she could get close to his multitude of alleged children.

Caz kept me company as we watched Gavin gut, skin, then hang the stag with a rope over a long, jagged rock that jutted out from the wall of stone. I watched, aware once again that I should know how to slaughter and prepare my own meat. Still, watching him was... brutal, but the way he worked was almost routine, as if he'd butchered hundreds—perhaps thousands—of animals to survive.

I watched blood drain out of the carcass. I'd heard Phillip talk about cleaning an animal to know it was necessary. I thought the sight of red would grip me by the throat and steal my breath, but it didn't. This was... different. Gory and brutal, yes, but this was survival. Maybe it was because *he* was here or simply because I wasn't alone anymore, but I wasn't afraid of the blood. I couldn't afford to be. Not anymore.

And I thought... maybe that's why he was doing this right in front of me. Because he knew that, too.

Still, there was one piece of the slaughtered stag that haunted me. It soured my stomach, but I forced myself to look at the deep gash in its neck. The killing cut. Where Gavin had ended its misery.

I jumped when Caz put his arm around my shoulder. He squeezed me, winked, and whispered in my ear, "Always entertaining to watch another man mark his territory."

I opened my mouth to ask him what he meant, but he was already gone.

"We will stay here for the day," Gavin announced to no one in particular. "The rain looks like it will clear soon." He turned to me, hands still bloody. "Once it does, I want you outside for training. Bring your knife."

Sure enough, the rain stopped about twenty minutes later. I shoveled down breakfast—the last of our bread and strips of jerky left over from Freyburn. I stared at the hanging stag as I passed it.

Gavin was still damp when I found him, but his wet, dark, shoulder-length hair was pulled back into a knot at the base of his neck, revealing more hidden scars, which I ogled longer than I should have. He was clean—no trace of the stag's blood on his hands or clothing. The amount of skill it had to take to slay, carry, and butcher an animal while only bloodying his hands…

I shivered.

"I brought my knife," I announced. "Just as you asked."

He looked up and gave me my favorite half-smile. "Good girl."

My body clenched from within. I redirected the tension elsewhere. To my anger. Mostly unwarranted, but useful.

"I'm assuming we are staying put today so you can spend all morning and afternoon running me ragged?" I asked, voice sharp and cold.

"Morning?" He chuckled. "The morning is gone. You slept it away."

"All afternoon, then."

He covered the space between us with four long, steady strides and looked down at me.

"What?" I snapped, straightening my shoulders.

"I slay an angry stag for you, and this is the attitude I get?" His lip twitched.

The bastard was egging me on.

"I didn't ask you to slay anything, and you did it for all of us."

He tsked. "Did I?"

My nostrils flared. Caz's words echoed in my mind. *Territory.* Is that what I was to him?

"Why do you have something against Caz?" I fumed. He raised an eyebrow, waiting. "He's my friend, and you don't like it."

"Caz is a flirtatious ass who wants to get under my skin."

"He's married with a baby on the way."

Gavin laughed humorlessly. "It's a shame you're naïve enough to believe that would stop most men."

"You're the one with the problem, not Caz." I scowled. "Besides, even if he wasn't taken, he's quite a bit older than me."

His nostrils flared. "I'm older than Caz."

"How old *are* you?" I snapped.

He froze, eyes narrowed down at me. If I didn't know any better, I thought he looked a bit unsure. "How old do you think I am?"

My irritation with him got the better of me. I arched a critical brow and made a point to scan his form from head to toe. "*Old.*"

That muscle in his strong jaw twitched—another telltale sign of his rage—and I knew I'd hit the spot.

"Feisty today." A sneer, instead of a smirk, darkened his features. "Did you wake up on the wrong side of your mat this morning, Your Highness?"

"No!" I snapped. I threw a punch toward his annoyingly rugged, handsome head, but he effortlessly dodged it. "You just piss me off!" I swung again, but he caught my whole fist in his palm.

"Good," he purred, the sound silky and dangerous. "Use it."

My back hit the stone, hard enough to hurt but not damage, before my brain registered that he had flipped me upside down. He was so fast, gripping my hand one moment and tossing me to the ground the next.

Asshole.

I lay still, temporarily paralyzed with my back against the cold earth. When his hand fastened around my arm, reflexes took over.

Because since the moment he'd taught me, I had memorized every movement—envisioning it in my mind over and over again while we walked, while I ate, while I lay awake—so that when this happened, I would be ready.

I leaped up, using all the new strength in my core. Landing cleanly on my feet, I used my momentum to jump onto his back, throwing my forearm around his neck and tucking my legs inside his. I squeezed to disorient him—just like he had taught me—and forced him to the ground.

And then I went one step further. In one swift movement, I spun to his front, straddled him, pressed the tip of the knife into the top of his shoulder. Then I let go of the handle to let it drop to the ground, showing I'd won.

"Shit," Gavin hissed through his teeth, then laughed, carefully shifting me off him. "Tell me how you really feel, Your Highness."

I realized I'd never heard the clang of metal on rock after dropping the knife. Confused, I looked down.

The knife hadn't hit the ground . . . because it was stuck in his body. I hadn't dropped it.

I'd stabbed him.

I gasped, the sight of blood on his neck and shoulder ripping the air right out of me. I had meant to touch against his shoulder and pull away. I hadn't planned on stabbing it into his flesh. His shirt was coated in dark crimson, wet on his skin beneath the tear of the cloth and under the place his fingers touched. I crawled to him, reached for him, threw myself onto him—

"No!" My hands on his hard chest were small and helpless. "I didn't—I didn't mean to!"

"A good hit." He used his uninjured arm to raise himself off the ground. "I think that's all I need to see for today, as far as training goes. If only for my own protection," he said, and chuckled.

"I don't know how I—" I panicked, the breath in my chest tight. "Oh, gods, I could have killed—"

"This won't kill me, Ella." He gave me an amused, reassuring smile. "Though I won't lie, seeing *you* so torn up about the thought of me dying is not good for my ego."

"How did I—what did I—"

"Unconscious desire to end me, I imagine." He winced as he shifted his left shoulder forward.

"No!" I insisted. "No, I would never—"

"Ella." He grabbed my hand with his uninjured arm and squeezed. Comforting me—*he* was comforting *me* right after *I* had stabbed *him*. "You hit muscle. That's all. If you wanted to kill me, you would have."

"What do I do?" I pleaded, touching his face as gently as possible. I had to make sure his skin didn't grow cold or flushed or pale. Tears welled in my eyes. He looked at my fingers so close to his mouth. "How can I help?"

"Well, for one." His eyes scaled the length of my body, starting at my neck. A coy grin spread across his face. "As much as I already regret saying this, you'll need to let me stand up."

"Oh." I looked down. In my worry, I'd straddled his left leg and my hand that wasn't touching his face was pressed firmly against the center of his abdomen, essentially pinning him to the ground. My heart raced. "I'm sorry."

I thought I heard him mumble, "I'm not," but it was too quiet to be sure.

His rumbling grunt, the squelching of bloody flesh as he pulled the knife out. It was all too much, but I made myself watch. Made myself suffer at the sight. It was only fair since I'd done it to him.

"Directly above the artery, but you missed." His fingers brushed over the gash. Blood was trickling out, but not fast. He ripped the forearm of his shirt and used the back of his sleeve as a rag to wipe the blood from his skin. To be so nonchalantly amused by a knife in his shoulder was disturbing. Impressive—but most definitely and much more importantly, disturbing.

"Why are you acting like this happens all the time?" I demanded. But with his clean hand, he gently took my chin between his thumb and index finger and smiled.

He lifted an eyebrow at me, like it was obvious. "This is hardly my first stab wound, Ella."

"I don't like that thought."

He shrugged, wincing at the movement. "Then don't think about it."

"That sounds like a very *male* thing to say," I mumbled, annoyed.

He chuckled. "I'm proud of you."

"You're proud of me?"

"Yes. It looked easy for you to put a knife to me, then through my flesh. You didn't have to think about it. That instinct is what you need to survive."

"I don't even remember pushing it into your shoulder. It *was* instinct, and I don't want to be someone who just kills without thinking. A monster." I felt his index finger brush my chin. "Not that you . . . not that you're a monster, I . . ." His eyes were soft, his fingers curled around my jaw. He smirked, and I leaned into his touch. "You're proud of me for stabbing you a few inches above your heart, as if killing should come easy to me."

"Yes, Ella, I *am* proud. You're improving." He cradled my face in his non-bloody hand. "And if killing came easy to you, you would have just stabbed me lower." He dropped his fingers to his side. "You must only hate me a little."

"I don't think I could ever hate you." But I'd acted like it. I'd marched right over to him, ready to fight, and I had. My shoulders slumped. "I just... I was frustrated. You frustrate me."

"Likewise."

But he was grinning as he approached a small, trickling stream of the clear water. The black corded necklace with two rings had been bloodied. I watched as he removed it from his neck and knelt to rinse the silver rings. They rested in his scarred fingers, a beautiful and delicate contrast to his roughness.

"Why do you carry those rings around your neck?" From a distance, I'd seen one thick and tarnished silver ring. It looked like it belonged to a man. Now a bit closer, I could see a second band—smaller, delicate, likely a woman's—with flowers and vines intertwined in the metal. Beautiful, precious work. "You usually tuck them in like you're hiding them. Are they both yours?"

When he turned to face me, his lips were drawn taut, skin paling.

"The larger one is mine."

"And the smaller one?" I asked.

My gut dipped, silently begging for an answer different from the one I dreaded. I had no right, but I threw out a desperate prayer to the gods. Let it belong to a sister, a mother, or no one at all.

Finally, he exhaled sharply, ran his wet fingers through his hair, and admitted, "It belongs..." He flinched. "It belonged to my wife."

Wife.

The word echoed inside me like a hollow wail in a dark, empty room with no windows, no doors. An unfamiliar, anxious chill slithered through my chest, threatening to wrap around my neck and choke me.

I hadn't imagined Gavin with a wife. He didn't seem the type. But he was old enough that he'd lived many adult years before coming to know me. Years filled with love, adventure, joy, and a plethora of other things I'd never experienced. Of course he had experience and history. He was a grown man, and I was barely an adult.

"Where is your wife?" I asked quietly.

"Lost."

And there it was—that glimpse of heartbreaking longing, that sadness that consumed him the morning he found me crumpled on the ground, a victim of the wolf. I looked away from him, uncomfortable, my heart settling under the weight of his silent plea.

"Lost how?"

"It doesn't—" He cleared his throat and placed the black rope and rings around his neck. "It doesn't matter. What's done is done."

It was a failed effort to move. To shift. To act like I was unaffected. The envy took root like a poison. Could I really be so bothered by the thought of his heart belonging to another? Certainly, I had no right, especially when I was betrothed to marry Elias.

But that *look* in his eyes. It hurt me, as if he loved her so much, as if he'd lost so much that his pain unfurled itself from a dark place in his heart and lashed out, striking me.

I feared such terrible pain. *And* I longed for it. To feel agony so deeply...surely, a love just as deep had to exist on the other side of it.

"What was she like?" My chest stung at the thought of her, sure she was a stunning woman. Strong, tall, confident, and alluring. I knew asking about her was a defense mechanism, my mind's impulse to remind my reacting heart and body that this tension between us—tension I likely misread was there in the first place—would not culminate the way I secretly hoped.

"She was perfect." He ran his hand over his mouth and avoided my gaze as he spoke. "Brought up in a prominent, wealthy family. Her father was a general, and her mother was..." His jaw clenched, and he shook his head. I glanced at him, brow furrowed, but he continued despite my confusion. "My wife was greatly cherished. Protected but...*stifled*." A grimace flickered across his face at the last word. "I was far below her status. Frankly, it was a miracle she ever looked at me. Her family didn't allow her to go out on her own, but she was rebellious that way, stubborn. One day, she snuck out and showed up in my blacksmith's shop." A warm smile finally graced his rugged features. "The day I saw her was the luckiest day of my life. She was the most beautiful thing I've ever seen."

When he turned to me, his gaze softened. It made me feel oddly warm, but conflicted. I swallowed a lump in my throat.

"She told me she needed a weapon and she needed me to teach her how to use it," Gavin continued. "I looked like a fool, I'm sure. Utterly speechless, dirt on my face, arms, clothes covered in soot." He laughed down at his hands. "I would have done anything she asked."

"What happened to her?"

"She was taken from me," he uttered slowly, lost to his thoughts for a brief moment before shaking them off. "But as I said, what's done is done."

"She must have been pretty remarkable."

He looked at me, the light in his hickory eyes devoured by sadness. Perhaps he regretted sharing his secret with a naïve young woman. Maybe he told me, then realized I would never understand. He reached for me regardless, and with his thumb beneath my chin, he guided my attention back to him, features now twisted with remorse. "Forget about it," he muttered. "All right?"

I forced a smile, knowing that forgetting this was impossible. Just like I couldn't forget Caz's wife. Or how Finn and Gemma still weren't together because of the obstacles our people faced. I could never forget what these people were sacrificing. For me. For a promise made by an ancient queen that *I* was expected to keep. I could never let myself forget.

He cleared his throat and shook his head, turning toward camp. As if he'd come close to losing himself in memories of her, and my presence brought him back.

I hated that it made him sad to be back here with me.

"Gavin?" I asked. I heard the crunch of rock beneath his feet as he paused and returned to me. I held back a sob at the terrible, heartbreaking hope I saw in his eyes. "I'm so sorry she was taken from you."

His shoulders slumped. His eyes—brimming red with emotion—darkened and pierced me, and his pain became my pain.

"I'm sorry, too," he uttered, his voice low and hoarse.

It was a simple response, one I would have expected from anyone who had lost the one they loved. But like most things he said, it sounded . . . different.

And it gutted me.

That night, when the others were asleep, I pulled my quilt over my head and cried silent, stupid, childish tears.

Chapter Thirteen

We camped outside a small village, which Gemma said was only half a day's walk from the town of Tovick. It was our last stop before a week's rest with Gavin's friend, whoever he or she was. Then, three more days of travel, and we would reach Brinnea. Where my *real* father waited for me.

I failed to hide my nerves. Meeting a four-hundred-year-old sorcerer was unbelievably intimidating.

Mentally, I wanted to prepare. Wanted to prove myself. An idea began to form, of spending a day alone in the forest, with only my hands and knife to defend myself. I needed to know I could be alone again. Alone, without fading away, without losing my grip on the woman I was becoming. The woman I was starting to like.

I had to try.

But I would have to convince him.

We skipped training the next morning. He hardly spoke a word to me that entire day, but I noticed he still hid the black corded necklace with those rings tucked beneath his shirt.

He was quieter this morning than he was tense or angry. A good sign, I told myself. So I followed him into a small cluster of red maple trees to gather wood while the others made camp around the fire.

"What is it?" he demanded when he saw me approach.

An invisible blow smarted in my chest at his words. "I was thinking that tomorrow, while the rest of you are in Tovick, I could stay back for a day and practice—"

"No."

"You didn't even hear what I was proposing—"

"I don't have to." He removed the cover from his ax and began to sharpen the blade. "You are not going or staying anywhere alone."

"Would you stop interrupting me?"

Gavin shrugged. "I will when you stop making foolish suggestions."

Anger prickled my chest. "You're an asshole, you know that?"

He blew out a low whistle and chuckled. "Language, Your Highness."

"You're not listening to me!" I snapped, angry tears biting at my eyelids, but I held them in. "I—"

"Enough!" His booming shout shook the trees and made me shudder. "This is not a discussion, Aryella."

"Gavin." His face immediately softened when I said his name, so I marched forward and grabbed his thick forearm in my hands. His eyes locked on my fingers touching him. "I need to know I can survive alone. And you'll only be in the next town over."

He sighed. "I promise you'll have plenty of opportunities to test yourself." He withdrew his arm from my grasp. "But not this. Not right now."

"You..." I clenched my fists at my side, not caring that I looked and sounded like a petulant child. "You told me to never let anyone take my choices from me. Are you going to take them from me now?"

His eyes narrowed. He studied me for a while, then rested the ax against the base of a maple tree and closed the distance between us.

My angry breaths left small clouds of mist between my face and his chest. I refused to look up, to give him the satisfaction of knowing how vulnerable I was beneath his glare. But I felt his lips brush against my forehead and my knees began to buckle.

"Of course not, Aryella." I felt the deep hum of his voice infiltrate my body as he savored each syllable of my name, like he could taste each one. "But if you *choose* to willingly put yourself in danger, stay alone in the woods where every living, breathing thing wants to devour you"—his nose brushed against my temple—"there will be consequences"—I felt the friction of his beard on my cheek, and the air around me thinned—"that you are far from ready for."

I shuddered. Out of pleasure or fear. Maybe both.

And I decided not to stay behind the next day.

To my chagrin, the small, dilapidated village just west of Tovick tested me in more ways than I had expected.

Freyburn had felt *warm*, despite the literal cold. That small city had been living and breathing and full of hope and joy, but this place was gasping for air.

Gavin didn't insist I hide my hair beneath my cap like he had in Freyburn. The people in this dying village paid no attention to our presence. As if they'd already surrendered to whatever dreadful fate had chosen them.

I shuddered, remembering that feeling.

The few children we saw weren't laughing or playing like the ones in Freyburn had. Here, they were thin, their shoulders and eyes drooping with exhaustion and *hunger*. Black smoke oozed from ashy chimneys attached to ramshackle houses, many of which were almost crumbling beneath their own weight. Shops were boarded up, men and women alike lay covered in thin, holey blankets next to buildings, and two skeletal and mangy dogs trod over a pile of trash in an alley between a closed, shabby tavern and an empty shop.

My eyes dampened at the sight of a little girl across the path, curled up on a threadbare blanket next to a burned-down building. Her old house, I assumed. Her eyes were closed, and she was shivering, covered only by a thin coat—with no hat, no gloves, no scarf.

"No." Gavin fastened his gentle but unbreakable grip around my forearm when I approached the girl.

I glared at him, anger choking my throat. "Either let me go alone or come with me." My voice trembled. "Your *choice*."

After a heavy pause, he unfastened his fingers from my arm and nodded toward the girl. The latter, then. The others watched as we crossed the path and I knelt down before her, ignoring the sharp bite of gravel on my knees through my pants.

Hearing me approach, she opened her dull brown eyes and sat up, brittle bones struggling to support her weight. Her dark blond hair was matted and dirty.

"What's your name?" I whispered, and offered comfort with a gentle smile.

Her eyes widened. She shook her head.

"Okay." I nodded, keeping my smile. "That's okay, you don't need to tell me."

I started to remove the luxurious green-gold hat, gloves, and scarf that Gavin had bought me in Freyburn, but he stopped me with a hand on my shoulder.

"Anything worth selling will get stolen off of her," Gavin muttered. "Could make her a target."

I glanced around and noticed I was indeed receiving greedy glares from a few men and women close by. All eyeing the scarf around my neck and the hat on my head.

My shoulders slumped, until I remembered that my old winter clothes were in my bag. Slightly tattered and fringed at the ends but still warm, still intact. They would help her.

To avoid startling her, I carefully lowered my knapsack from my shoulder and unbuckled it. At the bottom were my old hat, gloves, and scarf. I tried to hand her the blue-and-gray bundle. "Will you take these and wear them?" My nose burned from tears I tried to repress. "Please."

Her small, pale fingers were shaking. Fearful eyes darted between me and the towering force of a man behind me. A rough gust of wind ruffled her hair, and she flinched at the cold.

"We won't hurt you," I promised. "Please take them." I gently laid the hat, gloves, and scarf in her lap. She was so pale, thin, and cold. She looked afraid to *hope*. "You're cold. You—" I faltered, realizing she reminded me of myself. "You don't need to be so cold and—"

"Who are you?" The strained, smoky voice of a female on my right made me jump. "Get away!" I rose to my feet, arms outstretched in surrender, and saw a haggard old woman with a broken cane rushing unsteadily toward me.

"I just wanted to help—"

"Get away!" croaked the old lady, dragging the little girl off the ground and away from me. "Outsiders are not welcome here."

"I'm sorry," I breathed, stumbling backward until I hit a safe, warm wall of muscle. He rested protective hands on my shoulders and gave a reassuring squeeze. Relief soothed me when the little girl hugged the items to her chest.

Gavin steered me back to our group. Finn, Caz, and Ezra watched me with a mix of sadness and admiration. Gemma hugged me tightly and gently stroked up and down my back before smiling tenderly and taking my hand as we walked down the center road.

I swallowed vomit when I noticed blood staining the outer walls of some run-down homes and empty shops. The number of dilapidated buildings far exceeded the number of people left in this village.

"Insidions," said Finn. The farther we went, the more the village stank of carrion. But it seemed anyone who had been slain was laid to rest. So far, the street was empty of corpses. "They've been here."

Gemma gasped and covered her mouth with her free hand.

To our left, a man was strung up in a tree with a noose around his neck. His abdomen was cut open. His intestines hung out of him, rotting. He reeked of decaying flesh.

"Oh, gods." Ezra turned away and vomited behind a tree. I faced the sight even though my stomach begged me not to.

On the ground below the body was a small wooden sign with words written in the victim's blood. I sounded out words I'd never seen or heard before, but I recognized Molochai's name. My knapsack dropped off my shoulder to the ground. I needed to remove a tangible weight so I wouldn't buckle under the horror.

"'Molochai is king,'" Finn translated. "Insidions only use the ancient language to spite the Selvaren."

"Likely tried to resist Molochai's men." Caz sighed. "Left as an example for the others."

Hope couldn't trounce logic even in the most optimistic parts of my brain. Caz's nonchalance implied that a scene like this—though the first I'd seen—was all too common.

"Is this what's happening in my world?" Tears pooled in the corners of my eyes, but I refused to blink them away. "My . . . kingdom." The sound of that—*my kingdom*—felt ridiculous. But it was true. "This is what was happening while I was sitting in my cabin."

"Not your fault, Ary." Caz squeezed my shoulder.

But for the first time, I began to truly feel like this was mine to change.

"You don't need to see any more of this today." Gavin placed his hand on my lower back to usher me away. "Unfortunately, there may be plenty more of this to come."

"Let's not pretend ignorance is a privilege I still have," I replied, voice trembling.

He frowned but didn't force me to move, nor did he obstruct my view of the unsightly carnage.

"Can't be more than a day old," Finn noted, scowling at the corpse.

"It's recent," agreed Caz.

"That means Molochai's Insidions could be close." Gavin lifted my bag from the ground and threw it over his shoulder, next to his. "We need to keep moving."

"I want to bury him," I announced, feeling five sets of incredulous eyes slicing into me.

"He's long gone, Ary." Caz gave me a sad smile. "Smyth is right, we have to keep—"

"What if it was someone you loved?" I demanded, trembling with unbridled rage. I thought of Marin but didn't dare say her name or put that image in his head. "Wouldn't you pray a stranger might be kind enough to lay them to rest rather than leave them hanged, humiliated, splayed open like a pig in a butcher's shop? *Take him down.*"

Gavin's concerned gaze lingered on me before he nodded to Finn and Caz. "Dig a grave."

Gemma groaned. As Finn and Caz moved the body, the rotten stench of death intensified.

I wanted to help, but Caz and Finn didn't let me. Instead, I stood and watched, letting my anger simmer. I wasn't convinced that justice for myself—for my loneliness, for being unfairly pushed into this role—would be enough to motivate me. A sad truth, but a very real one. But this . . . *this* infuriated me.

I *would not* let myself forget sacrifices made by others for a better world. If this man had suffered and died for what was right, the least I could do was memorize his pain. Make it my own. Make it my catalyst.

I walked to where Caz and Finn had moved the body, held my breath, reached for the sack on his face, and said, "He shouldn't be buried with a bag over his head."

"Ary!" Gemma grabbed my elbow. "Ary, please don't—ah, shit!"

"I'm going to check on Ezra." Even Caz turned away.

I held my breath and removed the sack to reveal that the man's eyes had been carved from his skull, leaving gaping black holes drained of blood by gravity. Gemma's and Caz's footsteps shuffled away behind us. Finn followed, leaving only Gavin beside me.

"They carved him up, like an animal," I breathed, eyes burning.

"As they see it, anyone who doesn't follow Molochai's orders is less than human."

Gavin's knuckles brushed against my elbow, a welcome comfort.

"You won't turn away like the rest of them?" I looked up at him.

"I won't let you face it alone." He cocked his head and surveyed the corpse, looking eerily... *bored*. "And I've seen worse."

I shuddered at the horrific, senseless loss of life before me. I couldn't destroy Molochai today. Not a single trace of my power had shown itself, and with no clue where to begin, I'd be helpless against him for quite a while.

But there had to be *something* to be done about this, even a temporary solution.

Wasn't I the queen? Barely trained? Yes. Still small and mostly weak and anxious? Yes. But a queen nonetheless. A queen could give orders.

Some good *could* come of it.

"I want to take these people—these *survivors*—to the caves." I willed confidence into my voice and stared pointedly at the others. "I want them fed, sheltered, and cared for."

Caz, Gemma, and Finn traded apprehensive glances but proceeded to bury the man as they were told. Ezra walked up to me, shaking his head. "I wish we could save everyone, but... we can't. We can't just lead a hundred people all the way to the caves."

"What would Elias do?" I asked. My cousin clearly admired my betrothed, and by mentioning Elias, I hoped to win him over.

"He would tell you to make the smart call and not draw attention to this place." Ezra waved a hand around the dilapidated village. "If Insidions come back and find the survivors leaving, they will wonder who did it. There's a chance they'll track and follow us."

I looked to Gavin, who shook his head. "He's not wrong. We can't do it."

My shoulders slumped.

"But," Gavin added, much to Ezra's displeasure, "my friend in Tovick has connections. He can get word to the caves, to Winterton. This wouldn't be their first covert evacuation."

I gave a relieved sigh and squeezed his large hand in thanks.

The feel of his answering grip lingered on my skin for the rest of the day.

Chapter Fourteen

Weariness settled heavily in our bones while we made camp inside a small grove of maple trees. Our plans to stay overnight in the village had been thwarted. The villagers were too afraid to talk to us and they wouldn't accept our food. With all our efforts to help proving futile, not one of us could stand to stay there a moment longer.

To my surprise, everyone but Gavin lay down and fell asleep before I even tried. Well aware one pair of eyes were burdened with worry and locked on me, I stayed up, standing with my arms crossed before the fire, making every effort to burn the memories from today into my heart. I wouldn't forget the fear, hunger, and destitution of the innocent people I should have been able to help.

I looked up only when I heard steady footsteps and knew it was Gavin. His black leather jacket was spread out on the ground beside me.

"Sit."

I stared at the jacket. "On your jacket? It—"

"Sit, Ella." Unwavering will persisted in his gaze.

I hesitantly obeyed, lowering myself slowly, so as not to do further damage to his jacket.

As soon as I was seated—"Give me your feet."

"What?" I choked. He squatted before me.

"Do you think I don't see you limping?" He gestured to my legs. "You've been in pain every day for the last week, and you've said nothing. Give me your feet."

"You really don't need to—"

"Let me take care of you, Aryella." His brow was furrowed with ache—torment—as he added, "Please."

It was the first time I heard him say that word. I had a feeling he didn't have to plead very often.

With a quick glance over his shoulder, I made sure the others were asleep. I didn't need Gemma or Ezra to be disappointed in me for letting him get so close. When I was confident they wouldn't see, I heeded his demands.

He started with my left foot, removing my boots, then my wool socks. His strong, long fingers rubbed the top of my foot in firm circles down to my ankle, repeating from the base of each toe. I closed my eyes and sighed, letting my head fall back between my shoulders.

"I suppose I better enjoy this while it lasts." I snorted. "I'm sure the army commander won't have the time or patience to give me a foot massage."

"He will if he knows how lucky he is."

A fluttering in my stomach caused my pulse to stutter. Guilt, for even mentioning my betrothed when Gavin did not seem to like it.

"I'm sorry," I whispered. His flaring nostrils were the only sign of emotion on his stoic face. "I don't know why I—I shouldn't bring him up, I—"

"You don't have to apologize for saying what you feel, Ella." He kept his firm grip on my foot and moved his thumbs to the sole beneath my toes. "It's your life, I'm just happy to witness it."

"You're quite the wordsmith tonight—" I hissed when he pressed a particularly sore spot, and the pain was glorious. "You'll have to tell me what I did to earn such treatment."

His lip twitched, but something else—regret, maybe—got in the way. "Your compassion for those people…" He huffed out a humorless laugh. "Not many would bother." His strong fingers dug into the aching arch of my foot, eliciting a moan that I had to bite my tongue to repress.

I studied the furrow of his brow, how the scar over his right eye crinkled on his cheek when he focused. Heat pooled in my stomach, from his strength, his touch. The fear he could invoke contrasted by the care he took with me made me feel like I *wanted* him to keep touching me.

I forced a swallow and shoved it down. I was betrothed to someone else. I couldn't feel this way.

"Simeon wouldn't bother?" I pressed on.

Another dark, humorless chuckle. "No. Simeon would not bother."

"How well do you know Simeon?"

"Too well."

I lifted my eyebrows in surprise and added that to the list of questions I saved for another time. I was too tired and emotionally drained to process anything about my ancient sorcerer father.

"Well, you did," I said softly. "You bothered."

"Don't give me too much credit." He smirked. "I helped because it was what you wanted."

"No." I tilted my head at him and smiled. "You would have made the call on your own. You're a good man, Gavin Smyth."

True. At least, *I* knew it was true. From the pause of his hands and the widening of his eyes, I could tell he believed otherwise. Maybe no one had told him he was good for quite a long while.

"*I think he doesn't like himself very much,*" Caz had said.

I frowned. That Gavin would stand by my side in the face of terrible horror, the worst of humanity, was something I would never forget. But I was also disturbed by the look of indifference he wore when faced with such a brutal sight, and I feared for him. I was afraid of what he had seen and done and endured. To see a man gutted and hung up as a feast for crows and be wholly unbothered…

"Can I ask you something?"

"Yes," he answered.

"You told me you're good at killing."

"Yes."

"How many people have you killed?"

"Don't ask questions if you can't handle the answer."

My stomach dropped. I could handle more than he realized, but did I want to?

"Would you…" I shuddered, terrified by the potential truth. "Would you kill…for *me*?"

He didn't hesitate. "I already have."

I flinched and resisted the urge to retreat from him. Because I should, not because I wanted to. He shifted from my left foot to my right, where he repeated his ministrations.

"Why?" I breathed.

He pressed into another beautifully painful spot. "You are my queen."

That answer again. There was more, but I didn't know how to

convince him to share it. Maybe if I helped him find peace or happiness of some sort...

"After all this is over, after I'm deemed ready to lead by Simeon and delivered to Elias, what will you do?"

"Does it matter to you?"

"I just..." Nerves made my skin tingle, and my cheeks flooded with heat. "There has to be a way to repay you for all you're doing for me. I'm sure I can find a way to give you whatever it is that you want."

His strong fingers brushed across the top of my foot. "I can't have what I want."

"Really?" I lifted a critical brow. "You said you do what you want, and that certainly seems to be true. Why can't you have what you want?"

He slid my wool socks back on my feet, closed his eyes, and confessed, "Because the whole damn world has been hellbent on taking the only thing I truly want—what's *mine*—for a long fucking time."

My throat tightened. "Your wife?"

He gave no answer but met my gaze with hot intensity.

My stomach threatened to upheave the remnants of my breakfast. With the way he looked at me, it was easy to forget about the mystery woman he'd told me about. He looked at me like she didn't exist. He looked at me like there was only me.

"I'm sorry," I rushed out. "I hope you can find it in you to let go of the pain. If you want to," I added, forcing my throat through a swallow. "If you can."

"I don't let go, Ella." Goose bumps rose up on every surface of my skin at the biting iciness of his tone. "Ever."

A melancholic longing sluiced through me, and I withdrew from him out of impulse.

"Thanks." I stood and willed my voice to be steady. "For the feet."

But he fastened his hand around my wrist, holding me in place. And then he rose, towering over me, mere finger-lengths away. I could feel the heat of his body. His cedar and leather scent was so close…

"The first time I lost what I wanted, I was young and naïve." He locked eyes with me. My breathing came out weak and stuttered. "I let my guard down and it slipped through my grasp, but that will not happen again." His fingers twitched around my arm. "I may never have what I want the way I want it, but the day I let go will be the day I'm buried as deep into the fucking ground as they can put me. Even then." He lifted his knuckle to graze my cheek where I felt heat pulsing. "I'll be damned if I don't try to crawl my way back out."

I was wholly disarmed beneath the intensity of his stare and the weight of his words. Despite his brutality toward the world around us, I felt safe with him. He made me want things I'd never known how to want.

My feeble knees threatened to undermine me. I stared at his mouth. Full, symmetrical lips, rich with color, framed by a soft, dark brown beard. I wondered how those lips felt, how they tasted. They were parted, just like mine.

Hungry, maybe, just like mine.

But one word echoed through the heady fog in my brain, loud and clear.

Wife. His wife. And what he wanted, it—*she*—would not slip through his fingers again.

"Good—" I stumbled over the word, withdrew my arm from his grasp, and cleared my throat. "Good night."

After crawling beneath my quilt, I was afraid to look back.

I descended a staircase of elegant black marble, curved around a grand, brightly lit foyer. I felt like I was floating. But not the fun, light, airy kind of floating. No, I couldn't compare this sensation to flight. Parts of my body felt elsewhere. Dispersed throughout the room, fractured at odd angles, like shards of dull glass no longer capable of refracting light. Parts of me void of life.

And at the bottom of the stairs, Phillip and Oliver lay dead in pools of blood.

I screamed in the dream, but no sound came out. When I inhaled, the breath cut off halfway to my lungs. I was stuck on that staircase. Stuck in scattered pieces with half-breaths like I had been stuck in that golden casket and—

"Aryella."

I heard him, but the emptiness was swallowing me whole.

"Open your eyes, Ella."

I woke the moment I felt his hand on my face. My breath caught in my throat at the sight of his protective form kneeling in the dirt. The fire flickered behind him, stars were bright in the sky, but I saw only him. "Breathe with me." He led me through a few long, deep breaths. "That's it," he encouraged, softly stroking my cheek with his thumb, summoning a familiar, addictive warmth to my skin. "Good girl."

I reached up to grab hold of his wrists like I had after that first nightmare. My gaze drifted to where the others lay, but it was quiet.

Gavin shook his head, guiding my eyes back to his. "They're all asleep. It's just you and me."

I wondered how that was, having woken up the entire room during my last nightmare.

"Did I scream?"

"You were crying. It was quiet, but—"

"You heard me from over there?" I nodded to Gavin's sleeping mat on the other side of our camp at least fifteen paces away. Untouched.

"No. I was sitting next to you. After today, what we saw—what *you* saw—I just wanted . . ." He swallowed. A nervous Gavin Smyth was an oddly heartbreaking sight. "I wanted to be close to you."

My heart stumbled and sighed. I closed my eyes, knowing I could only handle either the tug in my chest or the comfort of his gaze. Both, and I might throw my arms around him.

"Do you want to talk about it?"

"Not really." But I continued anyway, like he drew the truth right out of me. "Phillip and Oliver . . . I found them dead, and ever since then . . . my heart feels like it has a fungus." My eyes burned and tears dripped off my cheeks. "And if I go back there. If I tell you. It'll just do the same to you."

"The damage to me is done." He stroked my cheek. "I promise. Better me than you, Ella." I closed my eyes and leaned into his warmth. "Give me your burden." My desperate need for his comfort was so overwhelming, I thought I might suffocate if he took it away. "All of it, so that you don't have to carry it anymore."

A sob wrenched itself free from my throat, and everything else spilled out.

"Their throats were slit, and they had X's carved into their chests. And it was done without passion. Almost without malice. Like it was just a means to an end. And I was glad they didn't suffer, but it was so, *so* senseless." I shuddered, the words a blur. "Ollie's sweet little face was so full of warmth and hope and joy, but he was cold and lifeless . . . and eerily peaceful." Gavin brushed a tear from my cheek, listening. "I tried to understand. I've been trying to come up with a reason. For Phillip, maybe he had gambled or angered the wrong person when he was drunk. But Ollie?" I cried. "Why Ollie?"

"I'm sorry." His eyes were red with pain. "I'm so sorry."

"And that's been my nightmare these past few months," I pressed on, despite my trembling. I hadn't known how desperately I'd needed to get this out. "But then lately, I've been having different nightmares where my body is trapped or I'm bleeding and crying and my soul is in multiple places at once and I can't find any of them. No matter what I do, I'm hollow. I hear things—like memories, but they're *not* memories—and they're confusing and terrible and they *hurt.*" I inhaled shakily. "It's like love and joy have been ripped out of me. Something is taken, but I don't know what. And because I don't know what's been taken, I don't know where to look for it. I'm just empty, like I'm not even a whole person."

"You are whole." He took my hand and kissed my knuckles. "This world is cruel and evil, Ella. People will take from you, they *have* taken from you, but *you* are *whole.*"

The hollow cavern in my chest eroded away by grief at the thought of their deaths filled with warmth. With him.

"Maybe." My breathing steadied on him. "It's not all cruel and evil." I cupped his bearded jaw in my small palm. He stilled when I touched him. "Do you have nightmares?"

"Doesn't everyone?"

Maybe I wanted to hear about his nightmares. Maybe I felt less haunted just knowing he had them. Solidarity in terrible dreams. I shuddered—whatever haunted *him* had to be worse than I could imagine.

"What do you do to get them out of your head?" I asked.

"I hold on to the first good thing I can think of." He gave me a soft smile. "Lately, that's been you. Safe, warm, fed, happy. And *you*, Ella... you pull me out of my nightmares and return me to my dreams."

His words and touch seemed to shatter an internal cocoon that had been trapping pieces of me I didn't know existed. Pieces that felt dormant. And I wanted *him* to shatter me, then put me back together and keep those broken pieces for himself.

"Do you think I'll ever find out who killed them? If it wasn't Molochai..."

He tucked a piece of hair behind my ear, his eyes somber. "I believe you will."

"Ezra mentioned someone called the Butcher of Nyrida." When I said the name, the color left Gavin's face. "He said it probably wasn't him, that he would have made it...messier. But I think it had to be someone terrible. Do you think they'll come to kill me? Or my friends?"

"I will die before I let that monster touch you."

Rage swelled inside him, seeped out, and wrapped me in a protective shield.

"Thank you." I placed my hands on his chest. His thick muscles tensed and hardened like stone beneath my fingers. I pulled back—feeling like I'd been shocked—and shifted to lie down. But when he started moving away—

"You can stay close," I rushed out. "If you want."

He didn't leave my side until morning.

I knew because I hardly slept. I was wholly preoccupied with the life-altering awareness that I was forming a dangerous attachment to him. One that inevitably had to break.

Chapter Fifteen

We all ate breakfast together the next day. The sense of normality, of friendship, overshadowed all we had seen that previous day and allowed me to forget who I was, just for a little while.

Who I had to become.

And what that meant for my heart. A heart becoming drawn to someone other than the man I was meant to marry. A man at least ten years my senior. A man tasked with teaching me to protect myself—to *kill*. A man taking me to my real father, who had likely hired him in some capacity. A man with a wife who was gone but *lingered*.

I had bitten away the skin around my thumbnail as I tried not to think about it. But I had counted the days since we left, and I didn't forget what day today was. I could put off the worry, just for today.

Today, I was twenty.

I felt a brush against my soft blue sweater and sighed as an extra layer of warmth that smelled of him engulfed me. His jacket.

So much for not thinking about him.

Gemma noticed him touching me. She looked ready to lurch over the campfire and use her momentum to mow him over, away from me. But she didn't, because she had seen me shivering as he had.

I looked up at him. "Aren't you cold?"

"No." Gavin sat down beside me. "Have you eaten something?"

"Yes."

"Listen to you." Gemma glowered at him over the flames. "She's a full-grown woman. You sound pathetic."

"Tremaine," Gavin snapped back. "You've mistaken me for someone who gives a shit."

I bit my tongue to suppress a reaction. It wasn't easy. The horrified, offended look on her face both amused and distressed me. I would have been angry at Gavin, for her sake, but she wasn't just distrusting him. She was doubting me because *I* trusted him.

"Wipe that grin off your face, Ary." Her expression was hard, but her voice softened. "And don't come running to me when you can't get this deranged asshole to leave you alone."

Gavin scoffed. I shot him a disapproving look. The corner of his mouth turned up into a smile. And then my breath caught in my chest when the broody, gruff mass of man took a swig of his canteen, winked at me, and mouthed, "Happy Birthday."

I lost my balance and almost fell off my log.

"Can we all just get along?" I half shouted, catching myself with my free hand and doing my best to take any attention away from my swooning.

"Sounds great to me!" Caz chimed in.

"We aren't the problem," Ezra muttered.

"Not when he's after my girl!"

"*Gemma*," I hissed back at her, cheeks hot.

She shrugged and smiled. "Extra attention on your birthday."

Caz, Ezra, and Finn looked at each other, mouths open wide with big, silly grins. They hadn't known.

I buried my face in my hands when they started to sing.

"No!" I groaned.

Gavin refused to sing, but he laughed, the sound deep and soothing. I endured their song and their attention. Joy shimmered in my chest. My limbs tingled with giddiness. An irrepressible smile drew my lips so wide, I wondered if traces of it would ever fade. I couldn't remember any of my birthdays.

Today was going to be a good day.

We arrived just outside of Tovick after a few hours of walking. It was the largest town I'd ever seen. We stood atop a grassy hill overlooking cobblestone streets lined with wood-frame buildings of varying heights. Townsfolk bustled about, dressed warmly to fend off the crisp air. But happy and energized.

A grandiose house of worship, complete with a towering steeple surrounded by twelve equal points—one for each of the twelve gods of Nyrida—sat at the center of town. Dazzling stained-glass windows, bold with color, wrapped all the way around the captivating structure.

It was an effort to believe this place could exist so close to the dilapidated hell we had seen yesterday. It made me uneasy, how Simeon could be content letting one settlement suffer while providing protection to another.

Gavin's friend was not at the tavern he owned on the east side of Tovick. It was closed, so we decided to camp just outside the town until his friend returned. A neighbor had said he would be back on the fourth of this month, so we had only one day to wait. We found a small clearing within a forest of oak trees and made camp.

After our midday meal, Gavin revealed he had a surprise for me. Gemma objected, but he promised to steal me only for an hour. I followed him toward the sprawl of shops and houses and people. I started to tuck my hair in a messy bun beneath my green-and-gold knit hat.

But he took my hand and lowered it. The feel of his skin touching mine heated my blood. "Leave it."

"Aren't you worried they'll recognize me here?" I frowned. "We're farther south. Finn says it's more dangerous the closer we get to the areas Molochai controls. And they've been moving north."

He assessed me quietly. "On our first day of training, I said you have nothing to hide. I meant it." He shook his head. "I don't want you living in fear."

I smiled and let my waves of silver flow down my back like a cape, unafraid.

"Besides," Gavin continued, eyes lingering on my hair and neck, "Tovick should be safe beneath Simeon's wards for now and I won't let them touch you."

With his hand on my lower back, he led me into a stable filled with a half-dozen horses. It was roughly the size of the house in Warrich, covered with a straw-thatched roof.

"Why is it just the towns that have wards?" I asked. "Why not other villages, like that village yesterday?"

"Simeon prioritizes places, people, things he deems vital to his cause: stopping and destroying Molochai."

"And what do you think of that?" I asked. "Why should he get to decide who gets to be protected?"

Gavin sighed. "I can hardly fault him for that. I would let the whole world suffer if it meant seeing you safe and free."

My mouth opened in shock. He was wrong to say such a thing, but the honesty in his eyes and clarity in his voice stole my ability to say so. And before I could—

"Have you ridden a horse before?" he asked me.

"Not that I—"

"Remember," he muttered wearily, reminded of the burden of my lost memories. "Well, you'll learn today."

"These are your horses?" I watched him stride confidently toward a stall on the left side of the stable.

"A friend's," he replied over his shoulder. I wondered if it was the same friend who owned the tavern. How many friends did a man like Gavin Smyth have?

"Is this my birthday present?" I ran to catch up to him.

"No."

I blushed, embarrassed that I'd mentioned a birthday present. I expected nothing. Why would he bother? Why would anyone bother, when there were so many more important concerns in this world?

Gavin stopped before a sleek black mare with a gray-speckled crest and tail. He opened the door to her stall, gave her a sturdy pat on the neck, dropped the bag he had slung over his shoulder, and fixed her with a saddle. He did the same with another horse before guiding them both out of the stable and into the open air.

I smiled at the mare. "She's beautiful."

"Yes." He looked at me. "She's always been my favorite." Gavin enveloped my left hand in his and guided it down the mare's neck, stopping at the reins. "Grab the mane with your left hand."

I obeyed, and then instinctively lifted my left boot into the stirrup and kicked my right leg over the horse's back.

"Yes." Gavin smiled proudly and rested his hand on my knee. My eyes lingered on his touch, but he kept it there. "I knew you'd be a natural."

The mare's ebony coat was sleek and fine beneath my fingers.

"Wait for me." Gavin started to turn toward his own chestnut brown stallion but paused to ensure I would obey. My attention was fixed forward on the well-trodden trail before me. "Ella," he warned, but the sensation of the horse's strong body beneath me felt right.

I grinned, collected the reins, squeezed my heels into the horse's sides, and leaned into her movements like I'd been doing it my whole life. "You'll catch up."

He cursed and faded behind me as the horse's trot climbed to a gallop.

She ran with a yearning for freedom I felt deep in my bones. Her graceful bounds, synchronized with my racing pulse, made me feel like I was flying. My body felt light, no longer weak or hungry. The powerful mare *carried* me faster than my worries as her brilliant black coat shimmered in the winter sun. She carried me faster than my burdens, running through harvested wheat fields. For a little while, we left the heaviness behind.

I steered her in a circle to go back the way we came and threw my head back in carefree laughter when I saw even mighty Gavin

Smyth and his stallion were struggling to keep up with me. We rode for minutes, but I could have gone for hours. I smiled and laughed all the way back to the stables.

Instinct was the only way I could explain how I knew to sit back, relax my hips, and sink my weight into the saddle to slow the mare down to a trot and then, when Gavin caught up to us, a complete stop. With my bottom lip between my teeth, I braved his heated glare to gauge the amount of trouble I was in.

His dark hair was disheveled from the wind and the muscles of his arms were straining the sleeves of his black leather jacket. His jaw was clenched tight, and while fury burned in his gaze, relief washed over the flames.

"You really did chase me." I grinned, breathless. "All the way there and back. And you only look a little mad."

"I will chase you to the ends of the earth, Aryella." A hint of distress darkened his deep timbre. He dismounted his horse and added, "Though I'd prefer it if you didn't make me."

Once more, I threw my head back and laughed, if only to keep my giddiness—at his voice, at those words—from giving me away.

When we were back inside the stables, I accepted his help dismounting my mare, wholly aware of my stomach's warm leap as his large, strong hands locked around my rib cage.

As he lowered me to the ground, a small burst of his fresh, subtly sweet breath hit my face. The very same moment that my breasts, peaked from the chill, brushed against his chest. Warmth traveled between my legs, and I inhaled, shocked by the sensation. I wondered if he wished to memorize the feel of our bodies pressed together as badly as I did. My pulse beat emphatically in my ears and I let my fingers brush against the hard wall of muscle protecting his heart.

"Believe it or not," he drawled, touching my feet to the ground, "I'm redirecting all of my energy to *not* be short with you today."

I bit my lip to block my smile from growing too large and curled my fingertips around the cloth of his linen shirt. A dark blaze of desire sputtered through his stare. It disappeared as quickly as it came.

"I didn't know you could be so generous," I teased.

"I'm generous with many things when I want to be, Ella."

"Thank—thank you." I took a step back and cleared my throat—self-preservation, to avoid combusting. His gaze followed my movements as I caressed the mare's long, sleek neck. "I know you said that wasn't meant to be a gift, but it was one."

"A precursor then, to your actual gift." He picked up his bag, withdrew a thick shawl made of animal fur, and handed it to me. "For you."

I ran my hand over the thick pelt, gray like the grim skies of fall, speckled with a tawny brown as warm as the fur felt beneath my fingertips.

It had been dark when I'd seen the animal, but…

"Is this—?"

"The wolf that attacked you in the barn," he confirmed. "I was going to burn the damn thing, but then I thought…" Gavin took a step closer. The cold, empty caverns of my heart yearned for his warmth. He used his thumb and index finger to tilt my chin up so I could meet his brown-eyed gaze. "How convenient would it be for you to wear this around your neck? My mark, of sorts." He took another step closer and brushed over my lips with his thumb. "And a constant reminder of what happens to anyone or anything that tries to harm you." I exhaled shakily. A muscle worked in his jaw in response to my quickening breaths. "Because, Ella?" he said coolly, brushing a piece of hair from my face, "I'll gladly skin them all."

My breath tightened in my chest. "That—that's crazy," I whispered, clenching my thighs together. No, no, no. The thought of him ripping apart my enemies should not excite me.

But it did.

Gavin's mouth widened into a grin. His warm fingers touched my jaw, and he chuckled, not denying my words. With a single movement, he brushed my hair off my neck and held my face in his calloused hands.

As he looked into my eyes with breathtaking clarity, his grin faded. The playfulness gone. "I do have one wish for you, on your birthday." He worked his thick throat through a swallow and held my gaze. The stroking of his thumbs on my cheeks sent delightful shivers up and down my spine. "May your light blind your nightmares," he said, "and your love burn away the life that confines you."

I sucked in a shallow breath when he leaned down and pressed his lips to my forehead. Closed my eyes and memorized how every part of my body was on fire and alive. How my heart was elated. Safe.

"Thank you," I whispered. Before he could pull away, I rose up on my toes and brought my mouth to his bearded cheek—quickly, even though I had the urge to linger. The sudden, gentle heat of his warm exhale graced my skin, causing me to dig my fingers into the solid wall of his chest and look up.

My heart lightened with relief when his smile returned,

gentle and soft. Another brush of his thumb on my cheek, and he answered, "Always."

We returned to camp an hour later, just as he promised. Despite Gemma's earlier objection, it turned out the others had their own motives for sending me off. They made a run to town during that hour we were gone, and I was welcomed back with a gift from each of them.

From Finn, my own professionally drawn map of Nyrida with the caves' location and Elias's army outposts marked in a secret code he created. In case it ever got lost.

From Ezra, a history book about Nyrida during the Rexus dynasty—before Simeon and Molochai.

From Caz, a set of knives designed to skin and cut apart an animal. Specifically a deer, he said. Or "my own" stag.

I purposely avoided Gavin's reaction to that one.

And from Gemma, a few pieces of artwork Oliver had made for us both during her time in Warrich. She held me for minutes while I cried into her shoulder.

The day felt surreal. This past time with my new friends felt surreal. I was tired from long days of travel and taxing weather. We all were, but we had otherwise avoided danger and enjoyed each other's company. They meant the world to me already, all of them. It struck me, sad as it was, that I had never even dreamed of having friends like this.

Maybe I could find more friends in the caves. With Marin Sinclair, Caz's wife. Maybe even with Elias Winterton. I could start as his friend, and then—

"I need to go into the market for a few things." Gavin's deep, commanding timbre eclipsed all thoughts of my betrothed. "You stay here with the others. Don't stray far."

I stood up from my spot by our campfire. "Can I come with you?"

"No."

"Really?" Lifting my chin and crossing my arms in defiance, I pressed, "Are you sure?"

He studied me, knowing what I would say if he denied me my *choice*. He'd trapped himself with that one. Watching him realize was like seeing a marble statue crack in real time.

"Shit," he hissed, running his hand over his face. I finally let loose my triumphant grin. "Listen, there are rules. You'll speak nothing but pleasantries to anyone. Do not give your name. You'll stay less than five paces from me *at all times*. Do you understand?"

"I thought you said you don't want me living in fear."

"I don't. That doesn't mean it's something *I* am capable of, however. Not when it comes to you." He gripped my shoulder and let his fingers curl possessively around the back of my neck like at the horse barn. Whatever had kept him from touching me these past few days seemed to be dissipating. Fast. "So," he pressed, recapturing my attention. "Do. You. *Understand?*"

I bit my lip and nodded. "Yes, sir."

"Good." He studied me from head to toe, contemplating. "And don't call me *sir*."

But the hungry gleam in his fervent stare made me wonder if he secretly liked it.

Our whole group decided to go into town. "No soldier left behind," Caz joked. Now, I stood in a small, stuffy shop of trinkets with Gemma and Ezra while Caz and Finn ran their own errands and Gavin discussed something important with the shop owner in a low, hushed tone.

Gemma caught me watching him.

"You're spending a lot of time with Smyth," she observed sourly.

I shrugged, still happy from the way his touch made me feel, and looked through an old book with stale, yellowed pages. "He's teaching me a lot."

"Uh-huh." She focused on a small but detailed wooden figurine of an eagle, its wings spread wide. "Don't be naïve, Ary. Men like Smyth—when they're finished using something, they leave it broken." She returned the eagle to its place on a cluttered shelf of similar wooden figures.

"I know you don't like him."

"It's not a matter of liking him." She faced me, fierce eyes blazing with ire. "The only reason I haven't found a way to force him very, very far away from *you* is because I trust that Simeon has his reasons. But Smyth? He is overstepping. He is getting too close to you. He is violent, crude, hired muscle, and you are our queen." She crossed her long arms over her chest. "And most importantly, he is *not* Elias, who already adores you, even without having met you."

My smile fell. "If Elias adores me so much, he should have come for me himself."

Fuming, I sought Ezra in the corner of the shop by the window, leaving Gemma to gawk at my words. She had just as much a right to decide Gavin Smyth's worth to me as Simeon had to decide that people in Tovick were more valuable than those in the ransacked, oppressed village we passed through yesterday.

No right at all.

Ezra glanced up from the history book he was scouring and gave me a brief grin. A clear but kind signal he didn't want to be bothered. That was just fine. I stood next to him in silence.

Not much time had passed since we left Warrich, and my friends' loyalty to Simeon and the Wintertons had become clear. The anticipation and excitement they felt at the thought of uniting me with them, with Elias, was palpable. I really wanted to feel the same, but I didn't.

I held on to the part of me eager to make friends with people like Marin. I held on to it, determined not to return to the cold, lonely girl I left in Warrich. I tried to let that hope be enough to give my heart some peace. Living free in the world was enough. My new friends were more than enough.

But I couldn't shake my instinct about those caves.

I couldn't shake the wariness I felt that Elias hadn't come for me himself. What kind of husband would he be? Would he let me fight, or keep me bound to the throne? Christabel's prophecy claimed *I* was the one who needed to destroy Molochai. But in Freyburn, Gemma made it sound like Elias would be reluctant to let me participate in his annual training.

Then there was my mother, who had left me to starve and claimed I needed to remain dainty and small. To fit Elias's preference, perhaps?

Maybe he *was* a good man, a noble man. My friends were good. If my friends adored him, surely he was good, too. Perhaps Elowen was the disturbed one, not my betrothed.

But I kept coming back to Caz's comment about that man Alec Gerard—how his importance to the army meant Elias would not move against him, even though he was suspected of doing something "unsavory" to Elias's own sister…

"It's stuffy in here," I muttered to my cousin, searching for a distraction to relieve the nausea in my stomach.

Ezra looked up from his book. A strand of his sandy blond hair fell over his eye as he frowned. "Do you want to make a run for it? We can go see the temple." He nodded toward my protector, who was absorbed in an angry conversation with the shop owner. "Now might be our only chance."

"He'll be mad."

Ezra shrugged. "Probably, but we'll be safe. It's not like we'll get far before he finds us anyway."

Five paces, he'd said. Five paces from him at all times.

But the pull of the outdoors, the crisp air of the sunny Wymaran winter, the thought of exploring a world kept from me…it called to me. Consumed me.

And I needed to know I could be bold without Gavin there to guard me.

I nodded at Ezra. We snuck out a side door beside a tall display case of leatherbound journals and antique fountain pens.

Warm sun caressed my bare face and neck. Ezra grabbed my arm and pulled me to a hard right. Laughing, I jogged to keep up with his longer strides while taking in the sights. A vendor selling fresh chocolate pastries out of a small wooden cart. A pair of musicians whose fiddling duet drew a few passersby into an energized dance. Preparations for the Solstice were all around us here, too. Fire lanterns—in blues and oranges and pinks—imitated the dusk of night.

If I hadn't been told about the spells of protection Simeon cast over this city, I wouldn't think it was real.

We crossed the cobblestone street to the temple. Ezra used his full body weight to push open the heavy door. Before entering, I took a moment to admire the matured, knotted walnut and intricate designs of iron on those heavy doors. The kind of skill and patience it would take to craft such beauty was unmatched.

In line with the twelve spokes on the temple's exterior, twelve arches made up the circular interior. Beneath each arch lay an intricate stained-glass depiction of each of Nyrida's twelve gods.

The cool, pale blue turquoise of the winter gods faded into violet, misty, viridescent spring. And then summer carmine—hot and bright—mixed with peach and sunlight so vibrant, I could feel it burning on my skin from all the way across the vast hall. Three autumn gods to my left, crafted out of rich, deeper colors, like cinnamon, grape, and chive green, completed the symmetrical shrine.

A set of benches facing each of the Selvaren occupied the center of the space and left little room for Ezra and me to stand. But we did, slowly turning, taking in the grandiose stained-glass illustrations that refracted the sun into rainbows on the floors and ceiling.

Finally, I turned toward the shrine to the final, strongest god, the one our current month was named for: Nyxar.

His eyes sparkled like amethysts beneath his hooded black cloak, as if he could blink and drown the world in midnight. The darkness drew me in. My fingers itched to be held by a night that wasn't evil or scary, but soothing. A calming darkness I might claim for myself one day, if I could conquer my nightmares.

Phillip and Elowen had spoken little of the gods, but I knew the basics from my books. Here, it seemed they were legends woven into the fabric of Nyrida's culture more than they were true idols of worship. No one else was in the temple, and it felt as if the power of all twelve deities concentrated in the center of the room where we stood. A power lost and seeking a home.

"Do you believe in them?"

I'd been so entranced with the god of tranquil shadows that I hadn't seen Ezra watching me.

"I don't know," I answered, filled with a strange sense of longing. For doubting something so sacred. "I feel like I should. Like maybe if I don't, I'm betraying them." My cousin looked left to the coldest of the goddesses—Nevelin—the namesake for our first month of a new year. Her eyes were bright diamonds against the pale blue of her skin. "How about you?"

"Not really," Ezra replied, no hesitation in his growingly bitter tone. "The idea of them is comforting, but if the gods existed, they would have stopped Molochai a long time ago."

Instead, the responsibility of saving this world was mine.

As if he sensed the heaviness I felt, Ezra grabbed my hand and squeezed, saying nothing. My cousin's silent fellowship was comfort on its own.

A minute or so later, we decided to head back to the shop and not risk Gavin's wrath a moment longer. But when we turned to go, Ezra's eyes went wide at something behind me.

My body was jerked backward by a pair of long, cold hands.

And I felt the sharp, cool knife against my throat before a husky feminine voice snarled, "Empty your pockets if you want to live."

Chapter Sixteen

There were four of them—three male, one female.

I focused on my breathing to keep from panicking, like this was only a nightmare and I was bound to wake up. One, two, *breathe*... and I could get my bearings.

"What do you want?" I asked, forcibly leveling my voice.

Two men stood with blades pointed at Ezra, his glare a silent warning to bide my time, not to do anything more compulsive than we already had in coming here alone, against orders.

A third man sidled up to where the female held me at knifepoint. Tall, thin, and balding, he loomed over me the way most men did. But I looked up defiantly as I'd learned to do when examined by a man of my own.

"That man you were with? He has money. And he looked at you like you were his little pet." The man grinned at me to reveal a set of yellow-stained teeth. "I'm sure he'd pay a pretty sum to get you back."

"Let her go." Ezra remained calm as he'd been trained to be

in Elias's army. This wasn't his first brush with danger. I remembered him saying they'd been attacked by thieves on their way to Warrich.

How Gavin had eliminated them single-handedly.

"I'll get you your money," my cousin promised.

The men behind him chuckled darkly, and the balding man, who I assumed was their leader, cocked his head at me. "I might want something more than money." My souring stomach brought sweat to my brow and turned my blood to ice.

"Don't you touch her!" Ezra moved to step forward but was held back. They each grabbed an arm and pressed the tips of their blades into his sides.

I was just about to throw my elbow into the woman's gut when I heard a wet *squelch* in my left ear, followed by one low, guttural gasp. A clang echoed, the knife at my throat disappeared, and a body collapsed beside me.

I looked down to see the female who'd held me at knifepoint now crumpled on the ground in a heap of limbs and black hair, eyes frozen open in terrible shock. Blood pooling beneath her head...

There was a knife in her skull, buried to the hilt. A knife that had been thrown from the doorway of the temple, where no less than thirty steps away, Gavin stood, drowning the vast, colorful space of worship in dark, uncompromising rage.

I let out a sigh of relief in spite of his rage, stumbling away from the dead woman as Gavin strode swiftly toward the center of the temple.

He didn't look at me when he passed.

"Get her out of here—to the tavern," he snarled in Ezra's direction. "*Now.*"

The three remaining thieves cowered, looking between their

dead female friend and the mass of muscled fury barreling toward them, horror on their ugly faces.

My cousin lunged for my arm. I tried to look back, but—

"Don't watch." Ezra forced my shoulders forward. "Trust me." He quickly led me out of the temple. The heavy door closed behind us, muffling the pleading cries of three grown men fated to a hell of their own making.

The warm sunlight and crisp air swirled around us, but a heavy weight descended, ripping away any enjoyment they could bring. "Will he kill them?" I asked.

"Yes." Ezra didn't hesitate. He dragged me down the cobblestone street. I took two rushed steps for every one of his long, lanky strides. I could barely register the bright world as it raced by.

We entered a tavern through a back door, where Finn, Caz, and Gemma were waiting, their worried looks immediately settling into relief upon seeing us.

Caz stepped forward, no sign of the usual relaxed merriment on his tanned face. He turned to my cousin. "That was stupid, Ez."

I stepped forward in Ezra's defense. "It was my idea, and we were gone for less than twenty minutes."

"It doesn't even take half that time for something to go wrong," Caz answered, shaking his head. He looked disappointed, not mad, which somehow felt worse. "You can't run off."

Gemma avoided my gaze, but I looked at her. Arms crossed, shoulders tensed, eyes glued to the ground. I could tell she wasn't happy, either.

"Just because Simeon put wards on this city to protect it from Molochai doesn't mean there aren't other dangers," Finn added, his voice calmer than Caz's, but no less disappointed.

Shame tried to cripple me. I fought it, because even though they were right, it wasn't fair.

Hair rose on my neck when the door burst open behind me. It slammed against the wall, unsettling dust that danced inside the invading rays of sunlight.

A startled gasp escaped my throat. Three strides, and the intimidating form of my protector was before me, assessing me for damage. The man was unnaturally quick in spite of his size.

"Are you hurt?" he demanded, cupping my face, eyes wild. "Did they touch you?"

"I—I'm fine."

His chest heaved with violent breaths. He studied me for a few more moments, searching for proof that I was okay, fearing for signs that I wasn't. Finally he turned, dropping his hands.

But I screamed when he grabbed Ezra by the throat and threw him up against the wall. Gemma gasped, covering her mouth with both hands while Caz and Finn both cursed and jumped.

"You brainless little shit!" Gavin pinned my cousin against the wall like a ragdoll. Ezra was tall but looked scrawny in Gavin's lethal grasp. "You put her in danger—"

"And *you* threw a knife at the woman—" Ezra choked, gritting his teeth as he tried in vain to pry Gavin's steel grip off his neck. "Right next to Ary! You could have hit her! You could have missed!"

Gavin laughed, low and cruel. "I don't miss."

"You're a fucking madman!" Ezra gasped for air.

"And you're lucky I don't rip your throat out, Hart!" Gavin spit out Ezra's surname like a curse. The others futilely shouted attempts to stop him, but he persisted, his deep voice thundering, "I don't care if you decide to throw yourself onto a flaming pit of spikes, but you do *not*, under any circumstances, put her in harm's way!"

"Enough!" I pleaded, eyes wide with horror. With every word he spoke, his grip on Ezra's neck constricted, and I realized it would only take one twitch of his hand to make my cousin a permanent casualty of his rage. My sweet cousin, who'd only wanted me to see the sights. "Gavin, you're hurting him!"

I felt four pairs of shocked eyes on me and realized it might be the first time they heard Gavin's name. To them, he was only Smyth.

Trembling, I lunged forward and threw my arms around Gavin's thick biceps, standing on the tips of my toes to reach it. I would hang there, use my feeble body weight, if it made him let Ezra go.

"Let him go!" I ordered, pulling on his arm with the full weight of my body. "Now!"

"Brawling in my pub already, Smyth?"

We turned to see a man standing in the doorway to a wider, brighter space. The main room of the tavern. He looked to be about mid- to late twenties, with an impressive head of chocolate brown curls above circular glasses.

"It's not even suppertime." He stepped forward and waved a lazy hand. "You could at least come out front, make a good show of it." The man's eyes widened when he shifted his attention to me. Then to Gavin. Back to me. He sighed, seized by quiet awe.

I gulped, realizing that Gavin's friend knew exactly who I was just by looking at me.

"Let him go," I said to Gavin, softer this time, relieved to see

Ezra breathing again as Gavin slowly relaxed his grip. "Please. Let him go."

With a deep, rumbling growl, he released my cousin and stormed from the room without another word.

Ezra crumpled to the floor with his hands at his neck. I hated seeing those soft blue eyes and gentle smile contorted by bitterness and pain. I knelt beside him, stomach sick with worry.

"Well, then." The man folded his hands and gave a wide smile, wholly unbothered by Gavin's abrupt exit. "On that note, welcome to The Black Badger."

Caz ran his hands over his face and through his hair, more distressed than I'd ever seen him. Finn and Gemma introduced themselves to our curly-haired host. I couldn't hear his name or what they said. I was too focused on the angry red marks on Ezra's neck, the damage that Gavin had done to my cousin, all because of me.

"Ary, no!" Ezra reached for me as I turned to follow Gavin, my face hot with anger. "He's out of his mind! Just let him go!"

But I slipped away after him into a dark room filled with bottles of wine and every type of liquor. Lining the walls were oak barrels filled with beer or whiskey imported from different regions across Nyrida, indicated by the rough scribble labeling each one. The rich aromas of smoke, caramel, and fruit packed into such a tight space burned in my nostrils.

Gavin was a masterpiece of brooding, standing with his mountainous shoulders flexed against the fabric of his black shirt, the shelving above his head groaning under the weight of his fingers. His forehead rested on a barrel of whiskey that jutted out from the top shelf. Even in the dark, I could see that his eyes were closed, his breathing unsteady.

Massive, but vulnerable at this moment. The sight almost sucked the breath from my lungs. But Ezra had been vulnerable when held against the wall moments away from suffocating. We all were vulnerable. All at Smyth's mercy.

I shifted my feet loudly enough to announce my presence. Gavin's eyes opened slowly. And I was about to reprimand him when—

"Did he make you go with him?" His shadow rose up behind him as he turned. A menacing, overwhelming spirit of rage.

"What?" I huffed out. "No, of course not."

"Was it his idea?"

"It doesn't matter whose idea it was." I stepped forward. "I wanted to see the temple."

"Then you could have asked *me* to take you there!"

"We were across the street, Gavin!" My voice slipped on his name. "For gods' sake, we were just across the street."

He lifted his scarred palm from his side. It was trembling. *He* was trembling. "And I told you five steps, Aryella! *Five!*"

"Those people were just thieves, not Insidions. Ezra and I were handling them perfectly well before you got there."

"Were you? Because it looked to me like you were about to get a rusty blade through your neck, and I could've . . ." He reached for my face, then pulled back, helplessly dropping his hand to his side. "I could've lost you, Ella." The terror in his voice stabbed at my heart.

At first, I was touched, but then I remembered the earth-shattering sadness I saw in his eyes was the same I saw when he spoke of losing his wife. I wasn't her. I would never get to be her. He cared for me, and this had only stirred up his past fears, the trauma he'd experienced from her loss. I understood these fears all too well. We all had them.

"Gavin," I said softly, resting a small hand on his elbow. "Just because you lost her doesn't mean you're going to lose me. I know you care about me, but I'm *not* your wife. I am your *friend*." The words rolled numbly off my tongue. Empty, but true. He stiffened like I'd struck him with a bolt of lightning. "And you do *not* get to punish other people for *my* choices just because they scare you."

When he turned back, his eyes had cooled into something dark. A shield of apathy.

"I see," he uttered.

He brushed past me without a glance.

I preferred his anger to this terrible coldness.

A hush fell over the back room of the tavern when Gavin emerged from the storage with me close behind.

Standing among our friends, Gavin's friend leaned against a set of stairs and wore a sly, relaxed grin. His brown eyes twinkled. He didn't flinch in Gavin's presence. Based on those things alone, I decided I liked him—and his tavern—immediately.

"I'm Damond." He lowered himself into a dramatic bow, eliciting a light laugh from me. "A pleasure to finally meet you, Your Highness." He nodded to Gavin. "I'm his—"

"He owes me a favor."

Damond chuckled, brown eyes sparkling with mirth. "Sure, we'll go with that."

"It's nice to meet you, Damond." I forced a smile and offered him my hand. I felt bold—I couldn't remember offering my hand so readily to anyone. "And just Ary is fine. Please."

"Whatever you'd like, just *Ary*." Damond flashed me a crooked grin and took my hand in both of his. "Shall I take you to your lodgings?"

The stairs to the upper level of the tavern protested beneath our feet as we climbed. This place was old, if the shallow indentations on the steps from lifetimes of use were any indication. A hallway, dimly lit with oil lamps, veered off to the left, revealing three bedrooms and a bathroom, complete with a black clawfoot tub, toilet, and sink.

At the end of the hall to the right, Damond opened the door to a large room with only four single beds and a well-used fireplace.

"I can sleep on the floor," I said upon entering, breaching the silence. "You have all done enough for me."

Beside me, Gavin grumbled, "Don't even think about—"

"Nonsense!" Damond interjected. My eyebrows rose in surprise. He was the first person I'd come across, besides myself, who dared to interrupt Gavin Smyth. "Do you take me for an unprepared host? This room is for the men. You and your saucy friend can have the room across the hall."

"Thank the gods." Gemma scooped up her belongings and disappeared.

Finn and Damond discussed the route we'd taken and our plans to go to Brinnea to meet Simeon after our time here. I got the impression they hadn't known each other until today, but both Sinclair brothers were skilled at making friends fast.

While they talked, the knowledge of Gavin's stare plastered my feet to the floor. I shivered, dreading the apathy I'd see if I looked at him. Unable to resist, regardless, I looked, only to find that the unfeeling ice from minutes ago was already thawing into silent regret.

"I thought you weren't returning until tomorrow," Finn told Damond, tossing his bag onto a bed covered in a blue-checkered quilt. Caz took the one opposite. Ezra gave Gavin a wide berth as he followed the others.

"Had a feeling I might be…needed." Damond winked at me. He carried himself gracefully in black pants and a dark green button-down. "Turns out I was right. At least *one* of you needs a tonic for a miserable attitude."

Caz snorted. Gavin ignored the blow.

"I've heard Molochai's men have been busy just outside the city with their…displays," Damond continued, leaning against the doorframe. The memory from yesterday made my stomach ache. "Did you see anything?"

Finn nodded. "We thankfully managed to evade them on the journey here from Warrich by rerouting slightly north. But about a day's walk west of here, a village was ransacked, a man strung up and gutted. Vile business."

Finn went on to describe some of the beasts they'd seen on their journey between the caves and Warrich. Elias's forces were effective at keeping the area around the caves safe, but as Molochai drew farther north, it was becoming increasingly difficult to protect settlements without wards.

As promised, however, Gavin instructed Damond to send word for Elias to send help to the survivors in that village. Damond told me to consider it done.

"Thank you." I took our host's soft yet strong hands and squeezed. Being bold was a work in progress, but gratitude was easy. "For your efforts and your hospitality."

"It's an honor, my queen." Damond smiled down at me, bright and genuine. "There's another bathroom and shower downstairs, if needed." With a nod toward the hallway bathroom, he said, "It seems your friend has already taken that one." He took a step back and gave another dramatic bow.

I left the men's bedroom and crossed the hall to the one I'd share with Gemma. There was an oak four-poster bed large enough for the both of us, along with a matching wardrobe and vanity. The sheets were ivory and the blankets were red. Gemma had already taken the liberty of lighting the room's fireplace. Before the hearth, a brown bearskin rug reminded me of northern Warrich. Gemma's bag rested on a chair in the corner, already open.

I started to close the door, but a large boot crossed the threshold, stopping me.

"Aryella, wait. Please."

His deep, gruff voice stopped me in my tracks. I opened the door, and his sheer size crowded the entry. Gavin's handsome features were wrought with concern, the scar over his eye crinkled with his brow.

"I need to apologize." His thick throat bobbed as he forced a swallow and stepped into the room. "I was—*am*—a fool. A hot-tempered, overprotective fool. You are not a child. You are not a pet. You are not a frail girl to be subdued and coddled. You're a warrior. A queen. A woman with choices, desires, and thoughts—beautiful, intuitive thoughts. And you are remarkable. You are… *breathtaking.*" A crack rippled through my heart at his trembling voice. "But it has been a very long time since something—*someone*—has truly mattered to me, so you will please forgive me if I sometimes lack the control and discernment to treat you exactly as you deserve."

My lips parted in shock. His words, a panacea for my rage, began to restore me. Maybe a little too easily, but I couldn't help it. I didn't want to be angry.

"Thank you," I muttered.

"And it is an honor to be your . . . *friend.*" He bit out the word like it hurt him.

It hurt me, too. My heart despised the word and its simplicity, far too small to describe the familiarity and tenderness between us. But thousands of people needed me to be a queen. Innocent lives were at stake, and I couldn't let myself consider the alternative. An alternative with him.

I vowed to keep telling myself that.

"Damond will prepare dinner for us." Gavin shifted in the doorway—a subtle attempt to draw my attention back. "Take your time. Bathe, change, relax. I'll wait in the hall and go down with you."

I nodded, but something else nagged at me. Someone else. Ezra.

If I had to stay within five paces of him, I would. But that didn't excuse what happened to my cousin.

"Gavin."

He returned to me immediately, dark eyes hopeful. "Yes?"

"You should apologize to Ezra."

His nostrils flared. I waited, standing my ground until he gave a long, deep sigh.

"Would that . . . appease you?"

I nodded. "Yes."

A muscle in his jaw flexed. "Then for you, I will."

The door to the bedroom closed and locked behind him.

I exhaled, sat down on the bed, and removed my boots. Part of me wanted to crawl into bed, throw the covers over my face, and let the black night that I'd seen in the eyes of Nyxar soothe me. The other part of me wanted to rise from bed, go downstairs, and experience every moment of life I could before going to those caves. Before my marriage with a man I wasn't sure I wanted. Before a war. Before I likely had to say goodbye to—

I winced, forcing away the thought.

First, a bath.

Chapter Seventeen

I let the men use the downstairs bathroom and waited for Gemma to finish. When it was my turn upstairs, I took my time.

Cold rivers and lakes had been our only source of water for days. The bath was hot on my skin, drawing sweat and tension and death out of my pores. Renewing me. It was glorious.

When finished, I changed into a pair of tight black pants that Gemma had lent me days ago. They were a little long, but I was able to tuck the extra fabric into the ankle of my boots to hide it. I found a sage green bell-sleeved shirt with a tight cross-wrap tie around the midriff and a very generous neckline. It was velvet, with a floral design in a darker forest green. The blouse was another gift from Gemma. She'd surprised me with a few items from Freyburn, but I hadn't had the chance to wear most of them.

I let my hair—still damp but brushed, smooth, and free from the binds of a braid or messy bun—fall down my back and across my shoulders.

The vanity's mirror showed me someone I struggled to recognize.

My breasts were fuller than I had realized. They felt... more sensual. Too large to fit in *my* small hand, but not too large for—

I sucked in a breath, then blew it back out, sending the suggestive thought with it.

If I failed to control my wandering imagination, I wouldn't last very long out there at all.

Always hidden beneath loose-fitting sleeping gowns and baggy shirts, I'd never paid too much attention to the curves of my body. Had never cared. But this outfit hinted that the curves I used to have were slowly coming back.

With my hand on the doorknob, I paused. As if to give myself a chance to change my mind. But everything was *covered*. And Gemma, who did whatever she wanted, wouldn't think twice about wearing this. I could, too, on my birthday.

I took a long, deep breath and opened the door.

Gavin abruptly straightened from where he leaned against the wall, eyes wide with panic. He wore all black, his short sleeves showing off every bit of gloriously inked skin.

"No." The sound he made was throaty, choked off, and foreign. Like a plea.

He audibly gulped.

"What?" I demanded.

"No, Aryella." Deep and firm this time—panic and plea nowhere to be found.

"No, what?"

"You are not wearing that."

I crossed my arms over my chest, and his eyes flared and heated. Blood rushed to my cheeks when I realized my movements had pushed my breasts together. "Excuse me?"

"No," he uttered, the sound a low distressed rasp as he shifted his stance, wincing. "No fucking way."

My stomach plummeted. I must have looked worse than I thought.

"What say do you have in what I wear?" I hissed.

"I don't care. Go change."

"I won't."

"Yes, you will."

It was an effort not to melt beneath his glare. To return that heat in the form of defiance.

"What are you going to do, take it off of me yourself?"

Sweat beaded at the nape of my neck as he lifted one eyebrow and took his time surveying me thoroughly. I swallowed anxiously when I realized he might be considering it.

And that maybe I didn't look bad, but... good.

I stepped closer, and instantly, his huge body tensed. Interesting. It seemed my mighty protector might not be the one in control, after all. At least, not tonight.

I narrowed my eyes and tilted my gaze. "Did you not just apologize to me an hour ago for being an overprotective hothead?"

A deep and growly rumble in his throat was his only response.

"Did you not mean what you said?" I pressed, taking another step toward him. He stiffened, sucking in a sharp breath.

"I meant every single word."

"Then why—" I gasped when he carefully adjusted my long hair to cover up my exposed neck and cleavage, careful to avoid contact with my skin. "Hey!" I slapped his hand away and pointed a finger at him. "Stop that! I can wear what I want." I was learning to defy him, and was getting quite good at it, too. But that didn't mean his dominating presence left me unaffected. "And I admit, this is a little more . . . revealing than I'm used to." My cheeks burned. "And I know what you're thinking—"

"*Do* you?" His eyes flashed.

"I want to feel normal!" I bit out. "Like a normal person. A normal twenty-year-old woman that feels . . . pretty."

His eyes shot wide in palpable shock. "Believe me, you don't need to—"

"It's still my birthday," I rushed out despite his protest. "And this is my choice."

"*Yes.*" The emphasis on the word was too long—too sinister—to be sane. "That is true. Your choice." He seethed, like he regretted ever using the word with me now that I was hellbent on using it against him. "But you see . . ." He clicked the roof of his mouth with his tongue and took three steps, now a mere arm's length away. I held my ground. "I have choices, too, Ella. I'll take note of every single man who stares at you. And later, after you're safe in bed, I'll choose to hunt each of them down one by one and very slowly, very painfully, carve their eyes out of their sockets."

Horror stole my breath. "You would not." He brushed my temple with his lips, causing me to tremble.

"Would you like to test that theory? It'd be far more fun for me than you think." My knees were weak, but I forced my eyes to narrow—a show of defiance beneath his tight jaw and warning stare.

Because for once, I had some leverage over this man who constantly claimed he knew what was best for me. Maybe it was wrong to keep him on edge, or maybe it wasn't my problem he was wound so tight. Either way, I couldn't help wanting to let this feeling linger.

I think I wanted him to crack, even if that meant losing myself a little. Temporarily. Just for now.

I knew what was right. What was smart. I could rationalize when I was alone, convince myself I could be good and dutiful and responsible and obey, but one second beneath that intense stare and I abandoned all reason.

"I'll be downstairs," I finally said. He cursed under his breath. As I passed a mirror on the wall, I saw him run his hands over his face and through his hair before storming down the stairs after me.

Candlelight chandeliers cast a comforting glow around the tavern. The interior was lined with wooden tables both round and long. The seats were cushioned with a deep maroon similar to the blankets in the bedroom. The tables were full of people—some ate, some played with cards and coins, and almost all drank.

My heart raced from the aroma of food, the smell of liquor, and the heat of so many bodies. I was surrounded by shouts of joy, banging on tables, clanging of glass, rowdy hoots, riotous cursing, and cacophonous laughter. In the quieter, darker corners of the room, there was drunken kissing and caressing. I tried to ignore that and focused instead on Damond, who stood behind the bar.

He knew everyone, and everyone knew him. It was impressive, watching him work without a hint of reticence in his kind brown eyes or gleaming white smile. He poured drinks with movements so smooth, he could have been dancing and even managed to spare a glance or two to check on me. I laughed when he flipped a bottle behind his back, caught it, and threw me a wink.

As expected, Gavin remained close to my side. If I didn't feel so safe in his presence, free to look around and take in so many sounds and people, I would have found him insufferable. Only I didn't, and each time his arm accidentally brushed mine or he devoured me with his gaze, I felt *alive*.

Damond served us dinner—roasted turkey, buttery potatoes, and asparagus with salt, lemon, and garlic. Dessert was a decadent apple pie, and my eyes rolled back in my head with every bite.

Wholly satisfied with the best birthday dinner I could remember, I turned to Gavin. He was drinking a pungent amber liquid from a short glass. Whiskey, if the sweet, grainy odor was any indication, and stronger than the stuff that Phillip drank.

"Can I please try that?" I turned to face him, the heel of my hand beneath my chin.

I was met with his usual mask—furrowed brows and scowl. His intent to hide whatever dark and angry truth lived inside him didn't faze me. I narrowed my eyes in retaliation. A challenge. I still trusted him with reckless abandon.

"No," he uttered.

"So grumpy." I sighed then nodded to the fading wolf's bite on my forearm. "You offered me alcohol a week and a half ago."

"That was different."

I rolled my eyes and pointed at Ezra on his second beer a few seats down. "So Ezra's allowed to drink alcohol and I'm not?"

"Ezra is older."

"By two years," I said, folding my arms across my chest and redirecting his attention back to my scantily clad chest. Like earlier, *want* burned through his expression at my movement, his brown eyes growing wide with frenzy. With a clear effort, he tore them away. "That's nothing. I'm twenty."

"Barely." His deep voice rumbled with disdain.

I looked around. Indeed, I could see why he had asked me to

change my clothing. The men around us made no attempt to hide their interest and were liberal with their gazes. And it wasn't just me. Farther down the bar, where Gemma sat with Finn dressed in similar tight, thin black pants and a light blue blouse, she was fending off a few admirers of her own.

But I did seem to draw the most attention, to Gavin's chagrin. There were eyes on me constantly. Within five minutes of sitting at the bar, two men approached me, both scrambling away the moment they saw Gavin's murderous stare.

It wasn't just that Ezra was older. He was male. He wasn't *me*. He wasn't—to the other men in this bar—prey.

A third man with bright red hair and emerald eyes was the final straw.

He sidled up to the empty seat to my right and brushed against my arm in a way so overtly sensual, so *persisting*, it had to be intentional.

"Good evening."

I forced a smile but slanted my shoulders away from him, ever so slightly. Maybe he would catch the hint.

"What are you drinking, beautiful?"

Hint not caught.

He was older than me, probably mid-twenties. He wore a brown leather jacket and his red hair was cut cleanly with matching scruff, all impeccably groomed.

"Just water."

The man laughed, and I noticed his gaze flicker to my chest. I forced an uncomfortable swallow. I really hadn't thought it would be this bad. Were most other men like this? I just wanted to enjoy my evening.

"That's no fun," he crooned. "Can I get you something more… relaxing?"

My protector's angry fingers restlessly tapped on the wooden bar top to my left. I could feel it in my stomach.

"No, thank you," I hurried out. "I'm fine."

"Nonsense." My red-haired admirer waved Damond over. "A glass of your best wine, please, for the lady." And then he put his hand on my arm.

Oh, no.

"Do you enjoy having hands?"

I closed my eyes and shuddered at the deep, dark voice that could make demons flee.

The man nodded at Gavin and, with an arrogant smirk, asked me, "Who's this? Your keeper?"

"How about legs? You like having those?" Gavin's stool groaned under the sheer weight of him as he turned to face me, to stare at the man with a cold, murderous glare. "Eyes? Ears? A cock?"

I gasped quietly.

Perhaps I shouldn't have pushed him on the outfit, after all.

The man scoffed. "I wasn't talking to you, asshole."

A deep, sinister chuckle rumbled out of the warm wall of muscle to my left. I found myself leaning toward him, drawn into his safety.

"Gavin." I whispered his name as a warning.

"It's merely a question," he purred in response, folding his hands before him. "A question our friend here seems quite reluctant to answer."

"Fuck off," the man sneered.

"Now, now," Gavin drawled, his lips curling into a sinister

smile. It was feline, strangely at odds with his rugged form, but just as dangerous. "Is that any way to speak in front of a lady?"

At that, I rolled my eyes. As if he didn't have the filthiest mouth I'd ever heard.

The red-haired man scanned me with his bright green eyes, as if contemplating whether or not I was worth it. "Let me get you away from this buffoon." He offered me his hand.

On my other side, Gavin leaned forward, close enough that I could feel the glorious strength and heat of him. Inhaled a hint of leather and cedar.

"Touch my girl, and you'll never see that hand again."

My veins flooded with a different kind of heat.

The man lifted an eyebrow, his gaze drifting toward my low-cut top. "Looks to me like she's asking to be touched."

My stomach lurched, my cheeks burned, and Gavin was on his feet, pushing me behind him in one swift motion. I fully expected a brawl. Or at least a one-sided battering.

A hush descended upon the room. He stood unwavering, a silent, rigid shield before me. I glanced at my friends, apologizing with my eyes because this—causing this scene—felt like my fault. It wasn't, I knew, but if I had just listened to him and changed into something more modest, then maybe—

"I suggest you hold your tongue before I take my time cutting it out," Gavin growled at the man, who stepped back slowly and held up his palms, clearly angry but smart enough to suppress a retort.

Only when the man was on the opposite side of the tavern and commotion resumed did Gavin relinquish his position as my sentry and gently lower his hand to my back, anchoring me.

He shifted to block the rest of the room from seeing me. "Are you all right?"

"I'm fine," I said, shoulders relaxing. "You don't need to start fights over me, you know. Especially over some vulgar words. He would have left me alone eventually."

He reclaimed his stool at the bar, his protective hand remaining on my back. "Ella, if you think starting a fight is the worst thing I'd do for you, you have not been paying attention."

"*Your* girl?" I mumbled quietly so only Gavin could hear.

He finally removed his hand, leaving an unwelcome cold spot in its wake. Giving only a grunt in acknowledgment, he motioned for Damond to refill his drink. I looked between his scowling face and his empty glass and counted. This was his fourth. No, fifth.

"Are you okay?" I asked, motioning to his glass. "Do you have a problem?"

"What do *you* think, Ella?" His voice was low, eerie. Quiet, calm. "*Do* I have a problem?"

"You sure drink a lot. Like Phillip."

"Hmm." He tapped his fingers on his empty glass and winced. "No. Not quite like Phillip." He motioned again for Damond, who began to shake with silent laughter.

"Then why?" I pressed.

"It takes the edge off."

"What edge?"

A dark, humorless chuckle rumbled out of him as he studied me with a deliberate glare, which made me shiver delightfully. "The edge that makes me want things I can't have."

My skin burned so hot, I could practically feel red blotches forming on my neck, my chest, my cheeks. Good gods.

"Careful, Ary." My eyes snapped to see Damond standing behind the bar, watching us. "Smyth here, he's an old man." He poured another knuckle's length of whiskey in Gavin's glass, winked at me, and added, "You might give him a heart attack."

Doubtful, considering the ridiculous shape he was in.

I turned on my stool when the sounds of dueling fiddles paired with a tin whistle filled the air, eliciting shouts of joy, followed by clapping. People rushed to the center of the room and began to dance. I watched with a silly grin plastered on my face. Minutes passed before I realized I was mindlessly swaying and bouncing to the music. It was intoxicating, with a mind of its own.

I didn't mind him watching me. I felt beautiful when he did. I felt free, and I wanted him to see it. To see me.

Gavin shifted in his seat beside me and cleared his throat as he asked Damond for another. Damond complied, and then placed a glass of a light brown liquid in front of me, too. I smiled and fully faced the counter. Looking a little too eager, perhaps.

"No!" Gavin said harshly, lunging for the glass the same time I did. Damond beat us both.

"Oh, come off it, Smyth!" He jerked the glass out of Gavin's angry reach. "Don't be such a grumpy old codger and let the poor girl have some fun! No one's going to come anywhere near her after your little pissing match."

I could feel Gavin's eyes on me, seething and worried, as I lifted the glass to my lips and tasted warm, sweet cinnamon with a hint of camphor. I threw it back, forcing the whiskey down with a grin while delicious heat threaded through my body. Damond shrugged, eager for my reaction. Nodding, I pushed the glass toward Damond and motioned for a refill like Gavin had done multiple times tonight.

"Ah! Attagirl!" Damond guffawed, clapped, and pointed at the furious man beside me. "Learning from the best!"

Gavin cursed under his breath, gritted his teeth, and threw back another finger of whiskey before slamming the glass onto the wooden bar top with a force menacing enough to startle those around us.

But the music was loud, the jubilation mighty, and even the bitter attitude of my teacher couldn't dampen the mood.

I drank the second glass, but when Damond served up a third, I found my wrist fastened in Gavin's grip. It was gentle, but too firm to break out of. "Just—" He released me immediately, realizing he'd stopped me on instinct and probably shouldn't have. He reached for a small basket of bread rolls from down the bar. "Eat two of these first and give it a few minutes." I lifted an eyebrow, and in response, he gritted out, "*Please.*"

To my chagrin, he was right. Within ten minutes, I could feel my movements growing loose and uncontrolled. I felt warm, light, and carefree, but I had seen Phillip drunk enough to know I wanted to keep my wits about me. I turned to ask Damond for water instead and saw a glass already waiting for me.

Moments later, Gemma skipped up to me. I tensed, thinking of our exchange in the shop earlier, but she took my hands and leaned toward my ear.

"I'm sorry!" she said, loud enough for only me to hear. "For what I said. I shouldn't have called you naïve. Shouldn't have been so harsh, I just—you're dear to me, Ary." She squeezed my hands. "As a friend, not just the queen, and I want to look out for you."

I grinned, wide and true. "You don't need to apologize for being my friend."

Gemma threw her long arms around me in a loving embrace. When she released me, her eyes were sparkling. "Dance with me!" I could dance to something slower, less complicated maybe. But the fiddles were fast and picking up speed with every refrain, climbing a never-ending staircase of rhythm and joy.

"I don't know how to dance."

"You've been dancing for the past twenty minutes, there on your seat!" She laughed, pulling me down from my stool. "Just do that standing up!"

I glanced back, only to witness the subtle flex of his hand, as if he'd reached for me as I left him. His glazed eyes were empty as they stayed glued to the seat I had occupied.

The bounding rhythms and rousing melodies took hold of me. Gemma held my hands as we jumped, spun, and laughed. It was surreal.

Just over a week ago, I'd hidden beneath heavy shawls, ashamed of my weak body, and buried myself in a bed of blankets on the floor. Now I was dancing.

If all the hard parts of this world led to moments like this, maybe being queen—being a *friend*—wouldn't be so bad.

Chapter Eighteen

I was too exhausted to last long. Before midnight, I started to sway where I stood, which was all the justification Gavin needed to escort me upstairs. He said little, only grumbling "Good night" and "Stay in your room" before making sure the door was locked behind him.

Despite my exhaustion, I couldn't sleep. The boisterous sounds of laughter and the clinking of glasses from downstairs, and the knowledge that I was the only one of my companions in bed, kept me awake.

A coat rack stood in the corner of the room, and upon the far wall, the moonlight cast a warped shadow shaped like a monster with spindly arms and a twisted torso. I glanced at the knife on my side table and envisioned rising swiftly, silently, and attacking the figure before it could best me. No wonder it seemed Gavin hardly slept. After a day spent on alert, it was hard to calm my mind.

The longer I lay awake, the more aware of my body's discomfort I became. The noise dissipated from downstairs, but Gemma didn't return. Elowen had always called me hyperactive during my restless nights, when I complained of a dry mouth, legs that wouldn't settle, an aching back, and a mind that refused to quiet.

She'd always fetched me water. I rose from bed, deciding a fresh glass might do me some good.

A draft blew from the north-facing window, and I saw that someone had left me a pair of wool socks at the foot of the bed. Though the room was comfortable and clean, the building was old, and Damond could only do so much to block out the elements. I rose, put on the socks, and pulled the curtains open slightly, allowing a sliver of moonlight to glimmer into the room. Enough to light my path to the door.

At the end of the hall, I heard voices from an adjacent room. Damond's voice. I pressed my ear to the door and caught the end of his sentence.

"—gotten yourself into quite the pickle, cousin." Damond's voice. Of all the connections Damond could have had to Gavin, cousin was not one I expected. "It's her?"

"Yes," Gavin replied. "Yes. It's her."

I frowned. They were speaking of the prophecy.

"An adorable, pint-sized spitfire of a queen."

"Watch it!" snarled Gavin, his deadly tone startling me. "I don't care if you're blood, Damond. Sniff around, and I'll play cat's cradle with your intestines."

Damond laughed, unfazed. "And you haven't bedded her?"

My stomach dropped and my ears felt hot. Gavin gave a heavy sigh that made me guess he was clenching his jaw so tight, he could split a molar. His usual.

"I'll take that to mean you wish you had." Damond chuckled. "You couldn't hide it if you tried, old man."

"She's barely twenty, Damond. Fucking—" Furniture shifted abruptly, likely kicked or shoved. "Twenty."

"And you were twenty-two."

I frowned when a long pause followed, without elaboration.

Finally Damond spoke. "What happened to your shoulder?"

"Oh." Gavin chuckled, his tone softening. "She got me."

"Is that what foreplay looks like for you these days?"

"Fuck you."

Damond laughed, then whistled through his teeth. "That's some inhuman willpower, my friend. Being alone with her, knowing who she is, and doing nothing about it. Must be hell."

"I'm trying not to think about it." I heard the clinking of glasses and guessed Gavin was pouring himself another one.

"How's that working for you?"

There was a pause and a grim, "It's not."

Damond burst into laughter, and my cheeks heated.

"Simeon is adamant she has no army without the Winterton boy," continued Gavin, his deep voice strained. "And I . . . I won't jeopardize it, not if they can help her."

"When have you *ever* given a shit what that old bastard has to say?"

"I know her." The words snapped out of him. "And though I wish she could turn a blind eye and say, 'Fuck it all,' she's not me. She could never find peace or freedom after leaving thousands of innocent people to die." I heard the forceful thump of his glass on the table and the footsteps that followed.

"If peace is what *you've* found, Smyth, then I sure as hell don't want it." There was a long pause before Damond continued, "So you're going to surrender her to Elias Winterton?"

"She's not a fucking pawn to be surrendered."

"Smyth." Damond sighed. "Man, you've got to—"

"Enough!" Gavin snapped, low and lethal. "I've made my intentions clear: to protect her and teach her. She's safe with me, and she knows it. For now, that will have to be enough."

I felt nauseous at the implication that there might be more.

"Smyth." Damond's voice leveled out. "What about—how do you know she's safe from Molochai?"

"He doesn't know she exists yet."

"How can you be so sure?"

"Because if he knew, he would have come for her already."

"What are you going to do when he does?" Damond asked, sounding grim. "What are you going to do if he tries to use—"

"Over my dead fucking body."

I turned away from the door, having heard enough.

Secrets. I kept none from him, but he kept plenty from me. Or at least half-truths that left me wondering if his touch, his care, and his protection were only a means to an end. He clearly felt *something* for me. Wanted me, even if just for sex.

Yet he had reason enough not to act on it. Gavin Smyth was beholden to no one, certainly not the Wintertons or Simeon. He could take what he wanted, and he said he did exactly that.

I sighed, frustrated, as I descended the stairs. It was dark, but I could see that the back room was empty, the storeroom door closed. I would need to go through the bar to the kitchen for a glass of water, which I resented because I was still in my nightgown.

As I turned toward the main room, a familiar voice, loud and full of life, squealed from behind me.

"Ary! What are you doing?" Gemma threw her long arms

around my neck and squeezed. Her breath was both sweet and sour from hours of drinking. I winced but put up with it, unable to suppress a laugh. At least she was sober enough to stand and speak clearly. "Aren't you supposed to be in bed?"

"I'm just getting some water." I leaned back and held her elbows, testing her steadiness, just in case.

"Hmm, well, don't go through the bar, it's closing up. Go through that door there." She pointed to the door on our left. "Quench your thirst and get to bed before you're seen. The last thing we need is you stealing the heart of some drunken lunatic before Elias can give you a proper ring."

My gut wrenched at the reminder.

"What about you?" I forced a laugh. "Are you coming to bed?"

She clicked her tongue and bit her lip, smiling. "Eventually. I was using the bathroom and then . . . on my way to spend some time with Finn."

"Ah." I smiled. She deserved it. "Good. Be happy."

Her bright grin widened. She kissed my cheek. "Good night, dear."

She left, and I made my way to the kitchen. Once I entered, I looked around. It was still dark, but I could see enough to search for glasses.

I drew some water from the sink and let the drink soothe my dry, scratchy throat.

A window with a pane recently cleaned allowed me to see out into the dark night. There was enough clearing that the stars twinkled bright. Beacons of hope in an all-encompassing void of unknown. Warrich was usually overcast. I saw more stars while traveling through Wymara than I'd ever seen in the sky above the cabin in Warrich.

Lost in thought, I barely heard the footsteps behind me.

"I was hoping I'd get you alone."

I spun around to see the man from earlier—with red hair and scruff—standing in the doorway.

"I waited, actually, all night." He sidled toward me. "I know my way around this place well enough to figure out where you'd be sleeping." He waved his hand around the kitchen we stood in. "But now you've made it easy for me."

With a shaky hand, I reached for the blade on my hip and found the fabric of my nightgown.

My knife. I didn't have my knife. "What do you want?" I tried to fill my voice with false courage but it sounded weak even to me.

He took two steps forward. "Isn't that obvious?"

"I'm not interested."

His huffed-out laugh, cold and grating, made my skin crawl. "Don't pretend to be innocent. I bet that barbaric beast has fucked you so many ways that you aren't even tight anymore." He gestured around the room. "Only he isn't here, is he?"

My eyes burned. Should I tell him that I'd never even been kissed? Would that disgust him, dull his interest, or make this even worse?

Frantic, I looked for an escape, but there was only the door I came through. He blocked the other and left little space for me to make a successful escape.

"Well." The man sighed, taking another step, even closer to me now. "I won't turn down sloppy seconds, not when they look like you."

I repressed my whimper, forcing my lips into a sneer.

"Yes, that pink mouth." His hot, sweaty hand reached for my

throat. My back hit the counter. And I felt his erection pressing into my stomach. He pushed it against me, invading me through multiple layers of clothing, his and mine. "Shall we see if it matches your cunt?"

"I—I'll scream." I failed to hide the fear this time.

"Good," he crooned, leaning so far over me, I feared my back would crack over the counter. "I like the screams of little sluts."

If I screamed, Gavin would hear me. I knew he would. But I wasn't sure I wanted to give this man that satisfaction.

Then again . . . I could fight.

Or I could do both.

With an angry, wild screech I kneed him square in the groin and lunged around him. He wasn't expecting me to strike. But even with training and surprise, I wasn't fast enough.

"You stupid whore!" he wheezed, grabbing me by the hair. Sharp pain lit up my skull as he yanked me back. My head slammed against the hard floor, vision blurring. I rolled to my stomach, unable to stand, and crawled away instead.

I felt a hand clasp the cloth of my nightgown, lift it up, and pull, while his clammy fingers gripped the hem of my undergarments and tore them clean off. Suddenly, I was bare between my legs.

"No," I cried, rolling back over, grasping blindly at my nightgown to cover myself up. As if that would do a damn thing. "Please!"

His sweaty hand swiped across my face, disorienting me with a sting, followed by the clink of a belt unbuckling, a sound I knew I would never forget if I made it out of this kitchen alive.

"I'll make you pay for that, bitch!" He shoved his hips between my legs.

But he was no longer touching me. He slammed into the

cabinets to my left, blasted with a force so swift and powerful, the wood splintered beneath his body.

Mouth agape, I froze at the sight of my protector standing over us, the image of terror. Wild and fuming, like I'd never seen him before. That look in his eyes—ice cold, all-encompassing and lethal—was beyond fury. I scurried out of the way, half naked, into the opposite corner of the kitchen.

I watched as Gavin grasped the man on both sides of his head, like he'd done with me during so many gentle moments. But now he tightened his fingers around the man's skull with punishing force—withdrawing a petrified whimper from the lips of his victim. He leaned down and stared directly into wide, pleading eyes.

"What did I tell you," he hissed, low and lethal, "about touching my girl?"

And in a single movement, quick and effortless, Gavin snapped the man's neck.

I gasped a choked-out rasp. The air escaped my lungs in reluctant empathy as life drained from my attacker.

Gavin let the man's body crumple to the ground. And then he sighed, merely annoyed.

He turned toward me. Panicked, I crawled backward until my back hit the cabinet beneath the sink.

"Twice in one day, Ella, you manage to scare the ever-living shit out of me." He squatted before me and reached for my arm, but I dodged him. He frowned. "Are you hurt?"

"I—I was getting some water," I panicked. "I was thirsty."

Again, he reached for my hand, but—

"No, no, no!" My voice broke, making way for the flood of

tears. I pulled my nightgown over my knees and my knees into my chest. "I don't—I don't want you to see me like this."

Or perhaps...I didn't want to see *him* like this. What I'd just witnessed...

"It makes no difference how I see you." He outstretched his hand. "He's gone. You're safe."

"He's not gone, he's *dead*."

"Aryella." He shifted to block the lifeless body with an unnaturally twisted neck. His voice was too calm after breaking a man's neck with his bare hands. "Come here. Please."

"Get away!" I wept, but I didn't try to retreat any farther. Part of me wished to, but the warmth of his body drew me closer and reminded me of safety, which I desperately craved. "You killed him and now you're angry with me."

Sadness passed through him. "Ella, why the hell would I be angry with you?"

"Because you told me to stay in my room, and I didn't listen." My breaths grew faster, panicked. "And now you killed him, and it's my fault!"

"I'm not angry with you," he replied calmly. "It is *not* your fault. And I can't...when someone wants to hurt you, I can't *not*—Ella, *sweetheart*, take a breath."

When I heard his command, I realized I *was* hardly breathing. I gasped for air. I closed my eyes and reached for his shoulder to steady me. He shifted forward, stroking my cheek as if to give my breathing a rhythm to follow.

It was impossible not to focus on the places I had been gripped, handled, thrown. I hoped they would heal fast, rather than lingering as a constant reminder of what had happened. Minutes passed before I opened my eyes and saw straight again.

"You killed him," I exhaled shakily.

"He was hurting you." His finger gently tucked a strand of hair behind my ear. "He was about to rape you."

"But you *killed* him. And you killed them today in the temple."

"Without hesitation." He carefully held my chin between his fingers and surveyed my head, face, and neck for injuries. "And I will do it again."

I shook my head. He told me he would kill for me. That he already had. It shouldn't have shocked me. But it was the ease with which he'd done it. The calm, unflappable tone in his voice mere minutes after taking another life that frightened me.

"You act like it was easy, killing them."

His dark eyebrows rose as he nodded. "It was."

"It—it shouldn't be."

He sighed. "Ella, there are people in this world who want what you have, who want to hurt you. I will gladly get rid of them. Every single one of them, until they're all gone."

"You can't just go around killing people, even the ones that hurt me—"

"I can, and I will. The world is better off without people like him."

"That's not your decision to make."

"I don't give a shit." His lethal resoluteness made me shudder.

"You should," I breathed.

He held my face with both hands, his burning brown gaze fierce and true as he said, "But I don't."

I leaned into his touch, wanting only his safety, knowing this was a battle for another day.

"I'm sorry for making you kill a man." I took his hands and lowered them from my face.

"You didn't make me do anything." He enveloped my hands in his like he didn't want to let go. "I have no problem killing a man for simply looking at you the wrong way. I would enjoy it, even."

I gulped.

He noticed. "I'm not a good man."

I opened my mouth to object, but before I could—

"And I'll never claim to be one. I will never be worthy of you. No one will." He lifted my chin with his careful touch. He could say he wasn't a good man—and after what I'd just seen, maybe he wasn't—but to contain such wrath yet take such care spoke to his honorable intentions.

With me, at least.

"I've seen things, horrors you cannot imagine, terror I will not be able to protect you from. I would give my life if it meant I could shield you from the darkness in this world, but I can't. I can only teach you everything I know; I can show you how to fight and live. And Ella," he breathed, stumbling over the emotion in his voice when he spoke my name, "I *need* you to *live*."

I nodded, soaking up his closeness. "I want to train more. Tomorrow. I don't want to be a victim to men like him. Because…" I croaked, afraid to admit the truth of that final moment. My fight had fled when I knew what was about to happen. "I'm not strong enough. Right now, I'm not. I think I would have given up, and I thought he was going to—if you hadn't shown up, Gavin—"

"But he did not. I am here, and you are safe." He stroked the tears from my cheek. "Please don't cry, Ella." He winced, his warm breath caressing my forehead. "You *are* strong, and…"

"And?"

He sighed heavily. "And it fucking guts me when you cry."

I wiped the tears from my cheeks with the backs of my hands and reached for his face. For the scar on his right eye and cheek, the rugged beard I longed to touch.

"Well," I breathed, touching him like he touched me. With gentleness and care. "I certainly don't want that."

His eyes shuttered at my touch, his breath became low and ragged. And with a shallow rasp, he removed my fingers from his cheek, squeezed, and pulled me to my feet.

"Let's get you to bed."

"Um." I pulled the edges of my nightgown tightly around my knees and pointed to the floor, where my panties, now filthy and ripped in half, lay crumpled by the stove.

I looked up to see Gavin's face, hard and otherwise unreadable.

"He managed to rip them off but didn't get any further." I leaned my shoulder into his chest, suddenly self-conscious of the fact that I was completely bare under my nightgown and concerned someone else might walk into the kitchen and catch a glimpse. "Thanks to you."

"Leave them, they're done for." His voice was strained.

"Yes, but I . . . I'm out." I'd packed a few days' worth of clothing, but we hadn't washed since that day beneath the rocky overhang in western Wymara. "We need clean laundry."

He released a long, heavy sigh. "I'll find you something."

I gasped when he bent down, tucked one arm beneath my knees and the other around my back, and lifted me up. In one swift movement, he managed to position me in his arms so that I was completely covered by my nightgown and he wasn't risking his hand coming remotely close to the part of me that was bare. It was these small but intentional gestures that made me crave his closeness. He was aggressive when he needed to be, which was most of the time. But when I needed care, he showered me with gentleness and respect. It felt like he saved that part of himself for me.

"Wait, what about the body?" I pointed behind him. He shifted so I couldn't see.

"Don't look. I'll have Damond take care of it."

"Is he used to *taking care* of bodies like this?"

Gavin didn't respond. He stepped through the kitchen, down the hallway, and carried me up the stairs like my extra weight was nothing.

The way I felt in his arms was everything. I could live there, engulfed by his strength and resting in his delicious comfort.

And then the indent of two silver rings beneath his shirt and my fingers reminded me that I couldn't.

I was quiet as he set me down carefully next to the bed.

"Stay here." He paused at the door to look back at me, his expression strict. "Did you hear me, Ella?" I'd caused him enough grief for one day, and I could tell he needed reassurance, so I nodded.

The bed was empty and the room silent while I waited. Dying embers crackled in the fireplace, and a chill—more frigid than before I went downstairs—descended upon me. This chill was the old familiar cold of loneliness. I shoved it out and reminded myself I wasn't alone anymore.

Returning after twenty or so minutes, he avoided my stare as he placed a pair of pure white satin panties with lace around the edges in my hands. I could tell just by looking at them that they would fit.

"Where did you get these?" I suppressed a snort.

"It doesn't matter."

"Do you carry these around with you? Have you had them with you this whole time?"

He cursed. "Of course not, Aryella. I have—I have my own space here, in Tovick." He ran his hands through his hair. And yes—*red*—that was red in his cheeks. I bit my lip, enjoying seeing the rare sight of a flustered Gavin Smyth. "I spend a fair bit of time here."

"And you collect underwear from each of your conquests?" I giggled.

He gave me an irritated scowl. "That's not funny."

"It's a little funny," I mumbled. I didn't know exactly how long his wife had been gone, but I expected he had experienced his fair share of women since then. I assumed any man would. Besides, his patience was alarmingly thin when discussing anything remotely intimate around me, but I was developing a mischievous streak.

"Would you just put them on and go to sleep?"

I jumped, startled by the panic I heard rising in his throat.

"Okay, okay," I mumbled, eyes wide.

He watched me tensely as I held the panties to my nose to check for odor. Because, well, they were mystery panties. They looked a little old but smelled fresh and clean, like lavender.

"They've never been worn."

"Why do you have never-worn panties—"

"*Ella*," he warned, pinching the bridge of his nose. "Fuck. *Please.*"

"All right, all right." I motioned for him to turn around to give me some privacy. "You have a filthy mouth, you know that?"

"You have no idea," he growled. My eyes widened in shock, and as usual, his words, actions, and presence all sent warmth from my cheeks to my belly.

I slipped on the panties, soft and comfortable against my skin, and muttered, "I'm decent."

He slowly faced me again, eyes glued to me as I climbed into bed. "Goodni—"

"Will you stay with me?" I rushed out, desperate to avoid the chill of that empty room. "Just until Gemma gets back from wherever she went. I don't really want to be alone."

He gave a hesitant pause before lowering himself into the chair in the corner.

"You don't have to sit so far away."

I was relieved when he stood, picked up the chair, placed it directly next to my bedside, and sat back down.

Silence settled around us. Not an awkward silence, but gentle and soothing, as we rested together in that dark room. I sat upright, unwilling to lie down just yet. Or to surrender a moment with him.

I fidgeted with my thumbs. "What if I can't do it?"

"Do what?"

"Kill." I shuddered. For the first time since Phillip's and Oliver's deaths, death truly scared me. Dancing with Gemma, laughing with my friends, and this—sitting, talking, and just existing with Gavin. I wanted all of it. I wanted to fight for all of it, but to take another life, to choose that I was somehow more valuable than another... "What if it's life or death and if I don't *kill*, I die?"

"You don't hesitate." He leaned forward in his chair. "Don't give yourself the chance to think about it."

"Gavin, I don't think I can—"

"No, do not hesitate, Ella." He grabbed my hand and held it.

"Do you hear me? You take whatever weapon you have and you stab, beat, or slice the life out of them. You do not hesitate. You live, because you are invaluable."

The weight of his words was heavy enough to level the expectations of all the people relying on me. And I needed that—something encouraging to hold on to so I could weather those expectations. Because without that encouragement, I felt empty, and I feared that emptiness in my chest was a starving monster destined to devour all good things before given the chance to plant their seeds and take root.

"Don't, for a second, think that I can't see what all this is doing to you." His deep, persistent tone summoned me back into his comforting atmosphere, and I came willingly. "Look at me, Ella," he commanded softly, lifting my chin with his forefinger, stealing my gaze. "I see the burden on your heart clear as day. These people you're meant to lead—they think they can define you. Don't let them. Don't let your value come from a crown on your head or the power in your veins, and especially not from having a fucking Winterton at your side."

I choked on a tearful laugh and leaned into his touch, my heart longing for him to continue. To fill with his assurances the part of me that felt empty.

"You are invaluable not because of your birth or your power or your blood," he continued. "You are invaluable because you're *you*. And you, *just you*, are more than enough to fight for."

I forced a swallow and nodded, unsure I believed his words were true. For him, maybe they were, but not for me. I knew I could remember his face, remember him and his words and his warmth, and for him I could *fight*.

He leaned back and motioned me toward him. "Come here."

I obeyed, and he pulled me into his lap. This time, I avoided the indentation of those rings beneath his shirt. There was no crime in holding me or wanting to be held. That was all this was—all I could allow it to be.

I pretended I didn't hear his pulse race at our closeness or feel his shudder beneath my touch. How my own heartbeat hurtled into dangerous territory. I pretended not to grow light-headed at the knowledge that he wanted to hold me. I let him, and that was enough.

"Gavin?" I whispered, fingers light on his beard.

"Yes?"

"You really do have a filthy mouth."

He shook with quiet laughter. "Yes."

I traced my finger along a scar on his neck. "But you make me feel like I can do it, you know. Be queen."

When he looked down at me, his scarred face was illuminated by moonlight. The warmth in his brown eyes made my eyes burn. Gavin rested his hand over mine and squeezed.

"And I will serve you, my queen, until the day I die."

Filled with pure warmth and safety, I started to drift off soon after, waking only when he lowered me gently back into bed. I crawled beneath the covers, wonderfully and acutely aware of his presence.

My grin was so wide and content that it made my cheeks hurt. Because when he was near, I wasn't afraid of closing my eyes. With him so close, my nightmares didn't scare me.

Not when I knew he would save me from them.

Chapter Nineteen

I woke as the early morning sun splattered its sharp light through the tree canopy and into the room from the window. Despite the stressful night, I slept well. Thanks to his presence and to the warm spot on my stomach, where something rested heavier than the blankets that swaddled me. I uncovered my hands to feel warm, calloused fingers attached to Gavin's scarred left hand.

He had kept his hand on me—protecting me, holding me—all night long.

My heart danced.

Gavin's focus was on a vial of dark liquid no larger than my index finger. He twirled it between the fingers of his right hand, lost in distant thought, staring at nothing.

I made a point to shift and yawn, fully opening my eyes. "Were you there all night?"

He snapped out of his trance, tucked the vial back into the pocket of his black linen shirt, sat up straight, and nodded. "Mostly. I didn't want you to wake up in an empty room."

To my left, Gemma's side of the bed was bare.

"Is she okay?"

He failed to suppress a grin. "I'm sure she's just swell."

"Where is she?"

"With Finn." He folded his hands in his lap. "Has been all night."

"Oh, right." Blood rushed to my cheeks as I sat up in bed. "Good for Gemma."

And then I began to ramble.

"Did you know Finn has wanted to be with her for years?" I sputtered out. "But refused to touch her until she turned eighteen, even though there's only three years between them."

I got up from the bed. The wooden floor groaned beneath him as he rose from his chair.

"Then she was summoned to Elias's barracks to participate in Commencement." I unbraided my hair. A muscle flexed in his jaw as he watched my hair fall over my shoulders. They were partially bare as my nightgown had drifted off-kilter while I slept. But he kept his distance. "Then, she was sent to me. Before now, Gemma felt they would never be able to express their true feelings and be together, that the timing wasn't right. But I'm glad for them now." With my brush, I made long, languid strokes. "They deserve to be happy. Finn is a good man."

"Finn is a better man than—" He cleared his throat. "Better than most."

Empathy flooded through me at what I knew he'd been about to say. That he had stopped himself from admitting the type of man he thought he was. I wanted to say something profound to comfort him, as he would me, but I didn't know what that was, and I wasn't sure he wanted to hear it.

Instead, I distracted myself with a look outside the window. Green and crimson Solstice decorations brightened the heart of the small city. Tovick townsfolk bustled about the cobblestone streets while dodging horses, rickety carts, and carriages, some simple, some grand. The temple was still beautiful but carried an impending sense of gloom for me after yesterday's events. It rose proudly above the homes and shops, some of which had shutters partially ajar to disperse the stuffiness inside with the crisp winter air.

"Will we do more training today?" My bag rested on the floor by the hearth, and when I went to it, I saw that all of my clothing was washed and folded.

"I'm thinking we should enlist some help from your friends," Gavin suggested before I could comment on the clean laundry. He leaned against the doorframe and crossed his arms. "I want to know what Winterton is teaching his soldiers before you go there." A troubled shadow snaked through his typically stoic expression. "Give yourself a leg up so you can defend yourself if need be."

I frowned. "Why would I need to defend myself against my own people?"

His nostrils flared, but he kept his cool repose. "After last night, I'll rest easier knowing you can."

It was an effort not to read into that. To hear how little he trusted the people in those caves. Because so far, he'd been right about all the threats to me.

"Gavin?"

With his hand on the doorknob, he turned back to me.

"I don't want the others to know what happened last night. Especially Ezra and Gemma. I don't want them to worry about me."

Because they would, and they would coddle me for it. He must have read this on my face, because he didn't object.

"Your secrets are always safe with me." A coy grin sent my heart aflutter. "I don't enjoy talking to them anyway."

I snorted and watched him go, quickly exchanging my nightgown with a pair of black pants and a matching black sweater. Oversized, but with the shoulder dropped off to one side, the style was cozy, cute, and comfy enough for sparring. Another outfit Gemma had snuck into my bag, no doubt.

My silver hair contrasted with the black fabric, and the freckles up and over the bridge of my nose were more prominent than usual against my green eyes. I twisted my hair into a long braid and was satisfied and hungry enough to follow the sweet aromas of breakfast downstairs.

Gemma, Finn, and Ezra were nowhere to be found while the rest of us ate eggs cooked with cheese, bacon, and sweet cinnamon cakes. Their absence angered Gavin—thwarted his plans to have me try and land blows on all our companions—but I told him to leave them alone. If I had a night like I assumed Gemma and Finn had, I'd want to sleep in, too. And Ezra was undoubtedly determined to avoid Gavin. I couldn't blame him.

Reluctantly, Gavin conceded, "Fine. You can practice with Caz."

In response, Caz caught my eye with a wink and a truly feline smile. I rolled my eyes and laughed.

And when I started to wonder if I would ever have a night like Gemma and Finn had, I shoved the thought away.

Damond came out from the kitchen halfway through breakfast to join us, mercifully refraining from any mention of the body he must have dealt with during the early hours of the morning. I listened while he and Caz discussed the rising threat of Molochai's Insidions as they pushed farther north. Villages that had once been safe havens were being decimated, and Elias's forces, despite their training, were struggling to keep up.

Something was drawing Molochai farther north than he'd bothered going before. The obvious answer was me, but they assured me that Molochai still remained unaware of my existence.

"But if they're that close, shouldn't we be going to the caves?" I felt the color leave my face. "I don't know if I'm ready or if I want…" I paused, sucking in a breath. My wants didn't matter when people were in danger. "But if they *need* me—need *us*—then why do we delay? Shouldn't we insist Simeon just meet us there instead of Brinnea?"

Caz spoke first.

"Simeon gave Smyth the order to bring you to Brinnea. He wants to meet his own daughter—speak with you, discover your powers—before you go to the army. Brinnea is safe." Caz shifted again, this time facing Gavin. "But—"

"But nothing." His chilling stare was locked on the empty plate before him. Beside that plate, his huge, scarred fingers drummed restlessly on the thick oak table. "We have time. We will go to Brinnea."

Part of me was worried, most of me was relieved, and I didn't object, even when Damond winced at his cousin's stern insistence.

Aware of my uselessness without training and practice, I was the first to rise from the table, venture outside, and begin to run—Caz and Gavin quickly following—into the towering canopy of leafless trees on the north side of the tavern, away from the city. The walking and running from traveling, coupled with the much-appreciated birthday rest I received yesterday, left me far less winded than I expected. Still, when we completed our warm-up, I frowned when I saw both Caz and Gavin breathing easily, as if they had never even moved.

More. I needed to run more, train more. I'd improved, but it wasn't enough.

Caz and I sparred for at least an hour while Gavin assessed us against a maple tree, muscular arms crossed over his broad chest.

"Dead." Caz held his hand at my throat in place of the blade he would use to take my life, if he held one.

I groaned. The amount of times he had "killed" me were well into double digits. Caz was tall, agile, strong, and well practiced. No threat compared to Gavin, but that was a comparison unfair to anyone.

I lunged and Caz dodged again. We repeated the dance for another half-hour, halted only by the commanding call of my name.

"What?" I snapped.

Gavin curled a finger and motioned for me to approach him. Leaves crunched beneath my boots as I stalked over, hands on my hips.

He smirked down at me. "You're holding back."

I shrugged. "I can't beat him."

Gavin furrowed his brow at me. "Wrong attitude, Ella. You're practicing just as I taught you, but you're a second behind him."

"Because I'm not fast enough or strong enough."

Another frown, but no denial. I was right, and he knew it.

He studied my face in silence. By now, he'd done it enough

times that I was less fazed by his appraising stare and more bored while I waited for whatever conclusion he formed in that mysterious mind. Maybe one day he'd tell me all he was thinking, but—

"Punch him in the throat."

"What?" I dropped my folded arms to my side. "No."

"Yes," he firmly replied. "Catch him off guard. See if he can block it."

It was a savage move, certainly not one to use on a friend while sparring. We only made the motions of attack and defense without landing actual blows.

"That's not fair."

"I'm not teaching you to fight fair. I'm teaching you to survive."

I shook my head. "I don't want to hurt him."

"You won't." He raised a brow. "Not if your *betrothed* is effective in training his soldiers."

With a roll of my eyes, I returned to Caz. His hazel gaze sparkled with humor as he shook a strand of black hair out of his eye. "Did he impart any grumpy wisdom upon you?"

In my best effort to be vague, I said, "He wants me to be… rougher."

Caz laughed, motioning for me to come at him. "Then by all means, do your worst, Your Majesty."

At least I had his permission.

I lunged again, and Caz dodged until I lowered my arms, pretending to give up. And then Caz, dear friend, let out a playful snort and shook his head. His attention left me for a second.

It was all I needed.

My arm unfurled like a snake and my thin knuckles met with the center of his neck, sharp and effective.

"What the—shit!" Caz wheezed. I covered my mouth with my hands, shocked and immediately regretful. Deep, booming laughter erupted from our left, where Gavin tossed his head back in amusement. "Did that asshole... tell you to do that?" Caz croaked, pointing at Gavin.

"Yes," Gavin answered for me, still laughing deeply. "But she—" He shook his head, grinning with pride. "So well executed."

"That's a shit move. I wasn't even looking." Caz rubbed his neck, where a red mark was forming. And then he smirked, coughing away his surprise. "Though I suppose being punched in the throat by my queen is an honor."

I bit my bottom lip. A failed attempt to suppress a relieved and confident grin.

"That's enough for today, Caz. Thank you." Gavin strode over to us and nodded toward the tavern. "Better put some ice on that."

Caz snorted and shrugged, agreeing. Both Sinclairs had the same unruffled demeanor. I thought for a moment how crucial it was for Gemma to be with someone like Finn. Someone had to temper her fire. But this morning, I was especially grateful for Caz. His awareness and self-confidence that kept him unbothered by Gavin's behavior. He whistled cheerily as he walked back to the tavern, still rubbing his neck. The man had to be quite comfortable with himself to be ordered around by someone so intimidating, who he hardly knew. Or maybe Caz was just smart.

"You did well."

I turned to see Gavin standing before me, arms crossed, eyes aflame with pride. He followed my every move, even as I emptied my canteen down my throat without tasting the water. I'd hardly had a drink since breakfast.

Something dark flashed across his face. "You're learning."

But I had been successful only after he gave me instructions. I wouldn't be very useful if I couldn't strike on my own.

"Maybe I'll be fine if I have someone to give me orders, but send me alone and—"

"Will you fight back if it happens again?"

I froze. His question was a nagging echo. If it happened again, would I fight? We had discussed this last night. In the moment, I had told myself I would, and yet there was still a part of me that wasn't sure.

"I . . ." I forced a thick swallow. "Yes."

He eyed me warily. "You hesitated."

My chest rose and fell with agitated breaths. "I don't know why. I just don't know how to find the drive to *hurt*. I don't want to *hurt* anyone—"

"I know, but you have to. For your own sake, you *must*." He dropped his gaze to the ground as he mulled over his thoughts. At least a minute passed before resolve steeled his expression and he met my gaze. "I need you to show me. I need you to show me you'll fight."

"How am I supposed to show you?"

His jaw tensed. "Pretend."

My hands began to tremble. "Pretend?"

"You trust me." He took a step toward me. "You know I would never hurt you. Yes?"

I gulped and nodded. "Yes."

He gave me a firm nod back. "Then I'm going to take you back to last night, and you're going to do whatever you have to do to stop me. You're going to show me you'll fight for yourself. Understood?"

I stared at him, eyes wide as he slowly approached. Fear tried to crawl from my stomach to my throat, to escape and consume me, wrap around me like a snake until I couldn't breathe.

I gritted my teeth together. I could see the value in what he was suggesting, but I was terrified of returning to that moment. This was going to make me hate him, even if it was only temporarily.

But if I was going to let my mind return to last night, I knew it was safest to do so with him.

"Understood," I said shakily.

He was on me before I could take my next breath. Iron grips fastened around my wrists and forced me to the ground. Within a second, he was straddling me, the weight of his body pinning me, helplessly bound.

I jerked and thrashed, but he was so impossibly strong. Maybe the force of magic could have pushed him off me—of which I had yet to feel even a flicker.

"What would you have done if I hadn't shown up?" he hissed.

"I—I don't know!" I spit back.

"Well," he said, gripping the fabric of my sweater and sliding it up, exposing my midriff. "You'd better figure it out."

"What the—" I panicked. His fingers were digging into my bare rib cage with more than enough force to bruise. "Gavin—"

"Fight!" he shouted, tearing my sweater open in two so I was left in nothing but my undergarments.

I screamed and clawed at his face. But my nails were bitten down to the quick—not long or sharp enough to do him any damage. Instead, I gripped his beard and pulled.

He bared his straight white teeth. "That's not enough."

"You... *asshole*!" I spit, swiping across his face. And though he did not take liberties with his touch, he didn't ease his hold on my shoulders, the grip on my ribs, or the pressure of his hips that pinned me to the ground, either.

Screaming, panting, I thrust my body forward and crushed my forehead to his mouth. He jerked back from the force, giving me just enough time to remember the knife wound in his shoulder—the one I'd put there just days ago. There was no blood, no sign of it, but I could envision it well. Too well. Intrusive memories of the bloody sight flashed across my mind.

I had been so terrified of hurting him, yet here he was, willingly dragging me back to last night. I'd given him permission to test me this way, but I still hated him for it.

Why was I so soft all the time? Could I not find an ounce of defiance inside myself?

"Fuck you!" I screeched. Gripping his thick, hard shoulder, I placed my thumb over the wound and pushed it in, shoving all my weight behind it. The bloody flesh squelched so horribly that I had to will my breakfast not to make a reappearance. But I clenched my teeth and pushed even harder.

Then I kneed him in the groin as hard as my small body would allow.

He grunted out a few curse words and was off me.

Seething, I scrambled to my feet and backed away from him, ready to strike if he tried anything like that again.

A gash on his lip dripped red from where I'd slammed my forehead against his mouth. His tongue darted out to lick the blood as his lips curled into a wry smile. A movement so unexpectedly sensual, it pissed me off even more.

"That's my girl," he hummed, rising smoothly to his feet. He wiped his mouth with the back of his hand, dangerously captivating eyes locked on me.

"You scared me!" I rasped out. "For a second, I really thought you were going to . . . to . . ."

His left eyebrow rose questioningly, daring me to say it. "Had to make some part of you believe it." He brushed a few dead leaves off his black sweater sleeves. "That fucker may have been the first to force himself on you, but he may not be the last."

I huffed angrily, at myself and at him. I knew I had needed that fear again, that panic, to fight back. He was nothing if not an effective teacher.

Still, eyes burning, body shaking with adrenaline, I gritted out, "Gods, you're a prick!"

"And I'll happily be a prick for the rest of my gods-damned life if it means pissing you off enough to make you fight for yourself!"

"That crossed a line!" I snapped back.

"I agree," he uttered, his voice coated with ice. "And it *worked*."

An unfamiliar sound left my throat—a growl, almost like his, but not nearly as menacing. I lunged to shove at him.

"Aryella!" He stopped me before I could make contact, gripping my wrists in his calloused hands, firm but gentle. "There is nothing I will not do to protect you! To make you protect yourself!" His eyes softened when he murmured low, "There is no *line* I will not cross for *you*."

I could muster only a huffed-out breath in response. So I stepped back—pointedly distancing myself from him—and folded the tattered pieces of my sweater over my exposed torso. I crossed my arms to hold the cloth in place and refused to meet his gaze.

In my periphery, I saw him lift his own black sweater over his head and cover the distance I'd put between us.

"Arms up." Still seething, I obeyed, eyes locked on the ground. Darkness enveloped me for a moment, along with the glorious, masculine scent of him. His shirt now hung down to my knees, covering up every part of me he'd exposed with his attack.

My first thought was that I never wanted to take it off, and I detested myself for that. Also for the breathless gasp that left my lips when I looked up and saw his bare chest.

My lips parted, mouth agape, stunned by his remarkable form. Rippling muscle stretched across the broad plane of his chest. I'd caught hints of the terrifying details of his physique that day he returned soaked to the bone from his hunt. But now, he was bare, and… good gods.

My breath was low and uneven in my chest. His tattoos—the tally marks… there had to be hundreds of them, looped around his forearm, elbow, and biceps, spanning across his rugged chest in rows before repeating the same design on his other arm. And scars. So many scars, some faded and white, some dark, some pink and fresh. So much history and pain and blood…

He was bleeding now, from the barely healed knife wound on his left shoulder. The one I had put there days ago and then reopened.

"I'm sor—"

"Don't you *dare* apologize." His deep voice was clipped, his jaw tight. "You will fight, you will survive, and you will apologize for nothing."

He stepped to the side and gestured for me to pass before him back to the tavern.

I obeyed, but for the rest of the day, I refused to look at him or talk to him.

I knew why he did it, and though I would never admit it to him, I was glad he had.

That burst of energy—that defiant eruption I felt upon thrusting my momentum forward to hurt my attacker—had been missing last night. And we both knew I needed to find whatever would make me fight. To kill. If pure self-preservation was not enough to motivate me, then I needed something else, another type of fuel. I needed to find it *now* before another worse predator came after me.

And I'd found it. Injustice. Against others. Even against me. Hatred of all things unfair. I loathed myself for hurting him by accident while he attacked me, provoked me, scared me, on purpose.

It felt *anything* but fair.

But he'd helped me find my strength in a space that was safe.

And though I was still pissed off, I was also grateful for that.

Chapter Twenty

After training on the third morning in Tovick, I waited for Gemma, hoping we might spend the day together, but she and Finn were nowhere to be found. Where they had hidden away, I didn't know, but I assumed they weren't both "sleeping" in the same room as the others.

Gavin remained close but quiet, probably sensing that I was still processing the events of the last few days. Training that morning had been awkward. I ran and sparred with Ezra without giving my teacher a single word or look.

After lunch, I sat on a tattered leather sofa in the back room of the tavern, happily out of sight from its daily customers. The book Ezra gave me for my birthday was informative but dull. I'd already read through it twice and could recite the Rexus dynasty rulers and the years of their reigns. Now, in the present, with all that lay ahead, it didn't feel useful.

And *I* needed to feel useful.

Eventually, my patience ran out. I asked for more books, and

Damond delivered, escorting me and a silent Gavin to a magnificent library a few blocks south of the tavern. There hadn't been many books in my old home in Warrich, and I had read through those not about the gods—which I hadn't been permitted to read—several times over.

But the towering red-brick cylinder with a glass ceiling crosshatched with iron had thousands.

I almost tripped when I entered, too focused on the lofty black iron staircase spiraling all the way to the top to notice two wooden steps beyond the entryway. I caught myself and turned in circles, eyes upward, gawking. I didn't know so many books could exist in one place at a time. I didn't know so many books existed at all.

Every space on the wall was a bookshelf, and not a single space was empty. Volumes bound with black and reds and blues and greens were all the decor this space needed. It would take years—lifetimes, maybe—to get through these. I wondered if Elias liked to read. If, after going to the caves, I could come back here again. Maybe he'd come with me.

Gavin strode past, sparing neither of us a glance as he grabbed a thick blue book from a shelf and sat, overtaking the majority of a brown leather love seat on the main floor near the door. Forever my sentry.

No, I reminded myself, chest tightening. Not forever.

I followed Damond to a circular table in the center of a room illuminated by chandeliers crafted with iron and green wax candles lit with bright flames. "Does he not trust you to be alone with me?" I muttered so only Damond could hear.

"He does, actually." Damond pulled out a chair and gestured for me to sit. "He's a possessive, jealous bastard when it comes to you. I've never seen anything like it, but *I*—" He clicked his tongue on the roof of his mouth, contemplating how to continue. "Well, Ary, you're not my type. I have... alternate interests."

I frowned, not quite understanding.

Damond merely chuckled at my confusion, waving a hand. "In any case, with or without you, I'm not sure you could keep him out of this place if you tried."

"Why not?" A twinkling smile gleamed on Damond's face, his cheek pushing against the bottom rim of his round glasses. "Because it's his. He built it."

My mouth fell open. I looked up at the iron features dominating the space. Likely crafted, at least in part, by a blacksmith.

"The whole library? He built the whole library?"

Damond nodded. "Blacksmith, stonemason, glazier, carpenter—Smyth is many things." He gestured around. "It's his home, actually. Here in Tovick. He's got living quarters downstairs. He could stay with me whenever he wants, but he stays away from The Black Badger whenever possible. My 'hedonistic shithole,' he so lovingly describes it."

I frowned at that.

"Although..." Damond leaned forward, folding his hands. "For the last few nights, I believe he's been lending *this* place to a few of your amorous friends."

My jaw dropped so far, I thought it might smack the table.

"Gemma and Finn have been *here*?"

I glanced over at Gavin—watched *him*, for once, rather than the other way around. He sat with his boot resting on the opposite knee. One hand resting on the propped-up leg. In his other hand, he held his book and he was focused on reading. His hair was clean, tied partially back in a knot. Beautiful and savage. A rugged scholar.

"That doesn't make sense. He can't stand them," I muttered, turning back to Damond. "My friends."

Damond shrugged. "Seeing your friends happy makes *you* happy, does it not?"

True. Warmth swirled in my belly at his suggestion.

"I don't agree with a great many of his choices," Damond continued, "and I'm unsure if he's capable of making smart decisions around you, but—"

"He's been committed to protecting me." The need to defend him felt like instinct. "He's saved my life on multiple occasions."

"I said *around* you, not for you," Damond clarified, chuckling. "Make no mistake—he'd gladly throw us all to the wolves to protect you, and he won't think twice about dying for you. But you'd have to be blind not to have noticed the way you make him lose his wits."

I forced a swallow and nodded. "I know he cares for me. And I would imagine Simeon has placed a lot of pressure on him to deliver me safely. But I would go to great lengths to protect him, too. He's my friend."

That word still felt wrong.

Damond studied me with a familiar stern look, giving little away. Finally, he asked, "Did you tell him that?" His lip twitched. "That he's your friend?"

"Yes."

He dipped his head, failed to suppress a snort, and looked up at me through his thick eyelashes. "And how did that turn out?"

"I don't... he didn't like it much."

Damond laughed and continued in a low voice, "Between you and me, Ary, is it a *friendship* you want from Smyth?"

Blood rushed to my cheeks.

"What? I... I don't... Damond, he has a wife, and Elias Winterton is my—"

"He told you he had a wife?" Damond's voice was clipped. He leaned forward over the table and crossed his arms, all traces of humor gone. It was clear by the way his eyes narrowed and his head tilted that he questioned Gavin's decision to mention her.

I nodded. I felt color leaving my skin. "But I—can we not talk about it?"

After an uncomfortably heavy pause, he answered, "Of course." Damond gave a soft smile and squeezed my hand. If he felt any lingering unease, he hid it well. "Why did you want to come to the library today, Aryella?"

I looked up, and around. There had to be something in this vast collection about the prophecy if it indeed was part of Nyrida's history. Something about the power I was meant to wield.

"Do you know much about the magic I'm supposed to control?" I asked Damond. "I don't want to wait for Simeon to teach me."

Casually, he rose from his chair and searched the first floor of shelves. A minute or two later he returned with a large black leatherbound book embossed in gold. I read the title.

The Book of the Selvaren.

"Our lore claims the gods each gave a piece of themselves to form our world. If your power comes from the Selvaren, I would start there. With the gods."

For three hours I scoured the book without once rising from that table. I'd known the names of our gods, how they corresponded with each of our twelve months, but I'd known nothing of their supposed powers. I wrote down each god and what they could do, and then I memorized them.

Nevelin, Goddess of Snow and Ice, could freeze anything with a single touch. Aurana, Goddess of Gravity, could levitate and move items without lifting a finger. Viridian, God of Healing and Regeneration, could repair the injured and dying and regrow limbs and organs.

I stared at my hands and couldn't help but smile at the amount of good I could do if that power was mine. I wondered what or who else I might be able to heal.

Rainar, God of the Seas, could manipulate water into whatever shape, wave, or weapon he desired. Floris, Goddess of the Earth, could wield the vines and branches of trees like extra limbs. Aesta, Goddess of Light, could illuminate her surroundings with a flick of her wrist.

Helios, God of Fire, could *burn*. Soltum, God of Animals, could communicate with creatures. Effusia, Goddess of the Mind, could manipulate emotion with a touch of her hand.

I looked up from the book and ran my hands over my face. Gentle heat caressed my cheek, and I could sense Gavin's eyes on me. I looked up to meet his worried brown gaze. The thought of all this power in my veins was overwhelming me. He only needed to look at me to know. But I pulled away, because this felt like something I needed to read and absorb on my own.

I forced a deep breath and pushed on.

Autumna, Goddess of the Hunt, could alter her appearance to go undetected by prey. Sussurro, God of Wind and Air, could steer the wind as he pleased.

And finally, the one who had entranced me in the temple with his soothing dark. Nyxar, God of Celestial Night, the strongest of them all. He could move the moon and the stars and engulf the whole world in midnight. Eclipse every other god and nullify the effects of their powers. I shuddered. To wield such remarkable power would be intoxicating.

After Nyxar's pages, there were thirteen more, and they were oddly blank.

"Damond?" I called, turning in my seat to see where he'd gone.

Gavin lowered his book at the sound of my voice. Our eyes met before I could stop myself. The heated, silent plea in his gaze was a catalyst to my pulse. It ricocheted around the chambers of my heart until I forced myself to look at Damond as he approached.

"Yes, Ary?" He sidled up to the table.

I pointed to the end of the book. "Why are these pages blank?"

"I believe all the copies are that way."

"Well, has anyone checked the original to make sure?"

Damond chuckled. "Only the Selvaren know where it is. It would be at least a thousand years old."

My brow furrowed as I looked down at my hands. There was no trace of these powers in or around the fair, lightly freckled skin of my fingers. They looked as weak and helpless as I had felt in Warrich.

Fuming, I scanned those ancient pages again and again. *The Book of the Selvaren* had plenty to say about the deities and their histories, but nothing to suggest how a mortal might wield their powers.

My hunger and thirst eventually overpowered me, exhaustion surpassing frustration. I broke the hours-long silence and told

Gavin that I was ready to go. When he sensed my chagrin, the concern in his face was clear, but I walked out before he could pry.

For the rest of that day, I fought the urge to get close to him. No matter how badly I longed to share my frustrations, to ask his input, I knew I had to get used to doing things on my own.

Still, what Damond had said about Gavin giving up his home for Gemma and Finn just to give them time alone stuck with me. It was kind. It was good. And if Damond was right, Gavin was generous not just for their sake, but for mine as well.

He made them happy to see *me* happy.

And while that *did* make me happy, it also made me *ache*.

We were in Tovick longer than planned, and I spent most of that time training or in the library. I memorized nearly every detail in *The Book of the Selvaren* and imprinted Finn's map of Nyrida in my memory. I was scared to forget any of it, like so many details of my youth. But perhaps those details weren't useful. My mind seemed to hunger for *this* information. Seemed to know that nothing else would matter more to me than this.

Daily, the others questioned Gavin why we had yet to depart for Brinnea.

I knew why they pushed him, why they wanted to go. My friends wanted to be done with him. Finn and Caz remained mostly neutral, but Gemma and Ezra were tired of his snide comments regarding Elias Winterton and the caves and the not-so-subtle hints that he hated the idea of me in a place of confinement. I'd be queen, yes, but I'd be required to be the type of queen Simeon felt the people needed—the dutiful ruler foretold in Christabel's prophecy.

Because if I did not become what was needed, if I didn't succeed in my duty, then people would die. The weight was heavy, but I carried it. And during the past week in Tovick, I did what I needed to do to make it bearable.

I insisted that all training sessions be group sessions. Sometimes even Damond joined us. While Gavin watched and instructed me, I made every effort to maintain emotional distance.

I wasn't cold or rude. I'd already forgiven him for his surprise attack the week prior, knowing I'd needed a push. But I gave him no more attention than I gave the others, and I stomped out any urges to spare a second of time alone with him.

More than once, he requested I join him on an errand or suggested an extra training session. I refused them all, tearing my gaze away from the rejection in his eyes before I could let it break my resolve.

Damond's lighthearted presence helped distract me. When we weren't in the library, he taught me how to use a bow and arrow. It was his favorite weapon but felt impossible to perfect. I missed, and I missed, and I nearly gave up. The dull ache in my shoulder was frustrating. But just like every exercise and movement I learned, my body adjusted, my muscles strengthened, and the pain gradually dissipated.

Ezra and I began each morning with a run. Of the men, he was the youngest and least experienced in combat—even though it had been two years since he passed through Elias's Commencement. I asked plenty of questions about my betrothed. Tried to make myself interested. I learned that he was born during the fifth month of the year—Floris—and adored his grandmother, Ophelia, above all else.

Except for me. A woman he'd never met. A prophecy. An idea.

So when Ezra told me how excited Elias was to meet me, I forced a smile and believed that my cousin thought it was true.

Gemma spent most nights with Finn in the basement of Gavin's library across town. Every day, they came to breakfast with smiles on their faces, and every day, I felt the same twinge of jealousy in my chest. But I kept it hidden. I was happy for them, but I couldn't help . . . *wishing.*

Gavin continued to place outrageous amounts of food in front of me. I ate without objection, both to avoid any confrontation and because I could feel myself growing stronger. And when I looked at my naked body in the mirror before a bath, my ribs were harder to see.

Besides, at least eight hours of training a day made me constantly hungry.

I managed to avoid the tension with Gavin and distract myself from the ache of missing his closeness.

Until one cloudy winter afternoon, three days before Solstice.

I sat cross-legged near the edge of a short cliff looking out at the field I'd ridden the black mare through on my birthday. The field was now covered in a thin layer of snow, which glistened beneath the winter sun's rays. It reminded me that seasons changed and moments were not permanent.

Riding free—with that black mare—was not permanent.

I heard the unmistakable footsteps, solid and swift, until they stopped behind me.

A coin landed in my lap.

"For your thoughts, Ella?"

I sucked in a breath at the sound of him, enduring a heavy, painful pause between us that spoke volumes of its own.

"Please," he added, voice hoarse.

I looked up at him and nodded. Relief poured out in a sigh as he lowered himself to the ground beside me, the stone scratching beneath the heavy soles of his boots.

Long minutes passed. Silent minutes that we spent sitting together, looking out at the field beyond the stables until he finally spoke.

"You've been avoiding me."

I forced a swallow. "Yes."

He turned to face me. "If this is because of our last training session—"

"It's not," I told him, shaking my head. "You made me angry—angrier than I've ever been, I think—but I gave you permission, and I know why you did it."

"You do?" His gaze followed mine to my fidgeting thumbs.

"Yes." The cooing call of a morning dove echoed in the woods behind us. I took it as a command from the gods to *breathe*. Breathe, so I had the courage to speak the truth. "I don't know how you can read me like you can, know my thoughts and see my fears." I tucked my knees into my chest. "I don't have to tell you I'm afraid to meet Simeon in Brinnea for you to know it. I don't have to tell you how uneasy I feel about those caves and all the people there waiting for me, or how much I dread being someone I'm not. I don't have to tell you anything for you to know me. You just do."

Distant wind disturbed a flock of birds in a forest beyond the field. They rose and scattered in a synchronized dance. I could feel his stare locked on me, calming me from the outside in.

"I want to help these people," I continued. "I want to fight. I'm becoming strong enough—I *think*—but I'm also starting to understand what—" I clenched my teeth, afraid to look at him. Knowing if I did, I wouldn't be able to say what I needed to. "I'm starting to understand what I'll be forced to give up, and that's why I've been avoiding you. Because it hurts to know that they'll make me give *you* up, won't they?" My breath shuddered. I blinked out a tear. "My teacher, my . . . friend."

Avoiding him had left an aching hole in my chest. When I was angry, I wanted to tell him. When I was afraid, I searched for the solace I found in his presence. When I was successful, I wanted his praise. When I was happy, I wanted to share it with him. I wanted to watch his face when I smiled. Despite his hardness and his violence, I craved him. His deep laughter and devilish grin. His safety and warm, gentle touch.

The way he made me want to fight.

I wasn't sure I knew what love was, but I imagined it had to be something like this.

In just a few weeks, I had found in him a soul that connected with mine. As if our bond had been declared by the gods long before a clairvoyant queen's prophecy. Sometimes I felt like he was an extension of me, and no amount of time or distance could sever the cord binding us together.

But Gavin Smyth was and always would be a man mourning his lost wife. He didn't follow the rules, and he would challenge authority. And the way he made me feel could not exist alongside Elias Winterton, the man I had to marry to keep my army, to beat Molochai, to save this world.

"When I go to those caves," I continued shakily, looking up at him, "they will make me say goodbye to you, won't they?"

His thick throat bobbed as he swallowed, and he stared straight ahead. The hard planes of his face revealed nothing, but sorrow weighed heavy in his gaze.

"Yes."

I let silent tears fall. And as if it was the last time I might ever get to touch him, I wrapped myself around his arm and held on.

Indeed, I could make this the last time I touched him. I could keep my distance as I had over the last week and a half. Or I could cherish the time we had left, knowing it was going to hurt to say goodbye either way.

"But we have at least a week." I pulled away and met his gaze with hopeful eyes. "We still need to go to Brinnea. And I haven't found my power. Surely Simeon can't send me to Elias until I find whatever it is they're counting on, so you can stay with me until I find it, can't you?"

His breath quickened, his eyes darted between my eyes and my mouth. "Aryella, I—"

The ground rumbled beneath us, and an energy that I could only describe as *alive* reverberated through my core.

To our right, fire, smoke, and screams erupted into a terrible cloud of destruction.

A booming shockwave right in the heart of Tovick, as the Temple of the Selvaren began to crumble.

Chapter Twenty-One

By some miracle—driven by fear—I was on my feet quicker than he was, though he was close behind. The explosion lasted only for a second, but I felt the wall of pressure absorb the oxygen around us like an inferno's eclipse.

As if hell itself had reached up through the center of that temple, ripped out its heart, and sucked the life and air back into the earth.

I stumbled through the trees, down the rocky hill, toward the temple. It was so close to the tavern where my friends—

My eyes burned. My pace increased.

My friends.

"Gemma!" I screamed, scrambling onto the cobblestone path.

Ash polluted the air. I coughed but sprinted through the airborne embers, not caring if they burned me. It would be a blessing from the gods if, just like the day Ezra and I had been there, the temple had been empty at the time of the blast.

I watched in horror as flames roared inside the temple. Stained glass shattered and boulders of stone crumbled as mothers grabbed their children from the streets and stumbled back from the collapsing splendor, screaming.

"Help!"

I turned toward the source of the scream.

"Please! My boy, my boy!" A short brown-haired woman knelt amid shards of glass as she cradled the limp form of a small boy.

I ran to them and knelt down on the boy's other side. He was four, maybe five, with sandy brown hair and freckles. Too sweet and innocent for this mess of a world. Collateral in a war fought by selfish people wanting power.

A strained whimper left my throat at the sight of a deep gash across the boy's collarbone, where he'd been struck with debris. It was deep—too deep—and near his throat. The blood pooled beneath him, the puddle growing.

The face of another little boy flashed in my mind.

I choked out a sob and lunged forward to cover the little boy's wound with my hands. Through my tears, I begged the gods for mercy. Whatever they had to do, whatever parts of me they had to take, I begged them to save him.

I begged for Ollie.

"Please," I wept, squeezing my eyes shut. "Please, please, please—"

Dread gripped me by the throat, air was torn from my lungs, and for a moment, I was floating. Glimmering onyx swirled in every direction. Ropes of void-like darkness snaked around my wrists and ankles, holding me somewhere where gravity couldn't exist.

Until I was dropped into the center of a twelve-spoked wheel.

Sharp pain burst up and through my ankles at the force of impact. I stumbled and winced, bracing myself with my palms on the ground, forcing myself to breathe in, out, as I opened my eyes to take in my surroundings.

Time stood still, and the Temple of the Selvaren surrounded me. Only now, Ezra wasn't with me. Neither were the assailants that Gavin had slain. And *Gavin*... I couldn't see him, but I could feel him there, somewhere, anchoring me to the present.

But the temple had just crumbled, so... this had to be all in my head.

The hall of worship trembled around me, as did each colorful shrine, and I began to spin. No, *they* did. Each spoke of the wheel was connected to one of the twelve gods, and while my feet remained in the middle of a small silver circle, the wheel drove the room clockwise around me. Faster and faster until the colors blurred into a violent, iridescent tempest.

Fear prickled the base of my spine. It was spinning *too* fast. The small silver disc I stood on couldn't possibly hold. It was going to crack, rip the wheel off its axis until each spoke was thrust outward to impale and shatter the stained-glass shrine of each god. And I would be launched up, away, back into the shadowy purgatory that brought me here.

I looked down, searching for a way out, or at least a way to stop it. My brow furrowed at the unnatural stillness beneath me. Somehow, the small silver disc beneath my feet was stationary. I, too, was still, melded with the silver into one piece, one center, and I realized...

It felt like my body was the axis. *I* anchored *the gods*.

The twelve gods spun, but if I remained, so would they.

Beyond, I heard the cry of the little boy's mother as she pleaded for his life, and I remembered why I'd come here. Panic snaked its way through my veins.

There was a tendril reaching out of his chest. I couldn't see it, but I could feel it.

His lifeline, begging for help. Begging for *me*.

Words dashed across my vision. I'd spent hours scouring *The Book of the Selvaren* for answers in that library. Fire, water, ice, night, wind, objects moved with the mind and... *healing*. I pressed my hands to my ears, pressure crushing my temples as I strained for the right spoke.

The mother cried again for her son, and I screamed a final desperate plea to the gods that this little boy not die, even if I, the axis of the wheel, had to splinter to save him.

My right hand shot out and reached for green.

The temple disappeared, and a flash of emerald light illuminated the black of my closed eyelids. I smelled iron-rich blood and flesh as it burned and healed over.

When I opened my eyes, I realized not what I felt, but *who*.

Viridian, God of Healing and Regeneration.

I gasped and yanked my hands from the boy, frantically crawling back and away. Afraid of the power I didn't know how to control, afraid of myself, of what I could do to him. Weakly, I stumbled into a warm wall of muscle, and familiar arms caught me.

"It's okay, you won't hurt him," Gavin promised, his mouth close to my ear. Quiet, so only I heard him, as he secured a steel arm around my torso, drawing me into him. "You would never hurt him, Ella." I felt his chest shudder. Not a cry, but a breathless laugh of relief.

I was afraid to look down at the little boy, but when I did, I saw what Gavin saw. The deep, fatal gash over the boy's little neck was gone. He lay in a pool of blood, but the flowing had ceased.

Little gray eyes flickered open.

The mother wailed and wept beautiful tears of relief, embracing her son as he turned into her chest for comfort. My heart cracked at the sight, and at the sudden awareness that I'd never yearned for my own mother that way.

"Thank you!" she cried, her eyes tearful orbs of wild gratitude. "You . . . our—our Silver Angel, *thank you*."

Words escaped me. Racked by tremors, I merely nodded at the woman and leaned into Gavin, letting him help me to my feet. I wavered as I rose, sudden waves of nausea and dizziness inhibiting my balance. It felt like healing had *taken* something out of me. Gavin wrapped his arm around me and all but carried me toward the tavern.

I looked around to see buildings singed by fire and struck with debris, townsfolk scrambling to put out the flames. Only a few buildings stood close enough to be badly damaged by the outward blast of fire.

But the front wall of the tavern had been blown out. With it gone, I could see straight through the dust into the wreckage. Tables and chairs were in pieces, debris strewn across the floor I'd danced on days ago. Shattered glass from Damond's chandeliers crunched beneath our feet. Dust from the blast floated inside streams of dusky sunlight.

I looked down and saw a streak of blood trailing from the tavern's threshold into the back room. As if someone had been wounded and dragged.

And then I heard a man screaming in agony.

Bursting through the door, I saw Caz on the floor, flat on his back, Gemma and Finn on each side of him. And his leg...his left leg was severed at the calf, connected only by a thin strip of tissue. Blood spurted from the stump.

I covered my mouth with my hands, swallowing the bile as it rose in my throat.

Finn remained remarkably focused as he fastened his own belt—a makeshift tourniquet—just below his brother's severed knee. It was a relief when Finn pulled the tourniquet taut and Caz responded with a groan.

"He was just inside the temple, and a boulder—" Gemma paled. "A boulder fell on him. We were here, just on the other side of the street." She gave me a quick glance before sliding a pile of books to elevate his bloody stump. "We found him, we got him out in time before anything else could happen, but—"

"I'll live," Caz groaned in pain.

Sorrow and rage bit at my eyes like hellhounds, relieved only slightly by the sight of unscathed Damond and Ezra rushing in from other rooms. Damond, with a bottle of water to cleanse the wound and Ezra with a blanket to cover Caz.

Indeed, my other four friends were fully intact, save for some scrapes and burns.

Gavin held my hand but stepped forward, face grim. "The leg. It's—"

"I don't think so," muttered Damond, gripping Caz's shoulder in one hand while opening the bottle of water with the other. "We can stop the bleeding, but the leg—he'll likely lose it. The healer here in Tovick won't be able to help. All we can do now is prevent infection."

With his leg now elevated, Caz was sitting up partway with a bag of barley at his back for support.

But if I could save that little boy...

I rushed to Caz, stumbling through unexpected weakness in my bones as I knelt beside him, gently placed my hands on his thigh and prayed for him like I did the child. Healing and regeneration—that bright emerald light. For at least a minute I tried, ignoring the objections and questions from my confused friends.

I reached for the temple, for the wheel, even for the suffocating black I had to pass through to get there.

There was nothing.

"No!" I groaned, chest aching. "It's not working, why isn't it working—"

"What isn't working?" demanded Gemma, gripping my shoulders from behind, searching my face for answers. "Ary!"

"My power!" I choked out a tired, angry sob.

Gemma shook her head, not understanding. "Your power isn't—"

"She saved a boy's life," Gavin explained. "Outside the temple, she healed him."

Gemma sucked in a breath, the rest of them growing silent. Rage slithered up my spine as I tried to reach for the green spoke, to summon that viridian light through my body, through Caz's leg.

"Caz," I groaned. No trace of jasmine in my nostrils, no rush of renewed life. No wheel. No temple. Nothing. "No, no, no! I'm sorry, I'm so sorry—"

"Stop." Caz reached for my elbow and squeezed. I barely felt it, he was so weak. A brave grin warmed his pale face. His gentle hazel eyes fluttered open. "Don't break yourself for me, Ary."

I took his hand and cradled it to my chest. The only way I could hug him and not risk hurting him.

Ezra stood beside me, fuming. "I thought Simeon had wards on this city!"

"Magic doesn't stop explosives," answered Damond. "Who knows how long those explosives had been under that temple? Decades, maybe."

"And you think it's a coincidence they went off today?" Gemma pressed a cool cloth to Caz's forehead. "We should have left sooner. They must know she's here." Calmly, Gavin shook his head. "They don't know that. They *suspect* it."

"How do *you* know what *they* suspect?" Her ebony curls trembled—an extension of her rage. "Are you one of them?"

Gavin turned on her. "Why do you think Simeon sent me, Tremaine? Just because I'm good with a blade?" He bared his teeth. "He sent me because I have seen and done shit your precious army commander would piss himself over. He sent me because I know evil, I know Molochai, and Molochai will want her"—he pointed at me—"for himself. So if Insidions knew she was anywhere near here, they certainly wouldn't risk blowing her up."

"Insidions have always gone after the temples first," Damond rushed out in agreement. "They despise the Selvaren. Tovick has been a bastion for years. It was only a matter of time before they decided to strike."

"Because of Ary," Finn said. "We need to get her out of here, and to do that, we need to split up." He wiped the sweat from his forehead, smearing his brother's blood over his skin. "We need to get Caz to the caves. For any chance of saving the leg, we have to get him to Nestor and Abram."

Trembling, Caz took a glass of water from Damond's hand and rasped, "I'll be fine."

"Shut the hell up! You got your leg blown off!" Finn shouted, running his trembling hands through his short black hair. "We have to go back to the caves, Caz and me, and at least one other."

Gemma glared at Finn. "We have to stay together!"

"Don't break yourself for me, Ary."

They argued, but Caz's words echoed in my mind, drowning them out. He *had* broken himself for me, risked everything—for me. They all had.

No more.

Just because I wasn't ready didn't mean they had to stay.

"Enough." I stood. "You will go home. All of you."

Gemma gave me a warning glare. "Ary—"

"The four of you will head west to Avendrel."

Conviction. I'd had to fake it many times before, but not this time.

"Caz will rest until dawn tomorrow," I continued. "And you will leave once the bleeding stops. You will take horses. Do not stop until you get to the caves. Smyth and I will go to Brinnea, to Simeon." I cleared my throat and looked up at him, hopeful. "That is what I want. Will you take me?"

Utter relief and awe stared back at me. "Yes, I'll take you."

"Let's all go," Ezra insisted, looking nervously between me and Gavin. "All of us, let's go home."

He meant all of us other than Gavin. But home, to me, did not feel like those caves. "I'm not ready." Whether or not I would ever be ready, I didn't know. At the very least, I knew I wasn't ready until I met with Simeon.

And I wasn't ready to leave *him*.

Gemma took my hand. "Ary—"

"This is not up for debate. I need to go to Brinnea. It is . . ." I forced a swallow, forced my fear and anxiety down. I knew I better start practicing. "It is an order."

Ezra shook his head. "Elias will—"

"If Elias didn't deem it crucial to deliver me to the caves himself, he can wait a few more weeks." The words burst out of me, angry and hard. Out of the corner of my eye, I saw Gavin's lip twitch for a moment before he tempered his pride with a clenched jaw.

"Caz." I knelt down, resting my shaking hand on his clean-shaven face. He was in and out of consciousness, so I wasn't sure he had heard. "You are going home. Gemma, Finn, and Ezra will take you home. To Marin and the baby."

His sweat drenched his skin—far too pale now. "Marin will disown me if I don't bring back her queen."

"Then you tell her you were following orders." I gritted my teeth, eyes burning. "*From* her queen. And that I will . . ." My throat tightened at the promise I was scared to make. "I will come when I'm ready." Then I smiled, because this next part was true. "I'll have to meet that sweet baby, after all." His responding grin was his strongest yet.

Finn and Ezra stayed with Caz in the tavern's back room, where they moved him to a sofa near the hearth. I watched as Damond fastened a metal lock on the door. Now that the front was incinerated and the main room open to the elements, there was direct access from the outside.

It was an effort to refrain from helping Tovick's townspeople sift through the temple rubble, but Damond assured me there had been few people harmed. Those remaining were under the care of the town healers. My efforts were better spent preparing our friends for their journey.

So I gave all my efforts in the kitchen, preparing food to send with them. Boiled potatoes, sliced bread, and meat. Hopefully the food would last to nourish them until they arrived at the caves. I wasn't sure how long it would take to get there on horseback, but surely faster than we'd traveled from Warrich to Tovick.

For Caz, they *had* to.

Heat warmed the kitchen from both the stove and the wood-burning oven. I cracked open the window above the wide metal sink basin for some crisp, fresh air to dry the sweat on my brow and heard Gemma's shouts.

Standing on the tips of my toes, I peeked outside to see Gavin, gathering and sharpening blades, preparing them to be stored on belts and in satchels. And Gemma followed him around the forested area directly behind the tavern. Arms waving, beautiful eyes blazing.

"She is not going anywhere alone with *you*!"

"She is." Gavin filled a quiver with arrows. "It's her choice. She wants to go to Brinnea. I will take her there. She is safe with me."

"Is she?" Gemma hissed. "Is she *really*?"

Gavin turned slowly, lip curling. "What are you implying, Tremaine?"

"Do you think *I* can't tell what a man wants?" she sneered, hands on her hips. "You want to keep her for yourself."

A lifted eyebrow and devilish smirk appeared as he said, "Perhaps I've underestimated your intuition, after all."

"You bastard!" she snarled, shoving at him, trying to rile him up. It didn't work. "You want to ruin her for your own pleasure. Get her to let her guard down and manipulate her. So you can fuck the young queen and say you did!"

Anger stewed in my belly at both of them. At Gavin, for not denying it. Laughing to antagonize her. At Gemma, for speaking of me like I was some mindless puppet.

"You even have the gall to laugh about it." She threw her fists into his chest. But he stood, an immovable stone wall, and answered her anger with an unbothered stare. "Why haven't you done it already?" She shoved him again, egging him on to a fight she would lose. Her free hand tightened on the handle of her blade like she was going to wield it. "Do you or don't you want to bed her before Elias Winterton?"

But Gemma couldn't catch him off guard. Her blade got no farther than the air in front of her face before he stopped her with a steel grip and a mean, acerbic scowl.

"You have *no fucking idea*."

I stumbled back two steps from the sink, fists and stomach clenched.

He hadn't done a very good job at hiding his interest in me. I was probably too sheltered and naïve but I did still wonder if he *wanted* me. He showered me with attention and care, and I couldn't help but be drawn to him.

Gemma burst through the door to the hallway outside the kitchen, leaving it wide open in her wake. She stopped when she saw me standing in the kitchen, her eyes pleading.

"I need more time," I told her. "It's my choice."

With a bitter scowl, she uttered, "It's a stupid choice," and stormed off.

Maybe it was, but I trusted my gut regardless.

Still, my chest sank into my stomach as I watched her go. I was quickly learning that I couldn't please everyone. Accepting this reality didn't soothe the ache of knowing how Gemma and I were leaving things.

Heavy footsteps drew my attention toward the kitchen door, followed by a cold rush of leather and sweet cedar blown in from the winter wind. Gavin stopped when he saw me. I sized him up—his intimidating form, dark hair pulled back with a leather strap. The way his sleeves were rolled up around his thick arms, revealing those tattoos.

I couldn't help but look at him and wonder what it would be like to be on the receiving end of his desire.

His face hardened when he saw me. He glanced at the open window, then back at me, then the floor.

He asked, "How much did you hear?"

Heat rushed to my cheeks.

"Enough."

"Enough to what, Ella?" Panic laced his voice.

"It doesn't matter." It was an effort to keep my tone steady. "I trust you."

That was true. For better or worse, I trusted him.

He took two steps forward, just into the kitchen. I retreated to give him room. He winced at my withdrawal.

"I will not touch you, Aryella. What she said…" He ran his hand over his face and huffed out a breath. "You are *safe* with me."

I knew that. Too well. I craved his closeness like a drug and loathed his self-control. Afraid of the resentful note in my voice, I merely nodded.

"It's very late." His deep voice turned gravelly. "If you're finished here, you should get some rest." Avoiding my gaze, he backed into the hallway. "We'll leave tomorrow for Brinnea."

"Will you talk to her?" I rushed out. "I know you don't feel the need to prove yourself to anyone, but anything I say…she won't listen. She thinks I'm helpless." My eyes burned. "But I don't want to leave her like this, with her angry."

"She has no reason to be angry at you, Ella. It's me she—"

"Please." I tied the ends of a knapsack and fidgeted with the strings. "She needs to hear it from you. Show her the man I see so she knows I'm safe."

He leaned one arm against the doorframe and ran his other hand over his scarred, bearded face. I'd started to give up hope when finally, he nodded. "I'll handle it."

Sighing in relief, I closed the space between us and threw my arms around him. "Thank you," I muttered into his chest, inhaling his scent, absorbing his warmth. He folded his strong arms around me—engulfing my body.

"Anything for you," he whispered, resting his lips in my hair.

Minutes later, I crawled into bed and watched as Gemma tamed her curls into a high knot. She hadn't spoken a word since our confrontation outside the kitchen.

Three firm knocks on the door snapped the rope of tension. She crossed the room in four long strides and jerked it open, revealing Gavin.

"Tremaine." His expression was hard and cold. He glanced at

me, gaze softening, before looking back at her. "May I speak with you?"

She scowled in answer and moved to slam the door in his face, but he stuck out a heavy black boot and scowled right back.

"Gemma," I called out from bed. "Please."

She glared at me, then Gavin. With an indecipherable grumble, she shoved past him into the hallway. Before following, Gavin gave me a pointed nod. A promise.

I heard the door to the men's bedroom across the hall open and close.

They were in that room for over an hour. There was no shouting, only the distant rumbling of indecipherable conversation. For long, torturous minutes I waited before finally succumbing to my nerves and deciding there was nothing I could do besides get some rest.

Almost asleep when Gemma finally came to bed, I heard her move quietly and carefully through the room. She climbed in beside me but remained seated upright as she rested her hand on my hip. Thinking I was asleep, clearly.

But I could see her face in the vanity mirror. Her worries stewed beneath the moonlight. Her caramel eyes were distant, glassy, sad. She looked like she was somewhere else.

Bile rose swiftly in my throat. I knew it was a risk, asking him to convince her. I knew he had secrets.

And I suspected he'd just told her one he had yet to tell me.

Chapter Twenty-Two

Caz's leg stopped bleeding early into the night, courtesy of Finn's tourniquet and bandaging. He slept on the sofa—where he now ate breakfast, slowly—while Finn and Ezra took up space on the floor to tend to him. He was weak and clearly in awful pain, but his humor and outlook remained steadfast.

If I ever suffered a near-fatal wound, I prayed to be half as brave as Caz.

Gemma was quiet this morning. Her feisty, combative wit had molded into pensive awe. When Gavin walked into her line of sight, she stared wide-eyed at him, gulped, and then looked over at me with a similar expression.

No objection left her lips when Finn described the route they would take to the caves.

I'd wanted Gemma to understand my choice, but I had expected more of a fight.

I thought of what Gavin could have said to convince her. He'd likely told her of his wife, and she now understood why he feared losing someone he cared for.

Or he had threatened her.

I wished the latter wasn't so likely.

Clad in all black, Gavin entered the back room after everyone had finished eating. Late into the night, he'd been preparing supplies, horses, and a cart to carry Caz.

"Finn, Caz, Ezra, Gemma. I have three horses prepared for you." He took up a post beside me and crossed his muscular arms over his chest. "One to lead, two to pull a carriage. If anyone asks about Aryella, you tell everyone that you've seen her head south, north, or west, I don't give a shit. Anything but the truth. Give them a false description."

I looked at Gemma. She gave me a sad smile. Relief and warning battled in my gut, but I rose from the table and followed them to the wooded area behind the tavern.

It was a misty, chilled morning. The wind was brutal. Gray skies threatened snow or freezing rain. The day was colder than any other I'd experienced in Wymara—but I wore the wolf's fur shawl around my neck. It kept the shivers at bay.

Ezra and Finn carried Caz to a bed on the cart, padded with blankets and hay. They both rolled their eyes when Caz cheerfully questioned what he'd done to deserve such "royal treatment."

He wore a fur-lined brown jacket borrowed from Damond and a dark green hat. I climbed up to where he sat and began to prod at the bale of hay behind him.

"You're fussing, Ary."

He smiled up at me with his straight, bright smile, but my throat tightened at his complexion. Too pale.

I ignored his comment and tightened his wool cap over ears that poked out beneath a mess of ebony hair. Definitely in need of grooming by the time he returned.

"Is Your Majesty *tucking me in*?"

I snorted. "You know I hate being called that."

But indeed, I was wrapping his whole body—besides his injured leg, which had a single, loose covering over the bandage—in blankets.

"I'm fine, Ary." He took my wrist and lowered it. I sat back on my knees. "Thank you."

Gemma called and motioned for me to come down. To the east, the early sun was trying to peek out over the horizon.

Turning back to Caz, I bit back tears and said, "Please tell Marin I'm sorry."

"I can try, but she might slap me. Both for getting my leg blown off and for letting you apologize when it wasn't your fault." Caz grinned when I laughed.

"Ary," Gemma called again, more impatiently this time.

I carefully wrapped my arms around Caz's neck. "Be safe."

When I pulled back, he winked at me. "Not very fun, but sure."

With one last eye roll, I hopped down from the carriage to face Gemma. She stood confidently in her black fighting leathers with knives sheathed on her belt.

"I'm worried," I began. "The temple will draw their attention, and you might bring them right to you."

"No second-guessing." She took my thin fingers in her leather-gloved hands and squeezed. "It's the right call."

My eyes widened, remembering her conflicting comment from last night.

"It is." She sensed my hesitation. "We'll move as fast as we can. If they catch up to us, you won't be there for them to find."

I tightened my wolf-pelt shawl around my shoulders with my spare hand. She turned away, but—

"Gemma?" I held her hand and lowered my voice. "I asked him to speak with you. I trust him, and I want you to trust him, but..." I winced. "What did he say? Did he threaten you?"

She laughed once, shaking her head. "No, Ary. No threats. I just didn't know that..." Her long fingers wrapped around mine again, and her breath was a ball of mist when she huffed. "He won't hurt you." Emotion brimmed in her eyes as she drew me in for a tight hug.

I returned the embrace, a few tears of my own spilling onto her shoulder.

"Come when you're ready." She pressed a quick kiss to my temple. "Do what you need to do... to find yourself. We'll all be there, waiting for you."

With one agile leap, she climbed in the front seat of the wooden carriage, her long fingers tightening around both reins.

I hugged Finn next.

Then Ezra. He walked to where Gavin stood by the white mare positioned to lead them. Despite the height Gavin had on Ezra, my cousin sneered up at him, unafraid. I was grateful when Gavin let Ezra say his piece with no more reaction than a lifted eyebrow.

Ezra climbed onto the white mare and gave me one last worried glance.

Beneath the orange and ocean blue of a winter dawn, I watched as they departed westward, toward Avendrel.

An hour later, Damond stood with us outside the horse stables on the outskirts of Brinnea. He planned on staying in town for a few more days before deciding whether to rebuild the tavern or relocate to the Winterton Caves.

The sun was bright in the sky, and I prayed the others were far away by now. I wished there was a way to know when they returned to their families. Safe, where Molochai and his Insidions could not find them.

Both our bags were slung over my favorite mare, and her sleek black mane glistened in the morning mist. Two bags were all we had. Most of our supplies had gone with the others. I'd insisted, confident Gavin would be able to get us whatever we needed on the way. Perhaps I would even try my own hand at a hunt.

"Time to go." Gavin led the chestnut brown stallion beside the black mare.

"We only need her." I rested a hand on the mare's sleek neck and looked at Gavin. "I'll ride with you. It feels safer that way."

And warmer. Even with gloves, hat, scarf, and the wolf's pelt shielding me, the wind bit at my cheeks.

"If that's what you want," he answered after a moment of jaw-clenching contemplation.

I turned to Damond, who took my face in his smooth, slender hands and gave me a peck on the cheek. "Sweet, brilliant, beautiful girl." He sighed. "Keep him on his toes for me, will you?"

I snorted, wondering if that was possible. But then I remembered what Damond said about my teacher losing his wits and returned his knowing smirk with a nod.

It seemed like muscle memory—the way I hitched myself up and over the black mare. She shifted her majestic form beneath me. Excitement rushed through me, as if it flowed straight from her body into mine. I waited while Gavin leaned over and muttered something to Damond—a command, by the way Damond nodded in response—and climbed onto the saddle behind me.

I sucked in a shallow breath at the way he felt pressed against my back—warm, powerful, dominating. Aware of every shift of his body, the way his strong legs locked on either side of mine, both of us straddling the mare. How, with every breath, his chest rose and fell against my back. My stomach quivered.

I shoved it away, quenching it with thoughts of something, anything else. This was going to be a very agonizing couple of days if I didn't get hold of myself.

"How long will it take to get there?" I asked, in dire need of a distraction.

"About two days by horse." Two days. That was all I had left with him before I was handed off to my ancient, sorcerer father.

"There are a few small villages on the way. We can stop each night," he continued. "I want you out of the cold if we can help it."

"I'll be fine with a campfire."

He gave no response, which meant no budging on that, apparently.

Changing the subject, I asked, "What did you tell Gemma?"

I waited through his silence. Gave him about a minute before speaking again.

"What did you tell Gemma?" I repeated, wondering if he'd heard me. "What did you say to make her trust you?"

He sighed and shifted around me, gripping the reins so firmly that I could see the tendons rippling in his hands. I shivered at a sight as terrifying as it was tempting. Thought of those hands on me…

He finally spoke, his deep voice firm. "I told her the truth, Ella."

"And what's that?"

"Gemma understands the lengths I will go to protect you."

"You scared her." I remembered the troubled look on her face beneath the moonlight. "She seemed strange when she came to bed last night."

"I didn't scare her," he replied calmly. "I just helped her understand the true weight of the burden you carry."

"What does that even mean?"

Silence ensued.

But instead of losing myself to the frustration his relentless ambiguity drew out of me, I searched my memory of Gemma the night before. I remembered how she lovingly rested her hand on my hip, as if she felt the need to comfort me. Concerned and aloof, but not horrified. Not traumatized. And I couldn't fight the feeling that, despite her uneasiness, she had an air of awareness about her. As if something, maybe Gavin himself, finally made sense to her.

"Fine. You're clearly not going to tell me." I looked down and fiddled restlessly with my gloves.

"Aryella." He enveloped both my fidgeting hands in one of his, stilling my anxiety with his certainty. "I promise you, Gemma and I arrived at a very agreeable mutual understanding where you are concerned."

"But you won't tell me what that understanding is."

He sighed. Still gripping both reins in one hand, he brushed a strand of hair from my face and shifted my hat down over my partially exposed ears.

"She knows... how I feel."

I gulped. "And how's that?"

He gave me nothing. But this time, I felt his chin brush against my cheekbone. My thighs clenched at the touch of his beard on my sensitive skin.

He pressed a sweet kiss to my temple, right below the edge of my hat.

A shuddering pant escaped my throat. I felt him tense and shift behind me, knowing he'd heard the unintended sound. Pulse quickening, I clamped my mouth shut and laid my head back, longing to rest in the comfortable crook where his neck met his shoulder.

But thick fur was in the way.

With his arms wrapped around me, I didn't need the wolf's pelt. I leaned forward and removed it from my shoulders, then set it on my lap, where it could warm my legs—our legs—instead. I shifted backward with every intention of getting as close to him as physically possible.

For warmth.

After a few minutes of my squirming, he locked one arm around my stomach like a steel cage. "I'm going to need you to stop moving, Aryella."

"Sorry," I muttered.

He chuckled softly into my hair, the sound lulling me into tranquility.

The entire time we rode, I thought of his confession to Gemma. That he refused to act on his confessed desire just made me want him even more. His care for me mattered more to him than satiating himself. Ironically, knowing that made me even more desperate to rush into his arms or his bed.

Not that I'd even have the slightest clue what to *do*, given the opportunity. I knew the basics. But beyond that, I was oblivious.

My irritated breath turned to fleeting mist as we moved. I hardly had time to discuss with Gemma what had happened between her and Finn. I'd filled my days with running, training, sparring, and reading, too tired to do anything but fall into bed most nights.

I was going into my marriage with Elias Winterton completely blind. I would be going into everything blind if it weren't for my training with Gavin and books from his library.

"What is it?" Gavin asked.

"Nothing."

"Ella," he warned. "Talk to me."

"Oh. It's not so fun, is it?" I snapped back. "When someone is keeping things from you."

He released a heavy sigh but didn't press.

The rolling hills and craggy peaks turned to staggering mountains, with blue lakes scattered among them. Some of the peaks were so huge, they touched the clouds. The air grew colder and the trees here were sparse.

The previous night, I hardly slept, so it surprised neither of us when I drifted off for most of the morning, lulled to sleep by the rhythmic trot of our black mare and the assurance of his strong body at my back.

My growling stomach woke me a few hours later. At first, I thought I was dreaming. Sometimes the way he soothed me felt too good to be real.

"Welcome back," he mumbled into my hair, his rich bass soothingly *real*. "You didn't last very long at all. I missed my conversation partner."

"Hmm." I suppressed a smile and leaned my head back against his chest. "Maybe you shouldn't be so comfortable."

A low, responding hum traveled from his throat to my core. I shivered, and his hand tightened on my ribs.

We sat this way for a while, until my stomach growled again and he felt it, or heard it, or both. He stopped and dismounted the mare with an agile leap.

"I packed us a little food." I reached into my bag for some jerky.

He stopped me, his hand covering mine. "Are you opposed to making a quick stop?"

"*Should* we make a stop?" The sound of his deep chuckle gave me goose bumps. "I didn't ask if we should. I asked if you were opposed to it."

I took a page out of his book and responded with a narrowed stare.

Unfazed, he asked, "Do you know how to swim?"

"It's winter."

"Dodging my questions again?"

He fished out the jerky for me and handed me a small bag of red berries that Damond had kept frozen from the previous summer, along with my canteen of water.

Before taking an eager bite of jerky, I answered, "I can't recall having ever gone swimming."

"Well, I know a place. A hot spring." Gavin pointed north.

"Is it dangerous?"

"Would I take you there if it were dangerous?" he countered, brow raised.

Just ahead, at the base of a mountain, I caught a glimpse of a small pool covered partially by a cave's opening. Steam hovered above the clear blue water, enticing us in from the bitter wind and gloomy skies.

"Have you ever been to the Winterton Caves?" I asked, dragging my eyes away from that beckoning pool.

"Haven't had a reason to." I watched him use a leather rope to tie the mare's halter to the one evergreen tree in the immediate vicinity. He relieved her of our bags, slinging them both over his shoulder in one effortless movement.

Feeling so at home with him while riding had given me some

reprieve from fretting over my friends, but now worry occupied my mind once more.

"I'm worried about them." I wrapped myself up in my wolf-pelt shawl now that my body was no longer protected by his. "About Caz."

"They'll be fine." He threaded his strong fingers with my free hand and began to move toward the hot spring. "Caz will survive."

"But his leg." My eyes burned, even as I followed, taking three steps for every one of his. "He's going to have a child. He won't be able to run and play—"

"That child will have a father—a present, *living* father—because *you* sent him back, *you* protected him before anything worse could happen."

We stopped in front of the hot spring. I folded my arms across my chest and assessed the cave opening framing the intimate pool, the expanse of rock so smooth, it looked to have been purposely built into the base of the mountain.

Swimming—something so relaxed—felt irresponsible and callous the day after my friend was nearly killed in a blast. When people were scared and suffering like that village near Tovick, where we'd buried that poor man. And that little girl…

"It feels wrong to let myself enjoy this." I fidgeted with the edge of my wolf's pelt. "When Caz is hurt, when people are scared and fighting and dying."

"What's the point of fighting, then, if not for good things?" Gavin dropped our bags to the ground beside the steaming springs. "If you're willing to sacrifice your happiness for the sake of thousands of people you don't know, then you deserve happiness most of all."

"But—"

"Just be here with me, Ella." He brushed my cheek with his

knuckle and removed my green wool cap with his other hand. "Allow yourself to *live*."

I closed my eyes, leaned into his touch, and heard the words he left unspoken.

While you still can.

"Here. Wear this while swimming." He placed a folded, clean black shirt in my arms. *His* shirt. "So your clothes don't get wet."

I let the black linen drape over my fingers and resisted the urge to hold it to my nose to see how strongly his scent lingered on the fabric.

When I looked up, he was removing his jacket, shirt, and boots. Mercifully, he kept his pants on as he stepped down into the water. Mercifully, because . . . well, I wasn't sure I could handle seeing any more of him without losing my breath.

Indeed, his bare broad shoulders, arms, and torso seemed even more brutally glorious at this distance. The tally marks inked across his upper body seemed infinite. His scars only made him appear more savage.

And I wanted to feel all of him beneath my fingers.

When I reached to lift my sweater over my head, he turned his back to give me privacy. Water droplets glistened on the scarred planes of his shoulders. His muscles *rippled* with each shift of his body as he waited for me to change.

I removed everything but my undergarments, then pulled his shirt over my head. His shirt covered me down to my knees.

Carefully, I lowered myself to the edge of the pool and dipped my feet into the water. Hot and refreshing, the water pooled up to my calves with a welcome caress. I leaned forward and slowly let my fingers drift beneath the surface.

The water rolled in small waves toward me. I looked up to Gavin watching me with a longing I had seen in him only a few times before. Once, when he had found me in that barn after killing the wolf. Again, when he told me about his wife.

I wanted to think of only the former moment, frightening as it was. The first time we met.

"I don't have a coin on me," Gavin began, drifting toward me. "But if I did . . . for your thoughts?"

I smiled down at my hands. "What were you thinking in the barn that night, when you saved me from that wolf?"

"Why?" My eyes darted to the rings on the leather cord around his neck. Now, that vial of dark liquid I recognized from when I'd woken to him sitting at my bedside our first morning in Tovick was on the same leather cord.

"Because I couldn't understand why you looked at me like . . ." My voice, along with my thoughts, drifted off, as I tried to relive that moment without the burden of near-death terror. "Like I was a ghost. And you said you *found* me."

He studied me, his expression giving nothing away. And waited, appearing to weigh his words very carefully.

"When I saw you," he said slowly, "I knew I was witnessing a miracle."

My heart fluttered, but I couldn't help laughing at the idea. "A few weeks ago, I was skin and bones, with hardly any knowledge of the world, no skills, and barely any motivation to leave my house."

Shadows crossed his face. "And I will never forgive them for leaving you that way." That angry tendon in his jaw pulsed. "In due time, they will pay for it."

I swallowed a shudder, forced it back down into my belly. Elowen, he could snap in half. But Simeon? An ancient sorcerer. He threatened him like it was nothing.

"Elowen," I muttered. "Don't—"

"I won't kill her, Ella. I know she means something to you."

I gulped. As if that were the only reason not to kill her.

"Can I ask you something else?" I watched him move closer to me. The water was not very deep. He was standing, and his head and shoulders were still well above the surface. Tips of his dark hair that had escaped from his leather strap clung to his wet shoulders.

He waded closer through the water. "Yes."

"What did Ezra say to you before they left Tovick?"

Gavin smirked. "He threatened to kill me if I hurt you." I gasped, to which he gave a responding chuckle. "I'm not worried."

"Why?" I demanded.

"Because if I hurt you, I'll beat him to it."

I frowned and watched the steaming crystal blue pool move in mesmerizing waves around my calves. Now that my legs had adjusted to the heat, the rest of me craved it.

"I don't like that thought," I mumbled.

My heartbeat thrummed in my ears when I felt his touch—calloused yet gentle—on my bare knees.

"Come here." His expression softened at my frown. "In the water. It's not deep."

I rested my hands on his thick forearms and let him pull me off my rocky ledge into the water. Instinctively, I wrapped my legs around his waist and my arms around his neck.

"This isn't swimming." His voice was low in his chest—breathless—as his hard, carved pectorals brushed against my breasts. My core pulsed with heat and need.

"I'm not worried. You're good enough for the both of us." I matched each of my fingers with five water droplets along his chest and collarbone. Our breaths swirled together. His eyes were on my mouth, those burning pools darkening.

"Swimming. That's why we're here." The strong grip on my waist tightened, and suspended desire crashed violently into the wall of my stomach. "Don't worry, I won't let you drown."

He lifted me off him and tossed me to the other side of the pool. I was holding my breath before I hit the water, and when I did, the waves surged around me in a glorious embrace of heat. Unexpected but igniting. I grinned beneath the water and swore I felt the power of Rainar, God of the Seas, reach through my skin to touch it.

When I came to the surface, I gasped for air and laughed.

"You have to teach me first. I can't swim!" But I was still smiling as I propelled my arms and legs down in circular motions against the water to stay afloat.

"Ella." He gestured at me as I treaded water, his smile warm and proud. "You *are* swimming."

He was right. The movements of my arms and legs kept my head above water.

They came to me naturally, just like riding our black horse. Some part of me already knew how to do things I couldn't remember learning. Things I learned before the accident, perhaps. Or was it the elusive power in my veins? A piece of each god that lived inside me, guiding me?

Maybe I'd never know, but at least I could do *this*. Floating on my back, I let the water lift me up so my hips were on the surface.

He cursed and sucked in a breath through gritted teeth. I glanced at him and saw he was reacting to the way his shirt's fabric stuck to the front of my body. The way the winter air above the surface pressed my nipples against the fabric…

He made no attempt to hide how he devoured me with his gaze.

I felt like a flame, white hot.

"What if Elias doesn't want me?" Like *he* wanted me.

The water rippled around me as he moved closer. Closer, even though moments before, he'd tossed me away from him like a sharpened blade he couldn't bear to touch.

"That's not going to happen," he replied, his rich timbre low and gravelly.

"How do you know that?"

He slid his hands beneath me in the water—one touching my neck, the other on my lower back—and drew me against his chest. "Because it's impossible not to want you."

I sighed. "What if he's not . . . nice?"

"If he's not *nice* . . ." He cocked his head in thought, darkness surging in his eyes. "I know more ways to kill a man than the days you've lived, and I won't bother making it look like an accident."

His words—so full of rage—were so at odds with how he looked at me, how he spoke to me. I lifted my fingers to his bearded jaw. He closed his eyes and leaned into my touch. When he exhaled, I drew his breath into my lungs.

"If you had one wish in this life," I began, "what would it be?"

Because as queen, I would find a way to grant it. I thought of his wife, even though I didn't want to. And I knew, if it was what he wanted, if it was even possible, I would use every resource to find her. Even if it hurt me to see him with someone else.

He leaned down and pressed his mouth to my temple. "Your freedom."

I let out a quiet chuckle. "No, that's for me. What do *you* want?"

"I just . . ." He cupped my face in his hand, searching my eyes until I couldn't breathe. "I just want you to know *me*...know who I am, Ella."

"I do." I rested my hand over his heart. "I know you."

His thick throat bobbed as he swallowed. A want-filled stare darted to my mouth. I feared his kiss almost as much as I wished for it. Because I knew it would enliven me and gut me all at once.

But more than I wanted his kiss, I dreaded the separation of our bodies. And I knew, if I leaned in any farther, he'd toss me to the other side of the pool again just to escape temptation. So, before he could force a safe distance between us, I wrapped my arms around his neck, my legs around his waist, and buried my face in his shoulder so he couldn't be tempted. So he had to hold me instead.

And he did.

My eyes and throat burned at the truth I was afraid to admit. I cried silently into his shoulder, realizing Warrich was no longer my home. Phillip, Elowen, and even Ollie, were not my home.

Those caves filled with my friends, my people, and my betrothed, were not my home.

He was home.

A home I could not keep.

Chapter Twenty-Three

He carried me out of the hot spring minutes later. When he separated my arms from around his neck and set me down beside my bag and dry clothing, his reluctance to meet my gaze hit me like a low blow.

"Why are you wearing that vial around your neck?" In an effort to distract myself from the sharp twinge of his averted eyes, I looked at the emerald liquid swirling with eerie life inside the confines of its small glass container. Until he turned his back to me and pulled the shirt he'd been wearing over his head. "I've seen it twice now. You've been wearing it with your rings since we left this morning."

"It's nothing." He tucked it beneath his collar.

"Secrets." I tsked. "You know, they might catch up with you one day."

He briefly winced but offered no response.

For hours, he said nothing. We rode in silence, and even though I wore my green wool cap, I felt cold.

Our black mare had incredible endurance, but even she had to stop and rest a few times. The steep and jagged edges of the Wymaran mountains were treacherous and took her longer to traverse. When she stopped, we ate the bread, jerky, cheese, and berries we packed.

We followed this pattern until dusk when, finally, we reached the outskirts of a tiny village consisting of a single tavern, an inn, and a few homes. From afar, it reminded me of how the small village outside of Tovick might have looked before the Insidions ransacked it. Wisps of smoke slithered out of the few chimney stacks, and though the dull, shadowy light of twilight had yet to disappear, candles cast a calm glow in many of the windows.

We dismounted our mare to search for a stable to shelter her from the cold. There was a thin cluster of evergreen trees around the village—more trees than we'd seen all day in the mountainous tundra. The map Finn gave me for my birthday was tucked away in my bag, but I had Nyrida's landscapes memorized enough to know the return of trees meant we were drawing closer to Brinnea and the sea.

I felt compelled to give our mare gentle strokes of thanks along her sleek black neck before retiring her for the evening. Her onyx eyes seemed to smile back at me.

When I turned to follow Gavin toward the village, I was stopped by something hard. His arm.

"Don't move."

Turning my head as little as possible, I followed his eyes and choked in a horrified breath. I saw the ugliest creature I had ever seen.

Just north of the village, at the edge of the tree line, stood an ebony beast with iridescent scales, razor-sharp teeth, and blades for claws on its four limbs. Twice the size of any bear or wolf.

"What is that?" I breathed, my fingers tightening on the sleeve of his black leather jacket. The beast had a head like a boar with two gaping holes for a nose and steam for breath. It had yet to see us, too busy feasting on a doe.

"One of Molochai's. I don't know what he calls them." He shifted, and I looked down upon hearing the faint swish of metal. With his free arm, he unsheathed a long, curved blade. A scimitar, I remembered one of my friends had called it. "I don't typically bother with introductions."

I shuddered. "I thought Molochai's creatures didn't come this far north."

With the arm that shielded me, he withdrew another weapon from inside his leather jacket—the one he usually wore, though I'd never given any thought to the things he stored beneath it. My stomach dropped when I saw the second weapon. The sheer brutality of it.

The hatchet blade was connected to a well-worn wooden handle. I had watched Phillip use something similar once to cut up our cow after she died. It was a meat cleaver. A butcher's knife.

"Looks like they do now." He tilted his head down toward me but kept his eyes on the beast. "Be quiet and stay out of sight. Let me handle this."

"Wait!" I hissed. "Gavin—"

But he broke into an agile sprint, propelled by sheer power. He ran right toward the monster with lethal quiet, making enough noise only to draw its attention—with a shrill, sharp whistle—after curving his path to draw it farther away from me.

Sinister eyes with a translucent third eyelid peered up from its prey. The creature let out a series of hair-raising, menacing clicks and lunged at Gavin. I had to cover my mouth to keep from screaming. My savage teacher snarled right back—a beast in his own right—and dodged the creature's claws once, twice, again.

I had seen him kill two people—the woman in the temple and the red-haired rapist. Both fights had been quick. But I could see from his menacing sneer and the vicious light in his eyes that, for him, sparring with this monstrous devil was *fun*.

Gavin moved with feline grace despite his large, imposing build. One swipe of his scimitar, and the beast was bleeding from its chest. Its bark of pain was sharp and dissonant, and scattered somehow—as if more than one soul cried out from within

The strike was not enough, however. Whatever armor lay beneath the scales on its chest and back looked too thick to penetrate deeply enough to kill.

Panic struck my core when I realized his blades might not be enough. The beast lunged again, layers of teeth gnashing—more unhinged now in its pain. Gavin played with the beast, exhausting it as its blood trickled out, slowly depleting its endurance. Three more swings of his scimitar, and it was bleeding more.

It got closer. Too close.

With one swipe of three razor-sharp claws, blood spattered off Gavin's chest, and he was thrust onto his back.

I barely registered his devious grin as he hit the ground, snarling through the pain like he fed off it. The rational part of me saw him grip his butcher's knife, saw how he was ready to wield it the moment the beast was off guard—thinking it had won. That rational part of me knew he'd planned it. I knew, because he'd taught me how to take a bearable blow, to bide my time in order to seal a kill shot. And three deep slices across the chest were evidently, to him, bearable.

But a spine-chilling scream erupted from my throat at the sight of his blood, as if I, too, had been carved by the beast.

All I could see was it raising its claws over him once more.

Not him. Never him.

A cry of defiance tore out of my throat, and I was back inside the strange space with the wheel where I had first discovered my power.

I landed squarely on the silver disc. The shock of impact wasn't as sharp as before, and I focused solely on my objective: obliterate the beast to save Gavin. Not healing, but destruction, which was easier. I could be more reckless, couldn't I? There were more powers to choose from. The wheel spun around me, and I held fast, reaching for something familiar until I felt something potent and powerful in the palm of my right hand. Something we had just shared, him and I.

Cerulean blue.

The same touch of the sea god's power I'd felt in that hot spring came rushing back. I thrust my arm forward as if Rainar himself was reaching through me. Water—whatever was left of it in my pores and the air around me—surged from my fingers at inhuman speeds. Liquid ropes that wrapped around the neck of that evil beast and squeezed.

The water's pull nearly brought me to my knees. I needed only to think it into being, and one infinite rope of water curled around the creature's jaw, into its mouth, and down its throat.

Its cries of pain were silenced. Its razor-sharp claws swiped through the air in a desperate attempt to grip the force constricting it. But it could not *grip* water.

It seemed only I could do that.

So *I* silenced that beast for the blood it had drawn from the man who held my heart.

Gavin made the final kill with one swipe of his butcher's knife across the creature's throat. It arched its back as if to howl, choking instead on water and blood.

The beast's body crumpled to the ground. Gavin dodged it as it fell.

Then, he looked up at me.

"Did I not tell you to stay out of it?" he panted through gritted teeth. But I saw how his mouth twitched as he fought a proud grin. As his trainee, I had disobeyed orders. But as his queen—and his partner in combat—I had won his admiration.

With a wince and a grunt, he was on his feet beside the dead creature. He hovered over the beast and cocked his head, assessing the damage. Shoving its scaly ribs with his boot, he chuckled. The water it drowned in was still pooled in its gaping maw.

"Brilliant," he muttered, smirking at me. "*You* are brilliant."

But I didn't want to hear the compliment. No, my eyes burned hot at the sight of the three deep gashes through his shirt. Blood. So much blood dripped through the slits of cloth. Not enough to kill or even debilitate but horrifying nonetheless.

"I have to admit . . . Rainar, God of the Seas." He bent down with a slight cringe to wipe the creature's guts off his scimitar onto the dirt. "Not what I expected out of you next."

My eyes narrowed, and I was too heated to ask which god's power he *had* expected. He saw me and stopped, following my gaze to his sliced-up torso.

"Ah, yes." He had the audacity to laugh at his own wound. My chest splintered when he began to walk toward me with a slight limp. I *hated* his pain. "I had a plan, you know. I was only letting it think it won."

Rage and disbelief twisted in my chest. His nonchalance was flippant and irresponsible. He frowned at the sight of my concern.

"It only smarts a little," he assured me.

"You could have died."

The corners of his mouth twitched again, but he repressed his smirk, sensing my anger. He wiped the blood off his hands on the front of his pants and nodded in the direction of the beast's corpse.

"Do you know how many of those ugly fuckers I've killed over the years?"

"I don't care," I uttered through angry tears. "You could have *died.*"

With a sigh, he closed the distance between us. "Don't cry for me, Aryella." He stroked my chin with one thumb and my cheek with the other. "I'm not worth your tears."

I grabbed his wrist. From the same depths that stowed Rainar's choking waves, I felt anger rise, equal in strength and measure. Felt it burn in my eyes. Prayed he saw it, too.

"Yes. You. Are!" I gritted out. Awe and surprise flashed through him. But Gavin showed no fear. "I may not get to decide what role I play in this world or who I marry, but I will decide who I *cry* for!"

After a moment of contemplation, he leaned down, brushed his lips against my temple, and—knowing precisely what would both irritate me and rouse me—muttered, "That's my girl."

Fuming, fists clenched, I growled, "You—"

"—need to eat and clean up," he finished for me, hoisting both our bags over his shoulders with a subtle grunt before turning to the mare. The horse had remained oddly unruffled during the violent encounter. "And I would imagine you're equally famished after that impressive display." He grabbed the mare's reins and moved toward the village. "Let's go."

I groaned, rushing after him. But even with his slight limp and wounded torso—he still moved faster than me.

The innkeeper was afraid of Gavin the moment he gruffly tossed a bag of coins on the counter and demanded a room with two beds. Shuddering, the poor man stared at his feet and confessed all rooms only had one. I had quickly become accustomed to others' fear, despite not feeling it myself. For better or worse, I'd never been afraid of my protector.

Of course, the blood that covered him wasn't helping.

We climbed a set of thin, rickety stairs lit by oil lanterns. Scenic paintings lined the walls of the hall, but it was too dark to admire any details.

I could see why no rooms with two beds were available. The room was so small, it could only fit one. But it was cozy and warm, lit by an oil lamp on a table beside the bed.

Gavin paid extra to request our meals be made fresh and delivered to our room. While he cleaned up in the small, attached bathroom, he insisted I eat. Beef roast, baked beans, sourdough bread, and milk—it was hot, delicious, and I devoured it all.

While I ate, I tried to fend off thoughts of him on the other side of the door. Tried not to wonder if he was naked in the bath just a few paces away. I struggled to imagine a full image of him bare beneath the bath water.

When he emerged from the bathroom, I was nibbling on my thumbnail with my knees tucked into my chest, empty supper plate beside me on the bed.

He wore dark pants and a clean white shirt. Unbuttoned, to allow his wounds to breathe. He was barefoot, and his dark hair was damp and loose.

Even with the open wounds on his skin, he was a sight I'd never tire of. Relaxed. Unbound. Content. And so *big*. His sculpted torso glistened beneath the moonlight streaming in from the window. I bit my lip. My breathing accelerated into quick, tiny pants when I saw the carved V of muscle above his belt and realized it led to—

A tiny whimper escaped my throat before I could stop it. Before I knew it was there. I inhaled sharply, horrified at myself.

He heard the sound leave my throat. He saw my chest shudder. He kept his focus on me, tension in those brown eyes, jaw clenched. I braced for a retort without knowing what to expect. But he gave no teasing or acknowledgment of my humiliating slip of desire.

I didn't look away, despite my embarrassment. After the fear of truly losing him, I decided to drink him in, memorize him—whatever he gave me—until I no longer could.

"The bath is all yours," he finally said, voice solid. Unaffected.

"You should eat," I rushed out, eyes widening at the heat between my thighs before reining myself in. I stood from the bed. "Your food is probably cold."

I moved toward the bathroom, but he gripped my wrist and held me still.

"I didn't thank you for helping me with that beast." His fingers twitched against my skin. "I should have."

I shrugged, my eyes lingering on the mesmerizing muscle beneath the tan skin of his scarred chest. The perfect amount of hair across his pecs, down his sternum to his navel, mixed with the ink all over him. He was savage. All *man*. I couldn't help it, the way he made me ache. Internal wildfire incinerated my senses before I could understand what I was feeling. "Like you said…you had a plan."

He tilted my chin up with his finger and met my gaze. "Thank you, Aryella."

I grinned at the memory of our first private conversation, and was reminded how I thanked him for saving me from that wolf, as well as his response.

"You don't have to thank me," I whispered. His smirk showed me that he remembered, too. "But"—I scowled at his chest wound—"do you want me to try to heal you? I don't know if I'll be able to, but I can try." Filled with guilt, I recalled my failure with Caz. "If not, I think you'll scar."

"Do the scars disgust you?" he asked, his deep voice pinched.

"No," I rushed out. I noticed that the scar over my heart was peeking out of the neck of my shirt, and I brushed my fingers across it. "Do *my* scars disgust you?"

"Nothing about you disgusts me."

My heart clenched. I smiled and brushed my fingers against his arm. "Well, I like your scars."

It was something I'd wanted him to know that first day in Warrich.

"If you like my scars..." I felt the responding graze of his fingers against my skin. "Then let it all scar."

My throat tightened. And I knew I wanted to—*had* to—feel him beneath my fingers, even if that was all I would ever have of him beyond our friendship.

"Can I see them?" I asked, rubbing the fabric of his shirt collar between my fingers. "Can I... touch them?"

His eyes were wary but heated. He nodded.

Slowly, I removed his shirt. Off his shoulders, down his arms, feeling his hot skin against my fingers. He was smooth in all the places that weren't scarred and rough, textured in the places that were. I gently ran my index finger along a pale pink line over his collarbone. And then I touched each scar, memorizing not just the way the skin rose and dipped, but how he reacted to me. With shivers. Of delight, I think. I took my time. Savored the way my body ignited, how desire pulsed through me.

One scar, wide and thick, rested at the center of his abdomen, below his open wounds. I let my touch linger there, and then rested my palm against his skin. He tensed and sucked in a breath. But when I made to pull away—afraid his skin was sensitive from his wound even there—he covered my hand with his, keeping me in place.

"You're incredible." My voice trembled in awe. He kept silent, but I felt his eyes on me.

I touched the tattoos next. Permanent, but smooth.

"How many are there?" I asked.

"Four hundred and two."

"Will you keep adding more?"

His voice turned grave when he answered, "Gods, I hope not."

I gave him a sad smile, refraining from pressing for his secret. His eyes grew haunted when he spoke of the marks, and I would not stab my finger into any more of his wounds.

I shifted my attention to a faded pink mark on his biceps. Too thick to be from a knife. A sword maybe, but more like he had been brushed by a flame.

"Is that a burn?" I asked.

"Yes." His lip twitched. "That one was... an accident."

I nodded and ran my finger along it. "From your blacksmithing days," I realized. "Which one hurt the most?"

I wholly expected him to say the scar on his face, over his eye and down his cheek. But he took my fingers and gently rested them on the open palm of his left hand.

"The one on your hand?" I looked to his right. "From when you cut it a few weeks ago?" I asked, surprised. He had put a gash in his right palm and acted like it was nothing.

"The one on *this* hand." He nudged me again with his left hand, seeing the confusion plain on my face. "But it was worth it."

The faded wound on his left hand looked like it still hurt. As if whatever evil put it there marked him far beneath his skin. His darkness, that unquenchable rage—maybe whatever had happened to cause this scar was the source.

I let my fingers sweep across his abdomen, around his side, until I stood behind him. My throat burned. I had seen these scars—how they formed cross-hatched patterns up and down his spine. But this close, I realized it looked like he had been whipped. I shuddered and blinked past my tears. And then, to comfort him for all the pain he'd endured, I kissed his back—the sensitive place between his shoulder blades where the scar tissue was thickest. When my lips touched his brutally textured skin, he released a deep, startled moan.

I felt a throbbing need between my legs as the deep sound of his pleasure rushed through me. That sound—low, coarse, and uncontrolled. I could memorize it. Savor it. Hear it forever. And instead of pushing me away, he pulled me around and held my head against his chest.

"Ella," he breathed, pressing a kiss to my hair. "My Ella." His name for me was a plea and a warning mixed together in one zealous breath. I pressed my lips to his chest and looked up at him.

"Earlier," I whispered, "you said you wanted me to know you, and I do. I see you." With gentle fingers I traced the corners of his mouth and brushed over his lips. "This world has taken its toll on you, but I see your heart, and it is *good*."

Though I could hardly see him in the dark, the dim light of the single oil lantern glimmered fleetingly across the sorrow marking his handsome face.

"You know yourself," I continued, "and sometimes I envy you for that." My voice faltered in a subconscious attempt to shy away from the words I probably shouldn't say. Words that would put my heart right on his chopping block. "I love the friends and family I know, but I've felt detached—just . . . *not right*—for so long. Truthfully, I've hated myself for it." I stroked his bearded chin. "But now there's you, and I *feel you* in ways I didn't know I could."

He cupped my face in his hand and tucked a strand of hair behind my ear. I lifted myself up on my toes and pressed my lips to his cheek. His beard was both soft and rough beneath my lips.

"So thank you," I whispered against his cheek, smiling, "for everything you've done, everything you're doing." A hot rush of air escaped his lips and caressed my skin, my neck. I wanted to memorize that feeling of his breath on me. His hands. His eyes. A few torturously long moments later, his gaze landed on my lips.

A million battles raged through him in a matter of seconds. I tried to read the unspoken words in his eyes, but I couldn't keep up.

So I made my own decision.

I kissed him. It was a delicate kiss: the gentlest touch of my mouth to his, and only for a brief moment. I had no idea how to kiss. But I shivered with delight at the unexpected velvet softness of his lips framed by the igniting friction of his beard.

I memorized how he felt and savored the heat of his sweet breath as his unsteady exhale swirled in the air between our mouths.

But he didn't kiss me back.

When I drew back and opened my eyes, I found that his were closed. His throat bobbed as he swallowed. Each rise and fall of his chest pulsed through my body as if his breath controlled my heartbeat.

He took my face in his hands, touched his lips to my forehead, and whispered, "Good night, Aryella."

He turned away and left me standing there. Feeling like I had been kicked in the gut.

"Why?" I demanded, my voice low and shaky. The door opened, but he paused with his hand on the knob.

He slammed and locked the door behind him, not before I heard him rasp, "Because I won't be able to stop."

Chapter Twenty-Four

In my dreams, he kissed me back. And then some.

In my dreams, his scarred hands were all over my body. *Inside* me. His mouth was heaven and hell. And when I woke up, I was panting and paralyzed, flat on my back. I shifted slightly, and my eyes widened at the ache between my thighs.

"Good morning."

I squealed and shot up in bed. I knew he had come back at some point in the night. In my drowsy state, I had heard a chair creak as he shifted in it.

This morning, he sat on a chair beside the bed, his ankle resting on his other knee, one hand curled beneath his chin. Narrowed eyes, watching me.

"How long have you been sitting there?" I asked, sweat prickling on the back of my neck. Playfulness glinted in his eyes.

"Did you know that you make noises in your sleep, Ella?"

"What..." I gulped. "What...what did I say?"

His lips curled into a devilish grin, but he gave me nothing.

I cursed under my breath and threw the covers off my legs. He rose from his chair when I stood. His powerful presence consumed me. We were close, the room was so small. Too close, too small for me to breathe steadily.

"Don't be embarrassed to moan in your dreams, Aryella." He leaned down to brush his lips against my ear. And then I *heard* the smile in that deep voice. "You do more than moan in mine." He pressed a chaste kiss to my temple and brushed past me, opening the door. "Get dressed for the day. We'll eat breakfast and be on our way."

Fire engulfed me, and frustration.

"You're cruel!" I barked, padding after him into the hallway. "You are *playing* with me, and it's cruel!"

He stopped. His fist curled and unfurled at his side.

Teasing. Taunting.

And I realized . . . I could play with him, too.

"Tell me, *teacher*. Is that what I should expect?" I crossed my arms over my chest. Blood simmered in my veins. "When I have *sex*, should I *moan* his name?"

He turned on me, jaw clenched, nostrils flaring, and I knew I'd set him off.

"Who, Ella?" Danger and envy threaded through his forbidding glare. He approached, towering over me with only inches between us. I had to fully bend my neck to match his gaze. "Tell me who the *fuck* you intend to let in your bed."

"I suppose if I'm going to marry Elias, I'll also be expected to—"

"From what I've heard," he hissed, bitterness lacing his tongue, "Elias Winterton is a smarmy little shit who sticks his cock inside anything that moves."

Dread made me shrink where I stood. I tried to tamp it down, but he saw it. Fury rippled through him at the sight of my fear.

"And if he touches you—"

"What does it matter if he touches me? He's meant to be my husband." My indignance burst through my timid walls, but it was short-lived. His possessive fire blazed through every last trace of my defiance, leaving me bare and needy.

"It matters, Ella," he uttered, low and lethal. "What you *want* matters."

"It doesn't seem to matter to you!" I snapped, my throat thick with tears, still hurt from his rejection last night.

How could I know what I wanted when I was so overwhelmed with him and the way he made me feel? Defeated and afraid, I turned away. But his strong fingers locked around my wrist, yanking me back. Flush against him.

"You want to know," he began slowly through gritted teeth, "what it should be like?"

My erratic breathing sputtered out in tiny bursts. His scent, his warmth, his safety, his blazing glare on my mouth, my neck. I couldn't form a coherent thought. "Y-yes."

Gavin captured my chin between his thumb and forefinger the way I always craved. Only this time, his large fingers spread around my jaw and throat. My eyes widened and exhilaration consumed me at the realization that I was completely at his mercy.

"It's very important to me," he purred, "that you remember everything I am about to say."

I swallowed and watched him tense at the flex of my throat beneath his fingers.

"Any man worthy of touching *you*," he growled, and my knees nearly gave out, "should make your toes curl. He should make you succumb to a need so voracious that you combust from the inside out. You should feel a euphoria powerful enough to make you forget where, what, and who the hell you are. You should *scream* as you come apart beneath hands that have no purpose but to pleasure and protect you." He lifted my chin. My pulse thudded in my exposed throat. My body begged for the air on the other side of my skin to cool my blood before it burned me. "You will be worshipped—mind, body, heart, and soul. You will accept nothing less. Do you understand?"

All the blood in my veins rushed downward to feed the pulsing need at my core.

"I—"

"Do. You. *Understand?*" he snarled, his fingers gently flexing on my throat. I gasped and nodded.

"What if that doesn't happen with Elias?" I breathed.

"Then he isn't fucking doing it right." He tore his hand from my throat, leaving it bereft of his touch.

"And *you* know how..." I gulped down the urge to offer myself up to him and added breathily, "to do it right?"

His knuckles cracked at his side a few times. Each time, his fingers threatened to graze my hips.

"Aryella." He savored each syllable of my name. "I need you to go inside our room and deadbolt the door."

"I..." My brain had to remind my knees to straighten and keep me standing. Every part of me was weak and willing, though I tried to feign defiance. "I don't want to."

"You are playing a very dangerous game, Ella." His eyes darkened. "Do. It. Now." Clenched teeth. Ravenous eyes. The hunger there almost dragged me under. My stomach stuttered and dropped at the animalistic mass of man before me. I took a careful step back from him and almost tripped over myself. One more second of his craving gaze on me, and I knew I was pushing my luck. His lips curled into a menacing snarl. "*Run.*"

I gulped down a stroke of exhilarating fear and obeyed. I turned and ran like I was seconds away from my final breath at the hands of a starving beast.

Perhaps I *was* about to take my final breath of this life. Or at least life as I knew it.

The door slammed between us too quickly for me to see if he followed. Panting, I thrust down the deadbolt with the urgency of desperate, adrenaline-fueled prey.

Because at that moment, my guardian became a predator.

Gavin Smyth was on the other side of that door, where I knew he would stay to ward off any and all danger, including himself. He would not touch me, and he would destroy anyone who tried.

He was my greatest threat. He was my protector.

He was both in one body, one soul.

I had never been so torn. Confused. Needy.

And I'd never wanted anything more.

I sat in the bath for an hour with my knees tucked into my chest. Last night, I'd taken a bath after he denied me that kiss, but I decided to take another one—a lukewarm one that was now growing cold. If only to quell my frustration.

And to cool . . . the rest of me.

The tips of my silver-blond hair were wet down my back and

over my shoulders. I watched my fingers drift from one side of the cast iron tub to the other and, every few minutes, tried to summon the power of Rainar and move the water without touching it. Nothing happened. Just as the healing power of Viridian had disappeared after one use, there was no sign of Rainar this morning.

How was I supposed to fight Molochai when I could only summon the powers on impulse? When I could reach for my wheel of power but had no control over retrieving it? And when I'd only wielded the power of two gods when I was supposed to wield twelve?

I knew the answer, though it irked me to admit it. And I could only thank the gods and Simeon for giving me more time before being sent to those caves to figure it out. I'd tasted a sample of my powers, but mastering each one? Finding control? The ancient sorcerer himself would have to teach me.

I would be stuck until I worked with someone who knew magic. Wielding mystical power was the one thing Smyth did not know. It had to be Simeon. And Brinnea was only one day away.

I slid farther into the tub and sighed. Then I tried and failed to reach for blue on my wheel. Tried and failed to craft simple shapes out of water for another twenty minutes, until it chilled to an intolerable cold.

A half-hour later, I emerged from the bedroom wearing black pants and the oversized black sweater Gavin gave me in Tovick. Why I chose to wear it today, I didn't know. To taunt him, perhaps. Piss him off? Make him happy? See him smile?

All of those reasons, I think.

My thoughts and feelings regarding Gavin were no longer rational. Maybe I wore it just to get something out of him before he was gone.

He waited outside the room, eclipsing the doorway and crowding the hallway with his intimidating size.

"Have you calmed down?" I asked, infusing my tone with annoyance. "Or should I *run*?"

Saying nothing, he stepped back and motioned for me to pass through the dimly lit hall.

His finger brushed against the loose fabric on my arm as I passed.

"What?" I demanded, jerking away. "Do you want your sweater back?"

He looked down at me, brow furrowed. "No."

I glanced down to see his right hand bandaged again, even though the wound from his possessive tantrum in the woods mere weeks ago had already healed. Before I could ask, he reached to take my bag. I dodged him and hurried down the stairs.

I would carry my own damn bag.

I had been too concerned about Gavin last night to pay much attention to the inn. It was clean and humble, similar to Damond's place, only smaller. The innkeeper was nowhere to be found. I wondered if he'd heard us—*Gavin*—coming and hid. We requested sausages and eggs from the elderly cook in the tiny kitchen beside the foyer, and we ate together in silence.

To my left, across from the innkeeper's desk, I saw the mirror that had been fully intact the day before. Today, it was broken. Shattered, like it had been punched. I glanced back down at the blood staining the gauze around Gavin's knuckles. He'd clearly injured it again between the time he rejected my kiss and I woke up.

My gaze moved between him and the mirror. "Are you going to pay for that?"

His jaw pulsed. But he kept his eyes on me while he fished a small bag of coins out of his pocket and dropped it on the innkeeper's desk with a deliberate *thump*. I let his gaze follow me to the kitchen, where I dropped off my breakfast plate, thanked the cook, and walked out the door.

He was cold and distant the majority of the day, but so was I. What we had become—roaring flames one moment, steel and ice the next—was not sustainable. I didn't know much about friendships. Hadn't had many of them. But I knew that much.

After we mounted the horse, I kept my wolf pelt on as a barrier between his chest and my back. As we rode southwest through thickening foliage, I remained silent and focused on the world around me. Staggering white pines, leafless maples, and mountain ash. The terrain was much like western Wymara—rocky, treacherous, and breathtaking.

If we were only a day from Brinnea on horseback, then we were nearing the ocean.

I had never seen the ocean. Gemma had been to Nyrida's western shores off the coast of Avendrel, but not as far east as Brinnea. She told me of a southern beach town called Peradine, where, in the summer, the women only wore thin strips of colorful cloth and went everywhere barefoot. They were eager and willing to bed when men came to visit. Thus, it was a spot frequented by bachelors from the caves when not on duty.

I was too afraid to ask how often Elias visited there.

"Are you all right?" His deep voice, rich with concern, washed over me. Startling me, for we hadn't spoken in hours.

"Yes," I lied. "Why?"

"You just paled about three shades." He lifted his thumb and grazed my cheek with it. "Something's bothering you."

I huffed out a disbelieving laugh. "Disturbingly observant." When seconds passed with no reply, I added, "I don't want to talk about it."

The breath of his sigh warmed my neck.

"For the record," he said after a while, "I don't mean to be… *cruel* to you. It's true that I will not touch you. It's equally true that I can't stay away. And my entire existence, Ella, when near you, is nothing but a battle between the two."

I released a heavy breath and relaxed a little against him. Still vexed but unable to resist. The cadence of the mare's hooves on the solid dirt trail set a soothing rhythm as we rode.

My frustration faded quickly. It was an effort to stay angry at him when he felt so secure. When he crushed my loneliness.

I fidgeted with the edge of the wolf's fur and sighed. "Tell me more about you."

His lips brushed over the crown of my head, and my heart leaped. "What would you like to know?"

"Where did you grow up?"

I heard the smile in his voice when he answered. "I grew up in Brinnea."

"Brinnea is home for you?"

"It was once, long ago. I've lived in many places since then, but I can't say I've called any of them home."

The dirt path dipped steeply into a ravine. Although the mare handled it well, I felt my body slide forward on the saddle. With both reins in one hand, Gavin fastened his arm around me to keep me from sliding any farther.

"Which place is your favorite?" I asked.

"I grew up in the Trades District south of the old palace, but

I built a cottage on the far southern outskirts of Brinnea, on the beach off the Windcrest Sound. That cottage is my favorite place."

"The palace?" I asked. "What palace?"

Gavin's hand flexed against my stomach. "Brinnea is where the Whitlocks lived. Simeon, Christabel, her husband, and—" He stopped and cleared his throat. "And their castle was built along the sea cliffs, overlooking the city. But it's all ruins now."

After four hundred years, I imagined it was.

"Will we be close to the ruins tomorrow?" The final word grated in my throat. Tomorrow was too soon.

"Yes. I can show you if you'd like."

I squeezed his hand. "Yes, I would—"

The mare let out an agonized groan, stumbling and losing her balance beneath us. Instinctively, I grasped on to the horn of the saddle to keep myself from falling.

"Fuck," Gavin hissed and had us both off the mare before I could register what happened. My feet hit the ground, but he kept me close to him.

The black mare fell to her knees, then to her side. I cried out when I saw the arrow in her shoulder. I tried to run to her, but—

"Insidions." Gavin grabbed my arm and nodded to a group of at least ten people clustered in the trees to our right. They wore black fighting leathers with a bloodred sigil—a bull's head—on the front. Some wore black cloaks with hoods. Others went without cloaks but sported sinister face and neck tattoos. Skulls and bones and symbols I'd never seen before were inked into their skin.

One of them, I noticed, wore an empty bow and a quiver filled with arrows just like the one lodged in the shoulder of our mare.

They were close—too close for us to run and remain unnoticed.

And they were coming right toward us.

I gasped when Gavin restrained me with my back against him and his cold blade pressed carefully but firmly against my neck.

"What are you—?"

"Do you trust me?" he whispered in my ear.

My voice was lodged in my throat, so I nodded.

He shifted his mouth into my neck so that my hair was covering it. I realized it was so they couldn't see him giving me orders. Despite my fear, with his lips against my skin, it was an effort to focus.

"Act terrified," he commanded, his voice low, "and when I say the word 'hunt,' you run as fast as you can. East, toward the river. Start counting and you *do not stop running* until you get to three hundred. Then, I want you to hide. When I'm done with them, I will find you." His steel arm tightened around my stomach. "Do you understand?"

They moved toward us quickly—twenty steps or so away now.

"Okay," I breathed through clenched teeth, too afraid they'd notice if I nodded.

Their leader wore no hood or mask. He was a tall, bald man in middle age, with pale blue eyes like ice and thin red lips. The rest flanked him, but all had their eyes on me.

"Hello, Smyth," the icy-eyed Insidion purred.

Bile rose in my throat. The familiarity in his gaze when he looked at Gavin . . .

"Cherno," Gavin acknowledged, his voice cold—evil, almost. I felt his mouth curl into a sinister smile against my temple. "It's been a while."

Chapter Twenty-Five

A violent gust of wind crossed the path where we stood. The trees shuddered, and so did I.

"Always a pleasure," their leader answered casually. "I've been wondering where you might be." His pale blue eyes lingered on me as he tilted his head, eerily curious. "But it seems you've kept yourself busy." He chewed something and then gathered his saliva with a nasty swirl before spitting a glob of wet, tar black gunk onto the ground. He grinned at my scowl and took a few steps toward us.

"She is . . . *delicious*." Another Insidion sidled up next to Cherno. His face was tan and tattooed with skulls, his eyes unnaturally dark. He licked his lips. "You'll give us a taste before you kill her, won't you?"

I stiffened in Gavin's grasp, but he gave me a reassuring squeeze. Trust him. I needed to trust him, but—

Gavin chuckled darkly. "You know I don't like to share my toys."

I sucked in a breath. The evil was too convincing on his tongue.

Cherno opened a switchblade and twirled it between his fingers. The other Insidions laughed, all of them inching closer.

"And *I* haven't had her yet," Gavin snarled and dragged me a step back from them. "She's for me...or no one at all." His blade flexed against my neck but didn't break skin. "Try anything, and I'll slit her throat. She'll be no fun to either of us cold."

Cherno's eerie orbs of ice scanned the length of my body. "I think she'd feel good at any temperature."

My eyes burned with tears that I did not need to fake. One fell off my cheek onto Gavin's hand beneath my jaw. And in response, I felt his rage ripple through his chest into my back.

"Mine," Gavin snarled. His rage turned possessive. "She is *mine*."

And *that*, I knew, was true. Cherno rolled his eyes. "Always a game with you, Smyth. So...irritable. You know, I've never actually *seen* you fuck a woman, despite your other unsavory habits."

"A man can't value his privacy?"

I whimpered unintentionally. Gavin subtly stroked my rib cage with his thumb in an attempt to console me.

Cherno sneered, head cocked. "How about you bend her over right here and let us all watch you make her bleed?"

Gavin gave a low, wicked laugh against my ear. And then, as if he wanted to steal the breath from my lungs, he pulled my earlobe between his teeth in the most unnervingly sensual way and purred, "Let's enjoy the *hunt* first, shall we?"

He threw me to the ground with convincing force. With a throaty grunt, I propelled myself up from the frigid earth and forward.

The sickening sounds of metal on metal and tearing flesh

erupted behind me. I counted but made it only to twenty before I looked back, just for a moment. I saw that no one was following me. He'd already killed three and not one made it past him.

There was a head on the ground among the bodies. Cherno's head.

I halted, knowing well he would scold me for it later. Still, I stopped, curiosity and terror winning me over. To my right stood an ancient oak tree. I lunged behind it, fully concealed by its wide trunk.

And I watched as he tore through the rest of them.

They were nothing to him. Nothing.

He killed fluidly. Different than he'd been with that scaled ebony beast. The beast had been massive, three times his size, and still he had *played* with it. These were just men, and no man was a match for him.

This time, he did not laugh as he fought. By the time he pulled his scimitar from the throat of one Insidion, his sharp cleaver was lodged into the skull of another. He knew where they were—every one of them—and he butchered them all.

I remembered Ezra's command at the temple. Advice that this time, I did not heed.

Don't watch. Trust me.

A fair warning. Gavin was pure death and rage and darkness, covered entirely in their blood. He wore it like armor. Like it restored him.

When the final body dropped, I stepped out from behind the tree. His eyes snapped to me immediately. At the sight of me, he thrust both blades into the ground and swore.

"I told you to *run*." He wiped blood from his face with the back of his hand and strode toward me. My body quivered with terror, but I refused to move. "You were not—" His pace slowed, brow furrowed with concern while searching my face. Assessing my fear. "You were not supposed to see that."

"I wasn't going to leave you."

"Leave me!" he gritted out. "Damn it, Ella, in a moment like that you *do* leave me. You leave me with a thousand blades at my throat. You save yourself, and you *do not* hesitate!"

I clenched my fists and shook my head.

He cursed and ran his hands over his face. I almost sprinted the rest of the way to him, almost threw my arms around his neck and held on. The chill I'd heard in his voice when he spoke to those Insidions held me back.

"How did you know them?" I waved toward the bodies strewn across the ground, though I tried not to look closer. I had seen enough.

He stepped toward me. I took a step back. With a pleading gaze, he admitted, "I've been known to play multiple sides."

"And which side are you *playing* now?" But I already knew. If I had doubted him, truly, I would already have run.

"Ella." He closed the distance between us, catching me with both arms.

"Molochai's side or Simeon's?" I demanded. "Because the things you said to them—"

"Wars are not won by men with clear and honorable intentions, Aryella. They are won by those of us willing to live in the dark." He took my left hand and placed it on his chest. "I am not on Molochai's side. I am not on Simeon's side. I am on *your* side. Only yours." Then he lifted my other hand, which held my knife, and positioned the tip of my blade over his heart. "If my loyalty to you ever falters, I want you to take this blade and drive it through my heart."

I lowered the blade. "What they said... about women..." A horrified sound slipped out of my throat. My heart knew, but I had to ask. "Please tell me you haven't—"

"The last woman I touched was..." His broad chest strained beneath the weight of his truth as pain rippled through his gaze.

"Your wife?" I whispered, saying it so he didn't have to.

"Yes," he answered softly.

But that gentleness vanished in an instant. He snarled as an arrow pierced his shoulder. Clenching his other hand around it immediately.

"Mother... *fucker*!" He sucked in a breath, held it, and removed the arrow. Blood spurted out of the deep hole it left as he shoved me behind him. One more Insidion stood a short distance away. I glanced at the hole in Gavin's shoulder and had never been so grateful for someone's terrible aim.

The remaining Insidion was larger than the others had been, rivaling Gavin in size. He tossed his bow to the ground and unsheathed a long, curved machete, but before he could raise it, Gavin hurled a powerful fist into his face. Then another, and another. The Insidion stumbled back from the force of each blow until he mustered the strength and power for one swing of his blade.

I screamed when the machete connected with Gavin's unwounded shoulder. It cut straight through his jacket and drew a river of blood. Instead of recoiling like a sane person, Gavin pressed his hand into the underside of the blade, resisting the pressure, and *smiled*.

I tried to summon my power. I imagined myself inside the temple, tried to reach for the wheel, but it . . . wasn't there.

But Gavin didn't need my help. He leaned into the blade. Panic rose in his adversary's eyes at my protector's sinister smile.

Then Gavin thrust the man's own arrow through his neck and tossed him to the side like a useless slab of spoiled meat.

He looked at me, and his soured indifference morphed into debilitating fear—fear I didn't know could exist in those beautiful brown eyes, now panicked and wide as he roared, "Behind you!"

He lunged for me, but for once, he wasn't quick enough.

It happened so fast, I had no time to decide.

A man attacked me before I could run or dodge or attempt a blow. His neck, at my eye level, was all I saw before I felt the hidden knife thrust out from beneath his cloak and puncture my flesh. I screamed. The sudden and acute twist of hot metal in my side became an excruciating catalyst.

I had to choose. My life or his.

Fueled by rage and pain and desperation, I screamed and plunged my own knife into my attacker's throat. Blood gushed over my hand, down my wrist, hot and wet. The scent of copper filled my nostrils.

Only then, after piercing his flesh, did I have a chance to see what he looked like. The Insidion, simply a *man* in his final moments, looked down at me, pleading. His dark, forest green eyes were what I would remember in my nightmares. Not the skull tattoos covering his face or the gruesome scar across his mouth. But his eyes. The fear in them. And how, as he took his final breath, that fear—along with any joy or peace or laughter he'd ever felt—disappeared.

The man fell to the ground.

He was dead.

A tattered wail left my throat, and I stumbled backward. The knife in my hand... *my hand*, covered in his blood. I watched *life* leave those green eyes.

"Ella." Gavin caught me from behind, one arm across my chest. I stared in horror at my crimson-stained hands. So strange that such small, familiar hands with violently trembling fingers could be the source of death. "It's all right. You're all right." His fingers inched toward the handle of my blade. "Give me the knife, sweetheart."

I obeyed, weeping through the sharp, burning pain in my side. When he'd taken the dagger, I dropped my hand to the wet, sticky spot of fabric at my waist.

My muscles screamed with each shift of my body, like a hot poker twisting inside me. I lifted my hands before my eyes. My breathing labored when I realized I couldn't tell the blood of the man I killed from my own.

Gavin turned me around in his arms and followed my bloody hands to the stab wound low near my hip. Within a second, his usually tan skin was white.

"No," he croaked. Hands that were steady while slaughtering over a dozen men now shook as he reached for the hem of my sweater. All of him in a panic. "No, no, no, no—"

"Gavin—"

"No!" he bellowed, lowering me to the ground, crumbling to his knees along with me. He yanked away the black fabric, his breathing distraught and uncontrolled. Every trace of that savage warrior I knew was gone. "Please, no, no, no—"

"Gavin, breathe!" I insisted, my voice stronger this time. The wound burned, but I pushed through the pain, caring little about it when I could see something inside him had just *snapped*. I had never imagined he was capable of feeling such debilitating shock.

The cutting pressure was awful to bear, but I was only a little woozy. I felt the blood seeping rather than gushing. The blade hadn't gone that deep. Tears blurred my vision, but I knew—

"I'm okay." I lifted my quaking hands to his face and forced him to meet my gaze. "I'm okay."

His wide, wild eyes studied the wound as he touched the skin around the puncture. As if he was trying to hold me together. Fix me. I had done the same when I accidentally stabbed him. When I thought *he* might die. I never wanted to feel that fear again.

And now I saw that same terror mirrored back at me, magnified a hundredfold.

"I'm okay," I whispered again, even as I cringed at the pain.

He huffed out a relieved breath, assessing the wound with clearer eyes. It would need to be treated quickly to avoid infection, but it was right above my hip where there were no vital organs or arteries. It hurt like hell, but it wouldn't kill me.

"Ella," he breathed.

"Yes."

"You're okay."

"Yes."

He gripped my face with his hands and pressed a kiss to my forehead. Neither of us cared that he was covered in blood.

"You're okay," he reminded me again, or himself, or both of us. One more stolen kiss to my forehead. He carefully laid me down and removed his jacket, folding it so the clean interior faced out and tucked it beneath my head. "Don't you move."

I obeyed, staring up at the gray sky of fading dusk, focusing only on my breathing. When he returned moments later, he knelt beside me with a roll of cloth bandages and his canteen. He gave me his hand to squeeze as the biting cold water cleansed the wound. I clenched my teeth but hardly made a sound. He stuck his hand beneath me so he could wrap the bandage around my waist.

I tried to lift a hand to his wounded biceps. "What about your arm?"

"Fuck my arm," he grumbled, grasping my hand, holding my knuckles to his lips, kissing them. My insides fluttered despite the flaming poker in my side.

"Is our horse okay?" I asked, distracting myself.

"No." He carefully wrapped another length of bandage around my torso. "The arrows were poisonous. I got mine out fast, but she's..." A quick glance toward where she lay, and he shook his head. "They got her twice. One in the shoulder, one in the neck." A few more wraps of the cloth bandage around my waist, and he was done.

"This will have to do for now." He lowered the hem of my sweater over the bandage to cover me back up. "I know of a cabin a few hours east of here on foot. No one will be there this time of year. It's not as far as I intended for us to make it tonight, but it's safe and remote. We can rest there."

I stood with his help and limped over to the black mare. Our bags were still attached to her saddle.

Her eyes were closed. Peaceful, as if she were sleeping. But her strong chest didn't rise and fall, and no misted breath blew past her nostrils into the cold air. Blood trickled from each of her wounds.

"Did she feel much pain?"

"From the initial arrow hits, yes." He kept a firm grip on my elbow while I knelt beside her. "But she fell asleep, and the poison stopped her heart. She went peacefully."

Cheeks wet with tears, I studied the long, powerful form of a creature that had been so wild and free. I would hold on to the sweet moments she had given me. And when I dreamed of freedom, I would think of her. It wasn't right for her to leave the world this way, not after what she had gifted me.

"What do you need?" he asked, seeing me search for my knapsack.

"My bag." The cold dirt crunched beneath his feet as he reached for it. "There's a blanket inside—violet and maroon." He reached over the mare's body, opened my bag, and withdrew the quilt.

"This is from your home in Warrich." He knelt down at my side and rested the quilt in my open arms.

"I don't know if that was ever my home." I unfolded the quilt and draped it over the mare's head and neck. "Is it stupid? It was—" I sucked in a tattered breath. "It was mine and Ollie's. I just want her to have it."

"No." He intertwined his gentle, calloused fingers in my disheveled hair and kissed the top of my head. "Not stupid, Ella."

I rested my hand on her side, shut out my tears, and prayed, "May you outrun all your burdens in the land of the gods."

For me, I added in silence, hoping that Soltum, God of Animals, would find a way to get those words to her, wherever she was. *Outrun them for the both of us.*

I turned to rise, using his thick, solid arm as support. "I don't know how far I can walk."

"We're not going to find out."

The ground slipped out from under me, and I found myself cradled in his arms.

Chapter Twenty-Six

I don't know how long he carried me. Hours, maybe. The burning pain above my hip had me struggling to stay conscious, and the crunching of gravel and dirt beneath his heavy boots lulled me to sleep.

By the time we arrived at the cabin, the air around me was pitch-black save for the bright stars and waxing moon in the night-time sky. He woke me with his deep, soothing voice.

"We're here." The entire cabin rattled from the brute force of his kick against the door. It slammed against the wall, and he carried me across the threshold.

"Was that necessary?" I winced at the pain my laughter caused.

"I have no free hands." The traces of a smirk illuminated his face, even in the dark.

"Whose house is this?" It was a clean, single room with a tiny kitchen, a double bed, a cast iron tub, a toilet, and a hand-pump faucet.

"Damond's family," he answered, setting me down on the bed. "No one will find us here."

"Damond is your cousin." He kept his hands on my ribs to ensure my balance as I settled and cringed at the resurging pain. "So *your* family, then?"

He grinned and knelt down before me. "He's a *distant* cousin."

Before I could object, he was unlacing my boots, then removing my wool socks. I glanced up to see a full-length mirror resting against the opposite wall of the cabin. Dusty, but clear enough that I could see our reflection. And his reflection was a sight to behold. Kneeling, head bowed as if in surrender.

"I didn't think I'd have you on your knees so many times in one day," I quietly teased. "Such a mighty warrior bowing before a feeble queen."

He stilled with his hands on the backs of my bare calves.

"You have no idea how easily you put me on my knees." He stroked the bare skin of my calves, up to the sensitive space behind my knees and back down. "You are a dream." He lifted his right hand to cup my cheek. Then he traced his finger from the curve of my jaw to my lips, parting them with his thumb. "There's not a chance I'll make it to heaven, but I pray the gods are gracious enough to send me to a place where I can see you. Just you." He wound his fingers in my hair. "Because if I can't spend eternity looking at you, I'd rather my soul cease to exist. You *are*," he breathed, "the single most breathtaking thing in this world."

My brow crinkled in confusion at how he could whisper such longings to me when I knew his heart still belonged to his wife. Yet I whispered past the ache in my chest, through the tightening of my throat, "All those sweet words, and you still won't kiss me?"

He shook his head, eyes filled with regret. "I told you why."

Yes. Because he wouldn't be able to stop. That wasn't a good enough reason for me. A very poor reason, actually. But if it was good enough for him, I had to respect his wishes. At least, I had to try.

So I lowered his hands from my face. I diverted my attention to the mirror behind him and regretted it. Before, I had been too focused on him to see how much blood covered my face, arms, hair, and neck. Blood from the man I'd killed.

Red. So much red.

"I need a bath." My voice dropped, low and cold. "To get it off." Even breaths transformed into frantic pants. I pointed at myself in the mirror. "I need a bath."

He glanced at the cast iron tub in the corner, then back at me. "You can't submerge your wound, not when it's so fresh."

"I—I don't care. I need to get him—the blood—off of me—"

He turned, stood, and strode over to the corner of the cabin to swipe a sponge off a small table beside the tub. Then, he dragged a bucket over to the bathtub faucet and filled it with water. "Undress." He opened the drawer of a small wardrobe and tossed me four clean towels. "Put two of these down, cover yourself with the others, then lie down."

"What?" I gulped.

"Take off your clothes, Ella, and lie down."

"What?" I choked. "What are you going to do?"

"I'm going to get his blood off of you." He reached for a bar of soap from a stool beside the tub and tossed it into the bucket. "Tell me when you're covered."

"I . . . I can do it myself if it's too much—"

"You are injured, and I will help you."

He started a fire in the hearth behind the tub. As soon as the flames roared, delectable warmth filled the cabin. I stared at the towels in my hand and sighed. This was probably going to hurt in more ways than one.

When I lifted my arms to remove the black sweater, pain rippled up and down my sides, then throbbed in waves. I cursed under my breath.

"Are you all right?" Still with his back to me, he removed his jacket, rolled the sleeves of his black shirt up to his elbows, and reached up to rub the back of his neck.

"Yes," I hissed through the pain and peeled the sweater the rest of the way over my head. "Yes, it just . . . hurts."

Somehow—slowly and carefully—I managed to strip off my pants and undergarments without falling to the ground. While I undressed, he took the sponge and washed his own face, arms, hands, so all traces of blood on him were gone.

The towels were ivory colored and smelled clean. Odd for a cabin this far out in the woods, but given Damond's fine taste, I wasn't too surprised.

"I'm covered."

He turned but kept his eyes trained down as he dragged the bucket, now full of water, to the bed's edge and knelt before me.

I shifted where I sat, causing the towel to shift down my left breast, not far enough to expose anything. "Do *not* drop that towel." His voice was clipped, his jaw clenched. "To . . ." He cleared his throat. "To keep the wound dry."

Yes, to keep the wound dry. My core tightened, well aware I was completely naked beneath this towel. He motioned for me to lie down.

"Wait." Warmth flooded my cheeks like rivers of shame. Letting him see me in only his shirt while swimming was one thing. I had been covered. And sitting here beneath towels, I was still fully shielded besides my shoulders and knees. But lying down would expose almost everything else. The rest of me... I was afraid to disappoint him. "I don't know what I look like to a man naked."

Danger and darkness spiraled in his stare.

"You said you trust me, Ella?" he asked calmly.

I nodded.

"Then I need you to trust me when I say your *last* fear in this life, or any life, mortal or eternal, should be that I won't like what you look like naked."

I stared at him—eyes wide, cheeks hot. Fire licked my core. I forced a trembling breath.

"Understood?" His deep voice was strained.

I nodded and forced a swallow through my dry mouth.

"Good." He motioned toward the bed. "Now lie down for me."

With an unsteady sigh, I lowered myself onto the bed, highly aware of every surface of my exposed skin. He watched me at first, but when the towels began to slip, he became very interested in his own boots. I readjusted the towels to cover my waist and breasts.

"Gavin?" I asked.

"Yes?"

"If you won't kiss me because you don't think you can stop," I rushed out, "I'm having a hard time understanding how this is going to be any easier for you."

"This is... practical." But his voice was still strained, and he stared at his feet while taking up space on the edge of the bed. "You need my help."

The desire that pulsed in my center and soaked me between my thighs felt anything but practical. I heard him dip the sponge into the water and held my breath, waiting for that first touch.

"It might be a little cold," he muttered.

"Probably for the best," I whispered. He chuckled in breathless surprise and touched the sponge to my forehead. I gasped and shuddered. Cold, indeed.

"Do you want to talk about what happened today?" he said, distracting us both from the weak pants passing through my lips. "With that Insidion." Our eyes met, and I knew the guilt and sorrow read plainly on my face when he added, "You were defending yourself."

I broke our gaze, closed my eyes, and focused on the cool touch of the sponge on my skin. He wet my hair, splayed out on the pillow beneath my head, and took his time washing out the blood.

"I know I had to do it," I said finally. "Or I might have died." He took a third dry towel and carefully brushed any remaining water off my forehead, nose, and cheeks. "But I'm afraid I'll see the light leave his eyes every time I close my own."

"For a while, you might." The sponge moved in careful strokes along my jaw and neck.

"But it gets easier?"

"I can't answer that for you." He rinsed the sponge and washed my left shoulder. "But it did for me. Though I suppose the first time I killed someone, I never regretted it to begin with."

"Who was it?" I looked at him and found no traces of warmth in his stare.

"Someone had been harmed and frightened. Someone I cared about very much." His wife, I presumed, but I was afraid to ask.

I didn't want any of our few remaining moments to be about her. Maybe that made me selfish. I wasn't sure I cared.

"You killed the person that did it?"

He languorously stroked the sponge from my shoulder down my left arm. I closed my eyes, lips parted, breathing shallowly, allowing myself to savor the touch.

"He should have been punished long before I got to him." He rinsed the sponge with one hand and softly dried my neck, collarbone, and left arm with the towel before repeating on the other side. "But he wasn't, so I took care of him myself." After what I saw today, I knew he hadn't hesitated. No remorse. Only death.

"When you were fighting that Insidion, it felt like you went… feral, almost. Like you went somewhere else."

He focused on my arm as he dabbed it dry. "I'm sorry I scared you."

"I'm not scared of you, I'm scared *for* you." I turned my head to look at him. "You're filled with so much anger. I'm afraid it will swallow you whole." He stilled, and I grabbed his hand. "I can't go to those caves until I know you'll be okay."

Scorn contorted his rugged features. "Aryella, you going to those caves is the last gods-damned thing I want to think about right now."

"I hate the thought of you alone," I pressed. "I need to know you'll be okay."

Shadows consumed him, his rage an entity with a mind of its own. It lashed out the moment I threatened it. Vying for dominance over me and anyone else who wanted to free him of it.

"Tell me how you got that scar, Ella." His voice was clipped. I followed his gaze to the old, faded white scar above my heart.

"I don't know," I stuttered, shifting the towel to cover up the blemish. "It happened when I was young. I asked, but Elowen never told me. Surely you don't remember some of your scars?"

His eyes brimmed with yearning. "I remember everything."

I searched for something to quell his rage, to relieve him of the tension in his body and heart. Tension that was ripping him apart. "That sounds like a lot of work."

He stilled. I held my breath.

Relief washed over me when he dropped his head between his shoulders and laughed. "Gods, I lo—"

He bit back the words, consumed by shock. My heart plummeted to the bottom of my chest, and a lump swelled in my throat.

But he stopped, which meant what he was going to say wasn't important or true enough to finish.

That was good, I told myself. Because he couldn't. *We* couldn't.

Gavin cleared his throat. "I'm going to check on your wound."

I nodded, afraid to trust my voice.

The ceiling of the cabin was bare and dull, but I furrowed my brow and stared at that ceiling like it was the most interesting thing I'd ever seen. Memorized those faded wooden grains. Anything to keep him from seeing the tears that threatened because of unspoken words and a reality we couldn't have.

And yet, as he tended to me, I felt the sadness subside and my body respond. As if my instinct knew him in a way my mind didn't, and no matter how hard I tried, I couldn't remain distraught in his presence. Only safe and free. My body reacted to his gentle hands on my stomach. A gentleness I felt he reserved for only me.

If he had lowered his hand past my navel, he would have felt the heat that gathered there. The sensitive, aching wetness that had me fighting to arch into his touch, despite my pain. One touch of his fingers was all I wanted.

My breaths quickened as my imagination ran wild. My hips squirmed with a mind of their own. Begging for him. And his palm rested on my stomach, steadying me. I felt him lean toward me, his hot breath on my skin. I couldn't think clearly. I opened my mouth to beg him to touch me between my legs just once, but—

He stilled. One of his fingers touched the curved smile of a scar between my navel and the place I ached for him.

The tension in the air snapped like a dry bone.

In one swift movement, he covered my body in the white bedsheet.

"What's wrong?" I gasped. "Is something wrong with me?"

"No." He squeezed my hand and tucked a piece of hair behind my ear. "You're perfect."

He avoided my questioning stare as he helped me sit up. "Elowen told me about that scar below my stomach from when I was little," I spit out nervously. "I had a growth of some kind. A physician removed it."

"A growth." The words sliced out of him.

I nodded. "I don't remember it. I was two, maybe three."

He rubbed the back of his neck as he stood. He turned to study the roaring flames, lost in thought, before instructing me to get dressed for bed. I slipped into clean undergarments and my white nightgown. When he heard me crawl back into the bed, he turned and went to the chair in the corner of the room.

The bed felt so cold.

"Gavin?"

He stopped and looked at me.

"Will you lie in bed with me?" I asked.

His eyebrows rose. "Aryella, that's a terrible id—"

"Please," I rushed out. "I won't tempt you. I promise. It's just... you make me feel safe and warm and... *please*."

He ran his hands over his face and through his hair with a tortured groan.

"Please," I said again.

"*Fuck*." He bent over to unlace his boots. My exhale carried the tension away, and I grinned even as he uttered profanities under his breath. But when he looked at me, his eyes were soft and yearning.

The bed groaned beneath his weight. He reclined next to me, hands behind his head. Too far away. He watched my every move like he was afraid I would spontaneously combust. With the way my skin burned, I thought I might. Careful not to irritate my wound, I slid deeper beneath the covers, facing him.

His body radiated heat so soothing that tension in my muscles dissipated when my body settled against his. I felt exhilaratingly aware. Free and elated. My cheek rested on his chest, altogether hard and soft, and I slid my hand over his broad, muscled torso, crumpling a piece of his shirt in my fingers. The urge to slide my hand under his shirt was almost overwhelming.

But I'd promised not to tempt him.

"Is this okay?" I whispered. The flames beneath the hearth were bright enough only to illuminate the tightness in his handsome features.

He gave me a single, sharp nod and lowered one arm. Like a collector would treat a treasure, he wrapped it around me and pulled me into his side. His fingers curled over my ribs, where he circled his thumb in gentle strokes but didn't dare travel up or down into more dangerous territory. Even if I wished he would.

I closed my eyes and surrendered to exhaustion in his arms.

It was the sweetest sleep of my life.

At one point in the night, I woke up to him spooning me. His arm was tight around me and our legs were intertwined. I gasped and stilled when I felt him gloriously hard against my backside. Through our clothes. Just from lying in bed with me. I didn't know much about a man's desire, but I knew what that meant. I swallowed and, even while drowsy, arousal rushed through me.

But when I tried to turn to face him, he locked me in position. "Be *good*," he grumbled into my hair, "and go back to sleep."

I forced a heavy sigh and obeyed.

When I woke the next morning, he was gone.

Chapter Twenty-Seven

I stared at his note for an hour. Paced back and forth in front of it. Thought about ripping it up and throwing it into the fire.

Gemma once told me about a man who'd left without a goodbye after a passionate night together. It was a shitty thing to do, she'd said, and should it ever happen to me, I'd be smart never to speak to the man again.

Nothing had happened between Gavin and me last night, not really. No passion, at least nothing pursued. We hadn't even kissed. We'd shared a bed. He'd kept me warm and gave me the best sleep of my life, nothing more.

And, of course, there was his... well, I think he liked lying with me.

Still, I stared at the note and felt anger and sadness grip me by the throat.

> I have some business to attend to. I will be back soon. I promise. I've left you food and water. Eat. Change your bandage around midday. You are safe here, but do not leave this cabin under any circumstances. Please.

I rolled my eyes after reading it for the twenty-fourth time, aware the final word had been nothing more than an afterthought.

The man gave commands, not pleas.

I trusted his word, that he'd be back, but that didn't stop anxiety from planting its sour roots in my belly.

My stomach's demanding growl dragged my attention away from the note. Indeed, he'd left me plenty of food. Bread, jerky, hard cheese wrapped in wax, canned pears, and a jar of walnuts. The water from the faucet next to the bathtub was clean, the fire was strong and comfortable. I even noticed a few books resting on the chair beside the wall—the chair he'd planned to spend the night in before I coaxed him into bed with me.

He'd left me with more than enough to sustain me for a day. The thought of him being gone longer than that filled me with dread.

I stared into the fire and frowned. We were caught in yet another delay, one Gavin didn't seem concerned about. Simeon was waiting in Brinnea, and although I was in no rush to say goodbye, I couldn't deny the nagging hope that I would not disappoint the father I had yet to meet. I wished I didn't care about pleasing Simeon. Or Elowen or Elias and his grandparents. I daydreamed over a breakfast of bread and fruit. Wondered what it would be like to live without trying to please anyone at all.

I vowed to keep these dreams close. These secrets of my heart were all I could *let* myself keep.

After I ate, I spent the morning reading the books he left me. The first was a short love story that made me blush and cry at the same time. The second an anthology of stories about multiple fictional female warriors who rebelled against expectations, defied odds stacked against them, and lived the rest of their lives however they wanted.

I smiled when I saw it marked for me in multiple places.

How subtle of him.

When I finished reading, the sun was near its zenith and my stomach growled. I decided to eat before changing my bandage so that the sight of bloody flesh didn't steal my appetite.

Today, the wound ached more than it stabbed, but that didn't stop me from flinching with each pass of the bandage as I unwound it. After washing the dried blood away, I could see into my own gaping flesh. But the fluid oozing from the wound was clear, not discolored. It was no longer bleeding, and though the flesh was swollen and tender, it seemed to be healing.

My bandage wasn't as neatly wrapped as Gavin's had been, but my wound was covered. If he didn't find it satisfactory upon returning, he could fix it himself.

After my bath, I grew restless. The longer he was away, the less likely it felt he'd come back. I studied the map of Nyrida from Finn and scoured it for ideas. Where Gavin might have gone, which route he might have taken, how long it would be before he returned.

I looked to the west, and my thoughts drifted to my friends. I *prayed* they were safe and wondered if they had arrived at the Winterton Caves by now. When I thought of Caz and Marin reuniting, joy soothed my nerves. Even if he lost the leg, he was alive. My eyes dampened with tears and guilt prickled my chest.

"Alive," I whispered to myself over and over again, until it was all I could hear.

The final book I found was a collection of accounts about

Queen Christabel's life, told by those who had the privilege of meeting her during her thirty-nine years.

My eyes blurred with tears while reading the very first account, from a middle-aged single mother who'd been unable to pay her tithe owing to an unfortunate yield of crops. Simeon, who she described as fair but not cruel, insisted the tithe would need to be paid. Christabel promised to pay the woman's tithe herself. Simeon had told her it was irresponsible. That others would expect the same. Christabel did it anyway. The queen's unbounded generosity, the woman called it.

" 'Life and sun and stars live in her smile,' " I read aloud with a smirk of my own. " 'She shares the same silver hair as her brother, they look quite alike…' " My smile grew. "Silver hair."

For the first time, I was unashamed of my silver-blond tresses. And I knew where they came from.

" 'The queen's brother may wield the magic that saved us from tyrants,' " I continued, " 'but it's her kindness that sustains us.' "

I felt a gentle tug in my chest as I read and reread the woman's words about the beautiful queen who came before me. I would never measure up to such resilience, but that was okay. Christabel gave me something to strive for.

Based on the date of this first entry, the tithing took place a few years before Christabel's death, which meant her generosity persevered after unimaginable pain. After Molochai succumbed to evil and blamed her for choosing the man she loved over him. After cursing her with a slow, excruciating illness. After murdering her infant child.

After realizing that generation after generation would suffer because of *her* choice.

The price she'd paid for the man she loved…

I shut the book with a sharp snap, unable to read on. And then I closed my eyes, lying in bed and trying to think of absolutely nothing.

A frigid chill had settled inside the cabin when I woke alone to the fire burning out beneath the hearth. The sun had set, and there was still no sign of him. Rising from bed, I grunted at the tears burning in my eyes, furious at how weak they made me feel. My emotions felt like burdens to my duty and purpose. I'd once yearned for feeling, but now I wondered if it would be easier to feel nothing at all.

My wound stung and pinched as I tossed the few remaining pieces of firewood one at a time into the hearth. More bread, canned pears, and jerky were enough to satisfy me for supper. There was plenty left for tomorrow and the next day, which I hated. With his tendency to lose his wits when I ate too little, a large stash of food likely meant he would not return for another few days.

I sat on the edge of the bed and looked around at the cabin—brighter now that the fire had returned to its impressive blaze. A small cabinet in the corner of the room caught my eye. Only tall enough to meet my knees. Plain, dark pine with two doors, which I laughed upon opening. After living with Phillip, I should have known a liquor cabinet when I saw one. On the top shelf were a dozen or so bottles of beer, and on the bottom, a few large glass containers of liquor. One in particular caught my eye—a half-full bottle with only *Damond* scribbled on it.

"Hmm." The sound of the cork popping bounced off the walls of the cabin. I took a whiff—it was odorless and colorless. Whatever was in this bottle couldn't be so bad if it smelled like nothing.

"Thank you, Damond," I muttered to no one but myself, uncorked the bottle, toasted the air—as I had seen my friends do—and took a swig.

To my credit, I forced it down. Even though it tasted like pepper lit on fire. The sweet cinnamon whiskey Damond had given me in Tovick was a far cry from this offense to the senses.

I decided to stick to beer.

When I finished my second, the pleasurable burn in my veins began to dull the pain of my wound and lessen the burden of my anxious thoughts. I changed into my nightgown early, preparing to stumble into bed when ready, and hummed the music I'd danced to with Gemma a few weeks ago in The Black Badger. Twirling around the cabin until sweat prickled the back of my neck, I let myself feel as light and free as possible. I bound my long silver hair into a bun atop my head, to let my skin on my neck cool.

Three beers, then four. For an hour, maybe two, I continued to dance and swirl around the small space.

Until I slammed into a solid wall of heat, cedar, and leather.

I hadn't even heard the door open. I craned my neck up.

He did not look happy.

"Ah." I sighed, taking an unsteady step backward. Irritation and relief washed over me in equal measure at the sight of him. I waved my hand to the empty room around me. "Look who decided to join my little *soiree*."

"What are you doing?" His words were sharp and cold.

I shrugged, swaying where I stood.

His nostrils flared. "Are you drunk?"

I put my free hand on my hip. "Maybe."

Pinching the bridge of his nose, he released a sigh, which

aroused my guilt. But I had nothing to feel guilty about, so I forced my shoulders to straighten.

"Did you know that alcohol impairs healing, Aryella?" He quickly and silently counted the few empty bottles scattered around. "How much have you had?"

I arched an eyebrow. "What does it matter to you?"

"What does it matter to *me*?" he growled, fury roiling through his muscled form. His angry gaze landed on the uncorked bottle of odorless, hot pepper hell I'd left on top of the liquor cabinet. His eyes shot open, stunned. He cursed under his breath and reached for the bottle in my hand.

"No!" I growled and held my fifth beer—just opened—against my chest.

He chuckled humorlessly. "Well, aren't you an angry little lush?"

"Don't call me *little*!" I snapped. I wasn't sure what a lush was. "And I didn't say I was done!"

"Okay, Aryella." He narrowed his eyes and nodded calmly. Too calmly. He stepped forward until his body was flush against mine. Those tiny, panting breaths—always impossible to control in his presence—began to flutter past my open lips. My already unsteady knees shook, threatening to collapse when he gripped my chin between his thumb and index finger, lowering his lips dangerously close to mine…

A squeal escaped my mouth as the bottle slipped out of my hand.

I gasped and shoved against his chest. The bastard had only done it to distract me.

"You are *done*." The command snapped out of him, low and deep. He kept his eyes locked with mine as he chugged the rest of my beer. He set the empty bottle on the liquor cabinet and nodded toward the bed. "Sit down."

Fuming, I saw no choice but to obey.

"Eat." He handed me a few pieces of bread. "I'm surprised you haven't thrown up all over this cabin." I took a reluctant bite and watched as he filled my empty metal canteen with water from the faucet. "Drink this. When you're finished, I will refill it for you, and you will drink another."

My shoulders slumped. "I don't want to."

"Then you'll regret it in the morning."

I scowled. "Is that a threat?"

"No," he bit out. "It's a fact."

The exhaustion in his eyes was palpable. My heart hurt to see it, especially as I didn't know why he was so tired.

"You were gone all day."

"And I have returned." He stood over me, arms casually crossed, his handsomely scarred face cold and assessing as he watched me chew and swallow every piece of bread he gave me.

"Where did you go?" I asked, lifting the canteen of water to my lips.

"I had something to take care of."

I scowled, set the canteen down on the side table, and crossed my arms over my chest. "I'm not eating or drinking any more until you tell me where you were."

Groaning, he ran his hands over his face. "Do you think I *enjoyed* being away from you, Ella? Do you think I *enjoyed* the panic I felt every moment, not knowing how you were doing?" he snapped. "It was hell. Being away from you is absolute hell, but I had to do it."

"And do *you* think *I* was enjoying *myself*?" I shoved at his chest again, only because I knew my strength was nothing to him. "Don't you think I was worried about *you*? Wondering if *you* had been hurt or killed?"

With a tired sigh, he reached to pull me close. "Ella, you don't need to worry about me."

"But I do!" I slapped his hand away. "You once asked me if it'd ever occurred to me that I might mean more to someone than a prophecy! Well, did it ever occur to you that *you* might mean more to *me*?" The world around me spun, tears bit at my eyes, but my voice was clear. "I had no idea where you were! If the roles were reversed, if I was gone and you didn't know where I was, what would you have done?"

Without hesitating, he answered, "I would have ripped apart the world until I found you."

"Yet *I* was stuck here waiting for you, just like when Elowen left!"

I regretted it as soon as I said it. Because it wasn't true. Gavin had left me warm and safe with plenty of food. He had left a note, promised to come back, and kept his word. Horrified awareness and regret cast a pall over him, his grim features illuminated by the roaring fire beneath the hearth. He opened his mouth to speak, but—

"Were you with a woman?" The words snapped out of me before I could think them through. I had no right to ask.

"*Ella.*" My name was his plea on his lips. "Gods, of *course* not!"

"Because I would understand—"

"I tracked down the Insidions' camp," he rushed out, his patience thin. "I was going to go last night, but you were hurt. So this morning, when I was confident you were all right, I tracked them down and went to that camp. I slit the throat of every single person in that camp to ensure there is no chance that news of you will get back to Molochai. *That* is what I was doing. So *no*, Aryella, there is no *woman*."

The cramping tightness in my stomach eased with relief I didn't think was mine to feel. But I felt it anyway. He rested both hands on my shoulders and rubbed gentle circles over the cloth of my nightgown.

"I didn't want to leave you. I didn't want to scare you. But I needed to cover our tracks."

"You should have taken me with you. I could have helped."

"You were *stabbed*, Ella," he bit out, fury shuddering through him. "I will not treat you like some helpless creature because you're far from one. But I also won't apologize for taking care of something myself if it might protect you."

I sighed, resigned. Indeed, I would have been no help. I wrapped my arms around his torso and breathed in the scent that had become my home. He pressed his lips to the top of my head.

"I'm sorry." His strong arms folded around me. "Forgive me."

My heart cracked wide open at his plea.

"I forgive you," I whispered into his chest. I had already forgiven him a few minutes after realizing he'd left. Inhaling him again, I registered that he felt and smelled clean. "Why don't you have any blood on you?"

He chuckled. "I bathed in a river on my way back to spare you the carnage."

"You bathed outside?" I looked up at him with sad eyes. "But it's so cold."

His gaze lingered on my mouth. "Cold baths are sometimes very necessary."

I sat down on the edge of the bed and pulled him with me. He followed, lowering himself to one knee—body tense and flush against my knees. I knew it wasn't fair or appropriate or smart...

But the alcohol gave me courage, and I felt inclined to take advantage.

"Ella," he warned as I guided his hands to my ribs.

I took my bottom lip between my teeth. His gaze—heated and hungry—darted to my mouth. I let my thighs open so there was nothing between us but the cloth of my nightgown and my underwear.

A deep, guttural sound formed in his throat, and I could tell by the tense air that passed through his lips that I was doing something right. Or... wrong. Tempting him to dangerous limits. My tongue wetted my bottom lip, and he followed the motion like he wanted to worship it. Worship *me*.

"Now who's being cruel?" he growled. This was the power I really wanted: the ability to bring *this* man to his knees with desire. No other man. Only him. I didn't care about manipulating fire or wind, communing with the earth's forces, or whatever else I was supposed to be able to do.

He removed his hands from my ribs, careful not to brush his thumbs against either breast. He cupped my face in his hands instead. I released a sigh, deciding as long as he was touching me, I was happy.

"Don't you think you deserve it?" I whispered. "Just a little?"

He hummed, the sound low in his chest. "Time to go to sleep, Ella."

But even as he said it, he wove his fingers through my hair. I let my face tilt up toward him, at his complete mercy. He could overpower me, kill me or kiss me, do whatever he wanted with me. But I was not afraid. He would protect me from everything and everyone, at all costs. Even from himself.

He shifted, and my eyes widened at the sudden realization that he was hard against my thigh. I sucked in a tattered breath and met his gaze—glassy and overcome with lust that he no longer tried to hide from me.

The lust he refused to act on.

"Yes." He hissed out a low chuckle when he realized I felt him. "By now, it should come as no surprise that I can't control my cock around you." His mouth curved into that devilish smile. "I know you felt me last night, Ella."

"Difficult not to," I breathed.

"Mmm." He hummed through clenched teeth. "I'd ask for forgiveness, but it would imply that it won't happen again, and that I don't enjoy lying to you." He caressed my chin between his thumb and forefinger. "But I *can* control myself."

He pressed a chaste kiss to my cheek and pulled away.

"Go to sleep." His gaze was stern as he covered me to my waist with blankets, but his voice was gentle. "*Now.*" I watched while he poured himself a few fingers of Damond's liquor and tossed back the whole glass.

"Will you come to bed?" My eyes and heart were hopeful when he looked at me and didn't immediately object. His hand flexed while he contemplated.

"No funny business," I muttered, fidgeting with the edge of the plain gray quilt in my lap. Funny business—something Gemma had once called *it*. But the words sounded silly on my lips. "I promise."

That handsome half-smile lit up his face. His broad shoulders relaxed, and a light chuckle rumbled in his chest. He unlaced his boots and motioned for me to make room. Happy to comply, I shifted farther beneath the covers. But instead of lying on his back, he positioned me to face away and slid into bed behind me.

Straight to spooning tonight, then. He would get no complaints from me.

His warm, soothing lips kissed the top of my head three times as he curled his body around mine. "Sweet dreams, Ella."

I sucked in a breath at the feeling of his arousal—massive, constrained by his pants—against my backside.

All night long, his desire for my body remained apparent. But all night long, he just held me.

Chapter Twenty-Eight

Relief washed over me when morning came and his warm body was still wrapped around me beneath the covers.

"Good morning." His deep timbre resonated delightfully against my back, followed by a long, quiet inhale.

"Are you smelling me?" I giggled, stomach fluttering.

"No." But I could feel him smiling into my hair.

I snorted. "What do I smell like?"

"Strawberries." His lack of hesitation plastered a stupid grin on my face. "And the sun."

I giggled again. "Well, what does the sun smell like?"

The warmth of his exhale covered my skin with goose bumps. "Everything that is *good*."

Tears welled in my tired eyes, and my heart pounded in my chest. I would lose this—all of this—so soon. I would marry my betrothed, perform my duties. Hopefully, I could learn to be fond of Elias. That would have to be good enough.

As Gavin and I lay together, the desperate silence between us spoke volumes. My chest ached, and though I didn't know much about love, I wondered if what I felt for him was something like it.

I needed one more day.

"We'll arrive in Brinnea today?" I quietly asked. After counting the days back, I realized what day today was. Winter Solstice.

"Yes. About a five-hour walk from here."

"Can we put off meeting Simeon until tomorrow?" I asked. "I know he might be expecting us, but Finn said there are grand celebrations in Brinnea, and I'd like to see them . . . with you."

A long pause ensued. "Yes. Whatever you want."

I let out a ragged sigh of relief and tucked his hand into my chest.

Minutes later, it was me who climbed out of bed and suggested we better start moving. I had a small headache from last night's overindulgence, but I was grateful. Without the bread and water he'd forced on me, it would have been much worse.

After I stood, his palm rested where my body had been. The flames in the hearth warmed the faded pine floors. I padded over to the sack that contained our food and unwrapped a bread roll. I filled a glass with water, sat down in the chair in the corner, and looked up to see him sitting on the edge of the bed, watching me. The longing in his eyes cut me like a knife.

My cheeks heated. "What?"

"Nothing." But his smile didn't reach his eyes. The floor creaked beneath his feet as he strode over to the liquor cabinet and poured himself some of Damond's potent liquor. His eyes were colder. Distant.

"Isn't it a little early to have a drink?"

He shrugged and took a sip.

"Do you ever get tired of it?" I asked, frowning. "The solitude?

The traveling? The fighting? And—" I followed the glass to his lips. "The way it makes you feel?"

"Yes."

I chewed and swallowed another bite of my roll. "What do you think about to keep yourself going?"

One more sip and he was done. "I think about finding you that day in Warrich." He set his glass down with a forceful thump. "I think about how the people who were supposed to love and protect you starved the life out of you so that they could rebuild you however they see fit. And it becomes very clear to me, again and again, why I'm still fighting."

"You didn't even mention Molochai."

"I don't need him to rile me up when your puppeteers do a fine job of that all on their own." The words cracked out of him like an angry whip.

"I'll be okay, you know." But he cringed at my words. "I'll—"

"Why didn't you try to heal yourself?" He gestured to my side. "With your power, you could have."

I leaned back in the chair and shrugged. "I didn't think about it. But even if I had…I think healing takes something out of me. Maybe that's why I couldn't help Caz after saving that boy." Another shrug. "I'd rather save my ability to heal someone who truly needs it."

Broad shoulders sank at my answer. His jaw pulsed as he considered my words. Three long strides and the space between us disappeared. He squatted in front of me, large hands on my knees.

"I want you to promise me something, Aryella."

"What?"

"I don't know exactly what this world—this *war*—will require of you, but I fear there will come a time when you feel the need to sacrifice yourself—in one way or another—to save others. I fear that your power will take too much from you, and that you'll let it." He cupped my face and a familiar heat pulsed through me. "Promise me you won't."

I thought of Caz and Marin and their baby. Of Gemma, Finn, Ezra, even Elowen.

Of *him*.

"I don't want to promise that."

"*Please.*" His appeal wrought deep tremors from his chest. With gentle urgency, he pressed his palms to my cheeks. "Gods be damned, Ella, do *not* sacrifice yourself for this world."

My lips quivered. I *was* afraid. But then I thought of Ollie and how I would still trade places with him if I could.

Despite the dread pooling in my belly, I knew my answer.

If I had to, I *would* give it all.

Begrudgingly, I lowered his hands from my face. "I will do what I have to do."

"I *know* you will." His fingers tightened around mine in my lap. "And I'm asking you—*begging* you—*not* to."

"And I'm saying no." Prying my hands from his strong grip, I stood and wiped my eyes. "I won't make that promise."

Soon, I wouldn't be his problem anymore. Soon, he would return to whatever it was he'd been doing before his agreement with Simeon. He would be relieved of this mess, though when the time came for battle, I believed he would join the fight. There was a chance I might see him again, but by then I would be married to Elias, and Gavin would be another soldier in my army rather than my teacher or my friend.

"Ella, sweetheart—"

"I don't want to talk about it anymore." And before he could contest, I added, "We should go if we want to get to Brinnea before the celebrations start."

When I started to lift my nightgown over my head to change for the day, he rushed out the door—as I knew he would—without a single look.

An hour into the final leg of our trip, my knees gave out. My wound pulled and ached with every stop up the steep, rocky hills. I couldn't do it. I tried and tried. And he let me try despite my struggling grunts, until one icy rock had me slipping, falling, panting. Had my hands gripping my wounded side while I bit back frustrated tears.

My tears were where he drew the line.

He shifted our bags to hang off his shoulder and carried me the rest of the way on his back, my extra weight no hindrance to his strong, agile movements. I almost fell asleep once or twice with my cheek pressed into his shoulder, but I refused to miss a single frozen waterfall.

They were everywhere. Long, perilous icicles, suspended in time—dropping off rocky cliffs into lakes of blue water so clear, they had to hold nature's sacred breath within them. Evergreens were scattered across the rough forests and reached up into winter's gloomy gray sky. Snow crunched beneath Gavin's feet as he walked, but the chill wasn't bitter. Just cold enough to freeze.

I memorized how it felt to have my arms wrapped around his muscular neck and shoulders. How his silky dark hair kissed my cheek. How his earthy, clean scent engulfed my senses. I hoarded these pieces of him, intending to draw upon them later. When he was gone.

I asked him to keep talking and telling me stories as he walked, but I didn't explain why.

To hear his deep, comforting voice. To try and memorize that, too.

Hours later, at the edge of the vast conifer-covered terrain, we saw the stunning ruins of a castle appearing to drop right off the edge of a cliff. And beyond the cliff, crystalline waters stirred beneath a soothing overcast sky.

The fresh salt and musk drifted across my nostrils. The crisp winter breeze stunned my lungs awake, and I sucked in a greedy breath.

When I released my gasp—unintentionally close to his neck—I noticed goose bumps prickle across his skin and I smiled. At least that went both ways.

"Is that . . . ?" It was so magnificent, I felt like my breath leaped out of me. "Is this where they lived?"

"Yes." He increased his pace. The closer we got to the ruins, the louder the squawks of seagulls grew.

Flourishing green moss crawled up the stone walls and back down the craggy cliffside. The place seemed tired, but not dead, for the foundation was strong and the rooms were still framed with resilient stone. I imagined a castle one day restored to its former self, rebuilt from the ashes of its original footprint.

He let me explore the ruins but followed closely. I stopped and turned, neck craned, when I came across a cylindrical structure lined with shelves, and on the ground, tattered remnants of what those shelves once held. If there had been treasures and jewels in the castle, thieves had taken those long ago. But they left a few of the books, destroyed and disintegrated as they were.

"Was this their library?"

He bent down and picked up a dusty, tattered brown leather book with the spine barely intact. "Yes." I grinned. "It's just like yours."

His answering smile heated my cheeks. "I modeled it after this one." He carefully flipped through the few remaining crusty and yellowed pages of another book—so worn that the writing was smudged and illegible. "When I was younger, these ruins were my favorite place to be alone and think." He gestured to the cylindrical walls, suspended in time, halfway crumbled. "This room, in particular, I'm fond of."

I could see why. If I had unlimited access to his library, it would be my favorite, too.

"The city is below." He waved a hand toward the edge, then took mine and led me there.

I could see the far reaches of the city as it poked out beyond the cliff's edge. These ruins overlooked the coastline and a sprawling settlement. A long, winding gravel path carved into the cliff led down to rows of stucco houses and shops. Buildings decorated with a variety of light, earthy tones lined cobblestone streets. A cheerful vision. As if beneath the shadow of the castle ruins, this place remained a timeless reminder of the unbroken world of the past.

I sighed at the sights and let the sea breeze wash over my face. Being here with him made me feel content. But when I looked over at him, his brown eyes rimmed silver with tears. A crack split through my chest. My smile vanished.

"What's wrong?" I asked him.

"I..." He cleared his throat, shook his head, and just like that, his sorrow was gone. "I just never thought I'd see the day. You." He gestured around us. "Here."

I beamed again at the ruins and the sprawling city below. "It's beautiful."

The sight *was* so ancient and breathtaking, and it felt like a part of me. Through my blood, I suppose it was. Despite the destruction and the scars from years of neglect, it was breathtaking.

"It's never been as beautiful as it is right now."

Featherlight flutters warred with ruthless fissures in my chest, because I could feel his eyes on me as he spoke.

If the gods' plan for me was to be their savior queen and marry Elias Winterton, why had they sent me Gavin Smyth? I didn't understand how they expected me not to fall in love with him.

I squeezed his hand. "Will you show me the rest of the city?"

He had given me plenty of rest by carrying me. The pain in my side was bearable enough to make it on foot along the path down the rocky prominence. But he held on to my hand like he was afraid to let go.

The greens and reds and golds of the Solstice looked even brighter in Brinnea. Fresh wreaths were on every door—evergreen mixed with pine cones and holly berries. Paper lanterns connected the roofs of each building, and dried orange slices dangled and swayed from fascias and porticos in tribute to the sun and as symbols of hope for its return.

Fresh oranges burst from baskets all around, too. One of which Gavin expertly peeled with a pocketknife and insisted I eat. I smelled the citrus as much as I tasted it.

We went into a few shops of my choice. My favorites were the candy shop, where he bought me some chocolate. I somehow knew what it was. I liked it but couldn't recall ever eating it. And a pottery studio, where the artist was hand-forming the pieces at a table for people to watch. I yearned to stay for hours.

The Solstice festivities commenced as dinnertime neared. He led me in the direction of the inn we would be staying on the northern edge of the city. A habit of his, I realized, to stay near the outskirts of a place to allow for a quick escape.

"Will you join me for dinner tonight?" His deep voice undercut the frantic and excited sounds of Brinneans engaged in last-minute preparations.

I frowned, and took a bite of my chocolate as we walked. "We always eat dinner together."

His forearm flexed as he rubbed the back of his neck. He cleared his throat and briefly—*very* briefly—winced. Was he... *nervous*?

"A special dinner, I mean."

"For Solstice?" I savored another bite of chocolate and tilted my head at him. It felt difficult to worry about much while eating chocolate.

"Yes." He chuckled warmly. "For Solstice."

I smiled back, my stomach fluttering. "I would like that."

A few minutes later, I paused outside a dress shop. A special dinner... for which I had nothing special to wear. Patiently, he stood by my side as I admired the dresses in the window. Pastel gowns of silk and satin, some covered with sashes of fur or silver and gold.

"May I please buy something?" I asked. Because even though I was queen, no one had bothered to give me any money but him.

He smirked, fished a heavy pouch of coins from the pocket of his leather coat, placed it in my palm, and closed my fingers around it. "Buy the whole shop if you like."

My constant sentry, he stood at the front of the store and kept an eye on every person who passed in and out of the shop, never letting me out of his sight. I perused the racks for something simple. Both because I was afraid I might look absurd in anything extravagant and because I didn't want to spend too much of his money.

There were several gowns I liked, but I needed to pick one. I bit my lip and groaned. If I couldn't even pick a damn dress, how was I supposed to make decisions for all of Nyrida?

Then I remembered that his favorite color was green.

After one glance at the silky, sea green dress, I knew that I didn't even need to try it on. I took it to the cashier along with a pair of silver heels and bought both.

Gavin took me to the inn and left me to get ready after starting a fire in the fireplace in our room. The floors were white oak, the walls painted a gentle gray, and the giant bay window—closed and curtained during winter—had a blue cushioned seat, which would be delightful to rest on during warmer months. I imagined myself reading there, windows ajar, bathing in sunlight as it sparkled off the sea.

The bathroom had a white tile floor and a shower. Gemma had told me about showers. Wealthy, advanced cities—including the caves and barracks where Elias trained his army—found elevated sources of water and then built pipes into the walls with pressure to allow for showers instead of baths. I savored the ability to cover my healing wound with a bandage to prevent it from getting too wet, as opposed to fully submerging in a bath. When I was finished, I slid into my dress and looked at my reflection in the wall's full-length mirror.

It didn't feel like too long since we'd left my old home. I couldn't believe it, because surely—compared to that pale, bony, lifeless creature who lived in Warrich—this was someone else. A stronger, fuller young woman. Despite the wound in my side, I was visibly healthier than even on our first night in Tovick.

I had gained a bit of weight thanks to Gavin's insistence that

I devour as much food as I could. But I'd needed it, and even a few pounds had made a difference. The natural curves I noticed in Tovick were accentuated. I never thought I was ugly, had never really cared much either way. But I smiled at what I saw. My green eyes were bright; my cheeks and lips were full of color. More… *alive*.

I really felt beautiful in this dress of sea green silk. My silver-blond hair—washed, dried, and brushed—draped over my shoulders in loose, natural waves. The dress had thin shoulder straps and hugged the curves of my waist. The sleek fabric hinted generously at the shape of my breasts. And beneath the silk on my chest, subtle hints of my peaks pointed in the chilly winter air against the dress's cowl neck when I moved. The look was elegant and daring, sensual yet regal.

Admiring myself in the mirror, I felt hopeful that he might give in to the desire between us. Tonight was my—*our*—last chance.

My pulse stuttered as I heard three firm knocks on the door.

"Come in," I called.

I turned when the door opened behind me. He'd donned black from head to toe. His beard was trimmed, and his clean, dark hair was tied partially back in a knot. If it weren't for those few wild features—escaped hair at his shoulders, the few scars decorating his neck and slashing over his right eye—he could have been a prince in his own right. A *king*, rather. Instead, he stood in the doorway looking like a tragic, fallen warrior. Staring at *me* like I was the last thing tethering him to this world. No trace of a smile on his handsome face.

"I thought…" Immediately, I questioned my choices. "This might be the first and last Winter Solstice I'll truly get to celebrate before…everything. And…dinner." I twirled once, blushed, and frowned when he still wasn't smiling.

Stupid. This was a stupid idea.

A muscle bobbed in his throat as he stared.

"Are you going to tell me not to wear it?" I laughed nervously.

"No," he answered, his voice hoarse.

"I found one that wasn't too expensive." I smoothed the fabric over my torso and hips. "When I get to the caves and have my own money, I can send some to pay you back."

He flinched. "I don't want your money."

"Then I'll find another way to make it up to you."

"You've made it up to me by letting me see you in it." He cleared his throat. "One glance in your direction, and every man in this city will be begging to fall on a sword for you." My mouth went dry as I watched him drink me in, his own lips parted. "You are exquisite, unbearably so. You are the most beautiful thing I have ever seen, Aryella, and you make it…difficult to *breathe*."

"That's not good." The words almost got stuck in my throat, the palpitations of my heart like flapping wings that dragged my voice and breath to the pit of my stomach. He made me just as breathless as I seemed to make him. "You should definitely breathe."

Looking down at his hands, he chuckled, and out of the pockets of his black jacket he pulled tiny, violet-blue flowers with bright yellow centers. Forget-me-nots. They were fastened into a delicate crown, green stems intertwined in continuous loops. He crossed the room and rested it on my head.

"There." He grinned down at me, looking satisfied. "A crown for my queen."

I smiled, felt the warmth in my cheeks, and—not caring that

I was blushing—leaned over to fasten the straps of the heels I'd purchased. When I moved, he inhaled sharply and took a step away from me.

My eyes darted to the reflection of us in the mirror. I realized I had bent down right in front of him, brushing my hip against his thigh. That he was tearing his gaze away from my body. From the curve of my hips and backside hugged by the silk fabric of my dress.

I stood, my stomach plummeting. "Gavin, I—"

"We should go," he said, averting his gaze, angling his body toward the door but offering me his hand. "We should go *now*, Ella."

"Wait." It was too cold to wear a dress like this on its own. But I had the shawl made of the wolf pelt, and I knew that would do. The night air here was frigid, but I wasn't afraid of the cold as much anymore. Not when I knew I'd be warm with him.

I reached back to where I laid the wolf's fur on the bed, tucked it over my arm, and we left the inn for dinner.

The white-brick tavern was right on the edge of the sea, accessed by a wooden walkway elevated just above the sandy shore. We were placed between a small evergreen hedge and the tavern. Our table was warmed by an outdoor bonfire. The flames roared at my back from a central firepit surrounded by a few more tables, each seated with two or more people.

Brinnea felt frozen in time, as if Molochai could never touch this place. As if he hadn't since the day Christabel died and he ransacked the city. It had been rebuilt, and now Brinnea's wards were the strongest in Nyrida. To Simeon, Gavin said, Brinnea would always be home. If the bulk of Elias's forces weren't needed in the central part of the continent to resist Molochai moving north, more of our people might live here.

Simeon preferred it this way, though. It was the only piece of his ideal world still intact, and he chose to keep it quiet and out of Molochai's grasp as best he could.

It was the last piece he had of his sister.

While gaping at the lights glimmering off the ocean and listening to laughter and chatter on the beach, at the tavern, and all around us, I decided I could hardly blame Simeon for needing to protect this city. Of all the places I had been these past few weeks, and as much as home could be a *place* for me, Brinnea felt most like one.

Gavin was quite funny when he wasn't so serious, which he seemed determined not to be throughout dinner. We enjoyed our meals in peace. Mine, a dish with chicken and tomato that nearly dragged a groan from my throat. But I remembered his reaction one time I'd moaned over a pastry and gracefully refrained.

He told me about the blacksmith and his wife—Isaac and Eden—who had raised him. How Eden taught him reading, writing, arithmetic, and science in place of a formal education. How he became Isaac's apprentice and took over the trade when he passed. He told me about the best friend he had as a young man, Victor. He'd died—I didn't dare ask how—but Gavin seemed at peace with the loss. He was happy to share stories of his youth with me, even if some of the details were sordid.

Only when the male server began to stare at my neck and chest did Gavin abandon his lightheartedness.

"Yes, she's resplendent, isn't she?" The growl deep in his chest fractured the air around us like thunder. "Gawk any longer and you might end up blinded by something far less pleasant than her beauty."

The server's skin paled at the threat as he scrambled for a thin piece of paper totaling the charges for our meal. I caught Gavin's gaze and lifted a brow. As if *he* never stared at me.

Gavin arched a playful eyebrow right back, swirled his glass of Scotch between his fingers, then nodded to the server, whose hands were now trembling. "Two sweet reds, please," he bit out before the server could escape.

My first ever wine was fruity with a richly sweet aftertaste. It sizzled through my blood and relaxed any remaining tension in my body. I sighed and gazed out at the ocean, watching the waves.

Minutes later, a string quartet tuned their instruments and began to play a soft, elegant melody. There was empty space on the portion of the walkway designated solely for the patrons of the restaurant. One couple, then another, meandered over to a space I realized was for dancing. I turned to see Gavin leaning back in his seat, wineglass at his lips, watching me.

"Will you dance with me?" he asked.

Heat gathered in my cheeks. I tried to envision this rugged mass of muscled warrior *dancing*. I tried—as he finished the last sip of his wine—but I couldn't.

"You dance?"

He rose to his feet, dropped payment for dinner on the table, and offered me his hand. "For you?" I accepted his touch, my hand so warm and safe wrapped in his as he guided me to my feet. "Until the sun comes up and then some."

A victim to my pounding heart, I focused on the feel of his

fingers as he led me to the platform, where two other couples swayed. My pointed heel slipped between a crack in the wood and caused my ankle to twist. I scowled at my new shoes, even though Gavin pulled me flush against his chest before I could fall. One of his arms curled around my lower back, the other hand held mine against his chest.

"I hope they don't make me wear shoes like these when I get to the caves," I muttered, glancing down at my delicate but increasingly unbearable footwear.

He tilted my chin up with his finger, and worry passed through his fierce stare.

"If they try to force you to do something you don't want to do, you tell them no, and you don't give in." He rested my palm on his chest and stroked my cheek with his thumb. "Promise me."
I nodded while savoring his touch. That, I could promise. A tear trickled down my cheek as, content in his arms, I pressed my body against the heat and strength of his. He scowled at the sight of it and caught it with his thumb.

"I have never despised anything as much as I despise this world for what it requires of you."

My palms moved from his chest to his back, where they rested between his jacket and his shirt. "Then just . . . remember me like this." I smiled up at him. Truly joyful, despite my burning eyes. "Remember me with you. Happy."

He pressed a soft kiss to my forehead and tucked my head into his chest. We stayed that way—him holding me, my arms wrapped around him while I listened to the quickening *thump* of his heartbeat. We remained like this for minutes that were too short.

No amount of time would be enough. His warmth and his

scent. The gentle sway of the music. The way he rested his cheek on top of my head and stroked my hair over my shoulders. I could live here with him forever.

"If a friend is all I ever get to be to you," he said, and sighed against my temple, "then you should know that you are the best friend I have ever had."

My eyes squeezed tightly to release my heartbreak, refusing to let my body feel the loss of him.

"I wish you could stay with me," I said, sucking in a tattered breath because I knew Simeon wouldn't allow it. Knew that Elias would see me look at my teacher once and know the truth of my heart. Another press of his lips in my hair gave me goose bumps. "I'll miss you, and I—"

"Aryella." With my ear against his chest, I felt his deep voice tremble. "Before you say anything else, there's something I need to tell you."

I rubbed his back, attempting to soothe his nerves. "Okay. You can tell me."

"Forgive me." His voice was no longer soft or affectionate, but... desperate. "Please."

"What?" I dug my fingers into his back. Holding on. "Gavin?" I whispered, begging my gut to stay silent. To stop trying to warn me. I didn't want to hear it. "What—"

"I lied to you."

My gut lurched. I stepped back, away from him. Craned my neck up to see the sorrow in his eyes. Sorrow that cut through me like jagged ice.

"Simeon is not here in Brinnea," Gavin said. "He never was."

Chapter Twenty-Nine

Devastating silence settled in my bones. Dread prickled at my heart and my neck as he looked down at me, face and jaw strained tight. I recoiled from him. All of me lost, alarmed and on guard—my stupid heart even more than my sense of self-preservation.

"What do you mean he's not here?" I stumbled backward.

"Don't run." He caught my wrists before I could fall and nodded toward the beach. "Please. Walk with me."

But I ripped my wrists from his grasp so hard that the violent friction chafed my skin. It wasn't smart to turn my back to him, but I did. I tore my heels off my feet and rushed toward the beach, even though it was far too cold to do so. I needed to be away from people, away from all the lights, away from *him*.

"I'm stupid," I hissed through tearful eyes. "Stupid, stupid, stupid—"

"Ella!" His deep voice was right behind me the moment my feet touched cold sand.

But I turned on him, wielding a heel in one hand. I stumbled again, losing my balance. "Simeon's really not here?"

His hand flexed as if to reach for me. "No, but—"

"Were you going to give me up? Is someone…" I looked around, frantic. No one was near us save for a few passing Brinneans distracted by celebration. "Is someone here? Do you make a deal and—"

"No!" Coarse pain rippled through him. "Never."

"Then I don't understand—"

"I wanted *you*. Just you," he insisted, hands open in supplication. "That morning the temple went down, I was going to tell you the truth, but you said you wanted to go to Brinnea with *me*, and I am a *selfish* bastard, Ella," he gritted out. "I am not the one that gets to have you, not in this life." His chest shuddered with emotion. "But I couldn't stay away, and I couldn't let you go, so I *took*—I took time, I took these moments with you knowing they're probably all I'll ever get."

"Me," I breathed, my chest split down the middle—confusion and distrust on one side, hope and love on the other. "You just wanted *me*?"

"Yes." Hesitantly, he reached for my hand. My recoil this time was only slight, but I kept my distance. "Are you *really* that surprised?" He huffed out a breath. "You see how I look at you. You hear me talk to you. When we're close, when we lie in bed together, you feel how I *want* you. I gave up trying to hide what I feel for you long, long ago."

The air around my head began to thin. I wanted to accept it. Go back to dancing, to just being with him, but—

"Did you have something to do with the temple in Tovick?" I demanded shakily. "To—to get me out of there and get me alone?"

His face twisted with pain. "*No.*"

"You intercepted the others on your way here and you told them Simeon sent you."

"He did send me. He sent me to retrieve you from Warrich and take you directly to those caves."

My stomach plummeted. But it had been Finn who revealed the plan to come to Brinnea, not Gavin.

"You told the others the plan was to go to Brinnea from the beginning." The air escaped my chest and left a cavern in its wake. "You had this plan before you even came to Warrich. Before you even met me."

"Yes," he confessed. "I did."

There's a difference between what I've been told to do and what I plan on doing.

I shrank back from him, remembering some of his first words to me. Words I had been too naïve to question.

"We only passed through Tovick to come here," I choked out. "If *Caz* hadn't been in Tovick—"

"I know." Remorse flickered through him. "But those brothers knew what they were signing up for by volunteering to escort you from Warrich back to those caves. They knew there were risks."

A gust of wind carried icy mist off the ocean and sent shivers through me.

"I would never have forced you to come to Brinnea, Aryella." He moved slowly, carefully, as he tried to close the distance between us—like he was afraid I'd snap if he moved too fast. "You wanted to come—"

"Under false pretenses!"

"Tell me you were ready to go to Elias Winterton!" Anger

rumbled in his chest. "Tell me you didn't want to come here with *me*!"

But I couldn't tell him that. The time he gave me allowed me to live, to train, to learn, to discover joy and separate myself from the bonds of the prophecy. Even if just for a few extra days or weeks. I was in no rush to get to those caves, to my betrothed, and we both knew it.

"It doesn't make any sense." I ran my fingers over my face, through my hair, throwing his flower crown to the cold, sandy ground, which bit at my bare feet. "You didn't even *know* me!" Agony rippled in his eyes. He took another step toward me. Reached for me, but I dodged his hand. "Make it make sense, please!"

"I was not going to let Simeon throw you to his wolves with no defenses, with no training, no idea who you were or what you could do, with no strength, no . . ." He bit back the torment the memory gave him. "No *food* in your belly or *life* in your eyes, Ella—"

"It wasn't your choice!"

"No, it wasn't!" The power of his brutal shout silenced the air around us. Silenced *me*. "And if that makes me your villain, then so *fucking* be it!"

I folded my arms around myself and rubbed warmth into my own skin. Unbridled laughter—distant, foreign, and carefree—sounded from the tavern behind me.

"If I ask to go to the caves, to Elias, right now," I began through chattering teeth, "will you take me?"

Gavin flinched but nodded. "If that's what you want."

"You said you'll kill Elias if he touches me," I said, calling his bluff. To not be fooled again. "You said you'll be his nightmare."

"Not if it's—" His chest heaved with angry breaths. His face paled, like it sickened him to say the words. "Not if he will make you happy."

"Swear on my life."

"Don't—I won't," he stuttered, scowling. "Your *life* is not to be bargained with!"

"Swear it," I commanded coldly. "On my life. That you would not, that you *will* not hold me here against my will."

Like Simeon. Like Elowen. I had friends, a community, *people*, and they had kept me locked away.

"I swear it on—on your life." My chest splintered at the stumble he took over the words, as if speaking them cut into his soul. I knew how that felt. "I will fight for your freedom and happiness as long as there is breath in my body, but..." His expression darkened with dread. "But do you *want* to go to him?"

"I have to."

"That's not what I asked."

"We can't *all* do whatever we want." The insult snapped out of me like the crack of a whip. When he opened his mouth to object, I held up my hand to stop him. "Don't. I need to think. Go back to the inn."

He shook his head. "You aren't walking back alone."

"I think I'll survive without you for once." My words were a finely honed blade slicing through us both.

"Aryella." He offered me his hand. I wanted to take it, but I refused. "I'm not leaving you out here."

"Then you will never see me again," I answered coldly. "I will find a way to escape from you. You will never touch me again. You will never speak to me again, and I will *never* forgive you." I wanted to crumble and weep, but I didn't. I clenched my teeth and glowered at him instead. "Do as I say, give me space, or I will *choose* to hate you for lying to me."

The threat felt venomous as it left my lips, but I knew it would work. And it did. His hand dropped to his side, defeat leveling the planes of his scarred, handsome face. I heard him shifting but refused to look up.

"Take this. It's cold." His black leather jacket brushed my arm. "Please take this, Ella, and know I'll be waiting for you."

Reluctantly, I accepted and put on his coat. It was large enough to fit over my fur shawl. I watched him leave in the direction of the inn.

For a while I stood completely still, numbly watching the reflections of lanterns and firelight off the ocean waves. Hearing the joyous sounds of Solstice celebrations. Laughter, cheering, singing. All of it felt separate from me now.

The mist bit at my cheeks and ruffled my dampening hair so it rippled around me and stung my face. His jacket, enveloping my body, blocked the shudders but couldn't soothe the ache in my chest. Behind me, I heard the carefree laughter of children and turned toward the source. Three of them—two young girls and a boy—skipped across and squealed down the cobblestone path, waving thin wooden sticks that sparkled with hot, dancing light.

I smiled through the ache in my chest when the boy laughed.

He sounded like Ollie.

I took in the children's sweet, unworried faces bitten pink from the cold, filled with joy. I knew my choice remained the same.

Simeon had placed wards on this city as he had on Tovick to protect these innocents. But they wouldn't last. Molochai was moving north, and he would eventually bear down on the last of

Simeon's defenses. Then, nowhere would be safe, not even Brinnea. Surely everyone in this world could not fit and survive in the Winterton Caves, if they could even be kept hidden from Molochai. None of this *good* would last unless I did something about it. I shouldn't have let myself forget that, not for a single moment.

I could be furious with Gavin for the rest of our last night together. Or I could be as grateful as I had been to Simeon when I thought it had been *he* who knew I needed more time.

But it had been Gavin who ensured I had time and space to *breathe*. To adjust. Simeon, it seemed, was ready to drag me out of one prison into another. Eight or nine days was all it would have taken to bring me from Warrich to those caves. I would be there now. I would have arrived to my people—my betrothed—weak, scared, confused. Without the strength in my body that I had now, the fire in my veins, the knowledge of the gods and their power. Had we gone straight to those caves... I would have gone in blind.

"I think about how the people who were supposed to love and protect you starved the life out of you so they could rebuild you however they see fit..."

I buried my face in my hands and muffled my screams. He'd lied. It was wrong, but it had been his twisted way of protecting that scared, weak, malnourished girl he found in Warrich. As much as I was angry at him for it...

I loved him for it, too.

With a heavy sigh, I dragged my tired feet through the freezing sand. When I reached the path to the inn, I slipped my shoes back on, unsure if the discomfort was any better than bare feet on the hard, stone ground.

Minutes later, I walked into the two-story inn and down the

lantern-lit, cream-tiled hallway until I stood in front of our room. I took a few deep breaths before opening the door. Upon my entry, he rose from where he sat on the edge of the bed. The door closed softly behind me. His eyes tracked my every movement.

"You shouldn't have lied to me." I shed his jacket and the wolf pelt, laid them on the chair beside the door. "But I know you were trying to give me time to adjust to everything. To gather some semblance of autonomy before going to those caves. So you were wrong," I repeated, reminding myself just as much as him, "but… I forgive you."

His chest quivered with a relieved sigh, and he was immediately moving. Reaching to pull me into an embrace. I stretched out my arms and stopped him, my palms flat on his hard chest.

"I also know there's more you're not telling me. And perhaps I'm a fool for it, but tonight, I don't *want* to know. Tonight, I want to pretend none of the rest of it exists." My instinct roared a warning at me. I shoved it down into those cautious depths. I didn't care. No, I didn't *want* to care. "Tonight, I just want you."

There was more than one war unfolding in Nyrida, and despite my status as the prophesied savior queen of these lands, the war I cared about *tonight* was the war… between *us*.

"Aryella." His voice was resolute. He wrapped his strong fingers around my forearms. "I am not going to bed you tonight."

"I want to. I want to give you that," I breathed. "It feels like the only part of myself that's mine to give."

"And I'm not letting you give that to me," he answered firmly. "Not tonight."

"But I have to go to those caves," I told him, pulse racing. "And at the springs, just days ago, you told me to allow myself to *live*, and that is what I'm trying to do *tonight*, with you. Because I've accepted that I have to go to my people and my husband—"

"He's not your *fucking* husband!"

The room shook at his lethal fury. I shrank back from him—not afraid of him or what he could do to me but afraid of whatever fueled a rage so hot and malicious.

Seeing my shock, he forced an even breath and added, "Yet. He's not your husband *yet*, and you are *not* his wife." The words rumbled out of him—a low, malicious growl. "To him, you're just an idea, but to me…" His hands were soft on my face before he twisted his fingers in my hair. "*You* are the air in my lungs. You are light and *life. You* are the reason I open my eyes every morning and brave this world. You are the tonic to my nightmares, the angel that defies my demons."

"Then be with me!" I placed my palms on his chest. "You took time, you took moments, so take *me*!" My fingers wrinkled his clean black shirt. "I know it's going to hurt to say goodbye, but—"

"You *don't* know!" he spit. "You have *no idea* how well I know it *hurts*!" My pulse raced, driven by the iron grip that restricted and caressed. Kept me at a distance, yet held me close. A push and pull that would shatter me. "I refuse to make this more difficult for you than it already is."

"It's *my* choice!" I pressed.

"And you don't know what you're asking me to do to you by honoring your choice."

"Yes, *I do*." I reached up to cup his jaw, savoring the rough feel of his beard beneath my fingers. "They've chosen Elias to be my husband, but right now, I want *you*." He scowled and tried to pull away, but I lifted my other hand to his face, keeping him there. "I can decide this for myself. I am *safe* with you." He softened at this, gently squeezing my wrists. "I'm whole, every part of me protected and cared for." I swallowed though nerves, forcing them back down to my stomach. "I want you to be my first."

I inhaled sharply at the sight of his rage—that lethal eruption of fury—that blazed in his eyes. "Your first," he uttered, scowling, like something vile touched his tongue. He loosened his grip on me and slowly retreated. "Your *first*?"

"Yes."

"No!" he snarled. I flinched, cowering beneath him, as if the voice of a god had thundered through the clouds to douse my stubborn fire with an even more unyielding storm. "*No.*"

"Please!" Sadness and anger splintered through my voice. "For gods' sake, tell me what I have to do to make you want to *fuck* me!"

Cold anguish stared back at me. Shadows whispered inside his deep brown gaze, begging to be set free. I had seen that look only once before. *Hurt.* Rejection. When I first dared to call him my friend.

"Is that what you want, Ella?" He took slow, dangerous steps toward me. I retreated out of instinct until my back hit the wall. "Do you want me to *fuck* you?"

Gavin pressed against me, his hands on both sides of my head.

His whole body hard.

"Yes," I breathed.

"You want me to *fuck* you so you know what it's like, before you go to your precious betrothed?" He hissed through gritted teeth and brushed his lips against my forehead. "Before you run off to marry another man?"

I blinked out a tear, fighting the ache in my chest, the need in my core. "Y-yes."

"And you ask me..." His voice was low and dangerous, rumbling through me. "What *you* need to do for me to *want* it?"

"Yes."

His response was a deep, growling hum.

"You need only exist for me to want to *fuck* you. *You* don't have to do anything. *I* have to do *everything* to *control myself!*" He slammed his fist into the wall beside my head, and I felt the world around me tremble beneath him. His breath, hot on my neck, sent goose bumps up my spine, and his fist caressed the length of my jaw down to my collarbone. "Let me tell you what I truly want, Aryella."

I blinked out a tear. He caught it with his thumb and wiped it away with a gentleness so at odds with his power.

"I want to *bury* myself inside you." His voice—dark as shadow—cloaked me in forbidden comfort. "I want you naked and writhing with pleasure beneath me. I want my name—*only* my name—on your lips while you come for *me.* I want my mouth, my tongue on *every* surface of your skin, and while I taste you, I want to hear your moans. Your precious, racing heartbeat. Those sweet little *panting breaths*"—he gripped my chin, his thumb on my lip—"so that I can lose myself in those sounds—in *you*—forever. I want you so full of my *cum*"—I gasped as his hand slid down my jaw and over my throat—"that there is no space for your power or this war. No space for the rest of this gods-damned world. No space for Elias *fucking* Winterton. No space for anything or anyone but *me.* Not your first, not your last, but your *only.*"

Quiet sobs wrecked me. He pressed a soft, soothing kiss to my forehead. I fought the urge to press for more even though I knew it would hurt me. But I lost that fight, because maybe if I could dream of it—of *him*—my future as queen wouldn't be so lonely.

"Would you," I breathed, trembling under his touch, "would you be gentle?"

"For as long as you needed me to be," he whispered, his lips against my temple. "But then..." His jaw pulsed with restraint.

"But...then?" I gasped as his calloused fingers flexed around my throat.

He growled and tore his hand away, retreating, shaking his head in warning. "By the will of the gods, Ella, one day I will have you—*all* of you. But not today."

"Why?"

"Because of the things you don't know. Because I refuse to make this worse, when I..." His hand returned, now light on my jaw while the other hand rose to cup my cheek. He drew a soft, whimpering sigh from my chest and stroked my skin with his thumb. "I *love* you so much more than I want to *fuck* you."

I squeezed my eyes shut, fighting in vain to fend off tears. He gently kissed each teardrop away.

"Yes. I love you." He pressed a chaste kiss to my forehead, then my nose, summoning more of my tears. "Gods, *I love you*, my Ella."

"You can't love me," I cried. Saying it aloud eclipsed any remaining hope. "You can't."

"But I do." He took my chin between his thumb and his index finger. "I've loved you for longer than you know."

"If you," I breathed, infusing my voice with strength, "if you love me, then you'll honor my wishes. Before I go to those caves and have to become everything they expect of me. If you care for me, Gavin, you'll do this one thing I ask."

Compassion and longing surged through his gaze, seized my heart, and coiled behind my sternum.

"I will not." His voice was too sure, too stubborn. "I will not yield on this."

"Gavin, people have sex with each other all the time."

"Not like this."

"Yes, like this!" I snapped, as if I really knew. "Gemma and Finn—"

"We are not Gemma and Finn."

"Then what are we?" Angry tears blasted through my remaining composure. But I was safe with him, with my wild and irresponsible emotions. "Because I've never wanted *anything* like I want you. I feel nothing but you, all the time, every gods-damned moment! You are the only thing that makes sense to me, and I'm not afraid of whatever it is you think is going to hurt me!" I captured his stare to prove it true. "And I know I can't have you forever, but I want you tonight!"

As he held my tearful face in his hands and looked down at me, apologetic but unwavering in his resolve, I knew his answer was still no.

"Then kiss me," I croaked out, mouth dry.

"I'm trying to protect you." He pleaded for me to understand, but all I could feel was the tingling heat his thumb left on my cheek. "I'm trying to protect your *heart*."

"And I'm *begging* you"—my voice cracked—"to give me something to remember. Something that only belongs to me. To *us*." My pulse pounded in my ears. I rested my palms on his face and soaked in the rugged feel of his jaw beneath my fingers. "We can't control my future, but we can control *this*. We can control tonight, and tonight"—I leaned closer—"it's just you and me. If you love me, the least you can do is kiss me."

He clenched his jaw in silent denial.

But I knew his jealousy and need for control were his catalysts.

It was a dirty game, but I was going to play it anyway.

Because I was desperate for him.

"Please kiss me before anyone else does." Guilt crept up my spine at what I was about to say. "Before Elias kisses me."

His growl was low and dangerous. And when there were only inches left between us, when the *starvation* was clear in his eyes, I prayed I might win, just this once.

His gaze darted to my mouth, his chest rapid in its rise and fall. A vast, breathing mountain, its impending avalanche seeking to crush and devour me. I waited. For long, torturous moments, he did nothing, and my stomach toiled with the ache of rejection. I gave one last pleading look and, accepting he wouldn't give in, turned away.

The ground dropped out from under me when he gripped the back of my neck, dragged me back to him, and crushed his mouth to mine.

We collided with brutal urgency, then stilled. Like he was afraid of what moving would unleash. The roughness of his beard against my sensitive skin, the hungry groan rumbling in his chest . . . More. I needed more. A pleading whimper escaped my throat, my heart and body begging for him.

"Gods be fucking damned," he groaned, his fingers trailing up the curve of my jaw, gripping my hair, tilting me back, "you're my heaven."

I sighed in delight when he slowly took my bottom lip between both of his. I shivered and pressed against him. He parted my lips with a dart of his tongue. Demanding entry.

With a shuddering gasp, I opened my mouth and let him in. At the taste of me, the flames between us roared.

I kissed him and his responding groan soaked into my skin. He feasted upon me like a starving man. And he tasted like honey and cinnamon whiskey and fresh air. I couldn't see or hear or feel anything but *him*.

He took my heart, my soul. And with the power and heat of his kiss, he ruined me. The world that had disappeared at the first touch of his lips, re-formed, tilted on its axis. My source of gravity became *him*.

And if I was his heaven, he was mine.

The glorious heat and sweetness of his tongue sent lightning bolts rippling through me. Each shift of his hard body against mine echoed through my pulsing core. A welcome invasion, a thousand beams of sunlight ripping through my ice-cold body on a winter's day.

I felt alive. I felt...*free*.

I used my own mouth to mirror his movements. Did the best I could without having done it before and hoped it was enough. He certainly didn't object. Each time I exhaled, he inhaled, as if my breath was sacred. All of me burned with fire and lightning until he pulled away. I gasped, my mouth, my hands reaching for him out of instinct. As if no piece of me could bear to part from him. The thought of it struck like a rusted dagger in my chest.

"Why did you stop?" The fear of disappointing him chilled my blood.

Burning brown eyes glazed, he parted my lips—swollen and wet from his kiss—with his thumb. He glanced at his hand, which he'd placed over my heart, over the bare skin of my faded mystery scar, and whispered, "I had to make sure you're real."

"I'm real." I pressed my chest against his. "Please don't stop."

He cursed under his breath and, with a surrendering, feral groan, plunged his tongue into my mouth. He wrapped his fingers around the nape of my neck, holding me in place as he led me, forceful and soft, rhythmic and calculated. He licked my tongue and devoured my lips. I followed his movements. As with so many other things, he taught me how to respond to him. He held me. Kept me from falling to the floor in overwhelming need.

I whimpered when he swiped his powerful tongue across the roof of my mouth. I responded, and the taste of him sent a jolt between my legs.

This feeling, with him, was the best I'd ever felt.

Somehow... still not enough.

"More," I breathed. "Please." I intertwined my fingers in his hair, pressed against him to show him how I wanted him to consume me, body and soul, and then capture the secret, vulnerable piece of me that was just a girl who wanted his love. The piece that was just me.

Just his Ella.

"Greedy little *queen*," he growled against my mouth. "Feel what you do to me." My pulse stumbled when he pressed his stone-hard length into my stomach. "Every time I see you, hear you, touch you, *smell* you. Every gods-damned moment in your presence, *this* is what you do to me. It is *torture*." He nipped at my jaw, then gently kissed the place it smarted. "And I don't ever want it to end."

I gasped at his hardness shifting against the thin silk of my dress. His arousal was no surprise. It wasn't the first time I'd felt it, but this time, my core ached with a terrible emptiness I'd never experienced, and only he could fill it.

So I took a chance. I gripped his shoulders, spun him, and pushed him onto the bed. He let me straddle him, groaning deeply when my knees tightened against his thighs. His hard length, even through his pants, was thick and bulging between my legs. I felt my own hot wetness. My body wanted him just as much as my heart.

"Ella," he warned but didn't stop me. No, he gripped my ribs with marvelous pressure, silently begging, pleading for me to keep going. Need pulsed in his fervent stare. He sucked a breath through his teeth and groaned when I ground over him with my hips. I took his hands and, without breaking his gaze, slid them beneath my dress, over my bare thighs, where they left a warm, tingling trail on my skin.

"*Ella*." He grumbled another warning but didn't retreat. His fingers slid over the curve of my hips, breaching the hem of my panties. I nodded, giving him permission, and with a hungry growl, he slid his strong fingers underneath, cursing as he gave in, his fingers cupping, squeezing, digging into my skin so vigorously, it hurt. A glorious pressure.

"*Fuck*, you're so soft." The desire in his voice quaked through me. I knew there was more there—what he kept *leashed*—as he hungrily kissed down the length of my jaw to my neck. "Every single part of you is soft and *good*." I pressed my hips into him, dizzy at the feeling of his mouth beneath my ear, his tongue savoring me in long, sensual strokes. Then biting softly at my neck as he wrenched panting gasps from my throat. Possessed by desire, I lifted up my dress, took one of his palms, and placed it on my bare stomach.

He tightened one hand on my ass, using his lips and tongue to hungrily lick, kiss, worship my neck. "My Ella, you have no idea," he breathed. "You have no idea how often I've dreamed this. Dreamed of *us* like this." I whimpered in response and kissed him, cutting him off, unable to be parted from his mouth for a moment longer. I couldn't think, could hardly feel beyond the places he touched me. The places I tasted him, and he tasted me.

"Touch me," I begged, leading his hand to my breast. "*Please* touch me." He shuddered at the feel of my stiff nipple under his thumb as he circled it, then did the same to the other. My hips bucked against him, pulling a desperate shudder from his chest. The deep vibration of his moan infiltrated every cell in my body. I almost came undone.

But with his hand in my hair, he parted us again, despite my frantic efforts to keep myself glued to him. He whispered against my lips, "I love you. Tell me you know." Our eyes locked together, and if it was possible for him to make love to me with his eyes, he *did*. "Tell me you know I love you, Ella."

A rush of emotion, of *love* overwhelmed me, too. But I didn't understand why he felt the need to part us, to tell me now, again, in the heat of it, when we were both getting what we wanted. When we only had one chance. This had to happen now, *tonight*, and we both knew that I . . . *couldn't* say it. Even if it was true, I couldn't say what couldn't be.

If I told him I loved him, if I admitted it out loud, I knew it would break something irreparable inside me.

So I refocused on his touch. His strength and his warmth. His body, and how he made me feel. Alive and warm and *safe.* I covered the hand on my breast and guided him down past my navel. He hissed through clenched teeth, breathing faster, his glazed brown eyes shuttering closed.

"Ella," he warned me. He knew where I was taking him. "*Ella.*"

But I needed him to understand. I needed him to feel what I felt.

"*Show me* you love me." I slid his fingers beneath the hem of my underwear, into my wetness.

"*Fuck!*" he gasped into my neck when he felt how soaked I was. A tortured, pleading, helpless groan so powerful, my core dropped even closer to the edge of unraveling. He was controlled violence, dominance personified, *trapped* in the prison he kept himself in, and I was determined to release him.

I breathed shakily, whimpering as I shifted on his fingers. It felt so wonderful—like light and warmth and tingling on the brink of euphoric explosion—even though he refused to move. And I knew, if he flexed them once, I would… I would…

"Please." Tears bit at my eyes, strangled my voice. "Take all of me."

With a tortured, raspy moan, he pulled his fingers from my wetness. With one hand, he trapped my wrists above my head. With the other, he gripped the back of my neck and held me still, kissing me again.

But this kiss was softer. Lingering. More… final.

When he pulled away, his eyes locked with mine. Brimming with remorse and loss and *love* but unwavering in his resolve.

"Ella," he pleaded, my name a desperate whisper. And I swear, my heart *split* in half at the sound of his shallow, broken, "*No.*"

Chapter Thirty

Ice crystallized in my veins.

He lowered me to the bed and turned away.

"I didn't want you to stop," I whispered, suddenly feeling like a shell of myself. Feeling *lost*.

"And *gods*, I don't want to," he groaned, and ran his trembling hands over his face. "But I have to, Ella."

I lifted my fingers to my swollen lips, where I could still taste him. Sweet, hot, and alive on my tongue. I looked down at the skirt of my sea green dress still hiked around my waist, leaving my thighs and the white underwear he'd given me in Tovick fully exposed. And I was suddenly very cold, very... aware of myself. Racked with violent shakes, I straightened my dress on my shoulders and covered my knees, face flushed. I grasped at the blankets on the bed and wrapped myself in one.

"You don't have to hide yourself just because I can't give you what you deserve, Ella."

I froze beneath the heat of his stare, afraid to look up. I didn't want whatever he thought I deserved. I only wanted him, but he didn't seem to understand that.

"You have *nothing* to be ashamed of," he insisted. But I didn't believe him.

"I thought..." I cleared my throat and finished folding the blanket over my lap, steadying my voice. "You said there was no line you wouldn't cross for me."

"Then I was wrong. Because this one..." He shook his head and pointed to the ground. "I will not cross this one."

"Because of your wife," I said, giving voice to what I already knew was true. "Right?"

He gave no denial other than a defeated shake of his head and a run of his hands through his hair.

I felt the blood leave my face. I'd become so worked up, so desperate to get what I wanted, that I hadn't considered that even though she was gone, he might feel like he was betraying her. Vile embarrassment unfurled in my stomach, threaded with guilt. Gavin had made his urges clear, but he was still a man missing his wife, and I was acting like a fool. A young, reckless fool trying to seduce him and satisfy my own selfish desires. Even his proclamation of love had been a defense to ward me off.

He was only trying to protect me from the pain of inevitable loss. Sex and the feelings it brought forth were things I didn't understand. But he did. And he needed to protect himself from the guilt of being with someone that wasn't her. His sorrow made it clear that she would always have him, whether in life or in death, and I never would.

"She's gone, but you can't let her go." I averted my eyes from his. "I understand, and I'm sorry."

"You have nothing to apologize for." He reached for my hand, but I withdrew it and shuffled back toward the headboard. "Look at me." I refused. "This is *my* fault, Ella. *Mine.* Not yours."

"I've been selfish." I focused on methodically intertwining my fingers one pair at a time until my hands were folded together. Mine were the hands I could rely on. Only mine. I needed to get that through my stupid, naïve little head. "I won't push you again. You made yourself clear, and I didn't want to listen. We will head to the caves tomorrow, and that will be the end of this."

I stared at my fingers, unable to look at him without shattering into a million pieces I wasn't sure I could clean up on my own. Out of the corner of my eye, I saw his hand shift toward my cheek, and for once, I hated his unwavering inclination to guide me back to him. He must have seen this because he halted and pulled away.

"I want to go to sleep." I let a foreign discomfort settle in my bones. "I don't think you should stay here tonight."

"Ella," he choked out. "Ella, sweetheart, please—"

"I am your *queen*!" The words were empty and raw. Finally, I listened to caution. I erected that wall of self-preservation I should have kept between us this entire time. "And as your *queen*, I am commanding you to *go*."

I sucked in a shaky breath as one last tendril of yearning rose out of my heart to seek him, trying to restore the bond between us.

But he left the room before I could utter a word and slammed the door behind him.

A pathetic sob wrenched free from my throat. That newly constructed wall of self-preservation shattered. Tears spilled to quell the firestorm in my throat.

He could say he loved me. He could look at me like I was the most important thing in this world. He could touch me. He could kiss me. He could probably even have sex with me. His passionate, breathtaking words and all-consuming presence could lay claim to my heart and soul for eternity, and it wouldn't matter. I would never be to him what she had once been.

He still didn't *love me* enough. Love me like her.

The people in this world wanted me for the blood in my veins, not the heart in my chest. They didn't want my words or my thoughts; they wanted the gods' powers I wielded. Even Elias Winterton, my betrothed, would never know me as Aryella, the girl. I would be his trophy before I was his wife. My wants and needs were secondary to the Queen of Nyrida. And though I had hoped and prayed it wasn't true, Gavin Smyth was no different.

I didn't get to have *who* or what I wanted.

And me? Without my crown or my powers? I was no one's first choice. I had been foolish—with all the burdens I carried—to hope that I could be.

He returned three hours later. When I heard the door unlock, I turned away from it even though doing so required me to lie on my wounded side. It hurt, but not as much as my heart. It had been weeks since I felt numb, but as I lay in bed, I wished for it.

I'd changed out of my dress into a dark green sweater and black pants, feeling too exposed to wear my nightgown and refusing to be cold. To have a reason to want him in bed with me.

The wind rattled against the rusty panes, making sleep impossible. At least there was the reflection of him in the window—vivid enough to make out his movements. He sat in a chair in front of the fire, watching the flames dance. He held a drink in his hand but never lifted it to his lips.

As I lay awake, I decided to plan for the morning. I would tell him we needed two horses and that we were to head directly toward the Caves. Whenever we stopped to rest, I would require my own space, and when we passed through Tovick, I wanted Damond to take over as my escort.

Maybe a clean break would hurt the least.

I had just finished wiping my eyes again when I heard a knock at the door. The chair creaked beneath him as he rose. Two long strides, and he was wrenching open the door with annoyed fervor.

"Smyth?" A timid male voice came from the hallway.

"Felix?" Gavin grumbled, then cursed before mumbling something unintelligible to the man on the other side of the door. I tried to remember if Gavin had mentioned Felix in any of his stories, or if the others spoke of someone with that name from the caves, but I couldn't recall.

I didn't bother sitting or turning to face Gavin, but he must have known I was awake, because his footsteps neared. "I will be right outside. Please stay here."

But after thirty seconds, I rose from bed and tiptoed to the door, where I could hear their voices in the hallway. Cringing, I turned the door handle as silently as possible to expose a crack. Gavin's back was to our room. He towered over Felix, but they were angled so that I could make out half of Felix's thin face and frame, blond curls, and pointy nose.

"He knows you have Simeon's daughter, and he's camped three hours south, by foot. He wants a trade." Felix nodded in the direction of our room and shifted anxiously from one foot to the other. "He's got your wife, Smyth."

Gavin's muscles tensed, a subtle change in his posture that signaled insidious danger rising to the surface. "Is that so?" he finally replied, a sheet of ice covering what I knew was a tsunami of rage beneath.

Felix swallowed hard, nodded, and said in a low, shaky voice, "Just give the girl up, you'll get what you want, and this will finally be over for you."

Gavin's left hand flexed at his side. After a long, terrifying pause, he uttered with a distant voice, smooth and cold, "Let's discuss this outside, Felix." He gave one nod toward the end of the hall, where a door led outside to the woods behind the inn.

I held my stomach with one hand and my mouth with the other to keep from throwing up. Beads of sweat and tears burned every surface of my skin. Silent sobs racked my chest. I should have known. How stupid I had been to say I didn't *want* to know. He'd said he wasn't going to give me up, but he'd already lied to me once…

Through my blurry vision, I made out his worn leather bag, which sat on the floor beside the fireplace. I lunged for it and began to dig. For anything. For proof that he wasn't going to betray me—give me up to Molochai, of all people, as Felix suggested he should. For proof that he *was*, because at least then there would be no questioning.

The leather-cedar scent I loved wafted from his bag, undeniably him. There wasn't much in the worn leather sack other than clothing and hygiene essentials—no different than mine or anyone else's belongings. With a frustrated grunt, I flipped the bag over to empty it fully.

An old leather journal fell to the ground at my feet, and out of the journal, a stack of papers bound with twine.

Letters, each one older than the last.

I began with what looked to be the most recent one.

Day 146,797
Smyth,
My father never returned, so I am writing on his behalf now. I think the old sorcerer murdered him before he could get to her. I will continue to search, but I won't challenge him, and I pray you won't ask me to.
Felix Morton

Day 146,243
I believe I've located her, sir. I am going to infiltrate and attempt to retrieve her for you. Perhaps you will finally be reunited with your wife.
Nigel Morton

There were many more, and they all said some variation of the same thing. These men, the Mortons, all looked for his wife, but not a single one of them could find her. My legs shook. Too weak to stand, I knelt before the fire and paged through the letters toward the bottom of the stack.

Day 96,114
I've had no luck these past few months. I don't suspect I will find any more than those before me. But I will keep searching for her, as I know you will too. I pray that she is still alive somehow.
Peter Morton

Day 83,902...

Day 69,899...

Day 47,039...

Day 28,562...

Day 19,421

I thought that I found a trail today, but the bastard's magic is too strong. He has concealed her. I lost it, sir. Forgive me.

Roger Morton

Day 17,256...

Day 13,469...

Day 8,931...

Day 2,583

My Dear Smyth,

There is still no trace of her. I will go further north this summer in the hopes of more clues. May the Selvaren comfort you. I will do everything I can.

Victor Morton

"Victor." I covered my mouth with my hands. His childhood friend Victor.

On each letter, the same handwriting—Gavin's—marked the date. And if the Felix at the door was the Felix Morton who wrote the letter on "Day 146,797," if she was still alive in the same way Molochai and Simeon were alive, she was likely still trapped there.

With Molochai.

"How long have you been looking for her?" I whispered, tongue dry, swallowing bile.

If Simeon and Molochai were so old, it should come as no

surprise that others could be, too. The math wasn't simple and I found myself calculating it repeatedly, hoping I would get a more realistic answer. I didn't. One hundred and forty-six thousand, seven hundred ninety-seven days was over four hundred years.

"Because the whole damn world has been hellbent on taking the only thing I truly want—what's mine*—for a long fucking time."*

A long time, indeed. A very, very long time.

I let silent tears fall. For him—for losing her so long ago. For being alone for so long.

And for myself. I mourned for what I would never have—the kind of love it took for one man to devote four hundred years to finding one woman. Four hundred *lonely* years, if the last woman he'd been with was her as he'd said. No wonder he had refused me. No wonder he hated himself for having feelings for me. I was in the way of *them*.

My betrothed wasn't waiting for me, but for an ideal queen. Gavin was waiting for the one he truly loved.

"Gods," I breathed, running my shaky hands over my face, hating myself even more.

I was stunned, heartbroken, and horrified. But I didn't have it in me to be angry. Not with him, not really. If he had planned to give me up to get her back, could I blame him? Wouldn't anyone make such a sacrifice after four hundred years?

I stared into the fire, let its heat dry the tears that kept coming, and tried to think of a reason not to do what I knew I needed to.

Despite the violent crack he'd put in my heart, all I could think about was his smile. His laughter, deep and warm and unrestrained. No more pain and longing in those warm eyes. After the kindness he'd shown me. The care.

He deserved happiness.

I thought of Finn and Gemma, Caz and Marin and their baby free to live without fear outside of those caves. Free to go wherever they wanted. And those children celebrating the Solstice. Many more to come, if I was successful. No more of Simeon's wards around the cities. No evacuations needed from Insidions wreaking havoc and death.

Maybe I didn't have to kill Molochai to free my people from him.

Molochai had been scorned by the woman he loved. He'd lost himself in the rejection. If the one thing that had driven Molochai off the edge was not having Christabel... maybe I could replace her. If I looked like Simeon—looked like *her*—maybe I was close enough.

Maybe the one thing that undid Molochai could put him back together just enough to end the suffering.

And I could feel free knowing the ones I loved were safe.

Indeed, I could get Gavin's wife back *and* save my people. I could make a deal of my own. Me and my power in exchange for Gavin's wife. I would convince Molochai to leave Nyrida with me and never come back. I remembered Gemma and Finn mentioning foreign lands across the eastern sea.

It hurt most parts of me to stand, but I did. I refused to promise Gavin I wouldn't sacrifice myself for my people. That was true. I would do what I needed to do. And for him, his happiness, and his peace, I would do *more*.

I had to do *something*.

With shaking fingers and blurry eyes, I wrote down what I wanted him to know. Then, I slid into my boots, climbed out the first-floor window, and stole a dark brown gelding from the stables of the inn. There were no other horses, and Gavin would have to follow on foot if he tried. I stopped at the edge of the forest. Gavin and Felix were nowhere to be found. I took one last look at the green and red firelights of the Solstice celebrations.

And I rode south to Molochai's camp.

Chapter Thirty-One

Gavin Smyth

Twenty-Fourth of Floris, 402 Years Ago

I had been working since dawn on a set of iron candlesticks and a detailed piece of silver art decorated with intricate vines and leaves. It was some asshole's last-minute gift to his wife for a forgotten twenty-fifth anniversary. Normally, I wouldn't waste my energy on some prick's urgent demands, but he was paying me triple to have it done within the day.

So here I was, well past any reasonable hour for supper, perfecting my trade for someone who would find my efforts unappreciated.

But a man had to eat.

The coals were white hot, the ashes like a chalky snow that would burn through flesh in fractions of a second. I knew that smell of burnt flesh well enough and had scars here and there to show for it, though it had been a while since I'd gotten too close to the coals.

"Excuse me, sir?"

A woman's voice broke the silence. That word, directed toward me, had me chuckling. I'd been called many things by many women. *Sir* was not one of them.

But spoken in *that* voice, I fucking *liked* it a little too much.

Generally, I preferred my women like iron and steel—flexible and willing when hot. Quickly chilled with ice-cold words and water when it was all said and done.

I wanted them eager to please and easy to part with. With their asses in the air, hair wrapped around my hands, and their faces effortlessly forgotten. I heard this woman's bleeding heart in her voice, and I could tell she was not for me.

I turned around to the source of that sweet voice with every intention of telling her to get the hell out before she regretted it. I opened my mouth to order her away, because I didn't like women in my arms. I liked them on their knees.

But one look at her, and I knew she would put me on mine.

My smirk disappeared. The breath left my lungs as if Sussurro himself reached inside my chest with his golden hand and ripped it right out. A pit—a cavern infinitely deep—formed in my stomach as I searched for adequate words to describe her. There were none, and there never would be.

Her eyes were a deep forest green speckled with gold, as if the sun were shining through the canopy of her soul. She had adorable freckles over the bridge of a button nose. And her silver-blond locks bound by a loose, long braid that curled around the curve of her perfect, kissable neck made me imagine things I would crush the skull of any other man for thinking.

A shiver racked my body, and I cursed quietly at the new territorial need possessing me.

She wore a dark violet cloak made of velvet, embroidered with black flowers. Thin, shiny black boots. She came from money; that much was clear. She embodied power and grace. Whatever realm of heaven dropped her into my blacksmith's shop was far too good for me.

I felt a panicked urge to force her away, if only to protect myself from the inevitable attachment that was already rooting in my chest. But I refrained, because within those first seconds, the desire to keep her right where she stood trumped the frantic fear of whatever deep, unknown agony this girl could inflict upon me should she wish.

She was young. Too young. No older than eighteen.

But she was mine.

And if *I* didn't pursue her... violent flames of fury erupted within me at the thought of another man. Because I knew men—I thought like the worst of them—and they *would* pursue her, lurch after her like starving sharks to fresh, bloody meat in the water.

I looked down at myself, sweaty and covered in soot. I immediately wished I had stopped working an hour earlier like I originally planned and taken a bath. Impressing a woman was something I'd never given a shit about. The ones I fucked were pretty, but they didn't require much wooing.

"What's your name?" she asked, a hopeful look on her stunning, heart-shaped face.

"Smyth," I replied, realizing I'd tell her anything she asked. She might as well have me in a trance. "Gavin Smyth."

"Gavin Smyth." She ran her index finger along the edge of the table I used to shape and carve wood. My eyes locked on that finger and I immediately wished I were the table. The gentle, curious look in her eyes proved she was too innocent to put any sexual intent behind her gestures. But she rounded her mouth and blew the sawdust off her fingertip and into the air. I thought of all the places I wanted those blushing lips...

"Gavin Smyth, I need you to make me a weapon," she blurted out. I had to reprocess the words a few times. All I had registered were her full lips in a circular shape and the words *I need you* coming out of her mouth.

"What kind of weapon?" I demanded a little too harshly, startling us both.

She crossed her arms and rubbed nervously at her elbow. "Something... sharp."

I cleared my throat and shifted my stance to better hide the one sharp thing I already had for her. I had a feeling that wasn't what she had in mind.

"Why do you need a weapon?"

Did she not have someone to protect her? Husband? Suitor? Lover? And could I kill them to make room for myself?

I shuddered. What she stirred in my bones was something foreign, animalistic, and desperate. I wanted to throw my body over her, become her human shield, and then tear her clothes off, free the goddess underneath, and claim her for myself.

She sighed and shook her head. "That doesn't matter. I need you to make me a weapon, and I need you to show me how to use it."

I raised an eyebrow. "You do know you can buy yourself any type of blade at more than one place here in this city, don't you? Besides, I'm a blacksmith, not a swordsman." I pushed back, not because I wasn't going to do it for her. I was. I resisted in the hopes that she would reveal more information about herself. Give me a reason to tell her to run.

I wasn't sure there was a reason strong enough to make me.

"It's not so much the dagger itself, it's..." She bit her lip, and tense heat flooded to my cock. "I saw you outside that pub this afternoon, fighting. The other man didn't stand a chance. You know what you're doing."

True. I had spent a good portion of my days roughing people up when they pissed me off. But that man owed me money, and I took what was owed to me. Still, I winced, realizing she had seen that. I hadn't exactly been merciful. He would be nursing his ribs and jaw back to health for weeks.

"Is your family nearby?" she asked, her fair skin growing pale. "I—I should have asked that first." Her green-gold eyes darted nervously around. "I don't want to bother you if—"

"No family," I rushed out.

Relief and sadness warred in her beautiful face.

And at the sight of her sadness, an unfamiliar rage simmered in my stomach. Fuck that sadness. Damn it to hell. I never wanted to see it again.

"Listen, I'm not supposed to be here. This is...delicate." She fidgeted with her thumbs. "I'm asking for help, and I don't really have anyone else to ask."

"Don't ask anyone else. I'll help you," I uttered a little too urgently. I cleared my throat again and forced my posture to relax. This dark need to possess her—I didn't know where it came from, but I couldn't show it, not if I wanted a sliver of a chance with her. "But where are you supposed to be?"

She shook her head. "My family doesn't like me going anywhere alone."

I studied the curve of her torso and waist, how the cloak hinted at the delicious shape of her breasts and ass. I could see why anyone who cared about her wouldn't want her going anywhere alone. I hardly knew her, and I didn't want her going anywhere alone ever again.

"How old are you?" I asked, flinching as soon as the words left my mouth. Sounding exactly like the predatory asshole I was.

"Eighteen." She swallowed hard, her beautiful neck pulsing. "And a half."

Ah, fuck. I knew it.

But it was only three years' difference. Plenty of eighteen-year-olds were married off to men much older than me. I winced at my own thoughts. Never, not *once*, had I considered marriage. For good reason—many reasons, actually—I abhorred the idea.

"How old are you?" she asked.

I cleared my throat. "Twenty-one." Less than two months from twenty-two, but twenty-one was still the truth and less likely to scare her off. Hopefully.

She looked around nervously, and my stomach lurched at her discomfort.

"You don't need to be nervous around me," I blurted out. And it was true. It didn't matter how much I lusted after her. I would cut off my own hands before touching her in a way she didn't want. I was rough. Definitely a coldhearted prick. But at least I could say I never gave a woman what she didn't want.

As I looked at her, my heart didn't feel rough or cold at all.

When she smiled, I almost choked on air. The way her green, gold-speckled eyes illuminated with gratitude. That perfectly kissable mouth.

If I hadn't accepted my fate upon first glance, I only had to see her smile to know I was completely and utterly fucked.

"I'll make you whatever you need and teach you everything I know, on one condition," I sputtered. She rubbed her left forearm with her right hand and waited for me to continue. "Let me make you dinner. Tomorrow."

A blush collected in her cheeks. All of my blood flowed south. I realized that—for the first time—I wanted to punch myself in the gods-damned face for my wolfish thoughts.

"What?" Her voice was high-pitched, surprised. I suppressed a smile.

"I want to see you again."

"You will." She twiddled with her thumbs. "For the weapon. And..." Her eyes darted to the side. "Training."

"I want dinner." I stepped forward. Another first, another thing I'd never bothered to ask a woman for. "With you."

And more. So much more. But we would start there.

Her mouth parted in shock, but she didn't object.

"So you'll be here, then?" It was a great effort not to sound overly excited. "For dinner?"

"Umm." She looked around nervously again. "I'm not understanding... why?"

I huffed out a breath, failing to contain my grin. She had no clue.

"Because you're the most beautiful thing I have ever seen." And I had seen a lot of things. A lot of *women* in various... positions. But I decided not to tell her that. None of them mattered anymore. "And if you say no, I think it might kill me." With the way my pulse roared in my ears—like it would explode right out of me—I wasn't lying.

Her lips parted and she inhaled sharply. That tiny, heavenly noise sent me spiraling through fantasies of what she would sound like with my mouth on her.

I was unhinged.

"Fucking hell," I growled to myself, shifting my pants at my belt again to try and make my hard-on less obvious. I had been attracted to plenty of women before, but my body had never reacted with so little control. It was mortifying.

"Excuse me?" she squeaked, eyes wide. Her gaze remained on my face, thank the gods. She hadn't noticed, though I still welcomed the undeniable need to submerge my entire body into a bucket of ice just to snap the hell out of it.

"Tomorrow?" I insisted, voice strained. "Will you join me for dinner?"

She looked to the left, then right, and checked the doorway, almost like she was afraid she was being followed. I fought the urge to hunt down whatever invisible threat she feared.

One glimpse of fear in those golden-green eyes and I was ready to kill for her.

"Okay." Her sweet, gentle voice calmed the storm of rage inside me.

"Okay?" I repeated, making sure I heard her correctly.

She nodded, and then she turned to leave.

"Wait!" I panicked, not ready to see her go. Hating myself for the fact that I had been so preoccupied trying to steady my heartbeat and calm my cock that I'd neglected to ask her name. "You haven't told me your name."

She paused in the doorway.

Without turning back, she said, "You can call me Ella."

Chapter Thirty-Two

Gavin Smyth

Present Day

Many years had passed since someone tried to cross me. Molochai himself didn't try without his magic. Admittedly, Felix's betrayal stung a bit more than I would've liked, considering I'd known him since the day he was born and was his sole provider of income and resources. Yet here he was, betraying me.

Needless to say, I didn't fucking like it.

Especially not where my wife was concerned.

The Morton family had done their best to help me find where she'd been kept over the years, but every generation had grown a little more feeble and flighty than the last. I'd all but given up on their efforts after the untimely death of Felix's father, Nigel. The family had been paid well by me for so long that Felix had taken over the search without hesitation, even though his father had been killed during my employment. But then, I found my Ella. I could have taken Felix off the search immediately. I should have, and I didn't.

I had been a bit . . . distracted.

Now, as I stood glaring at the shivering, gutless man before me, I regretted that.

I wouldn't regret killing him, though.

Deep into the forest, where I'd dragged him, no one would hear his cries for mercy. Most importantly, she wouldn't hear. I had upset her enough tonight.

"Molochai has my wife, does he?" I asked coolly, circling him slowly.

Felix kept his eyes trained on the ground and nodded.

"Have you seen her?"

Felix nodded again, but I saw his lip tremble before he sputtered out, "Just bring him the girl, and you'll get your wife back."

My fists clenched, knuckles cracked, and I stared at him blankly. Made it look like I was contemplating it.

"Simeon's daughter . . ." Felix swallowed nervously and nodded back toward the inn. "I see the appeal." I lifted an eyebrow, encouraging him to go on. To give me more reasons to enjoy killing him. "She's . . . she's something."

I chuckled and nodded. As if I didn't know. As if I didn't spend every moment in her presence trying to refrain from ripping her clothes off, laying her down in the middle of the fucking forest, and taking her for myself. Spreading open those soft, warm thighs and feasting on her sweetness until she screamed my name. Until she felt no pain, no fear, no sadness, no burdens. Only me.

Some things—like the way she turned me into a fucking animal—never changed.

"What does she look like?" I asked. "You said you've seen her, my wife."

"She's . . . beautiful."

"What color is her hair?" I pressed. "Her eyes? Is she short? Tall? Thin? Young? Old? If she's so beautiful, I'm sure you took your time admiring her, just like you did with"—my mouth curled into a sneer—"Simeon's daughter."

That fucking *lie*.

"I only saw her for a second," Felix rushed out.

White-hot rage seared through me and escaped in a frustrated, guttural growl. The feral flames of lust and love within me turned to fury.

He howled when I fastened my hands on his jacket and thrust him against the trunk of a thick oak. "What did he promise you, Felix?"

"What—what do you mean?" His useless fingers pried at my grip.

My hand twitched—yearning for the feeling of his thin neck crushing beneath it. Playing dumb. I didn't like that, either.

"I *said*"—my other hand clamped down on his shoulder—"what did Molochai promise you for facilitating this little trade?"

"N-nothing!" Felix panicked. "He didn't promise me anything, Smyth! I'm just trying to help you."

"He doesn't have my wife, Felix."

"W-what do you mean?" He tried to shift out of my grip, but I tightened my hold. "He does. He has her."

"I don't think so, my friend."

He screamed when the switchblade hidden in my sleeve made a spectacular squelch in the flesh of his side, between his ribs.

I loved that sound.

"How do you know?" he wailed as I slowly twisted the blade

into the weak muscle of his abdomen. The poor bastard whimpered and gasped for breath. The warmth of his blood on my hand soothed me. But it was still ice cold compared to the warmth of her.

Snarling, I gripped his hair and jerked him backward. Thrust my fist once into the center of his face. The bone in his nose crunched while unhinged whimpers left his throat.

"Because *I* have her, you fucking imbecile!" I roared, casting him down to the earth. "And no one will *ever*..." I bent down to flatten his hand on the frigid ground and readied my fingers to break each of his.

"Take!"

Thumb.

"Her!"

Index.

"From!"

Middle.

"Me!"

Ring.

"Again!"

Pinky.

"Please!" he howled. But I soaked in the sound of his agonized cries. Glorious retribution for even thinking of hurting my Ella. "I'm sorry! Oh, gods!" He was on all fours, snot and blood dangling in strings from his broken nose. "Gods, please!"

"Oh, I assure you"—I shoved him onto his back with my boot—"I'm as far from your gods as you can get." I squatted beside him and ripped my blade from his side. Gripped him by the hair and exposed his neck. "Time to go, Felix. Give your father my regards. For his sake, I am sorry." I clicked my tongue on the roof of my mouth, feigning reconsideration, and then sighed, shaking my head. "Just not sorry enough."

"It was money!" The greedy idiot had sold out my Ella for money. Fury roiled through me again. But *he* was so shockingly stupid that it became an effort not to laugh. "My family!" he gasped. "My wife and son, please don't hurt them."

"I'll see to it myself that your family is taken care of. They are safe," I assured him calmly. That was true.

"Unfortunately," I said, sighing, "you are not."

And I slit his throat.

Typically, I enjoyed spilling the blood of my victims. When killing was *my* choice, I made sure they deserved it. I'd slit enough throats to anticipate how the blood would spatter and pour, so I easily ended Felix without staining any parts of my body aside from my hands and forearms.

Tonight, I didn't want a mess to deal with. Tonight, I was eager to get back to Aryella, even if just to savor the peaceful expression she wore when she dreamed and watch the steady rise and fall of her body, small but tough as nails. I wouldn't get to hold her in bed tonight. I had gone and fucked that up with the truth.

But it *had* been inevitable, telling her the truth. Just like it was inevitable that I would need to tell her the rest of it.

In the morning, I decided. I would tell her everything in the morning.

With a weary sigh, I bent down and rinsed my hands and forearms in the nearby creek, immune to the cutting shards of freezing water that assaulted my calloused skin. My reflection made me scowl. A weathered, scarred version of the young man she had once married.

I hated that I had to take her to those caves. To Simeon, the liar, the manipulator. To Elowen, that soul-sucking cow. To Elias Winterton, the young, unscathed warrior prince intent on taking what was mine. But he didn't even know me. No, none of them saw my face when I butchered their loved ones. I made sure of it. They knew me only by the mark Molochai compelled me to leave on each of my victim's bodies. The Butcher's mark.

As much as I wanted to further delay delivering my Ella to a prison of Simeon's design, there was no more time to train her, teach her, or help her see her value beyond the crown and that fucking prophecy. Felix Morton's scheme to make me give up "Simeon's daughter" made it clear that Molochai knew she was under my protection. And now, thanks to Felix, Molochai knew I had a wife, too.

He wanted to trick me into trading Ella for my wife. He didn't know they were one and the same, but if he found out . . . if he knew her real full name . . .

I swallowed down the vomit pooling in my throat, and increased the pace of my long strides toward the inn. When I arrived minutes later, I noticed the empty rope dangling from the hitching post. Before I took Felix into the woods, there had been a horse there—a dark brown gelding.

Felix was dead, but his horse was gone.

And somehow, I could feel . . . she wasn't near.

No.

"Ella!" I shouted, frantic, nearly stumbling over myself through the back door of the inn. I covered the length of the hall in four long strides and burst into our room. "Aryella!"

An empty bed and empty room.

No.

Not again.

"ARYELLA!" I shouted, heart pounding in my ears, tears biting at my eyes.

I wanted to weep. Scream. Rip out my hair, gouge out my eyes. Any pain would be more bearable than what I felt at the thought of losing her again. I wanted to shrivel up and fucking *die.*

But then, I wondered if I should be relieved she got away. At least for a little while, hiding would keep her safe from me if Molochai made the order I couldn't refuse. If I acted fast, I could swallow that poison around my neck, end my own miserable existence before I was sent on an involuntary quest to destroy the only thing I ever loved.

That's what I would do. Drink the poison. And if that didn't work, I'd carve out my heart and pay someone else to burn it.

My heart belonged to her anyway. Without her, I didn't want it.

She was smart. She was fast. She proved she could ride a horse like she used to. Her body remembered even if her mind didn't. And now, after nearly a month of nourishment and training, she was much, much stronger. She could get to those caves on her own.

But...

"No," I breathed upon glancing at the mess of paper on the floor. "*No.*" My bag had been ransacked. The letters from countless generations of Morton men were strewn across the floor. A note in her undeniable handwriting rested on the bedside table. "No, no, no, no..."

Consumed by terrible dread, I picked up that note, reminded far too vividly of the last time she left me with one.

Gavin,

I know Molochai has your wife, and I'm going to make a trade. I'm going to get her back for you. He can have me and my power if he lets her go and frees my people.

I will make him promise to take me and leave this land.

You said you want me to be free, but I want that for you, too. I would never be as strong as I am now had I not met you, and I'll never be able to express how grateful you've made me. You've helped me become someone I'm proud of. And for that alone, I believe you deserve all the good in this world.

I know I can do this.

Please don't follow me.

Be happy.

Ella

I choked out a dry sob, then tears came. I broke all at once, stumbling toward the door, crumpling the note in my hand. "No, Ella, no!" I stormed outside into the forest and found the trail of hooves heading south. "ARYELLA!"

The fault was mine. All mine. I had opened my desperate fucking mouth once. I'd said I had a wife in a plea for her to remember she was *mine.*

This was no one's fault but my own.

She was on horseback. She would get to that camp in an hour. If I ran and didn't stop, I could get there in two. Finding a horse of my own could be faster, but I hadn't seen any, and by the time I found one…

So I ran, seeing nothing, hearing nothing else but her. As I ran, I roared her name into the woods again and again in the hope that she could hear me. That she would know, even if she would never remember.

In every life, I would find her.

Chapter Thirty-Three

Aryella

I counted to three hundred. That was how long I let myself cry.

Then, I wiped my cheeks and eyes with the sleeve of my green sweater and focused forward. Straight south with no stops. Hopefully I wouldn't have to search long for the camp. Best to get this over with before I changed my mind.

The gelding was old, smaller and slower than our black mare, but he galloped as fast as he could. Fast enough that peppering sleet from the dark, overcast sky felt like tiny, pointed blades on my skin. I thought of my beloved friends, smiling and happy. It was the only way I could stifle the fear and keep from turning around.

An hour passed, maybe a little more, before I spotted torches casting an eerie glow in the distance. The horse slowed without needing to be told, sensing the impending danger.

Indeed, dark figures and their shadows slinked in and out of tents so black, I couldn't make out where one started and another began.

I shuddered. The bitterness in the air around me was unnatural. It stole the breath from my lungs and turned it to ice as it passed from my lips.

I gripped the hilt of my dagger to provide myself with some sliver of assurance. Some, not much. I wasn't here to fight.

The Insidions on guard gathered around a fire on the north side of the camp. I decided to leave the horse a long walk away, hoping they might never find it. One of us should make it out of here. Each step toward that fire was an effort, but I took every one.

A tall, beautiful female with an ebony mane saw me first. Her black cloak was hooded, but the hood rested over her shoulders. Her long legs and torso were clad in fighting leathers, and she had a sword sheathed at her side. From the attire, I knew this wasn't Gavin's wife, but I figured she must look something like this—statuesque and alluring. I hoped the gods spared me from seeing her, just so that part would hurt a little less.

The raven-haired woman strode out in front of the fire, her four comrades standing to attention at her movement. A few others meandering about their tents sniggered and stayed put. I wasn't enough of a threat to require their attention.

Infusing false confidence into my voice, I announced to the raven-haired woman, "I'm here to make a deal with Molochai."

She cocked her head at me. It was too dark to decipher her eye color, but they looked...*evil.* Her bright red lips peeled back to reveal a disturbingly beautiful smile.

"And why shouldn't we kill you on the spot? Walking so willingly into our camp. Quite...stupid." She folded her long, slender fingers at her waist. "Though Lord Molochai may choose to *enjoy* you first."

"Because I am Simeon Whitlock's daughter." I forced my shoulders up, back, and hid my trembling lip. "I am the one Queen Christabel foretold." A few more Insidions—equal to her in rank based on the insignia on their black lapels—sidled up to stand with her.

Her smile vanished.

"You?" she uttered icily, her eyes drifting to my long silver braid still tousled from bed. She laughed—a shrill, grating cackle. "You're her? How... *underwhelming*."

"Now, now, Kiana, don't envy the pretty little thing," purred the Insidion beside her. Another woman—short with dull brown hair in a tight bun. I glanced to their left, where three men with brutish features stood. "What deal do you propose?" asked the brunette woman.

"I want to make a trade. Myself for Smyth's wife."

The raven-haired woman scoffed. The men beside her looked at each other and laughed. She held up a slender hand to silence them. "*You* would sacrifice yourself for Smyth?"

I gritted my teeth, not deigning to answer, and said, "I want to speak to Molochai."

The brunette sidled up to me and stopped before me, too close. Her nostrils flared with a deep inhale, and something hungry flashed in her black eyes.

"So young," she crooned. "So... *willing*. I can smell your desire on you."

"No games," I hissed. "Take me to Molochai."

The woman ran a finger along my jaw as her pale lips curved into a smile. "You're no fun," she complained, sighing.

She struck a sharp blow with her fist to the center of my jaw.

I hit the ground and saw only darkness.

I woke up tied to a tree and stripped of my clothes, the ground beneath me frozen. I sat at the base of the tree, arms spread fully open, bound by rope—unyielding around each of my wrists—stretched around the trunk of the tree. I could use the strength of my core to stand but couldn't turn, hide, or cover a single part of my naked body. The icy forest floor numbed the soles of my feet and bare bottom.

The cold *burned* the rest of me.

My vision cleared to reveal at least ten Insidion men admiring my naked form. A few of them had one hand down their leather pants.

I screamed and fought against my binds. As I jerked, silky warmth brushed against my bare nipples. I glanced down to see my long hair was loose from its braid and covered both my breasts and most of my chest and shoulders. One small mercy.

"Where is Molochai?" I demanded, crying, spitting at them. "I'm here for *him*."

They laughed at me.

"*Easy*, my dear," purred a deep male voice. A tall, middle-aged man, flanked by shadows, emerged from behind the wall of lechers. "They can look, but they can't touch." I blinked back my tears and remained still as he approached. "That's enough, gentlemen."

They scattered on command but watched from afar, leaving me alone with a man whose shadow flowed behind him like a celestial cape. For just a moment, it reminded me of Nyxar's soothing midnight, only this darkness was no glittering onyx, no companion to light. This darkness suffocated and devoured everything good.

It felt *corrupted*.

He wore a black tunic jacket embossed with gold on the lapels. Elegant designs—nothing like his Insidions' sinister bloodred bull head sigils. His eyes were a deep, beautiful brown, and his black hair—thick and streaked with gray—was slicked back over his head. A perfectly groomed goatee framed a disturbingly handsome smile.

"I'm Simeon's daughter," I rushed out through chattering teeth. "I can prove it to—"

"You don't need to prove it to me, Ary." His long fingers were tipped with black talons. I sucked in a sharp breath when he reached for my face. "Somehow, you're even more beautiful than my Christabel." He gripped my chin between his clawed fingers. "And the resemblance is... uncanny."

My stomach lurched with terror and relief in equal measure. Because if that was true, then my plan might actually work.

"It *is* a shame I'll have to kill you," Molochai said, and sighed.

I refrained from pulling away. For him to agree, I needed to be compliant. "You don't want to kill me."

"Why is that?"

"Because I have an offer I think will interest you."

He smirked and tightened his grip on my chin. "I'm listening."

"You loved my aunt Christabel." I flinched when he brushed his nose against my temple and inhaled my scent. "I look like her. I'm young. I've never even been with a man. I can be what you want."

His lithe shadows danced around us, hungry and thrashing.

"And what would you require in return?"

"Let Smyth's wife go. I know you have her." His cold finger traced my collarbone. I bit my tongue to stifle a cry. "Take me and my power, and we'll leave Nyrida and never return. Free the people in these lands, and I will be whatever you want." He brushed a cold thumb over my breast. "That is my offer. Agree to it, and I . . . I will be yours."

His eyes, eerily bewitching, studied me.

"I don't have his wife, Ary." Molochai grinned. "I'm not even sure who she is. *But* it was a good little trick, wasn't it?" Gesturing around, he added, "So where is he?"

My eyes burned hot with tears for Gavin. For my failure. But part of this could still work.

"If you don't have his wife, then free my people." I forced my chin up defiantly. "Take me, end this fight with Simeon, and leave this world in peace."

He chuckled. "Very enticing, Ary. More than you know." His shadows—cold, like ropes of icy wind—snaked around my naked, shivering body. Over my bare breasts and around my torso. "But . . ." His cold, taloned finger slithered along the base of my neck. "There's a larger war to be won than the war between two old friends. The power Simeon and I bargained for is nothing compared to the power of the Selvaren. The power . . ." His finger moved over my navel . . . to my hip . . . to my thigh, a venomous snake waiting to strike. "That is meant to be *inside you.*"

A gasping shriek tore out of my throat and faded into broken sobs when the sharp tip of his taloned nail stabbed into the meat of my thigh.

My blood iced over. Darkness shrouded my vision. And when I

looked at my veins, they were swelling with black, beginning at the place he cut me. His darkness was *inside* my body.

He was everywhere, invading me.

I could barely breathe.

"I have it!" I gasped, fighting the panic and terror that clamped down on my throat. "I have the power you want. Accept my offer. I'll do *whatever* you want, just leave this world alone."

"I'm *inside* of you, and your people are all you can think about?" Molochai hissed out a laugh. "I'll have to give it some more effort."

Sobs racked me—silent, void of air. He lifted his bloodied, taloned finger to my cheek, down the curve of my jaw, stopping at my collarbone. He dug each nail of his claws through my flesh, one by one, until he hit bone.

I screeched, but he clamped his free hand over my mouth, silencing me so he could whisper against my cheek, his hot breath a sickening contrast to his cold lips. "When Simeon and I made our bargain, we were told that when you kill someone, their power shifts to the killer. It's quite the valiant sacrifice you are willing to make, darling, but your offer is useless to me. I must kill you to get what I need."

"Then kill me, and let them go!" I pleaded. "I won't fight you."

Anything to get this horrid, blackened ice out of me. Death was surely better.

"Why so eager to *die*, Ary?" he sneered. "It would be such a waste not to take my time with you. Clearly, you're…" He violated my shivering, naked form with his slow, salacious stare. "*Divine.* A sacrifice for your people is one thing, but it's particularly *intriguing* that you would give yourself up for such a despicable bastard."

"He's a better man than you could dream of being!" I spit in his face.

"Is he?" Molochai laughed darkly. He wiped my spit off his cheek with his thumb and licked it off. "Hmm," he purred. "You *are* delicious. It seems Smyth thinks so, too. After all, my shadows can smell him on you. Smell...how you want him, too." His nostrils flared as he glanced down between my thighs. "I typically enjoy this, but you? No, I will not enjoy killing you." His lip and brow furrowed in mock sadness. "And it'd be a shame for Smyth to miss it."

"Leave him out of this!" I gritted out. "He has suffered enough!"

Molochai flashed a sickening smile.

"Let's see how fast your screams make him run."

"No!" I thrashed against my binds, but the shredding darkness stole my vision, and I held my breath to brace for what was to come.

The absence of all things good.

I lost sense of time and struggled to breathe. Every time I gasped for air, my lungs were crushed by a clamping fist of consuming darkness, that black void allowing in only enough oxygen to see and hear and survive. I was just conscious enough, aware enough to feel the agony. And awareness was a torture of its own.

The shadows that blackened my blood twisted through me like serrated snakes. Slowly, methodically, while my body begged for relief. I screeched—the sound terrible and foreign—until my throat felt shredded and I tasted copper on my tongue.

I screamed, but I didn't beg. I refused to give him that.

Briefly, mercifully, I lost consciousness, only to be dragged back into his hell of invasive shadows.

Again...and again...and again...

Time became a blur. My limbs stung and burned. Frostbite, maybe? It had to be. Devoured by exhaustion, my chin limply dropped to my bloody shoulder.

And I realized—*exhaustion*, stinging, burning . . . I was feeling something other than shredding pain.

Exhausted but mercifully empty of darkness, I tried to lift my chin and blink away the lingering tears.

And then warm hands—*his* hands—were on my shoulders. My arms, my face.

"Ella!" Gavin pleaded, through the shadowy, consuming haze. "Aryella!"

Adrenaline pulled my eyes clear open. I looked at him, damp with sweat and struck with horror, then down at my skin, now pale and bloody but free of that black sludge in my veins.

No more shadows . . . for now. But if Gavin was here . . . what Molochai could do to him . . .

"No!" I screamed, jerking, thrashing away from him. "You can't be here! You have to go!"

"I'm not going, Ella."

He severed the ropes that bound me with his switchblade.

"You have to! I'm sorry," I breathed, crumbling into his arms without the ropes' support. "I wanted to end this." My body shuddered with tired, pathetic sobs. "I thought giving myself up would end this."

"And it's my fault you thought sacrificing yourself was an option," answered Gavin, his powerful voice *breaking*. His warmth draped over me, a protective, comforting blanket. I felt his gentle fingers on my chin before the cold shock of metal on my mouth. "Drink." He parted my lips with his thumb. "It's water. *Drink*."

I obeyed, grasping both of his forearms as he held the canteen to my lips. Once my vision began to clear, I took in his scarred, shirtless torso as he knelt before me and realized that the blanket of warmth I felt was his shirt cloaked over my no-longer-naked body.

"Gavin," I choked and tried in vain to push him away. "Your wife isn't here."

"Yes, she is." He took me in his arms and pressed a desperate kiss to my forehead. I felt his cheeks wet with tears and realized he was crying.

"You need to put me down." I tried to wriggle myself free, shoving weakly against his chest, but his arms were unbreakable steel. "He doesn't have your wife. I'm so sorry, but she isn't here! You have to leave me!"

"She's here, Ella," he said again, searching my eyes as he cradled my cheek, silently pleading. "And I'm not leaving."

"You shouldn't have followed me—"

"I have followed you through four hundred years and I will follow you through four thousand more!" His eyes—full of love and fear and sorrow—burned into mine. "*You* are my wife."

His words, like wisps of air, were fleeting, impossible to catch or prove I'd heard them. I was willingly trapped by the desperate love in his fervent gaze, but what he'd said...

"What?" I breathed.

"It's you." His voice was strong and clear. I hadn't misheard. But it wasn't possible. "*You* are my wife, and wherever you go, I follow."

I tried to shrink away from him, but he was holding me, cradling me like precious goods.

Like he truly believed his own delusion.

"That's not poss—"

"You don't remember because it was another life, Ella, a life that was taken from you a very, very long time ago," he rushed out. "You were eighteen, I was twenty-two." He cradled my face and smiled through his tears. "You needed a weapon, so you came to me. You snuck out of the castle and came to my blacksmith's shop. You asked me to help you, and I couldn't *breathe* when I saw you." He let out a tattered sob and kissed me again. "Four centuries later, and you still take my breath away."

I grasped at his words, trying to make sense of his story. And then, when I couldn't, I tried to withdraw. But there was nowhere to go. I tried to *push him* away but I was too weak from abuse, heartbreak, and betrayal.

"I don't understand," I cried softly. "You're lying to me."

"It's the truth. I have no wife—no *love*—but you." He cupped the back of my head through my hair. "I should have told you, I was *going* to tell you, but I was trying to let you live *here*, in this life." He stroked my cheek and scanned my face like I was fragile and fleeting. "And I'm so sorry I let you believe for a single fucking second that you're not the only thing I've ever loved."

But it wasn't possible, and I would be damned if this was the last moment of my life. Watching the man I loved become so desperate for the woman he lost that he would insert me into some sick dream of redemption. Reality mocked my heart, taunted me with a love that came so close but I would never have. And now, the gaping pit of emptiness drilled deeper and deeper into my chest, hellbent on being the last thing I would ever feel.

"You're wrong," I whispered.

"I'm not wrong. I need you to remember." He kissed my

forehead, then my cheeks. "Please, gods, *please*—I need you to remember what you can *do*, or he will—"

"I'm so glad you've decided to join us, my son."

Gavin froze, his ruggedly beautiful features fracturing into sorrow and terror. His large form curled around me, shielding me.

" 'Son'?" I breathed.

He watched, sorrowful, as horror slithered through me.

"Put down our little pet, Smyth."

"No." Gavin's steel grip on me tightened.

"*Put her down*," Molochai gritted out, "or she will suffer for it."

Gavin looked down at me, brow furrowed with pain, eyes wet with tears. "He cannot know." His lips barely moved. "What you are to me, *who* you are. He cannot know."

He lowered me to the ground.

"Gavin?" I choked, a sob escaping from my throat. It was instinct, not logic, that kept me latched to him. Pure survival. My weak fingers gripped him like a child being torn from its mother. "Gavin!"

"Hate me," he whispered with a gentle kiss on my forehead, "and *use it*."

I cried—not because I was afraid of Molochai. I was, but I had accepted my fate, knowing that choosing to come here would end my life one way or another.

I cried because Gavin set me down like he was obeying Molochai. Like he belonged to him.

And learning that, if it were true . . . was worse than dying.

"Why?" I wept, defeated, lost in disorienting torrents of terrible possibilities. My wolf slayer. My protector. My teacher. The man I loved. He left me crumpled in a puddle of mud and blood, barely clothed. And though I wanted to trust him as much as I wanted to breathe, he left me, and it felt wrong. So, so wrong. "Why are you going to him?"

No answer. Just silence. I knew, in the deepest parts of my soul, that I had been deceived in more ways than one.

I tried to draw into myself. Attempted in vain to convince my body to be calm as I cried broken sobs and grasped at the version of him I knew. Not this man who left me to drown in confusion and lies.

"She looks just like my Christabel. We have similar tastes, it seems." Molochai violated me with a languid stare. I flinched when his lip curled over his teeth in a snarl that I had seen before. Before, it had belonged to Gavin. Bile slithered into my throat at the uncanny resemblance. How I hadn't noticed before…the snarl. The smile. The *eyes*. "Ary." Molochai cocked his head at me, tsked three times, and flashed a wicked grin. "Did he not tell you who he was? Did he not tell you he killed Phillip Gold and your little Oliver?"

My stomach twisted painfully.

"Yes," hissed Molochai, grinning at me as he watched me fall apart. "The Butcher of Nyrida. A son so loyal, he's done my bidding for four hundred years."

"I'm not loyal to you." Gavin's words were bitter.

"You *wound* me, boy," Molochai scoffed. He turned sideways, and following his gaze, I saw that Gavin's face was sickly pale, his eyes damp from tears. A shell of a man. "I would like to know how you convinced her to give herself up for *you*," said the dark sorcerer. "When your little rat of a friend—Morton—told me of the search for your *wife*, I was offended you never shared the wonderful news of your nuptials with your own father. You should have told me why you made a deal with me that day. I would have helped you find your wife."

I looked back and forth between them. Gavin's eyes were trained on me in a silent plea. He gave me a head shake so subtle, I couldn't be sure I'd seen it, and he mouthed something, but I couldn't process it... all I could hear when I looked at him was...

"He killed... your little Oliver."

When I'd mentioned the Butcher, he'd gone so pale...

And his knife. That truth had stared me in the gods-damned face.

How incredibly stupid I'd been.

"Shocking, I know." Molochai cocked his head and flashed me a devilish smile. "A little too trusting, are we, Ary?"

"Ella," Gavin pleaded. My name was all he had to say, no defense or denial. He tried to lunge for me, but Molochai trapped him in a prison of shadows. Even with his brute strength and size, he couldn't escape it.

"You've been working for him," I wept. "You're on his side?"

"I'm on *your* side!" he shouted, scouring my face with his gaze. As if he needed to memorize it. "Since the moment I first saw you, I've been on your side!"

"Then tell me it's not true! Tell me you didn't kill Oliver." But in his eyes there was no denial, just regret. All I had left was a low, distressed wail as I seethed, "I hate you!"

Molochai's laughter roared. This was nothing more than a show for him—my life and my heart, breaking.

"Good! Hate me! Fight for yourself!" Gavin reached for me again, but it was futile against Molochai's power. "You can, Aryella! You can fight him!"

Molochai's laughter abruptly ceased when a gust of wind blew my hair off my shoulders. The left side of my chest caught his attention. He tore Gavin's shirt away, leaving the full scar over my heart visible, along with my naked breasts.

Molochai's skin paled. Darkness rolled around him in waves, now wild and uncontrolled. He looked at my face, back to the scar, then back at me. He froze.

And in his eyes there was suddenly . . . *fear*.

"You . . ." Molochai whispered, running his fingers along the scar over my heart. "You aren't Simeon's daughter."

Behind Molochai, Gavin bowed his head. When he lifted it, his soothing warmth and any remaining traces of *hope* were gone.

Molochai shuddered, wrapping his cold, taloned hand around my throat. "You filthy little *mutt*!" And he squeezed. Rage and darkness devoured his guile. Panic bled out of him through trembling, angry breaths and wild eyes. "And you knew!" He glared at Gavin, betrayal threading through his terror. "Simeon kept her hidden away all this time, and you knew her—and loved her—and *she*"—he laughed in wild disbelief, pointing his other set of taloned fingers at Gavin—"*she* is why you came to me, so desperate." Shadows shrouded Molochai's eyes in deep onyx. "She is your *wife*."

Molochai stared at the scar above my heart. "Of course, you don't remember the day I gave you that scar," he snarled. "You *were* only three days old, after all."

Gavin strained against the ropes of darkness confining him. Roaring, snarling—the sounds of a rabid animal. And behind him were the sneers of Insidions as they gathered to watch our suffering.

Molochai's laugh was loose and maniacal. "Such a sad thing, your little wife. Angelically beautiful, yes, outside *and* in. I felt for myself." He arched an eyebrow and wiggled his taloned fingers, still caked in my blood from the places he'd sliced me open. "But *weak*, whiny…such a petulant *child*!" Molochai dug his claws into my skin and spit in my face. "It took a little longer than I'd hoped, but you and Simeon led her right to me."

"Take *me*!" Gavin shouted desperately. "Take my life, my soul, but not her!"

Molochai scoffed. "You'd wait so long for her, you'd suffer so terribly, just to have her for what? Weeks? Days?"

"Yes." Those deep brown eyes, rimmed with tears, gripped me. Held me. Promised me.

Molochai bared his teeth. "Is she really worth throwing away your long, miserable existence?"

"Yes." A tear rolled down Gavin's cheek. "Always."

"Special indeed." Molochai brushed his knuckle against my cheek. "Sheer, untapped power. I *would* have him kill you. Punishment, for keeping you from me." Molochai's thin red lips curved into a menacing grin. "But I would prefer to do the honors myself." He revealed a long, jagged blade from a sheath at his side. "Since you escaped it the first time."

The first time? Confusion whirled through me like my enemy's dissonant shadows.

"Ella!" Gavin roared. "Fight!"

Molochai tsked and shook his head. "It seems, my son, that you and I have managed to steal the fight right out of her."

The dagger bit into my hip and it felt like burning hot coals in my side. A scream ripped from my throat.

Gavin roared, a wild and desperate sound that brought a sinister grin to Molochai's face. But Gavin was paralyzed where he stood. Held back by shadows.

Molochai twisted the knife above my navel before slicing upward into the flesh of my ribs. So slowly I felt everything. My scream faded into a broken, weakening cry.

"NO!" roared the man I loved and hated, again . . . and again . . . and again. Each agonized shout was like a blade. Veins threatened to burst through his skin; the flex of his arms was deadly, his muscles tearing, as he vainly fought against shadows to get to me.

But I realized there was nothing—truly nothing—he could do against Molochai.

Which meant I was going to die.

I'd known this, though. I had understood the risk, offering myself up. Me for his wife. That was the deal I'd accepted.

"Fight him, Ella!"

Out of an instinctual compulsion to obey him, I began to reach for the temple, for my wheel of power, but then . . . I wasn't sure I wanted to.

The Queen of Nyrida had plenty to live for—a noble betrothed, devoted friends, thousands of people to worship at her feet, a war destined to be won in glorious victory. The power to heal, move the land, the oceans, the fire simmering in the earth's core, and the very air she breathed. But when I tried to summon something—anything—to save myself, nothing came.

I wasn't sure if any of those things were mine. Not really. Not when I couldn't even make sense of who I was.

I stared at the cold ground, empty and lost. Eyes wet with tears. Wondering if silence might be a relief. I prayed for calm, for Nyxar, for any of the gods to end it. I'd rather be dead than live without knowing myself.

But Gavin called my name, and something stirred in my chest.

A distant memory, not my own. An invisible string stretched out of me and latched on to him, refusing to be severed. It was...familiar, as if, even before he saved me from the wolf in that barn, it had lived within me, reaching for him. Only just now had I let it break, cleaved in two by my doubts.

"Eyes on me!" Gavin demanded. The invisible string grew taut, doubly strong. It heard his command, and the connection dutifully obeyed. And so did I. "Good girl, that's my girl." Violent trembling and suffocating tears racked my body, but Gavin held his gaze. "I love you!" He gritted his teeth through the fractured despair in his voice and became a stone pillar of strength. "And I'm going to follow you!" The sharp tip of Molochai's silver blade punctured my stomach. Whimpering screams tore through me, and he shouted over my agony, over his own voice breaking. "I swear on every star, every sky, every soul that has passed through this world, I will follow you! I will find you! Whatever it takes."

Those three words were all it took. And I was suddenly somewhere else.

"Whatever it takes."

It was odd, considering he'd said those three words before, and though they made an imprint on my heart, they had never taken me...elsewhere.

This time, I watched fragments of a foreign life reel across my memory, unfamiliar images taunting me with things that never were and never could be mine. Gavin with his hair shorter, face clean-shaven, younger, unbearably handsome, carefree, scarless, and full of hope. A small, cozy loft above a blacksmith's shop. A secluded field showered in sweet, summer rain. A small gray cat rubbing against my ankle. A silver ring on my finger. A metal blue jay on a string.

A promise never to let me carry the weight of the world alone.

The images disappeared as quickly as they came, torn from me while Molochai's jagged blade sliced into my chest. The pain was so bright, I couldn't see or taste or hear.

I screamed until there was no sound left. At some point, shock took over. I briefly tasted and felt the coppery warmth in my mouth, but my senses began to dull shortly after.

Molochai's voice . . . a sinister whisper.

"Your heart can't heal if it's gone."

My vision blurred. The scene . . . fading . . . in and . . . out . . . and . . .

He reached into my chest, and he tore out my heart.

My body was thrust through the air, swiftly and violently. I was launched backward, up, away from them both, over the edge of the cliff.

And all I could hear—somehow, even after my heart had left my body—was Gavin's agonized roar, fading in front of me, above me, then completely away. From another world.

Until my gutted body was plastered on the hard rock below.

I felt my body shatter. Not in a figurative sense. Not soul-shattered, or with a shattered heart, but physically splintered from head to toe, composed of bloody fragments. A broken shell.

As every single bone in my body broke, I thought that soon the shock would become overwhelming. A strange form of relief before death's consuming kiss.

But as I lay there on the hard rock, somehow still existing, I realized I'd been wrong. I felt it all, every agonizing wheeze as my body worked by some divine will to keep me alive. I wasn't sure how far

I'd fallen, but I'd suffered a jagged blade through my chest. And my heart…was *gone.* I felt no pulse. It was impossible that I was alive, but it seemed the gods had one more cruel thing in store for me.

Hearing him weep.

The scarred hands I had come to know slid underneath my body, and I heard his voice. "Ella!" he wept, lips against my forehead. He began to murmur something under his breath, something that sounded foreign—a prayer—and he didn't stop for…I don't know how long. I had one foot in consciousness and the other in death. Time didn't exist.

His trembling voice was so faint, a whisper. Or perhaps it was the angels, the gods, my ancestors calling me to my new home. "I love you! Come back to me, *please*!" Gavin shouted desperately, finally giving up on whatever peculiar phrase he'd been repeating, until all he could cry was, "Ella, my Ella, my Ella, my love, my Ella…"

Just let me die, I thought, because I couldn't speak. *Just let me go.*

Gavin didn't say anything else. He wailed. He roared. It was a horrific sound, like fragments of his soul reluctantly splintering out of the only home they knew.

It was all I heard.

The world around me went dark.

And I was dead.

Chapter Thirty-Four

The grass was warm beneath me. Sunlight, hot on my skin. A light summery breeze. I lay flat on my back, and when I turned my head and saw a familiar wooden house and barn with worn siding, I knew I was back in Warrich.

But if that was so, this sunlight and gentle breeze were not right. I rose up on my elbows and took in my surroundings. No clouds—the sky in Warrich had never looked so blue, even in summer. A flock of goldfinches danced through the clearing. The sharp chirps of their calls made a gleeful song in the peaceful air. One more thing out of place.

And then I saw Oliver.

He sat in the grass beneath the apple tree Phillip had cut down just weeks before their deaths. It had been our favorite spot, but the tree had developed a fungus, rendering it useless. Now, the tree was abundant with bright red apples.

"Ollie?" I stood but paused when I felt no pain. I rested a hand over my chest and found that my heart beat steadily in my chest.

I looked down at my clothes. A fluttering white dress with short sleeves, and I was barefoot. No blood. No fatal tear through my torso.

"Hi, Ary."

I bit back a broken cry. His back was to me, but that sweet voice—so clear, so happy. For over a year, I had only heard it in my dreams.

In one hand, he pushed around a toy wooden carriage painted green and yellow. Tucked beneath his other arm was a plush toy horse. Black, with a spot of white on its chest. I remembered the little stuffed horse from the day I found them. Even in death, he'd held it against his chest, untouched by the blood. But thinking back, I couldn't recall ever seeing that horse before that moment. My mind must have done what it could to block out any more details.

My tears were silent as I knelt in the grass at his side. I was afraid to touch him. For this to be a dream. That fear manifested in trembling lips and hands as I tried to understand how I got here.

I felt like I was stuck swimming beneath a thick sheet of glass covered with doors. Through each door, I could see up above the surface, into a different world, where scared and angry voices beckoned and begged for me. But only one door was real. Only one could be opened. And I would have only one chance to try.

"Are you real, Oliver?" I whispered. From the side, he looked happy and serene. "Are you . . . *here*?"

"Of course I'm here." His small hands wrapped around my arm and squeezed. "Where else would I be?" Ollie looked up at me without a single trace of sadness. "Did he find you, too?"

"Who?" I asked.

"The man with the scar on his face."

I worked my throat through a swallow to suppress the acidic burn of vomit. Oliver's shirt was clean—no sign of that X I'd seen carved into his chest the day I found them dead. I hadn't considered that mark might have been the work of the Butcher of Nyrida, but now…

"I'm so sorry, Ollie." I turned and cupped his face in my hand. His skin was even softer than I remembered—without a single blemish save for the cute mole on his forehead. Everything about him seemed lighter. "What happened to you—you must have been so scared—"

"I wasn't scared." Oliver looked up at me again, smiled, and held up the small stuffed horse. "He was nice. He said Papa was taking a nap, so he gave me some juice and this horse, too." He stood and hugged the horse to his chest. "Besides, it's better here. I don't ever get sick, hungry, or cold, and Papa isn't sad anymore."

"Where…" I worked my throat through a swallow and looked around. "Where is Papa?"

Oliver nodded toward the house. "Inside."

"Will he talk to me?" I wasn't sure what either of us would say, Phillip and I. But I felt the need to tell him how sorry I was for burdening his family. I also needed to demand the truth. Not Simeon's story or *his* story—it hurt to think of my teacher's name—but the untainted truth.

Oliver shook his head. "You can't go in."

"Why not?"

"Because you can't stay here." As he stood, he pointed toward the trees in the direction I'd gone with my friends on that day that felt so long ago. "You have to go back." He grabbed my fingers and pulled. "You have to get up."

"I don't know if I want to."

"Why not?"

Anger soured my stomach. "Because all everyone does is lie to me."

"Yeah." Oliver sighed. "I remember when they brought you home. Mama said you had been asleep for a very long time and that you were too weak to know where you came from, so I had to pretend you were my sister. Like a game," he added. "But I think she was wrong. I think you know who you are."

"I *don't*." He seemed confused by my denial, so I reiterated, "I *don't* know who I am, Ollie."

"Well, *I* do." Oliver threw his arms around my neck and squeezed so tight, there was no doubting that he was indeed real. I didn't know what plane of existence we were on. But it was *real*. "You're the strongest person I know," he said, and I could feel his mouth curve into a smile through the cloth of my dress.

I drew in a ragged breath and held him, knowing this was the chance to say the goodbye we'd never been given.

"I love you," I said, tearfully pressing a kiss to his temple.

"I love you, too, Ary." He pulled back, and his responding smile was as bright as the summer sun. This kind of joy would be unnatural in the cold and brutal Warrich I had once known. But here, he fit. "You can go now."

I burst into tearful laughter at his innocent candor and stood. It hurt to walk away, but I found peace in Oliver's happiness. And despite the unknowns and lies and calamity awaiting me, the pull to return to life was too strong.

"Ary?" Oliver called when I reached the edge of the tree line. I turned to see him hugging his horse to his chest. "Papa and I know you told the man with the scar on his face to be happy." Oliver's face brightened into a beaming grin that stretched from ear to ear.

A warmth settled in his eyes, too mature, too knowing for a five-year-old boy. As if Phillip—sober and clear-eyed—was speaking through him. "He told me to tell you he's sorry he didn't fight for your truth when he should have. He said it's okay to be angry because of what's been taken from you, and happiness…you deserve that, too."

Oliver turned toward the house. I watched him disappear through the front door. With his beloved stuffed horse in tow, he waved me a final farewell.

I took a breath, closed my eyes, and stepped into the dense thicket of trees.

Chapter Thirty-Five

The pain returned when I woke and found myself in the softest bed I'd ever known.

I groaned weakly at the terrible, throbbing ache in my abdomen, from my chest to my navel, radiating in waves through my rib cage and back. Sweat prickled the back of my neck, but my limbs felt cold. I looked down to see my entire torso wrapped in gauze bandages beneath a white cotton nightgown. Clean, no blood. But my chest…

Thump… thump… thump…

My heartbeat.

I let out a broken, grateful cry at the strong pulse in my ears.

"She's waking up." I heard a man's voice—Damond's, I thought—and the frantic shuffling of heavy footsteps in the room disappeared. I was too disoriented to see who had been with me.

My eyes darted around the quaint, tiny room. I was in a bed with cornflower blue sheets. In the far-left corner sat an oak wardrobe and, beside that, a matching bench.

A familiar growl rumbled in the hallway. Damond's responding voice was hoarse, and he sounded far away. "Let me talk to her first."

"Get the fuck out of my way—"

"Five minutes, Smyth!" snapped Damond. "Give me five min—"

"She is my *wife*!"

That voice. Once warm and soothing, now cold, threatening.

I could still hear their voices outside the door, but they had lowered them enough that I couldn't make out what they were saying. Through the glass window, I saw gentle blue and white foam washing over sand. A beach, and beyond it, the gray sky of a winter's day loomed.

The door to the small bedroom creaked, and I looked up to see Damond. He closed the door partway, turned, and gave me a contrite smile. He wore brown pants and a blue sweater. On his head, the same round glasses and impressive mop of brown curls. I'd seen him only days before, but it felt like lifetimes.

"Hey, Ary."

I eyed him warily, remembering the conversation with Gavin I'd overheard that first night in Tovick. There wasn't a single doubt in my mind that he'd known. Never again would I trust so easily. It would lead me to destroy myself. Not Damond, not a single one of my friends, not Simeon or Elowen or anyone in those caves.

And certainly not Gavin Smyth.

He read the doubt on my face and promised, "I'm not going to hurt you."

I grunted through the pain of hoisting myself from lying down to sitting.

"Try to stay still—"

I silenced Damond with a furious glare, nostrils flaring, lip curled, and I could tell I startled him.

"Molochai dragged a knife through my body."

"Yeah." Damond shuddered, lowering himself into a wooden chair beside the bed. "Yeah, he did."

"He ripped out my heart."

Damond nodded.

"And then he threw me over the edge of a fucking cliff."

Nervously, he shifted in his seat and nodded again.

"My heart's beating, Damond."

"Viridian." He gestured to me. "God of Healing... *and* Regeneration."

I gave a low, disbelieving snicker and shook my head.

"It's true, Ary," he contested.

"I was dead, *Damond*. I remember being somewhere *else*." The words snapped out of me. My throat pinched at the memory of Oliver. "How could I have *remade* my own heart if I was *dead*?"

"He told me he prayed to the Selvaren. Something ancient, in their language." Damond bent forward and clasped his hands in his lap. "He saw it with his own eyes. Your blood pooled around you, the ground tasted it, knew it was you, and then you breathed as if *your* blood commanded life itself."

"He?" I uttered coldly.

But I knew who. Had heard his rumbling voice just moments earlier on the other side of that bedroom door. He was here.

Molochai's son.

The Butcher of Nyrida.

Fragments of the dream I'd just woken from drifted back. I sat there and relived it all.

Oliver. His words. His... *peace*.

"The man with the scar on his face... He was nice..."

I shuddered and shoved away that impossibility.

"Have you known the whole time?" I demanded. "About… Smyth." To say his first name would have felt like I was betraying Ollie.

Damond's brow furrowed down at the cornflower blue bedding. "I'm his cousin, Ary," he reminded me.

"He's Molochai's son."

"Cousin on his *mother's side*," Damond emphasized with a lift of his brow. "But he *is* family, and he has an explanation for everything he's done."

"An explanation," I repeated, horrified. "He *murdered* Oliver and Phillip. An innocent five-year-old boy, Damond!" He killed Elias Winterton's parents and little sister. He killed and killed and killed my people. And I was beginning to feel even more alone than I had upon waking. If Damond knew, my friends might know, too. "Who else of my friends knows he's the Butcher?"

"He told Gemma everything before you left Tovick. The others—Caz, Finn, Ezra—they don't know."

Gemma *knew*. Not me, but Gemma. And she let me go with him. *"He won't hurt you."*

I shuddered at the memory. How very wrong she'd been.

"*You* could have told me the truth," I bit out, eyes locked on my fingers, which were gripping the blankets.

"Not my truth to tell." Damond picked up a glass of water from the side table and moved to take a sip. I watched him, appalled by his calm. He opened his mouth to say more but stopped when my attention shifted toward the door.

There he stood. My betrayer, my *heartbreak*. I could tell by the dark circles under his eyes that he hadn't slept in days. He wore all black, and his hair fell loose and messy at his shoulders. He towered over the rest of the room, but there was something exhausted and defeated in the way he stood.

"That wasn't five minutes," Damond muttered with a roll of his warm brown eyes. Regardless, he rose. "I'll be outside." Stopping briefly in the doorway, he shot me an apologetic glance before leaving the room.

Gavin appeared visibly broken, but the way he looked at me with warmth and love and sorrow still gripped my rejuvenated heart and squeezed. That longing stare hurt more than the jagged wound Molochai had left behind. Trust, love, forgiveness—these were things I vowed never to give him back. But the moment his eyes met mine, my vow began unraveling.

I hate him, I said to myself. *I have to hate him.*

So I chose to let more unbridled rage rise to the surface. Because it was easiest. Because it was the only feeling loud enough to smother the confusion wreaking havoc in my core.

"Get out," I choked.

But he didn't move. I shivered beneath his piercing, knowing stare. I remembered the things he knew. The things I should have questioned. Honey and green tea, my middle name, my mother's love for blue jays, my birthday...

"Because I know everything about you."

"Get...the hell...*OUT*!" I screamed, but it was a mistake. Sharp pain splintered up and down my torso with the speed and ferocity of a lightning strike. I gasped for air and tried to maintain clear vision through watery eyes.

"Please." He rushed immediately to my side. "Please don't do that. Your powers kept you alive, but barely. You have a very long road to healing. For your own sake, you need to try and stay calm."

"Stay calm?" I wheezed, gritting my teeth through the pain. "Stay fucking *calm*?"

The skin on his face, neck, and hands flushed and he raised his hands in supplication. "I know I have no right."

"Leave. Me. Alone. Get *away from me*!" I pleaded, shattering into sobs. "I never want to see you again! Go!" My plea floundered into a pathetic squeak.

"No." His face contorted in pain, but he didn't move. "Not until you give me a chance to explain. Ask me anything, and I will tell you the truth."

"It's a little too late for that," I croaked.

He snatched my blade off the dresser and—before I could scream or register an attack—he opened my hand, placed the knife in it, and knelt beside the bed.

"Give me a chance to explain myself to you." His deep voice shook with the strained desperation he drowned in. "If you still don't believe I'm on your side..." He watched me remember the moment after he killed those Insidions in the woods. "If, when I'm done, you still hate me enough to wish me dead, I'll beg you to kill me."

I would not listen. To do anything for his sake felt like betraying myself and those I loved. The brutal push and pull I felt in his presence was a curse. I just knew, after speaking with Oliver and taking this second chance at living, I needed to find the will to persevere. Even if this life was a gods-damned mess.

But I needed to know. Needed the pieces to fit.

"I will ask you questions. You will answer. And only then, if I choose not to kill you, you will *leave*," I rushed out to quell the hope rising in him, the waves of relief washing over him. "That is all you get."

"Yes," he breathed. "Thank you."

Patiently, he waited, and I had to rack my cluttered brain with where to begin. My eyes shifted to the silver rings around his neck.

"Am I really the wife you spoke of?"

Without breaking my gaze, he unfastened the black cord around his neck and placed it, and the rings, at my bedside. "Yes."

"Do you . . . do you truly love me?"

"*Yes.*" He dug his fingers into the bedding. He strained as he held himself back from me, tears brimming in his gaze. "Yes, *gods*, I love you. With everything I am, I love you."

I tore my burning eyes away from his. His confession of love opened the door to a place of tolerance I did not want to go to.

"How old am I?" I muttered.

"You've lived only twenty years. But if you count the years you've been trapped and asleep . . . four hundred and twenty-two."

"And you?"

"Four hundred and twenty-six."

"How many years have *you* lived?" A chilling pause.

"All of them."

I didn't understand how it was possible, but my heart still hurt for him. For that persistent loneliness in the dull brown eyes that just days ago had sparkled with love. The ache in my chest at the thought of him—or who I thought he'd been—alone for so long . . . I couldn't reconcile it with the things I now knew.

"Are you Molochai's son?" I pressed on.

"Yes." His voice darkened. "He raped my mother, and she died in childbirth."

I blinked out a tear. For her. Not for him. *Not for him.*

"Are you—" I looked up at him then, needing to see the look in his eyes when he answered this next question. "Are you the Butcher of Nyrida?"

His tormented gaze dropped to his hands, then back up to me, where it steadily remained. "I am."

"How many people have you killed?" I thought of the tattoos that wound around his body.

"I don't know." He swallowed hard. "I lost count."

"And you killed Phillip and Oliver?"

He flinched but nodded. "Yes."

I knew it. I did. But to hear him say it thinned the air in my lungs, what was left of it whipping out of me with every horrified gasp. He shifted toward me, hands flexing to reach for me, to comfort me. But I abruptly withdrew from him, causing the raw wound in my belly to burn. I cried weakly and held a trembling hand over my abdomen.

"*Breathe.*" His helpless gaze raced up and down my trembling body. It was killing him not to touch me. "Please breathe."

"Why did you kill them?" I groaned out, vision swirling, head dizzy with pain. "*Why?*"

"I made a blood oath with Molochai," he confessed. "I agreed to be his weapon. He says a name, and I don't have a choice. The oath takes over. I don't have much time before my body is no longer mine, and then I lose control until it's done. But Ella," he continued, compassion pouring from him like a warm silver stream, "when I was sent to kill the Golds, I didn't even know you were with them. Neither did Molochai. And it was *not* your fault they died."

I scowled, fury brewing low in my chest. He lied to me, turned my world upside down and left me hanging by my ankles, and *still* knew me. Still knew I blamed myself.

"It was *not* your fault," he pressed on. "They were descendants of

Simeon and Christabel's cousins—*your* cousins. Molochai wanted them dead, and it had nothing to do with you."

I refused to forgive him. Shook my head. Let rage infect my heart because it was easier than accepting the convoluted mess my reality had become.

"You let me confide in you about their deaths," I uttered hatefully. "You asked me to give you that burden, knowing you were the one that did it."

"Because it *is* my burden to carry, not yours." He reached for my hand, pausing to see if I would pull away. I should have, but I didn't. He touched me, and I didn't have it in me to recoil. As if my mind couldn't trust him but my body did. So this time, I let him touch me, and though I hated myself for it, he soothed me. Even as he spoke terrible truths, my breathing slowed, my pulse calmed. "It was never supposed to be yours."

He was so close, so warm, so rich with the scent of fresh cedar and leather that I wanted to bury myself in his chest. My source of pain and place of refuge in equal measure.

Murderer, I repeated in my mind, over and over again. *He's a murderer.*

But that was something I knew from the beginning, wasn't it?

"Why did you make a deal with him?" I jerked my hand away, resetting myself in resentment.

"Because it was the only way I could see you again." His hand remained on the bed, reaching for me. "I agreed to be his executioner in exchange for immortality."

Nausea churned my stomach. Molochai said he considered having Gavin kill me but preferred to do it himself. Indeed, in Tovick,

I'd overheard Gavin tell Damond that Molochai would want to kill me himself. And he had.

If murders hadn't been his choice…what a special kind of torture.

"Did you give Oliver a toy horse before you killed him?" I sputtered out.

He exhaled shakily, eyes wide, but he didn't ask how I knew. He nodded.

"What color was it?"

Without hesitation, he replied, "Black with a white diamond on its chest. I just…" His voice cracked. "I didn't want him to be afraid. The children, I…" He released a tormented breath. "The oath was never meant to apply to innocents. It wasn't what I agreed to."

A special kind of torture, indeed.

"And the prophecy?" I croaked.

"The prophecy is a lie, but your power is not. Four hundred years ago, shortly after we married, Simeon abducted you, put you in a deep, ageless sleep to buy himself time. He convinced this whole world—save for me, Elowen, and Phillip—that you were his and Elowen's child. Your people believe Christabel's child died at three days old. And until the other night, Molochai believed that, too. He's been looking for the power of the Selvaren since the day you were born. He can…sense it. But he had no idea you survived him. He had no idea that power is *you*. His ignorance is the only good thing that came from Simeon's lie."

"Christabel's child?" My tearful face contorted with confusion.

Molochai's words echoed in my memory.

"You aren't Simeon's daughter..."

"Filthy little mutt..."

"Of course, you don't remember the day I gave you that scar... you were only three days old, after all..."

Gavin nodded and gestured toward the scar on my chest. "That's where he stabbed you. Where he tried to kill you."

Nausea curled in my stomach. I remembered how angry he'd been when he asked where I'd gotten the scar and I hadn't known its origin. As if that knowledge had been stolen from me.

And when he'd told me about his wife, if it was true it was me or whoever I used to be...

"Brought up in a prominent, wealthy family... Protected but... stifled."

Then he had not lied about that.

I lifted my hand to the thin, faded scar and tried to remember my life so that I could prove him wrong. So I could prove that *this* was the life I knew. That this life had been *full*. But that was a lie. And I couldn't remember.

A part of me had always been numb, even when Ollie was my only source of joy. After his death, I was completely empty. I'd told Gavin as much that day he tended to the wolf bite.

Elowen had said it had been a fall that took my memories from me, and I wondered... how stupid I had been not to question that. Not to question so many things. Could a fall erase nineteen years? Could it erase memories of Oliver as a baby, if they'd existed? And I'd known she resented me for *something*. For being an unwanted burden—a responsibility.

And my nightmares... I always shoved away the feeling that they were horrible memories. I hadn't thought it was possible. But in those nightmares, I was trapped. Always torn. Always terrified. Always . . . *lost.*

"It wasn't a fall that erased your memories," Gavin said softly, glancing at my fingers on my head. "It was Simeon."

"Why would Simeon do that to me?" I whispered.

"He was afraid of you," Gavin answered. "You struggled to control your powers. *He* couldn't control them, and he feared what you might do if"—his throat pulsed with a hard swallow—"they were unleashed. He was not prepared to fight Molochai, and he didn't think you were, either. So he locked you up, hid you, erased who you were, took his time learning about your powers, gathered an army beneath that mountain to fight with you, and woke you up with every intention of using you as a tool to destroy his nemesis. He made you his blank slate."

I made every effort to not let that pathetic, devastated whimper loose from my throat.

I was a tool to these people. A weapon. An object to be used. When I thought of Elias and my people—though determined to help them—I already felt like a grand idea rather than a person with thoughts and feelings.

Perhaps I'd never been wrong for feeling uneasy about that.

"But my memories. Why?"

"Because I was Molochai's son, and you loved me. I was a distraction. A liability. Simeon couldn't have that," Gavin uttered. "But he underestimated the lengths I would go to follow you."

True. Four hundred years. For me. My chest burned with compassion, with hope, but I tamped those feelings down. "If he hates you so much, why did Simeon send you to me now?"

"After four hundred years of being the Butcher, if he didn't let me come to you..." His eyes darkened and chilled. "Well, let's just say I made the consequences of that choice very clear."

I shuddered at the man before me. What he was capable of. I realized now I could only imagine, and I did not want to.

"If it's all true," I whispered, "why didn't you tell me?"

"When I saw how afraid you were, when Gemma told you what happened between Simeon, Molochai, and Christabel, I decided I was going to. But then, despite your fear, despite your hesitation, you made the choice to help this world. You found purpose when you had none, and I couldn't bear to take that away from you."

"I could have found that purpose knowing the truth."

"You said you didn't want a husband." Rejection darkened his features. The memory of my own words back in Warrich—words I'd said about Elias—scraped in my chest. "And why would you, when you're barely twenty years old, with the weight of this world on your shoulders?" He shook his head. "I refuse to force our history on you, especially when I'm bound to Molochai, and I don't know how long I..." He trailed off, voice trembling.

"You should have told me," I whispered. "I wanted *you*."

"You just wanted me to *fuck* you." His face contorted in pain.

Tears bit at my eyes because he believed that was true. It wasn't all I wanted. It was all I had allowed myself to dream of.

"Ella, this is your reality now. I wanted to give you the chance to figure out who you are, what you want in *this* life."

"It was my right to know."

"And I'm a fucking coward!" The words cracked out of him, harsh and low. "I'm a coward for being so terrified to lose what affection you've had for me these past weeks. I couldn't stand the thought of being another person trying to trap you into a role you don't want."

He ran his hands over his face and paused, considering his next words.

"From the day you were born, others have determined who they want you to be. You have spent your life in shackles, Aryella, then *and* now." He wrapped his hands around my tired, trembling fingers. "There isn't a time or a life or a universe where I do not love you, but I will not tell you what I am to you *now*. You decide. I've tried—and likely failed—to show you the best of me, to show you how much I love you, but it is *your choice*." His face contorted with agony, and I knew he was thinking of the other things—the other *person*—I could choose. And it was killing him.

"Your life—what we were—was stolen," he continued. "And *gods*, when... *if* the time comes that I am free from Molochai, I pray that you choose me again." Desperation bled out of him like he'd been cut wide open just as I had. "But choose me in this life, not because of a vow you made four centuries ago in a life you don't remember. When I said the one thing I want most is your freedom, I meant it. I am many, many terrible things, but for you, I will not be another chain."

"Then you shouldn't have come." But the words sounded unconvincing, even to me. "If this is my life now, you shouldn't have shown up here." My throat tightened. I'd let him touch me. I'd begged him for more. I'd *wanted* more then, and a part of me I was scared of still did want him. "You shouldn't have let me... *feel* things for you."

"And I told you I'm a selfish bastard," he uttered darkly. "I couldn't stay away from you, Ella. If I was a better man, I would have, but I'm not. I had to know you could fight for yourself before going to those people. I had to try... for your *heart*... *gods*, I had to try. And I had to know *you* again if it was the last thing I ever did."

"But I'm not her anymore." I shook my head. "I'll never be whoever she—whoever *I* was—to you."

Though it was true, I only said it to remind him of what he'd lost and could never get back. I was lashing out, needing to share my hurt. And I knew he would sit there and take whatever cruel words I delivered.

He did. He took my beating and squeezed my hand, his gentle smile infusing me with familiar, soothing heat. "You will always be my miracle." A tear rolled down his face, over his scar and beard. "Simeon erased your memories, but he could never erase you."

I sealed my lips together, my jaw shut, to suppress the sob threatening to wrench free. I stared at his hands as they held mine. Those hands that sliced the blade through Phillip and Oliver Gold's throats were attached to *his* body. I also saw firsthand what Molochai could do and dared wonder if there indeed *was* a part of Gavin that Molochai controlled. Because when I looked at him, I *was* angry, but I couldn't tell if I was angry for me or for the both of us.

No matter how much I wanted to hate him with every morsel of my being, his touch, his voice, his presence all remained a welcome invasion. My body betrayed me. There was a pull inside me that couldn't detach from him, and it was stronger now than it had been before.

But right now, anger was the only safe feeling. It made sense, and I told myself I needed it to heal.

Weeks ago, I had been an empty canvas hidden away in my cabin waiting for the brightest paint to stick, and now I was nothing but muddled strokes of silvers and reds and blues and golds and *black*. That was what happened when you tried to fit too many colors on one canvas.

I didn't have to speak for him to see it seething from my soul.

I let the chaotic darkness bleed out so he could witness what he'd done, what they'd all done. You could only twist and pull a rope in so many directions before it snapped.

"I want you to go," I whispered. A lie, but I forced it out.

He hesitated, then released my hands.

"Please go." I spoke, this time to muffle the part of me that was crying out for him. "*Please.*"

Agony burned in his gaze, but his unrelenting love was stronger. He stood to go.

"I love you, Aryella." My gut twisted when, despite the hurt my words caused him, his gentleness endured. "I have loved you since the moment you walked into my blacksmith's shop, since the moment—" He huffed out a tearful breath, which cracked my chest wide open. "I have loved you since the moment I first saw you, and I will never stop."

He turned his back to me and stopped in the doorway, where he pulled a note from his pocket. It looked to have been folded and unfolded multiple times.

"Damond knows everything. Anything more you need explained, he'll tell you." He placed the paper on the chair by the door. "Please read this before you go to those caves." His throat flexed with a hard swallow. "And Ella?" He turned and met my gaze, passionate fury and plea brimming in those hickory depths. "Don't let this world take one more thing from you."

The door closed behind him, and he was gone.

I buried my face in my hands and cried the only weak, painful sobs my damaged body would allow. I wanted to scream. I wanted to drown everything and burn everyone until the only thing left in this barren wasteland was the truth.

But all I could feel was black.

Chapter Thirty-Six

A week passed before I healed enough to get out of bed. Whatever power kept me alive left nothing for healing of the supernatural kind, so it was slow. It turned out being gutted and thrown a great distance into a rocky ravine really took it out of a person. Even a person blessed with the power of the gods.

The icy month of Nevelin arrived, and a new year began. Gavin didn't return, which hurt more than it should have, and I let my self-loathing fuel my rage rather than my gloom. I grasped the bitterness well in the days after he left. Let the anger simmer long enough, and it began to char the good parts of me.

It made the days easier, though my fury wasn't directed at a single person. It just *was*. With all I had learned, I couldn't decide who to blame if not everyone.

Though I *was* angry at Damond for being complicit, I silently let him take care of me. In turn, he let me be angry. The cabin was one bedroom, but there was a light blue sofa by the hearth, where he slept, as well as a small bathroom and a kitchen, where he cooked for us. He accompanied me on my slow, uncomfortable walks along the beaches of the Windcrest Sound. The nastiest glares I could muster didn't deter him from staying by my side, and for that I was secretly grateful. I feared how far into myself I might retreat if left alone.

The cabin was hidden south of Brinnea between a thick line of trees and a small inlet off the sound. The cliffs were tall, and we were far enough away that I couldn't see a single part of the city. I was grateful for that. All of it was easier to process when I could pretend I had no responsibilities outside this cabin. Given how I'd been deceived by so many others, I couldn't find it within myself to feel guilty about lying to myself in order to cope. Just for a little while.

If Simeon himself deemed it necessary to keep me from my people and my duties for over four hundred years, I decided they could wait a little longer for their puppet queen.

I thought of Gavin far more than I wanted to, but his lingering effect on me was too intrusive to ignore. I saw, felt, and heard him everywhere. In the warmth and safety of my bed. In the frigid breeze off the sea. In the soothing whoosh of ocean waves. In the gloom of the sky when it was gray and in the heat of the sun when it shone. Sometimes feeling him made me scream and cry. Other times, memories of his protective warmth beside me were the only remedy for a restless night.

Damond told me that between the time he brought me to this cabin and I woke, Gavin didn't eat. Didn't sleep. Drank the water Damond forced upon him and did nothing but sit at my bedside and wait. Only when I began to wake did Damond convince him to briefly leave the room to spare me the initial shock of him being the first thing I saw.

Neither Damond nor I spoke of him after that until, three weeks later, Gavin sent me a little gift. Damond advised me earlier that morning he needed to run into Brinnea and would return before dinnertime.

When he called my name from out front, I rose from the afternoon nap my healing body still required and made my way outside, unenthused. Shoulders and neck wrapped in a plush olive green blanket, I stopped when I saw Damond holding a rope. At the end of it was some sort of silver-furred—nearly *iridescent*—wildcat cub.

My mouth fell open.

"Are you serious?" I grumbled, knowing exactly who this gift was from. "Is *he* serious?"

I could tell by the way she clumsily stumbled in the sand over her disproportionately large paws that she was far from full-grown. I'd only seen drawings of big cats in books. Lions, tigers, jaguars—she looked a bit like all of them, and also . . . not. She was long and lithe—or was going to be—with a head and jaw thick and strong like a tiger's. Her eyes glowed a deep, entrancing violet. Traces of a mane thickened the spots between and behind her ears. The longer I looked at her, the more I became transfixed by the shimmer of her fur. Almost like it was sentient and moving, flowing, shifting like molten silver, catching and refracting every color of the world around her.

"What is she?"

"She's called an umbra," Damond answered. "Incredibly rare breed. Frankly, I thought they were extinct." He cocked his head down at her. "They're supposedly unnaturally smart and fiercely loyal. Protective, too. And aggressive, but . . . she's small enough that she can't do too much damage for now."

"Who told you that?" I mumbled, entranced by thickly tufted silver paws, which I would've sworn were larger than my face.

Damond handed me a note and shot me a pointed look. I snatched the paper from his hands but refused to back down from our mutual glare. He nodded to the silver cub. "You should be able to communicate with her in a way no one else can."

I shifted where I stood. Soltum, the eighth of our gods. God of Animals. He was one to which I'd hardly given any thought. Only two of my twelve powers had shown themselves, and I knew it would be a while before I had the strength to find any more.

Damond bent down and picked the silver cub off the ground by the scruff, but she wriggled to be set free.

I cringed at her struggle. Felt it, somewhere deep. "Put her down."

He gestured to the note in my hand. "Then read the note."

With a reluctant grumble and roll of my eyes, I obeyed.

Aryella,

She was barely alive when she found me in northeast Warrich a month before I came to you. A friend of Damond's has cared for her these past few months in my absence. She can't be more than three or four months old now—still young enough to be impressionable. You must be strict with her in training. She's a weapon when you need her to be. She's a survivor, Ella, like you.

I named her Shera, after the cat you used to have. I know you don't remember, but I remember everything.

The silver fur is unique, of course, but I think the both of you together just feel… right.

Gavin

"Shera," I repeated aloud, hoping it might summon a lost memory. Nothing came. I dropped the note and my hands into my lap. "I don't want anything from him."

She let out a high-pitched growl in rejection of Damond's grip, kicking all four legs and contorting her strong torso back and forth in an attempt to escape. A swipe of her paws behind her head caught Damond on the wrist. He cursed at the cut of her claw and lowered her to the ground. Then, she ran to me, her massive paws sticking and sliding in the cold sand.

I met her hopeful violet eyes with a furrowed brow. She brushed against my legs, then between, and looked up at me. There was trust in her gaze as she looked at me when, for Damond, there was none. Through an instinct similar to how I imagined a mother might know her child, I felt . . . love.

"I guess it doesn't matter how she got here." I sighed, tilting my head as she batted around at a rock, pretending it was her prey.

"Like a kitten . . . Small, adorable, fearless, and born to be lethal."

I cracked a smile at the memory of his words, despite my best efforts. How he made me feel had never felt like a lie.

"If I'm keeping her, she's coming inside."

Damond sighed and tossed me her leash. "Whatever you say."

I knelt in the sand and let her sniff and nuzzle my hand before I removed the rope from around her neck.

"There." I tossed the empty leash into the ocean. "You can stay or go. Your choice."

When she brushed against my knee and rolled onto her back, her silver fur refracting rainbows in the winter sun, I laughed for the first time in quite a while. For the first time since that world-altering night in Brinnea, my smile was too big to contain. She would stay, then.

At night, my terrors were no longer returning to Phillip and Oliver. Or of being stuck in golden caskets or shredded into a mess of confused pieces I couldn't find, which I now suspected *were* memories trying to break through. I had one nightmare now: Molochai's cold, taloned fingers on my skin, his shadows inside my veins, that evil ripping apart my mind before taking his blade and cutting my body wide open. Most nights, I dreamed it over and over and over again.

Damond checked on me when I woke up screaming, but there was nothing he could do—nothing I wanted him to do—save for mixing me a sleep tonic. Sometimes the drink helped. Other times, it only made it more difficult for me to wake myself from the terror when it returned.

But those first nights with Shera, I slept fitfully and dreamlessly. For a three-month-old wild animal, she was incredibly calm. She had no accidents inside the cabin and scratched at the door every morning to ask to relieve herself. Perhaps there was nothing for me to *do* in order to wield Soltum's power. In the books I read in Tovick, Soltum's abilities weren't detailed like the other gods' had been. But Shera was relaxed when I was relaxed. For her sake, I forced myself to stop and breathe. With her, my mood seemed to be my power.

Another uneventful week passed with the three of us in the seaside cabin. Another week of peaceful, dreamless sleep. Another week of walking—faster and longer now—and growing stronger, but I still had a long way to go. My stomach still hurt when I moved, but it was a dull ache rather than a sharp wrench of muscle and skin that made my eyes burn.

Damond usually brought me breakfast in bed so I could take

my time recovering from the stiff discomfort of sleep before rising, but this morning I joined him in the main living space. There were more windows in this cabin than the one in Warrich. More light. Everything was bright oak.

I watched the waves of the Eastern sea wash up and recede on the shore of our little inlet, mesmerized by the fog hovering in the air.

Damond's voice broke me out of my trance. "You seem... *okay* this morning."

I shot him a perturbed glare, turned away, and poured myself a mug of green tea. "My only companions for the past three weeks have been you and a cat. Don't flatter yourself."

Damond chuckled softly and tsked. "You're not very pleasant when you're angry, Ary."

I took a sip of my tea and thought of how much had changed since Tovick. "Fuck being pleasant," I grumbled. "I'm not sure *pleasant* is something I can afford to be anymore." With that, I pushed off the wooden counter and took the seat opposite Damond at the two-person dining table crammed into the small kitchen. "I was an idiot, running to Molochai to sacrifice myself. I thought I was doing the right thing, the easiest thing for everyone, but my decision was based on lies."

Damond sighed, his eyes sad. "Love makes us do stupid shit."

"I don't lo—" My jaw snapped shut before I could say what we both knew wasn't true.

I loved him. At least, a part of him. Whether I wanted to or not.

But... never again would I make choices based on untested assumptions. Never again would I be so reckless and impulsive, even for the benefit of those I cared about. Never again would I lie to myself or let myself be lied to. Never again would I trust so easily.

I had accepted so many things that turned out to be lies.

No more.

Molochai had killed something in me that day: my blind optimism. I had grown a new heart, and despite the longing and love that remained, I needed to decide if I was willing to give this one away. To anyone.

I tightened a blanket around my shoulders and shifted in my seat. Shera brushed against my leg, sensing my distress. "Can you love and hate someone at the same time?"

Damond took a sip of his coffee and shrugged. "Two emotions rivaling each other in strength . . . I would guess so."

I ran my hands over my face. "I should feel nothing but disdain for him, and I am angry—I *am*—yet all I want is for there to be a reason to . . . *forgive* him." I shuddered as the self-hatred ripped through me. "Why do I want to forgive him, Damond? I should want to kill him. What's so terribly wrong with me that I want to forgive the man that killed people I love more than I want to hate him?"

Damond eyed me curiously. "Do you believe that he had any choice in killing them?"

If I hadn't gone to whatever plane Oliver existed on after death, I would have said yes. But I didn't think a man with a choice to kill a child would have been *nice.* Would have given him that toy horse. The agony Molochai had caused me with just his shadows . . . a power so great could accomplish terrible things.

When I'd found Phillip's and Oliver's bodies, they'd looked so very peaceful. Like they hadn't suffered, despite the blood and horror. Their calm was a detail I could never forget.

"No," I whispered. "No, I don't think he had a choice."

Damond looked at the second letter that Gavin had written

to me. I had left it on the table weeks ago and neither of us had touched it. "Have you read it?"

My throat worked through a swallow as I shook my head. "I have to go to those caves, but I won't go blind. I go on my terms, but those people—most of them," I added, thinking of everyone who wasn't Simeon and Elowen, "are innocent. I can't abandon the entire continent."

And whatever was in that letter would make finally taking up my role a whole lot harder. An uncomfortable pause split the air between us. I watched as Damond fidgeted with his thumbs. With a heavy sigh, he reached into the folded letter and pulled out a small piece of paper, featherlight, and set it before me. The scrap of paper was old and the writing barely legible. But I read it once, twice, again. Seven words had never held so much weight.

It was Simeon. Do not follow me.

I recognized the sharp curve of the *S*, the fat loop of the lowercase *f*, and how it read with some letters in cursive and some not. Those, among other traits, had always been consistent. I would know, because that handwriting was quite familiar.

That handwriting was mine.

I drew in a long, deep breath and whispered, "I wrote that?"

Damond nodded, his dark brow furrowing behind his round glasses. "You left it for Smyth after Simeon took you from him. Four hundred years ago."

"And he . . . followed me."

"Yes." Damond huffed out an awestruck breath and pushed both the note and the letter closer to me. "Yes, Ary, he followed you."

I had told him not to follow me to Molochai's camp. He had anyway. And then . . .

"I swear on every star, every sky, every soul that has passed through this world, I will follow you..."

Even in death, he promised.

"Tell me." I looked up at my curly-haired friend. I finally decided he was a friend at that moment. Not an enemy. "Tell me everything you know—every detail. My old life. Tell me about him, what we were. Who I was. I need to hear it from someone that isn't him. And then I'll decide what's true." Or *try* to decide.

Damond sighed in relief and leaned forward in his seat like he'd spent the last three weeks preparing for this moment.

"You've been told how Molochai and Simeon unlocked hidden power from within Nyrida to overthrow the old rulers? The Rexus dynasty. Tyrants." I nodded.

"The two of them made Christabel queen in their belief that the people would be more willing to accept a matriarchy."

"Yes. And Christabel fell in love with another man, married him, and it drove Molochai mad."

"Yes," said Damond. "But years before Molochai turned completely to the dark, while he still pursued Christabel and continuously failed to win her heart, he found ways to take out his... frustrations. One victim was a young servant girl named Louisa. Vulnerable, early twenties. She became pregnant. Something went wrong while she delivered the child, and she lost too much blood. The child survived, but she did not. Louisa had one older sister, but the sister and her husband rejected the bastard. Luckily, an older woman named Eden, who assisted Louisa in delivering the baby, decided she couldn't abandon an innocent child. She and her husband, Isaac, a blacksmith, took the child and raised him. That child was Smyth."

Eden and Isaac. He'd told me about them.

"I have loved you since the moment you walked into my blacksmith's shop..."

Damond's words were the loom pulling Gavin's truth together.

"She was the most beautiful thing I've ever seen..."

When he said that, he looked at me.

"Three and a half years later, Christabel had her husband's child," continued Damond. "And that finally broke Molochai. He killed her husband. Then he found the infant, a baby girl, and thrust a dagger through her heart at only three days old. And you now know... that child was you."

My fingers brushed over the two-inch-wide scar over my heart. The mystery scar that was no longer a mystery. Why else would Elowen have kept it from me?

"Only you didn't die. You survived, revealing traces of power so incredible that your mother and Simeon kept you locked up in that castle to protect you and keep Molochai from ever learning you were alive. That you were able to survive a dagger to the heart at a few days old..." Damond shuddered. "They loved you, but they were afraid of you. And though you were harmless at the time, just a baby, Simeon knew if Molochai could sense your power, if he *found* you, there was no telling what he'd do. Either try to kill you again or use you. So Simeon kept you locked up and then decided to use you himself. For... the greater good."

And there it was. The other villain in the story of my shattered past. Simeon, my uncle. Not my father but my *uncle*, my *real* mother's greedy older brother who sought control in his own way and held me captive for centuries.

"I'm one of the last people to defend that manipulative prick,"

Damond continued, "but I know—at least I think I know—that Simeon has always had good intentions. Smyth's even said so himself, though I don't think he'd hesitate to kill him if he could."

When I met Simeon, I wasn't sure what *I* would do to him myself.

"Why hasn't Simeon tried to kill Molochai?"

"Because they're *not* equal in power. He can't," Damond answered. "Simeon uses spells—like the one he used to erase your memory—and wards on all the large cities like he placed on Tovick and Brinnea. Molochai pushed the boundaries of the power they once shared. His darkness—those shadows—that's something deeper and darker than the power the two of them found four hundred years ago, and that's why Simeon needs *you*."

I shook my head. There was time for all of that later. I couldn't process it, not now, so I shoved it away.

"Gavin said I came to his blacksmith's shop asking for a weapon, and that's how we met."

Damond nodded. "When you were eighteen. He was twenty-two. He loved you, he pursued you, and you spent four months sneaking around together before Christabel finally succumbed to her illness. The curse Molochai placed on her. The city was sacked. Simeon had found out about you and Smyth by then, had forbidden your union, but instead of staying in that castle as he commanded, you ran away. To Smyth. You married him, and he brought you here."

I looked around and absorbed the calming comfort of the seaside cabin, seeing it in a different light. He'd told me about this place—his favorite place—and I could see why. The bright oak and gentle blues and greens in every piece of decor were soothing, and the sound of the ocean was a constant restorative.

"This cabin doesn't look four hundred years old."

Damond chuckled. "The stubborn bastard just rebuilds it every time it breaks."

Just like he had done for me.

"After you married, it took Simeon's men ten days to find you," Damond continued. "Smyth had left you sleeping inside to chop and gather firewood. When he came back, you were gone. With no sign of a struggle and only a single note."

I looked back down at the parchment. Foreign words written unmistakably in my own script.

"He chased after them, but at that time, he was just a blacksmith that liked to fight. They were faster, far more skilled, and Simeon knew how to cover his tracks. But Smyth never stopped looking, and after nine years, he found Simeon. He pleaded for him to give you back. Simeon told him what he had done—placed you in a deep sleep, so that the army of people within the Winterton Caves could grow large and powerful enough, fortified by generations, to support him in the fight against Molochai. And so he could take as long as he needed to learn about your power. He came up with his plan—a prophecy predicting a young savior queen, powerful, impressionable, and sacrificial. Your mother *was* clairvoyant, so to anyone who knew her, a prophecy was easy to believe. Simeon told Smyth this and ordered him to move on."

"I don't let go. Ever."

Of me.

I leaned forward and buried my face in my shaking hands.

"Obviously, Smyth didn't move on," Damond continued. "When it was clear that Simeon would not concede to his appeals, he went to Molochai. His father. He asked for a way to be frozen in time like Simeon, like Molochai, like you, so that one day he could see you again. He made his blood oath. He vowed to kill for Molochai in exchange for the power to make him ageless. To remain thirty-one forever. Molochai let him believe it would only be one kill, that the victim would be guilty. But Molochai tricked him. It wasn't just once, and it wasn't just the guilty," Damond uttered darkly. "He butchers whoever Molochai tells him to, and he's been bound by that oath for nearly four hundred years."

"What if Molochai gave him an order to kill me?" I looked up, pressure building in my throat. "What was his plan, then?"

"Molochai wanted to kill you himself." Damond gestured to my torso. "Even if that wasn't the case, to take another life, the oath requires Molochai to give a name, and to Molochai—when he first found out you existed—you were Aryella Gold. Simeon was smart in coming up with that loophole to protect you, I'll give him that. You were safe with Smyth as long as Molochai didn't know who you truly were."

"*He cannot know*," Gavin had said to me.

And I remembered that day we'd stumbled across a band of Insidions. Gavin had made a point to call me Simeon's daughter. Now, I gathered, to mislead the Insidions and Molochai.

Damond sighed and said, "Even *then*, Smyth had a backup plan. He had me following you both. I was far enough away to give you privacy, close enough to take care of you if he had to . . . he would have killed himself before hurting you, Ary."

"If I hurt you, I'll beat him to it."

Those words, about Ezra's threat to kill him. He was being . . . quite literal.

I blinked away a tear. Even if he didn't deserve it.

Hearing this story with a clearer mind, from someone other than Gavin, made it more real. I fought to believe it, refused to trust it. If true, it explained why Gemma would dare leave me alone with him. If I was indeed his wife and everything Simeon had told her had been a lie…

"*Come when you're ready*," she had said. "*Do what you need to… find yourself.*"

She, too, had meant that literally.

I buried my face in my hands again, rubbed my eyes to soothe the pounding in my head.

"Will Gemma tell Elias and the others the truth?" I whispered.

"Smyth asked her not to, though I would imagine she'll tell Finn." Damond sighed. "Simeon has controlled your life for too long. You should reveal yourself to them on your terms. With that, she agreed."

A wave of gratitude washed over me, for both of them—the two people that knew *me* best in the world.

"This is the truth?" I whispered, pointing to the table and the letter. "I need you to promise me, Damond, that this is the truth. Swear it. On your life, on the lives of everyone you've ever loved." I could feel power rumbling within me. I couldn't access it—not yet, in this body still weak, still healing. But it was there. "Because I *vow*," I uttered through clenched teeth, "I vow, here and now, that the next person that lies to me will need the protection of all twelve gods combined."

"It's the truth, Ary. I swear on my own soul." His lip curled into a sly smile. "And you know I love myself far too much to risk my soul."

Once more, I covered my face with my hands and focused on gravity holding my feet to the floor.

"Where is he?"

"I don't know," Damond replied.

"Will he come back?"

"He can't." He squeezed my arm. "He has to find a way to break the oath. You're not safe until it's done."

Tears pooled in my eyes. I wiped them away with the sleeves of my oversized blue sweater and straightened my shoulders. No more tears. I couldn't afford them. I had to stay strong for me, for my people. Even for him.

"You're not weak for weeping over him." The battle must have raged clearly on my face, as Damond gently lowered my sleeve from my eyes and squeezed my hand. "Gods know that man has shed four centuries' worth of tears for you."

My blurry gaze landed on that letter. Four hundred years.

The least I could do was read it.

Damond embraced me. "Do you want me to stay?" I shook my head, eyes locked on the paper. "No. I should read it alone."

One more squeeze and Damond turned toward the cabin's front door. I listened to the thump of his boots and—

"Damond?" I rushed out.

He turned back to me, hand on the doorknob.

I worked my throat through a swallow. "Would you forgive him for what he's done?"

His lips pulled into a tight line, then a knowing grin. He nodded. "I *have* forgiven him." In response to my furrowed brow, he continued. "My parents—descendants of Smyth's uncle on his mother's side—were spies for the Wintertons. They tried to infiltrate a band of Insidions but they were discovered. They got away, but Molochai gave Smyth the order to track them down and kill them. I was ten years old. He made sure I didn't see it happen, and after he killed them, he found a family in Tovick to take me in. When I turned eighteen, he bought me my pub. He's looked out for me ever since." Sadness glistened in my friend's brown eyes. "He's never had much family without you. And my parents...well, he knew them. They were his friends."

My chest ached. His friends. He had been forced to kill his friends, and if Damond had been able to forgive him for killing his parents when he was a child...I shuddered.

I thought of *my* friends. Gemma, Ezra, Finn, Caz, Damond. If I lost control of my body and had to kill them—had to *witness* myself killing them, fully aware of the horror but unable to stop myself—how would I go on? How *had* he persevered through the nightmare that was his life?

I sucked in a breath, remembering he'd told me.

"I hold on to the first good thing I can think of... Lately, that's been you. Safe, warm, fed, happy. And you, Ella...you pull me out of my nightmares and return me to my dreams."

Air. I needed air. I grabbed the letter and burst through the front door, loyal Shera at my heels. I looked around, but Damond was nowhere to be found. Most likely having guessed I would need solitude and fresh air to get through what I was about to read.

I opened the letter and forced a steady breath.

Aryella,

There is no greater truth to my existence than my love for you. You are the best part of me.

Please fight. Not for me, not for them, but for yourself. Fight for the life you want, not the life Simeon has forced you into. I taught you the basics in our short time together. Breathing, balance, how to throw a punch and wield a dagger. I hate that it was all we had time for, but I know you love reading, so I've prepared you a list of tomes with maneuvers, strategy, everything you need to become lethal. They are all in the Brinnea cabin. Study them. Memorize it all. Practice, hone the skills, ask Damond for help if you need it. Take the time to test your abilities. Earth, wind, water, ice, fire, healing—I thought I'd seen them all, but there are more. You have no limits.

Damond will not betray you, but he also knows you'll have to go to those caves eventually. As much as I wish to keep you from all of it, I know you can't rest when people are suffering. It's one of the infinitely beautiful things about you. It will be his goal to get you there once you're healed. But if you're not ready, do not go. Do not play into their hands. Don't give them what they don't deserve, because they sure as hell don't deserve you. Do what you need to survive and trust your instincts. If you think something is a trap, it probably is. Cover your tracks and run like hell. Hide in plain sight. You'll figure out how. Protect yourself at all costs, and when you swing your fist or your blade, don't you miss. Just like I taught you.

Be the queen you want to be. I promise, they will love you. It's impossible not to love you. You, my sweet love, are more than enough.

This blood oath and the danger it poses to you is the only thing keeping me away. Molochai knows by now—from the life and power he failed to take from you a second time—that he will need to find another way. That he cannot kill you with a blade. But that doesn't mean he won't try to use me to hurt you. So as soon as you are healed, leave Brinnea. Until the oath is broken, I don't want to know where you are.

I will free myself from Molochai one way or another, and as long as I am living, I will come back to you. I will be there for you however you will have me. But do not be mistaken . . . should I be freed, I will fight for your heart. I won it once, and I have every intention of winning it again.

I love you. You are a miracle too great for this world, with or without your powers.

Let no one convince you otherwise.

Gavin

P.S. I know you were eager to learn the meaning behind my tattoos. The tally marks are not kills, but years. Four hundred and two. One for every year I've lived without you.

Between my trembling hands and my salty tears, the ink on the paper in my hands was barely legible. It didn't matter. I had already stored his words in my heart.

The sun peeked from behind the heavy winter clouds and glistened on the ocean—blinding in spots, even through the blur of my tears. Just like the hope in my reborn heart. Blinding, too much to process, but persistent.

It would be a disservice to my new chance at life to lie to myself about who he was to me. My instinct had known, I think, that his protection, his guidance, his strange longing looks, his desire, his intense and mysterious words, had all been his way of trying to tell me what I meant to him. It just hadn't made sense. I'd thought he had been waiting for some elusive, alluring woman. But it was me. She was me, and now I had to be someone else.

I didn't know how I would fulfill my duty to these people, but I would take back the time owed to me and figure it out. My way.

Simeon had failed to mold me, like clay, into his weapon of choice. In taking my memories, he had taken away the very foundation of who I was. But Gavin gave me the tools to rebuild it here, in the present. Despite the oath that bound him to my enemy. He let me figure out my strengths on my own without tying me to a centuries' old union he wasn't sure I would want. He was far from a perfect man.

But he had been there for me.

And once, long ago, even if I couldn't remember, he had been mine.

That was something no magically forged identity, no evil curse, no ancient duty or charming betrothed, could make me forget.

I wasn't sure what to believe. Who to trust. But I stared out at the endless ocean and thought of him.

I let the brush of two silver rings—our timeless bond—soothe me as they moved against my neck in the cold ocean breeze.

Epilogue

Elias Winterton

When I was five, I memorized every single crag and angle of my rocky bedchamber ceiling. And then I spent every night thereafter tracing the edges and lines until I fell asleep. For twenty years, it worked. Lulled my methodical brain to rest while I planned every detail of my future, of this war, of the life I would give to my wife. The queen.

Until those plans—my lifetime in the making—fell through.

Two weeks. That's how long it had been since the Sinclairs, Ezra Hart, and Gemma Tremaine returned without her. Caz Sinclair, the poor bastard, without his leg. He was honorably excused from duty in my forces. I made sure of that. An explosion of the temple in Tovick had done it, Finn explained. When I asked what the hell they'd been doing in Tovick, they looked at me like I was insane. Simeon's orders, they said.

Tremaine had remained remarkably quiet—something I'd

never known her to be. Given she knew the queen better than any of us—perhaps better than Elowen herself—her continued silence was unnerving.

Ezra Hart arrived fuming about some big, arrogant fucker named Smyth—Simeon's last-minute addition to their group that I certainly hadn't agreed to. Apparently, this Smyth buffoon had taken it upon himself to drag my betrothed halfway across Nyrida, teach and train her, all without my permission. Ezra said Smyth forced my betrothed under his wing, followed her around like a damn guard dog, and did the gods know what else to her.

Gemma didn't have much to say about him, either.

When I sat up in bed, the pretty blonde beside me stirred. I ran my hands over my face and cringed. I'd forgotten she was even there. For months, I had resisted being with a woman out of respect for the queen's impending arrival. But after no sign of her and no word from Simeon, I . . . faltered.

My pulse throbbed in my ears from too much whiskey the night before. I groaned at the crystal decanter shattered in pieces all over the maroon-and-gold rug my grandmother had gifted me for my twenty-third birthday. It was expensive—imported from wool traders in southern Wymara—and matched the deep scarlet bedding and upholstered sofa that sat before the dwindling hearth. At least none of the red oak furniture from Peradine had been destroyed during last night's passionate spree. But that rug . . .

"Shit." I pinched the bridge of my nose and rose to clean the mess.

"Eli?" A warm, thin hand brushed against the back of my thigh as I stood.

With a roll of my eyes, I sternly corrected, "It's 'Commander' outside the bedroom." She reached for my hand, but I refused to turn around.

The husky sound of her laugh chafed my ears. I heard her shift in bed behind me. "Well, we're still in the bedroom, *Commander*." She snaked her hands around my waist and brushed her naked chest against my back. "But I'll call you whatever you want if—"

"Get out." I shrugged out of her touch and exhaled heavily through my nose. "Please," I added, cringing at the harshness of my tone. Last night had been nice. Hot, wild, loud, and rough.

I even considered one more round with her when, without a single objection, she left my bed and tiptoed around the shards of glass on the rug. Her spectacular tits bounced with every movement; that long, lean, tan body was . . . delectable. And her tight, round ass was still red from my hand. She caught me watching and gave me a bashful smile while slipping into the joke of a red silk gown she'd flaunted last night.

"Tonight?" she asked, lingering by the door with a grin plastered on her beautiful face.

"I don't know." I sighed, irritated as I folded the rug into four squares to keep the shards from escaping. "I'll send for you."

"As you wish," she crooned, taking her time with the doorknob, "*Commander*."

The door closed behind her, and I paused to massage my temples for a moment of quiet solitude. But mere seconds later, four angry knocks made me jump. I cursed under my breath and contemplated my next words to her. Cruel enough to keep her away just for a week or for good?

I opened the door and felt relief, instead, when I found my

friend, who required no sexual attention and certainly no post-coital cuddling, which I thoroughly despised.

Valda's slim, ebony neck tilted as though she was looking down at me in disapproval, despite being just shorter than me. Thick black locks shifted on her shoulders. She glanced in the direction Larisa had gone and lifted an unamused eyebrow at me.

"Morning, Val." I smirked, stepped behind the door, and opened it for her to enter. She strode in, confident and strong. When the door closed, she groaned at my still-naked form. She'd seen it before and would see it again. I owned a mirror, and I had no reason to be ashamed.

"Would you put some damn pants on, you *rake*?"

I laughed but slid on a pair of trousers to appease her. "You know better than to assume I'm decent before sunrise."

"Yes," she hissed, crossing her long, toned arms over her chest. Her lips pursed as she scanned the full length of my body. Unimpressed. "Since all you do is drink and fuck your sorrows away."

My eyebrows shot up in surprise and amusement. That Valda's tongue could cut as sharply as her blade was one of the reasons she was my best friend.

"What's your issue today?" I asked. There was apprehension in her dark brown eyes. The air left my lungs. "Is there word of her?" I scrambled for my boots.

Val reached in the pocket of her black leathers and handed me a letter. "From one of our spies east of Tovick." I tore open the letter and began to read. "He was watching Molochai's camp a few weeks ago, south of Brinnea." I froze with my eyes locked on the paper.

Valda delivered news gracefully, but I could tell she was nervous. "He saw our queen there," she added gravely.

My eyes drifted back up to Val. "*What?*" I gritted out.

"She was in Brinnea, Eli. She—"

"What the fuck was she doing in Brinnea?" I shouted, running my hands through my hair. First Tovick, then Brinnea. Why the fuck hadn't Tremaine and the others told me this? It felt as if someone had devised some twisted plan to keep her far, far away from me. I grabbed yesterday's shirt off the chair—where I'd thrown it last night in a fit of carnal need—and slid my arms through the sleeves. "Every detail, Val—every *gods-damned* detail—was supposed to go through me! Shit!" I smashed a wooden chair to bits with my boot. "Simeon!" I hissed, turning on Valda. He had some explaining to do. "Deploy the forces—all of them—and find Simeon! Find *her*!"

She flinched. "We aren't going to find her." Her normally hard demeanor softened. She took an apprehensive step toward me. "Somehow Insidions got hold of her. And what our informant saw…" Val shuddered, horror painting her sharp face. "Molochai killed her. He…he ripped out her heart."

A cacophony of sounds rang in my ears. I closed my eyes and slowly shook my head, rejecting the image. "That's not… no, it wasn't her." My pulse pounded, brutal and painful in my veins. "The prophecy. She has power. She's more powerful than Molochai."

"I thought the same thing, but the Butch—" Val choked on the name, then took a deep breath. "The Butcher was there. The man named Smyth…the one who joined the mission late. Based on Ezra's description and the things he said he could do—the way he *killed*—we think they're one and the same. He tricked them into thinking he was working for Simeon and took her to Molochai instead. And after Molochai killed her . . . the Butcher stole her body."

I met Valda's rigid gaze to search for a sign of insanity or dishonesty. As usual, no trace of either. "They wouldn't have been that stupid," I uttered. "Not the Sinclairs, not Ezra, and definitely not Tremaine."

"If the Butcher has managed to keep his identity hidden from us for four hundred years, *you* would be stupid to think he couldn't trick even our best soldiers."

"*No.*" Not *him*. Not that devil-spawned monster. "Simeon wouldn't let that happen." I paced back and forth in front of my fireplace, white shirt hanging loosely off my body. Hair wild as I stirred it with my frantic hands. "It's not possible."

"We haven't heard from Simeon in months, Eli!" Valda pressed. "We've been *waiting*, *vulnerable*, and until we hear from him, we have to assume, based on what we've seen and heard, for the protection of our people, that she's—"

"Val!" Vomit stirred in my stomach, rose up my throat. I halted mid-step. The vile things that beast would do to her. Even after she was . . . *dead*. "*No*, Val." I pointed an angry, trembling finger at her. "Don't you *fucking* say it!"

But Valda was the only one of my soldiers who didn't fear me. The only one I knew who would tell me the truth regardless of what I wanted to hear.

"I'm sorry." She clenched her teeth, biting back sorrow and rage of her own. "But if it's true, our queen is gone, and we have to act."

My knees almost gave out. I pressed my palms into the edge of the wooden table while my shoulders trembled beneath the weight of it all. My purpose in life had been my army and the prophesied queen sent by the gods to save us. Nothing else mattered. Nothing else ever would. Without her, I…there was no solution without her. Tears bit at my throat—tears for a beautiful young woman I had never known.

This was not possible. This was not real.

I centered myself in the rhythm of my breathing. As I'd been trained to do. As I'd trained countless others to do. Behind my closed eyes, I saw my sweet little sister and my parents. They were good. They were all *good*, and the Butcher had taken them from me.

Now he had taken *her* from me, too. My betrothed. My queen. Dutifully, rightfully *mine*.

When Val rested her hand on my arm to comfort me, I jerked away and held up my own in warning. She waited, stone-faced, for my command. I recalled that eerie quiet from Tremaine, who was never silent. It had nagged at me from the moment she returned.

She knew something.

"Bring me Gemma Tremaine."

Bonus

"I found you": Chapter 3 from Gavin's POV

My heart hammered in my ears, threatening to break free from my chest. I couldn't remember the last time I felt nervous about anything. There wasn't much that made me *feel* anymore. Survival had silenced my nerves and dulled my compassion—but lately both had come roaring back. At the thought of her.

I typically followed after any companions I was traveling with, to give myself a wider view of surrounding threats, but today I was the first one in that house. I looked around the inadequate little cabin, wishing I'd never seen it before. Bile rose in my throat when I didn't find a flash of silver hair or green eyes anywhere.

"Where the fuck is she?" I snapped at the dark-haired woman who'd arrived before me. She'd been sent early and tasked with protecting her. I leveled a death glare at her. I didn't know who she was, she didn't know who I was, and that was just fucking fine.

The woman blanched, then shot me a dirty look. So she *would* be a problem, then. "Ary went to the barn to see if the hens laid any more eggs. She should be back any minute now."

Outside? Alone? In the middle of the night? Surrounded by unforgiving darkness and a cold that was bitter enough to leave the strongest of men cowering by the fire?

Fuming, I turned and lurched back into the icy blackness. I slammed the door behind me and strode toward the barn.

When I heard her scream, the last four hundred years fell away.

Panic choked the breath from my lungs. I broke into a dead sprint toward the barn. I burst through the door in time to see an adolescent wolf toss a small figure with silver hair headfirst into a feed barrel. The wolf was too feral, and too focused on her, to notice when I entered. Thankfully, it wasn't that big, and it looked like it hadn't eaten for weeks. I didn't let myself think about what would have happened to her if this beast had been at its full size and strength. But even at this age, it was driven by instinct that told it to rip apart its prey.

Without needing to think, I unsheathed one of my knives and threw it into the wolf's hip. It struck true, and the animal yelped and stumbled. That was all I needed to lunge forward, grip it by the scruff, and jerk it away from her. I ripped my blade out of its muscle and struck again, this time in its neck. The wolf yelped again and thrashed against me until I leveraged my grip on the knife, with my other fist around its snout, and jerked with punishing force.

The sickening crack of its neck snapping was a sound I prayed she hadn't heard. I was more than used to the sounds of violence, but she wouldn't be. I shoved the wolf to the side and turned.

Her lantern had extinguished when she'd dropped it in the struggle with the wolf, and it had rolled into the opposite corner of the barn. She cowered against the wall now, one arm tucked limply into her side, the other held up in meek defense. That she blocked her own view of me was a small mercy. It allowed me an extra moment to gather myself. Pulse pounding, hands shaking, I took a step toward her—

"Please!"

The word made me freeze. Her entire body quaked with fear. It was a monumental effort not to beg her to speak again.

No matter how desperately I'd tried to hold on to every single part of her, I had failed.

I had forgotten the sound of her voice.

My eyes burned with tears. I ached to move closer, for her to give me one more word before she inevitably saw me and cowered in fear like the rest of them.

She didn't speak. But she lowered her arm to look up at me, and the breath left my body.

Green eyes with golden specks, like sunshine. Freckles over the bridge of her nose. The sweet, pink mouth I'd spent centuries dreaming of tasting once more.

Mine.

The force it took to bite back my anguished cry had me stumbling forward until my knees gave out. I thrust away my blade and dropped to the ground before her.

For her, I would always kneel.

Before I could think better of it, my shaking hands went to her face. I had to touch her. I *had* to, or else I couldn't be sure she was real.

She was real and here and *perfect*. She would always be perfect.

I couldn't remember when—one hundred years ago, maybe

two—I'd started to doubt I'd ever have the chance to look into those eyes again. But there they were—there *she* was—peering up at me through the light of the moon, full of gratitude, warmth, and goodness.

And *fear*. Fuck. Such heartbreaking, debilitating fear.

I forced my hands to still, because she needed me steady. Her skin beneath my fingers was *cold*, like ice, and though she was just as soft as I remembered, her cheeks were pale and gaunt. The hollow of her delicate throat was far too deep, and her collarbone was too visible beneath her skin.

What the *fuck* had they done to her? How could Simeon have let this happen?

My teeth clenched with a force nearly strong enough to split them to pieces. Because I knew how, and I knew why. Simeon Whitlock had deprived her of strength and nourishment. And he'd done it to deprive her of the power she couldn't even remember she could wield. He'd done it to keep her weak, controllable, and small. She had always been small, but not like this. She'd been full of life and light and quiet strength.

This was different. This was emptiness. Confusion. Mourning.

He had stolen the will to live right out of her.

Ella. My name for her—the one she'd given only to me—was on the tip of my tongue, but I couldn't say it.

She looked so *young*, barely any older than the day I married her.

I, on the other hand... my stomach plummeted. The last time she saw me, I'd been barely twenty-two, with a mischievous streak and hardly a scar in sight. Self-consciousness lurched through me. I had no way of knowing what she thought when she looked at me now. Disgust, most likely.

What would I do if she feared me? If she recoiled? I had survived vile, horrendous things, but the thought of those green eyes looking upon me with contempt made me want to press my knife to my throat and slice it right open. To bleed out and finally leave this world. If she was repulsed by me, would I truly be able to stand it? My chest fucking *ached* at the thought of seeing repulsion in eyes that had once held nothing but love.

I knew it was unlikely she remembered me, but I had so much to tell her, so much to explain. I didn't have much to do with the gods. I hated them for giving her to me and then taking her away, but for her memories, I would beg them.

Please, gods. Please—

"Who—who are you?" she stuttered out.

Who are you?

My ears rang at her words. I shuddered as my heart crashed into my rib cage, and acceptance settled like a heavy stone in my gut. She shifted away from me—though her recoil was weak and unsure, as though unsure whether I was friend or foe. But she truly had no idea who I was or what we once were.

Maybe I should have let go of her. Maybe I should have backed off completely, but I couldn't. I gave her the space I was capable of giving her—I lowered my hands to her shoulders and rubbed, desperate to warm her up. My chest burned at the thinness of her arms. It was a miracle that the wolf hadn't snapped her in half.

She had asked who I was, and I needed to give her an answer. All the things I needed to say rushed through my mind.

I've got you.

I'm here now.

I won't let them do this to you anymore.

I know you're lost, but I'll find a way to bring you home.

I'm sorry. Gods, I'm so sorry.

I missed you. I love you. I love you so fucking much.

But I couldn't say any of those things. All of them were true, and none of them were fair to her. She was lost. She was about to be saddled with an impossible burden, and any semblance of the truth about our past would only make that burden heavier. In time I could tell her, but not now.

I looked into those soul-saving eyes and tried to say it all with three words.

"I found you."

She tensed. Her body continued to shake. I clenched my jaw to fight my tears. Fuck, what I wouldn't give to pull her into my arms and let her rest there. Scoop her up and run, save her from all of this. I carefully reached out to brush my fingers to her cheek. That had always calmed her.

She should never have been here. She should have been with me.

When her bottom lip trembled, I had the overwhelming urge to punch my fist into the barn wall, rip away a plank of wood, and use it to bludgeon every single person complicit in this fucking ruse.

"You're safe," I promised her.

Her brow furrowed at me. The moment was brief—a split-second break in her fear and confusion—but *I saw it*. The love. The knowing adoration. The quiet reassurance that she'd chosen me and we were in this mess together. My heart swelled with relief. She was there. My Ella was *here*; I just needed to find a way to bring her home.

Our moment disappeared when she glanced behind me at the body of the wolf and whispered, "It's dead."

I cleared my throat. "Yes. Are you hurt?" Blood trickled down the right side of her face from a gash in her temple, but it wasn't deep. "You hit your head?" She nodded. I looked down at the bite on her arm. I would dress that wound the instant we returned to the house. I lifted my eyes to hers again. "Is your vision blurred?" I could see her pupils in the moonlight, and they looked fine. I'd be keeping a close eye on her, that was for fucking sure.

"I . . . I don't know," she answered.

I held up three fingers. "How many?"

"Th-three."

Good. "Can you walk?"

I wasn't sure why I asked. I had every intention of carrying her back to the house, even though it would take a miracle of will just to set her down again once we got there.

"I . . . I . . ."

I lifted her off the floor and had to bite my tongue to keep from cursing, because I wished lifting her hadn't been so effortless. She weighed next to nothing, and I could feel her spine against my forearm. Rage began to rise back up my throat. What if I had arrived two weeks later? One week? Would she have even made it that long? She was fucking starving to death.

Despite my anger, I nearly stumbled when she wrapped her weak, trembling arms around my neck and laid her cheek against my chest. She'd always been able to eradicate the anger from my body with a single, gentle touch. I calmed her. She calmed me. It had always been our perfect give-and-take, the way our souls and bodies had always intertwined and rested together.

My lips were inches away from her hair. It took everything in me not to bury my face there and promise her she was done being hungry and cold.

I paused before the door of the house, so briefly I didn't think she noticed. Now was my chance to take her and run. It was beyond tempting.

Would she believe me when I told her about us? Would she forgive me for all I'd become?

Even if the answers to both questions were in my favor, that didn't change the reality that she was only safe with me for a short period of time. The moment Molochai knew her real name...

I wanted to be everything to her, but I couldn't. Not until I found a way to free myself. I hated that she would need to rely on others. But that was fucking selfish beyond belief.

I forced a deep breath and opened the door. As the pleasant warmth of the indoors consumed us both, I reluctantly lowered her to the floor but kept my hand at her back to ensure she remained steady.

"Ary, there you are!" The dark-haired woman rushed forward. "These idiots just arrived while you were out, and—Shit!" She gasped at Aryella's battered and bleeding form. "Are you all right? What the hell happened?"

I could sense it coming. The few minutes we had spent alone together meant nothing to her and everything to me. That brief moment when I could have *sworn* her love was alive would be passed over and forgotten, overshadowed by a false prophecy and a young, unscarred prince who she was bound to fall for.

My hand flexed involuntarily against her back. It was instinct's way of keeping what mattered to me close by. But I had no way to keep her with me that wasn't by force. I had no claim to her in this lifetime.

Sweat broke out on my brow. One, because it was hot as hell

in this room with the fire roaring and four too many people. Two, because I wondered if she noticed my touch. If it made her feel anything at all. The thought of her being numb to me—or worse, repulsed by me—had what remained of my cold heart shriveling up in my chest.

"There was a wolf in the barn." Ella cleared her throat. "The chickens are gone."

The sadness in her voice worsened the ache in my chest. Of course she was devastated. If her heart was anything like it used to be—and I sensed it was—she would have let herself wither away before harming those animals. She was selfless to a fault. She always had been.

The dark-haired woman pulled her away from me, into an embrace, leaving my hand cold and empty. Caz, Finn, and Ezra stood up from the table. The hairs on the back of my neck stood to attention. The feral, possessive beast in me came to life as I was suddenly reminded of what it felt like to have other men look at her.

Pure torture.

Caz Sinclair was married, Ezra Hart was technically her cousin, and I was pretty sure, based on a few comments I'd heard from Finn Sinclair, that he wanted to fuck Ella's friend, the dark-haired woman hovering over her. I still wanted to drive my fist into all three of their faces. They weren't even looking at her with lust. Not at all. Only reverence, concern, and care.

And yet I was jealous. Jealous that they got to share oxygen, time, and space with her when I'd been deprived of her for so long. Jealous that, in all likelihood, she would smile at these kind, light-hearted young men before she ever smiled at the scarred, older brute staring at her like he was obsessed. And I *was* obsessed.

"Ugh," Ella groaned softly. At the quiet sound of her discomfort, my head jerked back in her direction. The dark-haired woman had released her and she was looking down at the wolf bite, which was bleeding through her tattered sleeve.

"May I?" I asked her, putting myself directly in her path.

She let out an adorably startled noise. If I hadn't been so worried that I'd frightened her, I would have found it impossible not to smile. Something I hadn't done in a very long time. Instead, I reached for her unwounded arm and led her to a chair by the fire, taking a knee on her right. I didn't trust a single person in his room besides myself to take care of her.

"That bite needs to be treated." I kept my voice gentle but firm. I was ready to rip the sleeve off her delicate arm and ensure it wasn't worse than I expected, but doing that without her permission would only scare her. I needed her to trust me.

Gods, I needed her to trust me.

Our eyes met and locked, causing my heartbeat to accelerate to unhealthy levels. I wanted to get lost in those eyes and never come back, but that wasn't what she needed from me.

"Let me help you," I told her, praying she knew I wasn't just referring to the wound on her arm.

She inhaled sharply in response. The sound was soft and sweet, just like the rest of her, and I clenched my teeth in frustration with how my body reacted. This was not the time, but I couldn't help it. Every part of me missed every part of her.

She carefully pulled back the sleeve of her shirt. When the other woman saw the wound, she covered her mouth and gasped. I fought the urge to turn and glare at her. I couldn't punish her as she deserved with my eyes. Did she really expect me to believe she truly cared about Ella? If she cared, that bite would never have happened. If she cared, she would have been here weeks ago, while Ella had been fucking starving to death.

I wrapped my fingers around my wife's wrist, flinching at how thin and breakable she felt, and grabbed a bottle of liquor from my bag. I gripped the cork between my teeth and pulled it out. Not giving her a chance to retreat or even think much about what was happening, I poured the liquor over the wound to clean it. She winced and sucked in a shaky breath. I fought the urge to wrap my arm around her and pull her into my chest. To shield her from the pain.

I made quick work of bandaging the wound, not wanting her to stare at it for too long. I knew better than most that dwelling on a wound only made it hurt more.

"The bandage will need to be changed no later than this time tomorrow," I told her. "Sooner, if it bleeds through." I carefully closed it over her arm, tying it as gently as possible while still being firm. Her flinch was minuscule, but I caught it. Guilt washed over me, and my eyes darted to hers. "Then you should change it daily, or more often if it gets wet, until you heal."

"Thank—" She cleared her throat and whispered, "Thank you."

I clenched my teeth, biting back the word I wanted to say.

Always.

But that would be too much. *I* was too much, and I needed to make every effort not to be, or she would think I was insane and want nothing to do with me at all. I had made a deal with Simeon before coming here. I would let these people tell her the lies that they didn't know were lies, about who she was and where she came from. I would let her believe them. And in return, I agreed not to go on a slaughtering spree.

I would tell her the truth in time. When she wasn't starving and afraid. When she could handle the weight of what had been done to her—to us—without crumbling. That wasn't now. Right now, her will to live was thin, and she needed a purpose. I was still bound by an oath that could make me kill her. I couldn't be her purpose. As much as I wanted to be.

I didn't trust my voice not to falter, or spit out something I shouldn't say. Instead, I gave her a firm nod, stood, and stepped back. For now, my only choice was to back away, to stand there in silence, to let them tell her lies.

And pretend like she wasn't the only thing I had ever loved.

Index and Pronunciation Guide

Notable Characters

Alec Gerard: Al-eck Jer-ard
Alistair Winterton: Al-is-ter Win-ter-ton
Ary/Aryella Gold: Are-ee/Are-ee-ella Gold
the Butcher of Nyrida: the Butch-er of Near-uh-duh
Caz Sinclair: Caz Sin-clare
Cherno: Chair-no
Christabel Whitlock: Kris-tuh-bell Wit-lock
Damond: Day-mund
Eden: Ee-den
Elias Winterton: Eh-lye-is Win-ter-ton
Elowen Gold: Eh-low-in Gold
Ezra Hart: Ez-ra Hart
Finn Sinclair: Finn Sin-clare
Gavin Smyth: Gav-in Smith
Gemma Tremaine: Jeh-muh Tre-mane
Marin Sinclair: Mare-in Sin-clare
Molochai: Mah-low-kai
Ophelia Winterton: Oh-fee-lee-uh Win-ter-ton

Shera: Share-uh
Simeon Whitlock: Sih-mee-un Wit-lock
Captain Valda: Val-duh

The 12 Gods of the Selvaren

the Selvaren: the Sell-var-in
Nevelin: Neh-veh-lin, *Goddess of Snow and Ice*
Aurana: Or-ah-nuh, *Goddess of Gravity*
Viridian: Ver-id-ee-an, *God of Healing and Regeneration*
Rainar: Rain-are, *God of the Seas*
Floris: Floor-iss, *Goddess of the Earth*
Aesta: Ay-stah, *Goddess of Light*
Helios: He-lee-os, *God of Fire*
Soltum: Sole-tum, *God of Animals*
Effusia: Eff-you-shuh, *Goddess of the Mind*
Autumna: Aw-tum-nuh, *Goddess of the Hunt*
Sussurro: Suss-er-oh, *God of Wind and Air*
Nyxar: Nix-are, *God of Celestial Night*

Places

Albertha: Al-buhr-tuh
Avendrel: Ay-ven-drel
the Barracks: the Bare-icks
Brinnea: Brin-ee-uh
Freyburn: Fray-burn
Nyrida: Near-uh-duh
Peradine: Pare-uh-deen

Thesa: Thees-uh
Tovick: Toe-vick
Tugaf: Too-gaff
Warrich: War-itch
the Windcrest Sound: the Wind-crest Sound
the Winterton Caves: the Win-ter-ton Caves
Wymara/Wymaran: Why-mahr-uh/Why-mahr-uhn

Notable Terms

Commencement: *Final series of challenges, which take place at the Barracks, after which the trainees are matriculated into the armed forces.*
the Dark Ages: *The time in which Nyrida was ruled by the Rexus family prior to being overthrown by Simeon and Molochai.*
Insidions: *Molochai's forces.*
the Rexus dynasty: *Ruthless ruling family during Nyrida's Dark Ages, who controlled their people with fear and lies.*
the Selvaren: *The pantheon of twelve gods.*
umbra: *Allegedly extinct breed of wildcat with unknown magic.*

Acknowledgments

First, I owe a great deal of gratitude to you, reader, the one holding this book in your hands. Thank you for taking a chance on me, and Ary, who, like many of us, is just trying to find her place in a difficult world. If you feel inspired and touched by her story, please consider leaving a review on Goodreads, Amazon, Instagram, TikTok, or your favorite social media platform.

A massive thanks to Sable Sorensen, who took the time to chat and field a laundry list of questions about indie publishing. I truly would not have known where to begin without your guidance.

A huge thank-you to my ARC team, who saw my request for early readers and gave this story a chance. I am so grateful for your kind words and the way you've loved this world and these characters.

My beta team—where to begin? An unending heap of thanks goes out to all of you, who gave the time of day to a random writer on Instagram. I didn't even have a bookish account yet, but you took a chance, and I am forever grateful. This would not have been possible without any of you. Thank you for believing in me. Thank you for the network you helped me create. Thank you for fielding my random social-media-illiterate questions and pushing me to get this story out into the world, especially on days when I doubted if I should.

Thank you for every single bookstagrammer and influencer who took the time to read and review *The Silversmith*! Thank you to my amazing street team who helped spread the word up to and after release! Word of mouth is so incredibly valuable to indie authors, and I'm forever grateful for the efforts you all put in to help this book gain traction.

Many thanks to my editors, Jack Renninson and Junessa Viloria at Second Sky and Forever, my marketing and publicity teams, and everyone at Hachette who has believed in this story enough to take it on. Thank you to my wonderful agents, Katie Reed and Andrea Hurst, for guiding me and advocating for me through every step. I cannot wait to see what the future holds.

Thank you to my entire family and all my friends for loving me. To all the friends along the way who encouraged me. To my parents and brother for always pushing me to be better. To my green flag husband, who took a self-imposed crash course in formatting every part of this physical book. Thank you for being my best friend and thank you for pouring your energy and time into helping me make this happen.

Finally, I am so grateful to God for giving me the writing bug and a chaotic brain with the drive to create.

And to my two wonderful, beautiful children, thank you for inspiring me every day. May you always chase your dreams, no matter how long they take to achieve. Never, ever give up.

A Letter from LJ

Thank you so much for reading *The Silversmith*. This story has been with me for a long time, and it's been so much fun bringing it to the page. I hope you enjoyed reading it as much as I enjoyed writing it. If you did enjoy it, and want to keep up with my latest releases, please sign up for my newsletter at the following link. Your email address will never be shared and you can unsubscribe at any time.

www.secondskybooks.com/lj-claren

My favorite part of writing is seeing and hearing reactions from readers. Did you feel and sympathize with Ary's struggles to find her strength and voice? Did Smyth make you swoon? If you enjoyed the story, I would be very grateful if you would leave a short review. I love getting feedback from readers, especially when it helps persuade other readers to pick up my book for the first time in the hopes that they love it as much as I loved writing it.

Ary's story is just getting started. There is so much more to come! I can't wait to continue this journey with you.

Thank you for reading!
Love, LJ

About the Author

LJ Claren is a lifelong dreamer, avid reader, and a grateful wife and mother of two. She writes powerful stories about heroines who get up when knocked down and the flawed, beautiful souls who love them. *The Silversmith*, in the Selvaren series, marks her adult romantasy debut. When she's not writing, you can find her reading or wrangling her husband, cats, and children.

You can learn more at:

www.ljclaren.com
Instagram @ljclaren
TikTok @lj.claren